Praise for Penelope Janu

'Encapsulates everything I love about the romance genre and so much more. A go-to author for rural romance for the head as well as the heart … '

—Joanna Nell, bestselling Australian author

'A rural story that has it all … simmering romance, international intrigue, a complex heroine and a swoon-worthy hero. What's not to love?'

—Karly Lane, bestselling Australian author
on *Clouds on the Horizon*

'Penelope Janu's fresh, bright, funny new twist on rural romance is an absolute delight. Her wit is as sharp as a knife. She is one of my absolute must-read authors.'

—Victoria Purman, bestselling author of *The Women's Pages,*
on *Up on Horseshoe Hill*

'Intriguing characters and a colourful setting: if you like romance and a little mystery, get ready to enjoy this novel.'

—Tricia Stringer, author of *Birds of A Feather,*
on *On the Right Track*

'Take a break from the news and spend time in Horseshoe Hill. Well written, interesting and filled with heart, *Starting From Scratch* is the perfect weekend read.'

—*Better Reading*

T0363359

ABOUT PENELOPE JANU

Penelope Janu lives on the coast in northern Sydney with a distracting husband, a very large dog and, now they're fully grown, six delightful children who come and go. Penelope has a passion for creating stories that explore social and environmental issues, but her novels are fundamentally a celebration of Australian characters and communities. Her first novel, *In at the Deep End*, came out in 2017 and her second, *On the Right Track*, in 2018. *Up on Horseshoe Hill* was published in 2019 and a novella, *The Six Rules of Christmas*, in 2020. Penelope enjoys exploring the Australian countryside and dreaming up travelling and hiking breaks, and nothing makes her happier as a writer than readers falling in love with her clever, complex and adventurous heroines and heroes. She loves to hear from readers, and can be contacted at www.penelopejanu.com.

Also by Penelope Janu

In at the Deep End
On the Right Track
On the Same Page
Up on Horseshoe Hill
The Six Rules of Christmas (novella)
Clouds on the Horizon

PENELOPE JANU

Starting from Scratch

mira

First Published 2021
Second Australian Paperback Edition 2021
ISBN 9781867240082

STARTING FROM SCRATCH
© 2021 by Penelope Janu
Australian Copyright 2021
New Zealand Copyright 2021

This is a work of fiction. Names, characters, places, and incidents are either the product of the author's imagination or are used fictitiously, and any resemblance to actual persons, living or dead, business establishments, events, or locales is entirely coincidental.

Published by
Mira
An imprint of Harlequin Enterprises (Australia) Pty Limited (ABN 47 001 180 918), a subsidiary of HarperCollins Publishers Australia Pty Limited (ABN 36 009 913 517)
Level 19, 201 Elizabeth St
SYDNEY NSW 2000
AUSTRALIA

® and TM (apart from those relating to FSC®) are trademarks of Harlequin Enterprises (Australia) Pty Limited or its corporate affiliates. Trademarks indicated with ® are registered in Australia, New Zealand and in other countries.

A catalogue record for this book is available from the National Library of Australia www.librariesaustralia.nla.gov.au

Printed and bound in Australia by McPherson's Printing Group

To my children, Philippa, Tamsin, Ben, Michaela, Gabriella and Max,
who listened avidly to the stories I told them at bedtime.

CHAPTER
1

Most people see colours, but sometimes I think that I see them more clearly.

I've worked at the long timber bench at the farmhouse for the past two hours, pressing crepe paper petals into shapes so they're ready to form into flowers. *Gompholobium grandiflorum.* Large Wedge-pea. The petals, in four shades of yellow, are lined up neatly in rows.

Saffron, lemon, amber and gold.

When a gust of wind rattles the window and sneaks through a gap in the frame, scores of petals fly into the air and fall to my feet like sunbeams. As I collect the petals and put them into a shoebox, I imagine Gran at her old kitchen table, the surface obscured by reams of crepe paper.

'Don't be so particular, Sapphie,' she'd say, as I fussed over shade and sequence. 'It's the imperfections that make the flowers perfect.'

I pack away supplies—glues and tapes, forestry wire and scissors, the yellow-coloured crepe I've cut into strips and the moss-green pieces I'll shape for the foliage. A screech shoots through the silence. Possums in the red gum. I wish they'd eat there every night and leave the orange trees alone.

Another gust of wind, stronger than the last, rattles the window again. The latch is fastened but the timber is weathered and the screws are loose. One day, when this farmhouse is mine, I'll replace the windowsill and fill in all the gaps. I'll hang curtains to keep out the cold, plaster the cracks in the cornices and repair the rotting skirting boards. One day …

I turn off the overhead lights and lock the front door behind me. A butterscotch moon, low in the sky, throws shadowy light on the gardens—camellia trees, azalea bushes and tangles of bare branched midwinter roses. The trunk of the red gum is palest pink, the low-lying branches heavy with foliage.

When the breeze catches my hood and pulls it back, the air is cold on my face. I thread loose hairs through my plait and secure it under my collar. My breaths are white as I step through the shadows on the porch. I could walk by road to the school where I teach and live, but I prefer to hike cross-country. High silky clouds, grey and teal, obscure the pinprick stars.

Tree roots have lifted cracks in the path at the side of the farmhouse and the water tank near the raised bed of herbs is ringed with rusty stripes. Ten empty pots, stacked in a wobbly tower, lean against the greenhouse. Was it Barney who hid the marijuana plants behind the tomato vines and trellis? My heart sinks. I don't want it to be him, or any of the teens and children who come to the farmhouse to help with the horses or just hang around, but Barney has shown particular interest in the vegetable gardens in the past few months.

I glance at the compost bin. The plants were mature. Was it safe to uproot them, cut them up and shove them in there? Tomorrow I'll add worms to the bin and fill it up with horse manure.

Skirting around the mandarin and cumquat trees, I bypass the horses napping near the yards and slip between the rungs of the wide metal gate. The track through the paddock is fairly straight and the grass is low and scrappy. More difficult to navigate is the scrub that borders the creek; I push back the branches, jump over a ditch and skirt around thistles. The creek is low and the meandering flow, black in the shadows, is interspersed by ridges of rock. I jump over two shallow crevices before leaping over the band of deeper water to land on my feet and scramble up the incline.

I'm still crouched low, my hands on the ground, when I see a man walking through the paddock from the direction of the school. He's dressed in city clothes. His shoulders are broad. He's tall. If I stand, he'll see me. Does it matter? Horseshoe Hill is my home. I haven't done anything wrong.

As I push myself upright, I touch a dandelion weed, the long, fleshy leaves soft on my fingers. I recall the marijuana. Barney is only fourteen. I don't think he smokes or drinks. Was he cultivating the weed for somebody else? This track leads directly to the farmhouse. Is the man sneaking in to check out the crop?

I scramble back to the creek bed, running along the bank before tackling the incline again. There's little cover on this side of the creek, only two gum trees. The closest tree isn't very tall, but there's a much larger tree next to it. I stand on a boulder and leap to the first tree, taking hold of the branch and swinging a leg over the bough, before hoisting myself onto it and sitting astride. I wriggle to the trunk, wrap an arm around it and stand. The adjacent tree's lowest branch, narrow and straight like a bar, is higher than the one I'm on, and only a metre away. I bend my knees and jump, grasping the branch with both hands before looping my legs around it. The branch, bowing under my weight, tilts towards the ground. Yikes.

Hanging by my legs and arms, I shuffle towards the trunk. It's too wide to wrap my arms around, but the knobbly remnants of a long dead branch provide a handhold. I grasp it as I pull myself up and sit, legs dangling beneath me. I check my phone. Almost ten o'clock. I peer through the leaves.

The man is only twenty metres away. His coat falls past his thighs; the collar is turned up. I can't make out his features, but I think that he's young with short dark hair. He doesn't have the look of a teenage druggie and, as he's not shady and thin, or thickset and threatening, he looks nothing like the dealers I've seen. But … there's something familiar about him.

When he stops at the end of the track and looks in my direction, I hold my breath. He shouldn't be able to see me. My hair is dark brown, I'm dressed in black and grey and obscured behind the tree trunk. But just in case, I yank up my hood, pulling the toggle tight so it sits above my mouth.

I hear steps through the undergrowth, branches pushed aside. Silence. My heart thumps hard against my ribs.

'Hello!'

His voice is deep. Does he know I'm close? Why else would he call out? Should I answer? If he's walking around in the dead of night with criminal intent, I have no interest in talking to him. He might not know exactly where I am and even if he does, my branch won't hold his weight. I feel for my phone again. Reception isn't great, but I can threaten to call for help if I have to.

He scrambles down the bank to the creek and walks alongside it, his eyes on the ground until he reaches my tree. He stops, turns and looks up. The moon sneaks through a crack in the clouds and shines on his face. My breath catches.

Matts Laaksonen.

A strong jaw, high Nordic cheekbones and deep-set, intelligent eyes. A crease through his brow when he frowns and a twitch to his lips when he smiles. A scar on his chin.

It's a face I could never forget.

'Who are you?' he asks.

A wave of unhappiness tightens my throat.

The girl who loved you a lifetime ago.

'Come down,' he says.

The school is hundreds of metres away, securely locked up for the night. The old schoolhouse where I live is even further. In the distance, I see headlights: a truck on the loop road. It's probably Freddie, who's often late home from the markets.

Matts scrambles up the slope and pulls a phone from his pocket. When he activates the light, the bright silver beam triples my heart rate. Should I stand on my branch? It would hardly make a difference.

'Sapphire?'

His shoulders are broader than they used to be. The stubble on his face is even and neat.

I sit taller and loosen the toggle on my hood. I draw it back, pulling out my plait and flicking the long end down my back. I blink against the glare. 'Turn off the light, Matts.'

He puts the phone in his pocket. 'Why are you up there?'

'Why are you down there?'

'I came to warn you.' He crosses his arms.

'What about?'

'Not now,' he says. 'Get down.'

One of my hands is on the tree trunk. The other is on the branch near my leg. I wriggle my fingers, stiff with cold. I want to get down, but—

'How did you know I was out here?'

'I looked for you at the school. I was sent to the farmhouse.'

'By who?'

'The hotel barman.'

When I'm teaching children to sound out words, I draw out the letters. I elongate them. *Ba ... aa ... rr ... mm ... aa ... nn*. Matts does the opposite when he speaks. His native language is Finnish. He's fluent in English, but his words are short and sharp.

'Did my father send you?'

He can't reach the branch, but steps as close as he can. 'How did you get up there?'

When I don't answer, he looks from my tree to the other tree, then speaks through his teeth. 'Still taking risks?'

'Calculated ones.'

'You can't go back that way.'

I glance at the ground, three metres down. It falls away steeply. I'll have to swing wide, and drop to higher ground. Even so ...

'I'll manage.'

'You'll hurt yourself.' He takes a few steps down the incline and braces himself. 'Jump, Sapphire. I'll break your fall.'

'Leave me alone, Matts.'

'You haven't changed, have you?'

'It's been eight years. How would you know?'

There's a rustling in the leaves above me. A ringtailed possum scampers headfirst down the tree trunk. When I yelp and pull back my arm, he freezes. His coat is speckled grey, his startled eyes are bright.

I put my hands on the branch either side of my legs as I inch away. 'I'm on your tree, aren't I? It's okay. I won't hurt—'

The branch dips sharply and I lose my balance. I fall.

If I'd jumped, I would have landed on my feet. Matts would have stopped me falling down the slope. As it is, my arms flail in midair as I try to right my body. But I don't have time. I don't—

I'm moving too fast for Matts to catch me so I land on my back and tumble helter-skelter down the slope towards the water.

'Sapphire!'

Pebbles and gravel dig into my skin. My chest burns and I fight to suck in air. My eyes water then tears trickle down my cheeks and into my ears.

He crouches by my side and runs his hand, barely touching, up my arm. 'Are you winded? Take small breaths. Fill your lungs slowly.' He puts a hand on my shoulder and frowns. 'Don't move.'

He takes my wrist and feels for my pulse. When he looks at his watch, his breaths are steady. His eyes are dark like storm clouds. He smooths hair from my face and it sticks to my cheek.

'Ow.'

He frowns again. 'I'm sorry. It's grazed.' He shrugs out of his coat and lays it over my body, tucking it closely around me from my neck to my toes. 'Breathe, Kissa.'

Kissa is Finnish for cat. When I was a little girl, he said I was a pest, but tolerable. Only he wouldn't have said tolerable. What did he say? That allowing me to follow him around was far less trouble than forcing me to leave.

'I want to check nothing is broken.'

I squeak a response.

He carefully presses down the right side of my body—shoulder, ribs, hip, knee and ankle—his touch impersonal and clinical. His hand goes to my left side. He feels down my shoulder and arm. I flinch.

He frowns. 'What? Did I hurt you?'

There's scar tissue on my inner arm. And other scars as well. 'No,' I croak.

When he's finished looking for broken bones, he sits back on his heels. The shadows shift. I shudder. I suck in tiny breaths. His shirt is long sleeved, but cotton. He must be cold.

'Can you move your hands?' he says. 'Your feet?'

I feel the weight and warmth of his coat as I stretch out my fingers and rotate my ankles. 'Yes,' I whisper.

'Your head. Your back and legs. Do you feel pain? Numbness?'

'Just ... winded.'

He watches as I draw air into my lungs, and bend and straighten my legs until they feel like mine again. When I attempt to get up, he puts firm hands on my back and waist and shifts me onto my side.

'Stay there.' His phone buzzes. 'Laaksonen.' He speaks in Finnish, just a few words.

I roll, without help this time, onto my hands and knees. I smell eucalyptus, dust and leaf litter.

Matts stands easily and holds out his hands.

I shake my head. 'I can get up by myself.'

'Prove it.'

We're at the base of the slope. The creek gurgles next to us; the trees tower above us. Where is the possum? I dig my heels into the ground, draw up my knees and rest my forehead on them—as if I'm lightheaded, as if I need to think. I *do* need to think.

'Give me a minute.'

The air is cold on my cheek. I tentatively touch it; sticky with blood. The children in my class range from seven to ten. I'll tell them I climbed a tree because I had to ... what? Spy on someone? I could have stood on the ground and hidden behind the tree trunk. That would've been adequate. Sensible. Why go to so much trouble?

I look up, straight into his eyes. Slowly shaking his head, Matts kneels, rearranges his coat around my shoulders and fastens a button.

'What a stupid thing to do,' he says, as he unclenches my fingers and brushes stones from my palms.

'Ow!' I snatch my hands back and press my palms against my knees. He frowns and, muttering under his breath, he stands again, undoing the buttons of his shirt and shrugging it off. He's wearing a white T-shirt underneath. I blink when he grabs the hem with both hands and pulls it off.

'Matts? What are you—'

He's slender but strong. Even in the half-light, his pectoral and abdominal muscles are clearly defined. Holding the T-shirt between his knees, he slides firmly muscled arms back into the sleeves of his shirt. I look away.

'Wait here,' he says.

His coat hugs my back as I rest my head on my knees again. His footsteps crunch on the gravel. Within a minute he's back and holds out his T-shirt, wet but neatly folded.

'Clean your hands and face.'

The fabric is soft. When I hold it to my cheek, it smells fresh. His shirt is buttoned again and neatly tucked in. My skin is suddenly warm.

'Thank you.'

Besides the wind in the trees and occasional movement in the undergrowth, it's quiet. I take care with my hands, ignoring the stinging as I brush the dirt away. The fabric is smudged with blood. I don't want to give it back but I don't want to hang onto it.

As if he reads my mind, he takes it from me. I clumsily undo the button and hold up his coat. 'Thanks.'

'Keep it.'

A shiver passes through me. 'I'm okay.'

After shoving the T-shirt into a pocket, he puts the coat back on. He holds out his hands and I take them. I wait for my hands to hurt again, but all I'm aware of is the press of his palms against mine. A second passes. Or is it a few? Our hands have grown. We're adults now. His touch feels the same, yet different. Slowly and carefully, he pulls me to my feet. He's still much taller, but our height differential is far less than it was. When I tug to free my fingers, he tightens his hold. He checks that I'm steady on my feet before he lets me go.

I nod stiffly. 'Thank you.'

The clouds shift. They're thinner than they were—gossamer sheets of iridescent pearl. Light catches his hair and turns the tips gold.

There are golden eagles in Finland.

Kotka is Finnish for eagle.

That's the name I gave him.

CHAPTER

2

Matts and I don't touch as we walk up the slope to the paddock, but he stays close by my side as if afraid I might fall any minute. I've wrenched my shoulder. Every step hurts because of the bruise on my hip, but I'm determined not to limp. I pull up my hood in an attempt to keep the cold from my cheek.

'You might as well tell me why you're here, Matts.'

'You're hurt. It can wait.'

'You said you wanted to warn me.'

'I'm also here for work.'

We skirt around the dam. The water, ochre in daylight, in moonlight is sepia brown.

'What work?'

'You're a teacher, aren't you?' I feel his gaze on the side of my face as, holding my hip to support it, I step over a ditch. 'And the chair of Horseshoe's Environment Committee.'

'Did you look me up?'

'Have you heard of the Ramsar Convention?'

'It's like a treaty between governments, isn't it?'

'It focuses on the conservation of wetlands. I'm the European representative on the secretariat that administers it.'

'What did you study?'

'Environmental engineering. I specialise in wetland biodiversity.'

The moon, bold and dark yellow, peers through the clouds again. Matts, who used to take one step for every two of mine, is walking deliberately slowly. If I close my eyes and open them again, will he still be here? What do I feel most intensely? Hurt? Pain? Betrayal?

When our arms bump, I skitter away. Fear?

I clear my throat. 'The creek leads to the Macquarie River, which runs through Horseshoe Hill. There are wetlands at the end of the river, aren't there? The Macquarie Marshes are on the convention's Ramsar List.'

'They form part of our study. We're consulting to your federal government.'

I push my hands into the opposite sleeves of my jacket, hoping to warm them. 'My father is a member of parliament. Is there a connection?'

'To my work, no.'

'What's the warning about?'

'Something that happened when we lived in Buenos Aires.'

I skirt around divots made by sheep and cattle hooves as we walk in single file towards the perimeter lights that mark the fence of the school. An owl hoots. Matts looks down. The scar on his chin is silvery now.

'Do you want to rest?' he asks.

'I'm fine.' When we near the end of the track, where the clearing is wider and the walking is easier, we step side by side again. 'Argentina was such a long time ago.'

'Not to me,' he says quietly.

'Did you do your year of military training?'

'Most of it in military intelligence. I hated it.'

'I live at the old schoolhouse, but I guess you know that already.'

'Buenos Aires, Sapphire. I'll come back tomorrow. What time?'

'I don't have good memories of it.'

'Because of your mother?'

I don't want to lead him through the shortcut to the schoolhouse, so I take the path to the road that leads to the town. We pass the ironbark tree, the trunk thick and rough, the leaves long and thin.

'And other things.' I step carefully over tree roots. 'How did you know I was in the tree?'

'I saw a light. Why were you hiding?'

A brushtail possum steps onto the power line that runs from the road to the school. He crosses the span as if he's on tiptoes before he leaps onto the roof of the school hall. His claws scratch and scrape as he scampers along the gutter.

'Is the warning about my father? I have little to do with him.'

'You changed your surname.'

'I didn't want to be a Beresford-Brown any more.'

He runs a hand roughly through his hair, thick and straight like it always was. 'You're still running,' he says.

When an aching tightness snakes up my chest, I walk to the school sign and grasp the post. I speak over my shoulder. 'I'll be at the farmhouse tomorrow afternoon. You will have passed it when you drove into town. Can we meet at five o'clock?'

I feel his eyes on my back as I walk up the steps of the original schoolhouse to the porch. As I kick off my boots, I lean against a timber desk, marked with stains from fountain pens. A century ago, children would have hung their hats, coats and satchels on the rows of brass hooks on the opposite wall. Tumbleweed, meowing loudly, leaps up the steps and jumps onto the desk.

'Hey, puss.' When I take him into my arms, he purrs against my neck. 'You'll never guess who I saw tonight.' My eyes sting with sadness as I stroke his fur, the stripy shades of brown fading with age. We pass through the living room and into the kitchen, built at one end of the verandah that overlooks the school grounds. He waits on the threshold as I walk gingerly down the back steps and along a crumbling concrete path to the toilet, a slightly modernised version of the old outhouse.

My muscles have stiffened even more by the time I return to the schoolhouse, holding the door open for Tumbleweed to follow me through. When he curls up on the rug in front of the fireplace, I pick him up and lay him on the couch in his favourite spot, covering him with a mohair throw. He looks at me balefully before curling up again. 'Sleep tight.'

The bathroom is a prefabricated unit, slotted between the living room and bedroom. I flick on the light. The graze on my face runs from my cheekbone to my jaw. It's not deep, just messy and dirty. I soak a cloth in warm water, holding it against my face as I pull the elastic from my plait and unravel my hair. My face is pale; my eyes are navy.

I *was* Sapphire Beresford-Brown. Now I'm Sapphie Brown.

It's after eleven o'clock by the time I sit on my bed in pink pyjamas, my laptop on my knee, a glass of water on my side table and a packet of frozen peas, wrapped in a handtowel, pressed against my face. The bed is only a double. Even so, it's impossible to get anything out of the cupboard without closing the door to the living room first. I pull the quilt more firmly around my waist and open my browser.

Matts Laaksonen.

How many times have I got this far? Typed his name but never hit return? He no longer had a place in my life.

He has no place in my life now, but he'll be back again tomorrow.

He did an undergraduate degree in Oulu and postgraduate studies in Helsinki. With his Ramsar work he's based in Switzerland, but seems to travel all over the world. He has no social media presence, but there are plenty of images attached to his name. In some photos he's dressed in boots and a warm winter jacket. In others, he's wearing jeans with a T-shirt, his face and arms tanned. He's in mountainous regions in France and Italy. He's thigh deep in a Yorkshire bog—with a lift in his lip that could be a smile. He's lying on his back with an arm across his eyes, one leg bent at the knee, on a grassy slope in Finland. There's a village in the distance, multicoloured houses and a bright blue lake.

Occasionally, he's wearing a suit. At the front of a lecture theatre. At a horseshoe-shaped table at the UN offices in Geneva.

When the peas soften, I put them on my side table. I gingerly touch the graze as I scroll through more images.

There are photographs of Matts with a number of different women—beautiful and leggy with curvy silhouettes and nicely rounded breasts. Holding hands, arms linked.

When salt stings my cheek, I reach for the tissue box, pluck out tissues and press them against my eyes. I sniff, swallow and wipe my eyes again.

'Why did you have to come back?'

When we met, I was seven and Matts had just turned ten. He told me later I had pigtails in my hair. One was higher than the other, but when he tried to even them out, I pushed his hand away and said I liked them as they were. Our fathers both worked in Buenos Aires. Leevi Laaksonen was the Finnish ambassador to Argentina and my father was a bureaucrat from the Australian Department of Trade. Matts's house was white with a terracotta roof in a hundred shades of orange, and my house was yellow with a kaleidoscope of colour in the garden. We lived in the same tree-lined street and attended the same international school. Our mothers became best friends.

Matts was thirteen when his mother died. My father thought I was too young to go to Inge's funeral, but Matts insisted he wanted me there. After the service, the mourners were directed to the embassy gardens and Matts took my hand. He held my fingers so tightly they hurt. He walked so quickly that I ran to keep up. He pulled me into the shade of a jacaranda tree, the canopy heavy with soft purple blooms. When his shoulders trembled, I stroked his arm. He swallowed a sob and I gave him my tissues. He blew his nose.

I rubbed his back.

He wiped his eyes.

'Don't scrub so hard,' I whispered to him. 'You'll make them go red.'

When he gave the tissues back, they were so soggy and torn that they fell apart in my hands. I rolled them into a tight little ball and hid them in my pocket.

We were always together.

We cared for each other.

Kissa. A cat. Kotka. An eagle.

I'm yawning as I unlock the door and let in the morning sun. When I see Barney sitting on my fence, I double back to the kitchen for my mug and shove my feet into sheepskin boots. I jiggle the string of the teabag as I walk down the path towards him.

'You're up early,' I say. 'It's not even seven.'

He pulls his long legs free of the railings and jumps to the ground. When he kicks a patch of dirt where the grass doesn't grow, his shoe disappears in the dust. His blond hair is sticking up like he's just got out of bed.

'Reckon it was you who binned them,' he mutters.

'Can you be more specific?'

When he looks up, his mouth drops open. The swelling in my cheek has gone down, but the graze is fiery red.

'What happened?'

'I fell at the creek.'

'Were you climbing?'

'The marijuana, Barney. That's what I'm concerned about.'

His shoulders sag. 'I shouldn't have moved it behind the tomatoes, miss. Sorry about that.'

'Sorry you moved it, or sorry you grew it at all?'

'My mates gave me the seedlings months ago. They'll want what the plants were worth.'

'What mates?'

'It was only weed.'

'You did it for your Dubbo cousins, didn't you? They're older than you. Why don't they grow their own illegal substances? Were they planning to sell it? That's dealing, Barney. You'd be in serious trouble if you were caught.'

'My mates couldn't do it at home. They were worried about the cops.'

'The police come to Horseshoe too, you know. And you'd be the one in possession. You're fourteen now. What would your mum say about juvenile detention? What about Archie?'

'Mum would be gutted. Archie too.'

'You're right about that.'

Archie, Barney's younger brother, is eight years old and has been in my class for the past two years. Shelley, the boys' mother, is raising her sons on her own and works at a factory in a neighbouring town. Archie is very bright, but has ADHD and struggles socially. The brothers are close.

'Will you go to the cops?'

'That's not all you have to worry about. You could be expelled from school.'

'I have to do another two years to get an apprenticeship.'

'Assuming you'd get one with a criminal record.'

His face is flushed. 'I don't know what to do. If I don't get some money to them, my cousins, their mates, they'll kill me.'

The kids know I support them, that I give second chances, and third ones and fourth. They know I do what I can to protect them when they've done something wrong. Some take advantage of that, but others do better in the future. I sip from my mug. The steam rises, stinging my cheek.

'Your mum could talk to her brothers,' I say eventually. 'Let them sort it out.'

'No! My cousins—they'll think I dobbed them in.'

'Just tell the truth: that I found the weed, destroyed it and blamed you. With any luck, your cousins will think you're not much good at crime and leave you alone in the future. And if you're upfront, your mum will see you're taking responsibility for your mistake. Reassure her it won't happen again and she'll be relieved you've learnt your lesson. Shelley works hard for you and Archie. You're old enough to help her out, not make things more difficult.'

He lifts his chin. 'When I've finished my apprenticeship, I've got stuff I want to do for her.'

'She's told me about that, how you're going to build her a house.'

'Reckon I can, when I run my own business.'

'I think you can too, Barney, provided you keep out of trouble. You're great with Archie, you don't muck up at school and you work hard in the holidays. Your mum cares about you a lot. She trusts you.'

He shuffles his feet. 'Your mum's not around, right?'

'My mother's not relevant to—'

'You were talking about my mum before.'

I blow out a breath. 'Mine died eight years ago, when I was nineteen.'

'She was a druggie, wasn't she?'

When we moved to Buenos Aires, Mum was sociable and vivacious. She enjoyed the expatriate life, caring for me and supporting my father. But after Inge's death, even though Matts and his father went back to school and work, Mum was tearful, unsettled and anxious. She rarely laughed, and only entertained when she couldn't get out of it. She wasn't the woman my father had married.

At his insistence, she went to a doctor and he prescribed sleeping pills. Maybe she took more than she was supposed to? One night when my father was away, she fell. I found her in the hallway between our bedrooms, disoriented and unable to speak. She'd injured her neck. Physiotherapists. Naturopaths. Chiropractors. Doctors. Painkillers.

She tried to get off the drugs too many times to remember. Or maybe not, because I think I remember them all. Withdrawal. Pain. Relapse.

I blow on my tea a few more times before I answer Barney. 'My mother had a drug addiction, yes.' I take a sip. 'Where did you hear that, anyway?'

'School. That's why you're a foster kid, why you went to the Hargreaves.'

'When I was sixteen, but … I was better off than a lot of other kids. I wasn't abused. I could have gone to England with my father.'

'You're against drugs because of your mum.'

'You sure it's carpentry you're passionate about? You don't want to be a psychologist?'

'What do they do?'

'They snoop into other people's lives.'

He grimaces. 'I wasn't saying your mum was on meth or heroin, nothing like that.'

'My mother abused painkillers and other drugs. Some she got on prescription, others she didn't. But addiction is addiction. It's brutal and dangerous—for you and the people you care about.'

Two stitches down, four stitches across.

Matts was sixteen when he got the scar on his chin. It wasn't long before our families left Argentina for Canberra, Australia's capital city, and Mum was worried she wouldn't be able to get everything organised without the drugs she'd run out of again. Matts had followed me along the backstreets of Buenos Aires and down to the ports, and refused to leave without me. When an argument started between the dealer and Matts, the dealer pushed Matts from the wharf.

When I saw Matts the next day, his arm was in a sling and he was propped up in bed. He couldn't eat because his face was swollen and he could only drink through a straw. It was painful for him to move, but he shifted on the bed to face me. He never raised his voice, even when he was angry.

'You're thirteen, Kissa,' he said. 'If you do that again, I'll tell your father.'

'You wouldn't!'

'You're growing up now. There are many ways the dealers can hurt you.'

'Mum needs my help.'

He must have clenched his jaw, because he winced and held his good hand against it. 'I need you too.'

I walked to the side of his bed and picked up the glass. 'Please, Kotka, don't say anything. I promise I'll be careful.'

He frowned. But when I held the straw to his mouth, he covered my hand with his.

'What happened, miss?' Barney kicks his shoe against the fence. 'Did your mum take an overdose?'

'She bought pills on the street in Canberra.' Clearing my throat, I focus on the long strappy leaves of the kangaroo paw I planted near the gate. 'The coroner couldn't work out whether she took too many or the batch was bad, but she became disoriented and ended up in the middle of a road. She was hit by a car, but it wasn't the driver's fault. End of story.' There are no buds on the kangaroo paw, but perhaps it will flower in the spring.

'Sorry about that, miss.'

'You have to tell your mum what I've told you about my mother. Otherwise, I'll have to do it.'

'I'll tell her.' He stands a little taller. 'But not my mates.'

'Thanks.' I throw the rest of my tea into the garden bed. 'And while you're talking to Shelley, how about you own up about the weed? I know she'll do what's best for you.'

'I hope she don't kill me.'

'Trust me, she won't.'

'Well if she does, it'll be your—'

'Hey! Quit while you're ahead.'

He scuffs his feet. 'Are you going to the farmhouse now, to your horses and flowers and stuff?'

I look over the paddocks to the fuzzy outline of the sun in the distance. I can't see the farmhouse from here, only a glimpse of the trees either side of the creek. 'It's not mine yet, Barney.'

'But it will be one day, right? That's what Mum says, because of all the work you put in.'

It was only after I was given a permanent position at the school and had financial security that I applied to the council for an option to buy the farmhouse. But when the youth centre needed somewhere to run its activities, I pushed back the purchase. Delaying also gave me more time to save up, so I wouldn't have to borrow as much from the bank.

'Yes, it'll be mine.'

'Can I go now?'

'You've reminded me of something.' I turn my mug in my hand. It was a gift from a student and is printed with red and bronze banksia flowers. 'We rely on the council's permission to run the youth centre at the farmhouse and to keep my horses there.'

'It's free.'

'On the condition it's used for community activities. What if they'd found out about the marijuana? You not only put yourself at risk, you put the program at risk. And you know better than most how important it is to a lot of the kids who go there.'

'Best day of the week for Archie, hanging around with Freckle and Sonnet.' He looks away and kicks the dirt again. 'I get it.'

'Bring your mum over to talk to me, and you and I can forget about this.' I raise my arm. 'Deal?'

He slaps my hand. 'Deal.'

'Ow.' I hold my hand close to my side as I walk down the path. 'See you tomorrow morning.'

I'm sitting on the end of my bed and brushing my hair, a second cup of tea steaming on the side table, when Tumbleweed jumps onto my lap. I tie a ponytail, before twisting it into a bun and securing it with pins. I push stray ends behind my ears. My eyes are darker than my mother's, but we shared the same colours in our hair.

Chestnut, cinnamon, coffee, chocolate.

Gran, my paternal grandmother, once told me that the way I see colour is my superpower. When I laughed, she pointed to a newly opened flower—a gardenia—that I'd picked from her garden that morning. She asked me to describe the shades of the petals.

'There are a lot, but ...' I turned the flower in my hand. 'Porcelain, frost, cotton and pearl.'

'Even as a toddler, you wanted to know about the colours.' She smiled. 'Your mum did her best, but it drove your father batty.'

'I must take after you, Gran.'

'In a few days' time, the flower will age. What colours will it have then?'

'I won't know the shades until I see it.'

'Because every flower is different.'

'Flying would be a more useful superpower. What do I do with this one?'

Her blue eyes twinkled. 'Treasure it,' she said.

I reach over Tumbleweed for the tea and hold the mug with both hands. I blow on the surface and sip. The first school bell rings, letting the children know they can play in the grounds. Through the window, I see mothers, fathers and children on the footpath, chatting and laughing.

When I meet Matts at the farmhouse this afternoon, I'll listen to what he has to say. After that …

I'll pretend to forget him all over again.

CHAPTER

4

After lessons are finished for the day, I go back to the schoolhouse to change before returning to the school grounds. A group of girls kick a football around the oval.

'Hey, Miss Brown,' Amy calls out. 'Are you taking Strider out?'

I fasten the buttons on my jacket before carefully stepping over the low wall to the netball court. 'I won't have time tonight.'

'Can me and Mary look after Jet's ponies tomorrow?'

'Freckle and Lollopy would love that. I'll see you in the morning.'

I unwind my cotton scarf and drape it more loosely around my neck. Closing the gate behind me, I follow the track through the paddock. The clouds are heavy and grey, but there's no rain forecast for another few weeks at least. I blow against my hands and put them into my pockets, cross the creek and step sideways up the incline, supporting my hip as I climb through the fence. Horseshoe Hill, the final bump in the Horseshoe Range, forms a backdrop to the farmhouse. The corrugated iron roof catches the light and shimmers; a rooster perches bravely on the lopsided weathervane.

I'd lived in Horseshoe for only a week when I first saw the farmhouse. My high school was thirty minutes away and I had to catch a bus there and back. When another student peppered me with questions about why I'd been fostered, I got off the bus early, reasoning I couldn't get lost if I followed the creek to the river in town. I'm not sure why I looked up, but when I glimpsed the chimney, sandstone gold against the bright blue sky, I changed direction. The twenty hectares of land surrounding the farmhouse was in reasonable shape because a neighbouring farmer leased it to graze sheep. But when I climbed over the gate on the far side of the paddock closest to the house, all I could see was an impenetrable wall of foliage. Only it *wasn't* impenetrable, and the further I pushed through it, the more curious I became. First I found the small orchard, almost smothered by vines. Next I found the gardens, a mix of introduced and native plants. It was early spring and the wattle trees were in flower. The daffodils near the water tank, fighting through layers of weeds, were like dabs of yellow paint. The roses at the side of the house had wild thorny branches and tightly furled buds. The lilli pilli fruits were as big and shiny as cherries. I couldn't see the boronia flowers, but could smell their crisp sweet scent.

By the time I found the steps to the verandah, my arms and legs were scratched and my hair was a tangled mess. My school uniform was torn where the pocket had snagged on a branch. I peered through the windows and tested the latches; I pushed against the doors and rattled the knobs. I couldn't get in but I knew I'd be back.

I liked the weathered sandstone chimney and the shutters on the windows. I liked the red gum and the flowers and the rippling waves of grass.

The verandah was mostly in shade, but the sun had found a way through the trees near the steps. I faced the house, lifted my hands and combed my fingers through my hair.

I liked the sunshine on my shoulders. I liked the thousand shades of green.

The farmhouse was neglected and friendless, damaged and abandoned. And so, I'd thought, was I.

This could be my home.

The trees in the farmhouse orchard are old and gnarled, but there are apples in autumn if the cockatoos don't get to them first and, subject to the possums, there are oranges, cumquats and lemons in winter. The fruit on the tree closest to the back verandah is bright against the timbers. I pluck an orange, small but sweet smelling, from the lowest branch. After I've fed the horses, I'll—

'Sapphire.'

Matts is standing a few metres away, wearing faded blue jeans and a navy blue sweater. His boots are city boots, shiny and brown with matching leather laces.

I raise my chin. 'You're early.'

'I'll wait.' I couldn't see his eyes clearly last night, but in daylight they're the same shades of grey I remember. His gaze slides from my eyes to my cheek. 'How do you feel?'

'A little stiff, but … I'm well, thank you.' I glance over his shoulder towards the sun, breaking through the clouds but low in the sky. 'I have things to do before it gets dark.'

I walk past him to the paddock at the side of the house where the horses spend most of their time. When I round the corner, Lollopy, a Shetland cross with a woolly black coat, nickers as he presses his chest against the gate. He belongs to my friend Jet Kincaid, as does Freckle, a grey pony even older than Lollopy. While Jet and Finn are in Scotland on their honeymoon, I've drafted the ponies into the equine therapy program.

Unlike a lot of people around here, I didn't grow up on a horse, but I was more determined to ride than make friends when I came to Horseshoe. Jet's father was patient and encouraging when he gave me riding lessons, pretending not to notice how unhappy and uncommunicative I was. I'd been riding for over a year before he let me ride Chili Pepper, his late wife's chestnut warmblood. Tears filled his eyes as he hoisted me onto his back. 'You've got a good seat and gentle hands,' he said. 'Annabel wouldn't mind a bit.'

Sonnet ambles towards me. He's in his twenties, a slow and placid ex-racehorse, perfect for building confidence in the kids who might be too anxious or aggressive to come into contact with other large horses. Strider, another gelding, and Prima, a mare, are thorough-breds too. I found Prima at the knackery. She's bay, with a brown coat and black mane and tail.

When Strider, black with one white sock, trots towards me, stopping only metres away, I hold out my hand. 'How are you, boy?' I stroke his neck before picking up his feet to check his hooves. They were split and an abscess had formed in one of them by the time he was rescued, so it's no wonder he was lame. Even though he doesn't often go on the roads, I have him shod once a month to get his feet back into shape. I trace the brand on his shoulder. He made money for his owners for a number of years, first on the city tracks and then on the country ones. But when he couldn't earn his keep any more, he was sold as a pony club horse to a family that didn't know his background. Within a month, he was sold again. And then again.

He hasn't thrown me off for a couple of months. 'We'll go out to stretch your legs tomorrow,' I tell him.

I ruffle Lollopy's fuzzy black forelock as I pass and, holding out a hand, walk towards Prima. Only slightly less skittish than she was when she arrived, she doesn't distrust only people but other horses—even Lollopy, who only reaches the tops of her legs. If she won't settle, she'll never work as a therapy horse. It wouldn't be fair to Prima or the kids.

'How are you, girl?'

She takes a couple of steps towards me before shying away. She's clearly aware of Matts, standing by the fence. He's a stranger to her.

And also to me.

When I double back and walk to the small timber shed, Matts follows again, watching silently as I load biscuits of hay into a wheelbarrow. If we'd had more rain, there would be plenty of grass for the horses. I spread the hay in a pile for the ponies and in two different piles for the geldings. I take Prima's share to her and after she's taken a few mouthfuls out of my hand, I encourage her to follow me to the solitary grey gum, away from the others. As she eats, I latch a lead rope to her halter and stroke her glossy neck.

'I hope you're not too chilly at night.' Being a thoroughbred, she doesn't have a thick winter coat like the ponies, and she's too fearful of the other horses to huddle with them for warmth. When I tried to rug her, even though she must have been rugged before, she was terrified, so I hang a rug over the fence near the feed trough to get her used to the look of it and the sounds it makes when it flaps in the wind.

Ignoring Matts doesn't mean I'm not aware of him. He crosses his arms and leans on a post as I run my hand down Prima's legs and over her rump. She's tall for a mare, well over sixteen hands, and is slowly gaining weight. I unclip her lead rope and thread my fingers through her mane. From the corner of my eye, I see Matts straighten.

'I think he's had enough of waiting.' When I lift my hand to stroke Prima's neck, she shies, skittering out of reach. Her wide brown eyes follow my movements as I slowly back away. 'Wish me luck.'

Matts leans against the gate as I walk across the paddock. When I throw my leg over the railing, he takes a step back.

I'm the girl who loved you a lifetime ago.

CHAPTER

5

My family moved back to Canberra not long before my fourteenth birthday. The leaves on the deciduous trees, liquidambars, poplars and maples, changed colour every day.

Russet, burgundy, peach, pumpkin, ochre.

Matts's father had been appointed ambassador to Australia by then, so he and Matts lived in Canberra too. Mum and my father were officially still together. Unofficially, besides the social engagements my father couldn't get out of, they led separate lives. Just as we'd done in Buenos Aires, Matts and I attended the same private school.

For that first year, we saw each other almost every day. When Matts wasn't at my house with Mum and me, I was at his. He was conscientious and dependable, arrogant and protective. I clung to him fiercely. Relied on him. Adored him. Until, soon after I'd turned fifteen, Matts told me I shouldn't turn up unannounced any more. He said he was busy studying and playing sport and going out with friends, so I should call before visiting. But sometimes we'd make a time and he'd cancel, or have someone else with him. It was like it was no longer enough to be just the two of us.

I missed him. I was hurt, angry and confused. My feelings for him were as intense as they had ever been, but our relationship had shifted. I resented his girlfriends. I wanted him to look at me.

It was the last day of term when Matts secretly followed me to the lane behind the suburban row of shops, where trucks made deliveries and the skips were kept. It wasn't the first time I'd handed money to the skinny man with the expensive black runners. He gave me a package, the drugs Mum had run out of again, and I handed over the envelope of cash. Mum would have preferred to do a bank transfer, but dealers didn't work like that. Anyway, her account was linked with my father's and he kept tabs on everything.

When I walked around the corner, Matts was leaning against a wall. He was a school prefect and usually wore a blazer, but it must have been in his bag. He straightened, watchful and suspicious, and rolled up the sleeves of his shirt. I hadn't put the package in my school bag yet, so it was easy enough for him to snatch it from my hand. He walked to my house and I followed, begging him to give back what was mine, but he was taller and stronger and I couldn't get it out of his grasp. His face was set and he refused to even look at me. So I pleaded with him not to upset Mum by making a fuss. I told her she knew it was wrong and would never do it again, that *I* would never do it again.

His lips were tight. He shook his head. 'Your mother puts you at risk,' he said quietly. 'I can't pretend not to see it any more.'

I was surprised he didn't continue to tell me off for the ten minutes it took to get to the front gate of my house. But then again, I was doing what he wanted me to do.

I saw my father through the glass of the wide double doors that led from the formal front garden, sheltered from the road by a tall pine hedge, to the lounge room. As the gate clicked shut behind me, I thought: *He's never at home on weekdays.* Mum, wearing a fitted black dress with a wide white belt and oversized buttons, was standing at his side, facing him. When she grasped his arm, he didn't turn towards her, he shrugged her off.

Which was about the time I worked out what was happening. It was a set-up. My father wanted to confront Mum by using the evidence Matts held firmly in his hand.

I stopped dead on the travertine path. Matts stopped too. When I held out my hand, it was shaking.

'Give it to me, Matts. I won't give it to Mum, I'll get rid of it, I promise.'

'I can't, Kissa.'

'He'll use it against her. He'll say she's unfit to look after me. That's what he's been threatening.' When Matts's lips tightened again, I took a step back. 'Is that what you think too?'

'She puts you at risk.'

'She's my mother.' I pointed to the window. Mum had her hands pressed against the glass and was crying. My father was standing next to her with his arms behind his back.

'She needs help.'

'And why do you think that is?' I said, fighting back tears so I could get my words out. 'He's finished with her. He wants to be free of her.' I took a shuddering breath. 'She's so sick she can't leave the house. She's of no use to him now.'

'What she makes you do, it's dangerous.'

'That's for me to judge!'

'You're too young.'

'I'm fifteen!'

I dropped my bag and scratched at his hand, trying to open his fingers. I grabbed his wrist with both hands and tried to pull him back to the gate. He walked on as if I weren't there, stumbling along behind him. The front door was open by then and my father was standing on the threshold. As I let go of Matts, my father grasped me by the tops of my arms and bundled me inside.

'Let her go!'

I'd never heard Matts raise his voice. I suspect my father hadn't either. He released me so quickly that I staggered and fell against the wall. Matts held out his hand but I punched it away. I shoved him in the chest, again and again, as hard as I could. He didn't defend himself; he stood with his arms by his sides, silently flinching.

'I never want to see you again!' I shouted.

I saw an expression on his face, pain or anger or hurt or maybe all three, that I didn't recognise.

My father cleared his throat. He took the package from Matts's hand. 'You care about Sapphire very much, Matts. I am her father. So do I.'

It was only then that I heard Mum's sobs from behind the door that divided the lounge room from the hallway. When she opened it wide, the architrave framed her. She was wild eyed with withdrawal. Her face was smudged with make-up. She'd got alcohol from somewhere; I could smell it on her breath.

For years my father had told the same story. How he'd seen a woman on a billboard and had fallen in love at first sight. Mum had been twenty-four, a successful model with a warm heart who liked expensive clothes, overseas travel and boutique hotels. My father was thirty, had a string of degrees and was a well-respected bureaucrat. Mum had given up her career so she could be with him and within a few years, I was born. A number of miscarriages followed.

'Darling?' The tips of Mum's fingers were stained with mascara. 'Don't be frightened. Come over here.'

'Sapphire?' Matts said quietly. 'I want to stay.' His eyes were clear, with black and silver shards.

'Get out.'

'Matts.' My father came between us. 'This is a family matter. Please leave.'

When Matts looked from my father to me, I took a step back. Mum held out a hand and Matts took it respectfully. 'I'm sorry, Kate.'

She hugged him. 'Inge would be cross with me to see you so upset.' She sniffed delicately and attempted a smile. 'All will be well, I promise.'

Matts turned at the door. 'I'll come tonight, Sapphire.'

'No!' I swiped tears from my face. My nose was streaming. 'You've got what you wanted! Go!'

Matts treads carefully up the wobbly timber steps as he follows me to the front door of the farmhouse. The hallway is crowded with plastic tubs filled with riding hats and boots, and crates overflowing with halters, lead ropes and grooming equipment. Three saddles, one behind the other, are balanced on a rail. When the new youth centre opens in a couple of months, the gear will be stored over there. I'll be able to replace the worst of the floorboards and paint the walls and ceilings.

'Excuse the mess,' I say, as I close the door to the first room on the left. When his steps slow, I imagine him reading Mary's poster. *Keep away from the flowers or else! This is Miss Brown's (Sapphie's) room. Private!*

'How often do you come here?' he asks.

The living room at the back of the house is set up as an office, with a battered filing cabinet, an old timber table we use as a desk and an odd assortment of chairs. I collect the folders I'll need for tomorrow, tapping their ends to line them up.

'I come every day, usually twice a day. I have an agreement to buy the farmhouse and land from the council, and my horses live here. We run youth centre activities on Saturdays, and sometimes in the holidays. Kids come on other days as well.'

'The horses are part of this?'

'In the equine therapy program, yes.'

'How does it work?'

'Adolescents who've been in juvenile detention and younger children with developmental and other differences interact with the horses. The sessions help with communication skills, impulse control, anxiety, anger management, things like that. Psychologists and social workers take care of the treatments. I provide the horses and coordinate the volunteers.'

He looks pointedly at the chairs. 'Can we sit, Sapphire?'

When I put the folders on the table and perch on an upright chair in front of it, he turns another chair so he's facing me. He's clean-shaven. He has very faint lines at the sides of his mouth.

'What work are you doing for the government, Matts?'

'For your government, I'm advising on wetland strategies. For mine, I'm doing a comparative study on diminishing rainfall and wetland biodiversity.'

'Right.'

'In the last drought, the Macquarie Marshes dried up. They're relevant to both projects.'

'They're hundreds of kilometres from here.'

'Four hours by road.'

I link my hands in my lap. 'What did you want to warn me about?'

'You see your father rarely.'

'I won't forgive him.'

'He was concerned when you ran away.'

'I was sixteen. I wasn't gone for long.'

'The first time?' His gaze goes from the cracks in the walls to the crumbling cornices. 'Six weeks, two days and fifteen hours. It felt like a long time to me.'

'I—' A white late model four-wheel drive is parked near the gate. Two galahs with pastel pink chests and dove grey wings peck at the ground near the tow bar. 'I should have contacted my father. It was wrong not to do that.'

'You ran away again.'

'I stopped running when I came to Horseshoe.' My nails are short and neat, but grubby from the horses. 'I see my father in the week after Christmas, and sometimes for my birthday. When he emails, I respond.'

'You feel the same about him as you did?'

'He gave up on Mum. He put Gran into a home.'

Matts frowns. 'She had dementia.'

'So? I looked after her.'

'What about when she fell?'

When my hand shoots to my breast, I awkwardly cross my arms. 'The oil caught fire while we were cooking. She could have come home, with a little more help, when she was better. She was happy in her own house. *We* were happy.'

'You went to school three days out of five.'

'How would you know that?'

'I communicated with your father.' He stretches out his legs.

'Why?'

'I cared about you.'

I don't want to look at him, but I can't look away. I know him yet I don't. I clear my throat.

'My father fell out of love with my mother. I understand that now. But what came later was different.' I cross one leg over the other. The sole of my right boot is almost worn through at the ball of my foot. 'His new wife has children of her own, young children. I don't want to be a part of their family. It wouldn't be fair to her or the children, because I can't pretend that the past never happened.'

'You hold me responsible too.' His eyes are clear and direct.

What's the expression in mine?

'You thought you were protecting me.' I reach behind me to the desk, pick up the folders and place them on my lap. 'I don't need that any more.'

The sun is going down, but rays of light shine through the window and lighten his hair.

Kotka. Eagle. Kultainen. Golden.

He leans his forearms on his thighs. 'You must remember my mother,' he finally says.

I'm not sure what happens first—the stillness of his body or the tears in my eyes. Inge was softly spoken and elegant. She wore her fair hair in a chignon, and always had fresh flowers on her dining room table. Matts didn't cry in the months after her funeral, but sometimes I did. He'd look into the distance, shove tissues in my direction and change the subject. We'd pretend it never happened. But I'd always chastise myself afterwards. I knew that Matts's father was too upset to even hear Inge's name. If I weren't brave, there'd be no one Matts could talk to.

I blink a few times and study my hands. 'Of course I do. Is your father still working?'

'He retired from the diplomatic corps, but consults to the government.' He runs a hand around the back of his neck. His sweater has a fine weave. It's not tight across his body, but firmly clings to his shoulders and chest. When he took off his shirt at the creek …

I swallow. 'Did he ever remarry?'

'No.'

'Please give him my regards.'

He frowns again. 'Your father, Sapphire. Are you aware of the allegations against him?'

'What?' I shake my head. 'No. What's happened?'

'When he was with the Department of Trade in Buenos Aires, Robert headed a multi-country working party, briefed to negotiate major infrastructure projects. The contracts were worth billions.'

'He was always at work.'

'It's been alleged that, in the course of negotiations, your father accepted a bribe.'

'What? Who from?'

'One of the companies that tendered for the projects, Hernandez Engineering.'

'My father wouldn't do something like that.'

His brows lift. 'You'd defend him?'

When I look down at the folders, my hair, neatly pinned back this morning, falls over my face. I push strands behind my ears. 'I don't think he'd take a bribe.'

Matts watches me closely. 'The Argentinian Government is holding an inquiry into the conduct of Josef Hernandez, the founder and majority shareholder. Hernandez has denied personal involvement in your father's case, but has claimed that, consistent with business practice in Argentina at the time, your father was given a gift.'

'A gift or a bribe?'

'Both would have been illegal under Australian law. Transfers of any type have to be declared. In any case, Robert denies receiving anything.'

'Why were the gifts handed out?'

'For many reasons: access to documentation, details of competing tenderer's bids, a friendly ear. Money and valuables were placed in deposit boxes in a Geneva bank. The recipients were given a key to a box.'

'Why do I need a personal briefing about this? Why are you involved?'

'Our fathers were in contact, professionally and socially, at the time the payment was allegedly made. A few weeks ago, Robert asked my father to verify details about business appointments and official engagements.'

The red gum near the window is blush pink in the sunlight, a silhouette at night. Repressing a shiver, I pull up my collar and blow on my hands. 'Did he find something?'

'My father had his own records, and also my mother's. He'd kept her personal items, letters and official diaries. When he looked through these, he found a key. It meant nothing to him seventeen years ago. Now it did.'

'Was it a deposit box key?'

'From the bank in Geneva named by Hernandez. My father didn't know whether it had relevance to the accusations against your father, but feared that it might.' Matts stands and walks through the shadows. He glances at me, holding tightly onto the folders on my lap, before flicking on the overhead light. He moves his chair closer to mine before sitting again. 'My father inherited my mother's estate, so was given access to the box. It held fifty thousand euro.'

'Oh!' I blink. 'What did your father do?'

'He reported what he'd found.'

'But weren't the allegations against my father? What did Inge have to do with it? Was it her money?'

'You won't like what I have to say.' His eyes are guarded.

All the buttons on my jacket are fastened, and the room would be no colder than it was twenty minutes ago. Nevertheless, my teeth chatter.

'Go on.'

'There's no record of the person who made the initial deposit, but the bank had other records. Before my father, only one other person had accessed the box.'

'Inge?'

'She was in Buenos Aires with my father when the box was opened. Your father was there too.'

'Who, then?'

'Passport records confirm that your mother was in Geneva. The bank has her signature.'

When I stand, holding the folders to my chest, he stands too. He comes so close that I smell his soap. Or is it the scent of his skin? I wish I weren't aware of him. I wish I felt nothing.

He takes a folded piece of paper from his pocket. There are three lines of handwriting, my mother's, on the photocopied page.

Dearest Inge,
Empty the box and keep everything safe. All will be well, I promise.
Love, Kate

'What does it …' my voice wavers. 'What does it mean?'

'Kate was in Geneva for a day. She didn't have a bank account in her own name and might not have had the time—or documentation—to set one up, so left the contents of the box as she'd found them. We believe my mother, who subsequently arranged to meet my aunt in Lausanne, must have agreed to help. Kate gave my mother the key only days before Inge died. She never had the chance to use it.'

When I step backwards into the chair, it tips and hits the table. It balances there, not up and not down. I breathe deeply as I right it.

'My father is going to drag Mum into this, isn't he?'

'It's cold in here, Sapphire. Let me drive you home. We can talk there.'

'No!'

He sighs. 'Sit down then.' He indicates the chair.

I shake my head. 'No.'

He closes his eyes for a moment. 'Establishing what happened is the only way to clear your father's name.'

'My mother will be collateral damage. I know what he'll say, what you'll say.'

Matts's feet are slightly apart. He puts his hands behind his back. 'Kate changed, Sapphire. She did things she wouldn't have done before.'

'The drugs, everything else, that only happened *after* Inge died. Before that, she wouldn't have needed extra money.'

He walks to the window. 'Shall I close it?'

'It's jammed.'

He examines the mechanism before opening the window wide and realigning the sash. Leaves rustle; a car drives past. When he puts both hands on the frame and pushes down hard, the window slams shut. Silence.

'Kate's behaviour after Inge's death was attributed to grief,' Matts says. 'There could have been another reason.'

'She had nothing to do with my father's work.'

'She was popular,' he says quietly. 'Everyone knew her. She also had access to documents and other material your father should have had locked up.'

'He didn't need to lock them up.'

'So he thought.' He blows out a breath. 'Now he thinks otherwise.'

'He accused Mum of neglecting me. He forced her to relinquish custody. He'll say anything to get out of this.'

'He was concerned about you.'

'And his career!' When my eyes sting, I turn my back. 'Whatever happened in Geneva, he'll blame Mum. She wouldn't have done something like that. She wouldn't have sold information.'

He hesitates. 'She was capable of worse, Sapphire. You know this.'

I swallow the lump in my throat. 'You have no right to say that.'

'You blame your father for what happened. You blame me. Never her.'

'She wasn't capable of defending herself. Not then. Not now.'

He stalks back to the window and looks outside. He grips the sill; his shoulders are tight. He turns his head and I see him in profile.

'Your father believes he'll be cleared of the bribe allegation, but fears the political fallout.'

'That doesn't surprise me.'

'Robert told me that if you refused to help him voluntarily, he could force you to do it. That's why I came.'

'How could he force me?'

'He wouldn't say.'

'I don't rely on him, Matts. I don't rely on anybody.'

He nods stiffly. 'You've made that clear.'

'I'll defend my mother. You tell my father that.'

When I walk to the door, Matts follows. Our footsteps are loud in the hallway. I stand aside to let him through the front door first, and he does the same. We touch and I jump.

His jaw is tight. 'Call him, Sapphire. It's the best way to protect yourself. It's the best way to protect Kate.'

Grey eyes on blue. Grey-blue. Blue-grey.

'You ...' I turn away. 'You cared for her once.'

I stuff the folders in my bag and rummage for Gran's old key-ring—the enamelled rosebuds in pale pink and crimson that snagged on my school tights in winter. The key is brass with an oval tip and a long, toothy shaft. I line it up with the keyhole.

Clunk.

What did Mum hear when she locked the deposit box? Was she afraid? Did she have something to hide? Was it night time or day time? Were the boxes at street level or deep underground?

My father didn't know whether Mum wanted to be buried or cremated. Neither did I. She would never have spoken about something like that. Even in her darkest times, she'd tell me that life was worth living. I'd tell her that one day, when the farmhouse was mine, this was where we'd live and …

As I throw the keyring into my bag, Matts touches my arm.

'Sapphire?'

When I turn, my hand is still in midair. He takes it, his fingers cold but mine far colder. He puts his other hand on my shoulder and peers at my cheek.

'Did you see a doctor?'

'I didn't need to.' The warmth of his body keeps out the chill.

'Let me drive you home.'

'I don't like—' I shake my head. 'I'd prefer to walk.'

'Call your father.'

My chin brushes against his fingers when I shake my head again. And all of a sudden, I'm hot and flustered and—

I take a jerky step back. 'Thanks for the warning. I'll think about what you said.'

As I walk past the water tank, his car door slams. The engine starts up. Headlights flash for a moment and then disappear on the road. Skirting around the orange and lemon trees to the paddock, I climb onto the gate and sit with my legs to one side. Freckle, ghostly in the shadows, lifts his head and softly neighs.

The weathervane's rooster looks into the distance. What does he see? What can I see?

I can't rely on Matts and never will again.

I refuse to do my father's bidding.

I have to protect my mother.

CHAPTER

7

Almost two weeks have passed since I saw Matts at the farmhouse. Every day, I've weighed up the pros and cons. Do I have to face my father in order to protect my mother?

Yesterday I messaged my father, asking him to call.

After morning tea, the children, chattering like pigeons, file into my classroom and sit at their desks. I clap my hands to get their attention.

'Mary? I think it's your table's turn to talk about native flora.'

She flicks her long plaits over her shoulders. 'Yes, Miss Brown.'

'Who would like to go first?'

Mary considers the other children at her table: Archie, Benji and Amy. Archie, who has multiple items lined up neatly in front of him, jumps to his feet.

'Archie,' she says firmly.

Horseshoe Hill Primary doesn't have enough students or teachers to separate the year groups, so the children in my Year 2 to 4 class are aged from seven to ten. Mary is nine and, as the youngest of the three Honey girls, she enjoys being the eldest on her table. Archie, Barney's clever younger brother, is eight. ADHD can make things difficult at school, but he responds well to Mary's bossiness. He methodically sets up his items on the table at the front of the room and I attach his poster to the whiteboard with magnets. He holds up a large strip of bark.

'This is from a paperbark tree,' he says. 'Who wants to hold it?' He laughs and spins around excitedly when all the children put up their hands.

'Thank you, Archie.' When I extend my hand, he gives me the bark. 'I'll pass this around while you talk about the tree you've selected.'

Archie has a phenomenal memory. He crosses his arms and recites, 'The botanical name of the paperbark tree is *Melaleuca quinquenervia* …'

When it's time for Benji to talk to the class, he walks nervously from his chair to the front of the room. Benji is the son of the publican, Leon. He's the youngest in the class and barely said a word at the start of the year, but is quietly growing in confidence. He holds up a small branch tipped with green-centred, feathery white flowers.

'I got this with Mum near the river,' he whispers.

'What type of tree is it from?'

'The river red gum.'

'What colour is the bark of that tree?'

He frowns in concentration. 'Brown.'

'It's all different shades of brown, isn't it, Benji, depending on whether the bark is new or old. Did you notice the colour of the trunk under the bark?'

'A whitey colour.'

'Excellent. Can you tell us some more about the flower?'

'You get seven buds or nine buds ...'

At the start of the year, Amy's parents were concerned when I put her at the table with Archie and the much younger Benji. Since then, they've realised that Amy is far happier at this school than she was at her last. She works hard and independently, without the anxiety she used to have that she couldn't always keep up with the children in her year group. When she reaches the front of the room, she methodically takes six different species of grasses from her bag.

'What a great idea, Amy.'

She smiles. 'Dad says these are the ones that grow best at the farm. They have seeds and they spread them by ...'

After the lunch bell sounds, the children file out of the classroom. I open my desk drawer and pull out my phone, but there's no word from my father.

'Miss Brown?'

Mary stands at the open door, awkwardly holding a sheet of cardboard half as tall as she is, with foliage and flowers stuck all around the edges. I think it's supposed to be a border, but it obscures most of the writing in the middle. 'I'm doing wattle,' she says proudly. 'Can I put my poster on the whiteboard now?' Mary wasn't much more than a toddler when her parents' marriage disintegrated. Her older sisters, settled at school and mad about horses, wanted to stay with their father, and her mother agreed that would be best for Mary as well. Peter is a great dad, but busy on his farm and not one for helping with homework. All Mary's work is her own.

I attach the cardboard, heavy with wattle, to the whiteboard with as many magnets as I can find.

'Do you like it, Miss Brown?'

I lift a thick bunch of slender leaves to find a hand-drawn diagram at the bottom of the cardboard. Straining to see through the smudges, I make out the words.

'You've labelled the anthers and filaments and all the other parts of the flowers,' I say. 'I can't wait to hear your talk after lunch.'

'I'm the same as you, Miss Brown. I love the flowers best.'

I can't remember a time when Gran wasn't making crepe paper flowers. Even before I went to Buenos Aires, she'd taught me how to follow a few simple patterns. After we'd moved back to Canberra, where she lived, I'd take the bus and visit her on the weekends.

I stayed with her permanently after my father took Mum to the clinic that specialised in drug and alcohol abuse. There was nothing wrong with the treatment she received, but in-patient programs rarely work if people with addictions don't go there voluntarily. Mum hated leaving me and the few friends she still had, but went along with my father's plan because she couldn't think what else to do. In the end, she said she didn't care where she lived, so long as my father allowed her to see me. He thought my refusal to live with him would be a temporary thing, that I'd change my mind and move back home, and then to England when he was posted there. He thought I wouldn't last five minutes at the local government school. But I was determined to avoid him and live with Gran at her house. It was only a short bus ride to Mum from there.

And Gran, who had liked my mother and didn't agree with my father's approach, was happy to have me. We'd sit opposite each other at her laminate kitchen table and, as I cut and shaped and glued, she'd talk about the times when she was young and married to my grandfather.

'Even then he had his head in the clouds,' she once said.

I trimmed the lacy petals of a pink and white carnation. 'Why do you say that, Gran?'

'He was a classics professor at twenty-nine, and from a good family. His people were hard up, but very well respected. Who'd have thought a Beresford-Brown would want to marry me?'

'He was no better than you were,' I told her. 'You didn't have the advantages he'd had, that's all.'

She winked. 'I was a pretty girl, don't forget that. It was important to the Beresford-Brown men. Your father was the same, he always liked the pretty girls.' She leant across the table and patted my hand. 'You're not only clever, Sapphie, you're pretty as well. You can marry whoever you want.'

I'd only been living with Gran for a few months when she started to ask the same questions over and over. She'd lean across the table and touch the petals of whatever flower I was working on. 'Where is your mother, Sapphie?'

'She's still in the clinic. Remember?'

'That's right, the clinic.'

Gran was only in her early seventies. No one else had any idea how severe the dementia was or that, on a bad day, her memories came and went like early morning mists. She'd lived in the same house and neighbourhood for the past forty-five years, so was good at finding her way around, and remembering most of the things she needed to know. And what she didn't know, she made up in a believable way.

Most of the concerns my father had about Gran he attributed to her perceived eccentricities. She'd always cooked, sewed and made things with her hands; she liked watching game shows on TV and reading trashy magazines. He'd looked after her finances for years, ever since Grandfather had died. Uncle James lived on a property in Queensland and deferred to his older brother. It wasn't in Gran's interests, or mine, to tell her sons how forgetful she'd become—particularly after Dad hinted that it might be time to think about aged care facilities—so I kept her failing memory to myself.

'I don't want to live longer than nature intended,' Gran used to say. 'I want to die in my own home.'

I selected school subjects that didn't challenge me too much academically, which meant I could mostly keep up with my school-work, and I took Gran to the doctor when she wasn't feeling well and made sure she filled her prescriptions. I used to put paper and templates on the table in front of her in the mornings, before I went to school.

'Lovely, dear.' She'd pick up pieces of crepe. 'You have a good day now.'

'Good luck with the dahlias.'

'Roses today.' She'd smooth out the folds of whatever petals I'd carefully made an hour earlier.

I knew that by the time I got home from school, she wouldn't have progressed with the flowers. Even though she generally remembered things from long ago better than things that had hap-pened only recently, she had little memory of how to cut and shape the petals, let alone how to put them together. She'd make herself cups of tea all day, get out ingredients but never cook anything, and potter in the garden. Then she'd go back to the flowers, fold and refold the paper, and rearrange the templates. She *thought* she was busy, and that was the main thing. Elderly neighbours often dropped by to have a chat. And once a week, the community bus would take her to and from a local club, where she'd catch up with friends and play bingo. She couldn't shop alone any more, so I took care of that, or we'd go out together.

The accident happened on my sixteenth birthday. I knew she'd want me to have something special, so I suggested we make hamburgers. For the patties we bought minced rump steak and mixed it with grated carrot, zucchini and onion. Her secret ingredient was homemade tomato paste, with parsley and oregano from the garden.

Before school that morning, I picked and chopped the herbs and assembled everything we'd need to make the hamburgers. The rissoles were rolled into balls on greaseproof paper and stored in the fridge with the salad. The bread was in the pantry.

Gran wasn't good at initiating anything much by then, so I thought I'd arrive home to find her in front of her favourite TV game show with an unread copy of a magazine on her lap. I planned to change out of my uniform, cook the rissoles and set the table. Gran and I would load our hamburgers with cheese, lettuce, beetroot and tomato.

I'd had a milkshake with my friends after school, so I caught the late bus home. As I checked the letterbox, I wondered why the light in the kitchen was so bright. And then I saw the flames. I dropped my school bag onto the path and *ran ran ran* towards the house. The blind was on fire; flames licked at the glass in the window.

'Gran!'

I'd left the rissoles in the fridge and the frying pan in the cupboard and the oil in the pantry. Had Gran remembered it was my birthday? It's not like she didn't have prompts, because I'd hung a *Happy Birthday* banner on the living room wall behind the television and my father had sent flowers and a card. Friends from my class had given me a bunch of helium balloons and I'd tied them to the table in the hall.

Or maybe it was nothing to do with that? Maybe Gran had remembered it was my birthday all on her own—even though it had slipped her mind that morning—and she was determined to cook a favourite meal.

She must have known something was missing. Was she waiting for me to come home to tell her what it was? Did she turn on the gas at the stove and add more and more oil to the pan as she waited? By the time I ran into the kitchen, the window was blackened and the blind was incinerated. Gran had already fallen. She was lying near the pantry.

'Can you help me up, dear?'

The pan of oil was bubbling like a deep-fry basket at a fish and chip shop. Flames licked the cornice and curled to the ceiling. My phone was in my bag but that was on the footpath, so I ran to the living room for the landline. I had the phone in my hand and was talking to emergency services when I noticed the oven mitts on the bench. If I could turn off the gas and take the pan off the heat, the oil would stop burning. I was giving the operator Gran's address when I lifted the pan and put it into the sink.

I was sixteen—just. I should have known better. There was water in the sink. Oil and water make steam. Boiling oil bounces and splashes.

By the time the fire engine arrived, lights on and sirens blaring, the fire was out. The police officers came next and asked a lot of questions. Gran's tendency to defer to anyone in uniform took precedence over the pain in her hip, but she couldn't remember what had happened. When the officers called her local doctor, the doctor gave them my father's number. He was living in London by then, but promised to book a flight back to Canberra.

'Your son will be here within the week, Mrs Beresford-Brown,' the officer said. 'We'll save the rest of our questions for then.'

'It was my fault,' I told the officer. 'I was cooking and the fat caught fire.'

'You were on your own?'

'We were cooking together.'

I didn't feel much pain then, but my uniform was darkened with oil and water. 'Were you hurt?'

'No!' I held my left arm tightly by my side and crossed my right arm over it. 'My uniform got a bit splattered, that's all. I'll go and change.'

I pretended not to hear when he called me back. By the time I'd stripped off my uniform, rolled it up and shoved it under my bed, and dragged a T-shirt over my torn and blistered skin, the officer was outside with the ambulance.

I had second-degree burns from the steam, and third degree burns from the oil, but it was two days later, when the pain made it impossible to sleep and my father was due to arrive, that I went to the emergency department at the hospital. 'You can't tell my father about this,' I reminded the plastic surgeon. 'I'm sixteen years old, so you won't, will you?'

U

The children keep me busy all afternoon, so it's after three-thirty when I check my phone again. My father sent a text two hours ago.

> *Sapphire,*
> *I'm on my way to Horseshoe Hill, so we can meet at any time from five (I'll stay overnight in Dubbo). Please let me know when and where would suit.*
> *Dad*

I text back immediately.

> *I'll see you where we usually meet in Dubbo, the pub on Elizabeth Street near the park. Is six OK?*

I start when I see Mary inside the door, her hands pressed together as she bounces up and down. 'Did you like my talk?'

'Very much,' I say, as I shepherd her out of the classroom. 'And I'll tell your dad all about it when we have our parent–teacher interview. He'll be even more proud of you than he is already.'

She skips into the sunlight, her plaits bouncing merrily. 'Thanks, Miss Brown!'

Sapphie Brown.

Sapphire Beresford-Brown.

Dubbo is an hour away, and I haven't driven a car since late last year. How do I get to my father by six? When I dial Pa Hargreaves's number, he answers straight away.

'Hello, Sapphie. How are you, love?'

CHAPTER

8

As I wait for Pa Hargreaves at the schoolhouse gate, Tumbleweed winds around my legs. I smile and rub under his chin.

'I'd prefer to stay here. You know that, right?'

I found Tumbleweed mewling behind a skip in a shopping centre carpark when he was seven or eight weeks old. He was just a scrappy ball of fur with a pink nose and sharp, pointed teeth. We shared a meal together—the tuna sandwich I'd stolen from the supermarket. When workers from a charity service picked us up the following night, they had no idea Tumbleweed was with me until they took me to the refuge. I begged to keep him and was told he could stay until the morning. I worried about that all night, trying to work out how I could feed him properly on the streets. Kittens needed milk and warmth.

The day after I found Tumbleweed, Ma and Pa Hargreaves found me. They were in their mid-fifties by then and the last of their foster children had left home. Ma was having problems with her knees and Pa was working twelve-hour days in the supermarket, but they thought they could manage one more troubled teen. The agreement was that they would take me and my cat so long as I was prepared to move to Horseshoe and communicate with my father. It was hoped I'd see things differently after a break and that we might reconcile. Twice a month, Pa arranged eight-hour round trips to Canberra so I could see Mum and visit Gran in the nursing home. My school grades improved and I learnt to ride. Most afternoons after school, I walked home via the farmhouse.

When Pa's van pulls off the road, I put Tumbleweed onto the grass. 'Go inside and stay warm, puss.'

Pa, who has very little hair, wears a peaked woollen cap all through the year. He leans across the gearstick and opens the passenger door. 'I've got the heater on full blast, love.'

I take deep breaths as I remove my coat, throwing it with jerky movements onto the back seat. I haven't seen the psychologist for a month, but her advice rings in my ears. *Face your fears. Meet the anxiety head-on.*

Reaching for the handhold above the door, I pull myself into the passenger seat. 'I'm sorry to put you out, Pa. I hoped there'd be a delivery truck that could give me a lift to Dubbo.'

'And how would you get home again?' Pa says, raising his brows. 'Not another word, Sapphie. Ma's perfectly happy to close up the store, and I'll pop in to see old Artie Jones in the hospital while I'm waiting.'

As soon as I've fastened my belt, I focus on my exercises. *Breathe slowly and deeply. Use your abdomen when you exhale. The anxiety is a creature in your mind. Face it and push it away.* When we turn off the loop road and onto the highway, my hands clench the seatbelt more tightly.

Pa smiles sympathetically. 'How's it going then?'

I swallow. 'It's been seven months. Sometimes I worry …'

'You hit a kangaroo, Sapphie, and your car was written off. That can happen to anyone. You'll be driving again soon, don't you worry about that.'

I grit my teeth and open my fingers, loosening my grip on the belt. 'I get anticipatory anxiety before I get in the car. Then I get full-on anxiety. After that, I get post-anxiety anxiety.' I take more deep breaths. 'Being a passenger is better than it was.'

'There you go, then. That's good news.'

'My psychologist says I have to reprogram my brain to accept that nothing bad will happen.'

'We'll take it slowly. Your dad will forgive a short delay.'

'Daylight helps.'

'You're nice and high in a van. You get a better view of what's happening around you.'

'I'm not sure whether that's a good thing or not.'

'You were a careful driver, Sapphie. It wasn't your fault.'

'I've been feeling more confident. It's just—' I swallow down the acid that comes up. 'I've had a few things to think about in the past couple of weeks.'

'You're always busy with one thing or another.'

'Can we have the radio on, please?' I tip back my head and close my eyes, but that makes things worse so I open them again. The bitumen is smooth and there's barely any traffic. The paddocks either side of the road are mostly cleared for crops. Visibility is good.

There's not a single kangaroo in sight.

I shortened my name to Brown well before I moved to Horse-shoe, and changed it by deed poll after I turned eighteen. I don't tell people I'm the daughter of Robert Beresford-Brown unless I have to, but I never deny it if they ask. If I'd met my father at the schoolhouse or the pub, the locals wouldn't take much notice. But Horseshoe is my home. I don't want my father there. I don't want unhappiness on my doorstep.

'This will be fine, Pa,' I say, pointing to a layby near the park. 'I'll walk from here.'

'Right you are, love,' he says as he pulls over. When he switches off the engine, I open my door to get some air before I reach into the back for my coat. 'Your dad sees things different from you, Sapphie, always has. But he tries to build fences.'

'Some of the time.'

'I'll see you here in an hour. You sure that's long enough?'

'Positive.'

As soon as I cross the road, I see my father sitting at a table near the window. He checks his watch and raises a hand in salute, and I half-heartedly wave back. When I walk past the few patrons to his table, he stands. Our cheeks touch lightly.

'Sapphire.'

'Robert.'

'You look well.'

'As do you.' I shrug out of my coat. 'Sorry I'm late. I didn't get your message until school had finished.'

'I was prepared to drive to Horseshoe.'

'You've already come a long way.'

He pulls out a chair and gestures that I sit. 'The wine selection is basic, but there are excellent craft beers on tap. What can I get you? Would you like a bite to eat?'

'Lemon squash will be fine, thanks.'

'You still don't drink?'

'No.'

'Perhaps I shouldn't have started.' He pats his stomach, perfectly flat. 'Last year I turned sixty. I'm getting to the age where I ought to mind my weight.'

I hang my coat over the back of my chair as he walks to the bar. He's wearing suit pants, a cotton shirt and a navy jacket. A small gold pin, presented by the Governor-General a few years ago, sits on his lapel. *Achievement and merit in services to Australia or humanity.*

His hair is grey, but thick and well cut. Not long after he'd gone into politics, a journalist, parodying his upright posture and careful wording, dubbed him Robert the Robot. The name has stuck. He chats to the barman and two other men sitting on stools at the bar. One of them slaps him on the back and all of them laugh.

He returns with the drinks. 'Thank you,' I say.

He sips froth from his glass while I swirl ice with a straw. When two of the men at the bar clink glasses, Robert glances their way before putting his glass on the coaster.

'Hear me out, Sapphire.'

I blink. 'I haven't said anything yet.'

'You will.' He frowns. 'You've seen Matts Laaksonen?'

'I'm sure you know the answer to that.'

'It was good of him to brief you. I understand your reception of him was cool.'

'The first or the second time?'

'What?'

I shake my head. 'It doesn't matter. He said he was here for work.'

'He's doing exceptionally well. How old is he? Thirty-one?'

'Thirty.'

'He travels widely.'

'Did you come here to talk about Matts?'

He looks towards the bar again. The two men, both dressed in black pants and white shirts, appear to be reading from a folder. Maybe they're salesmen? Or missionaries.

'This bribery allegation,' Robert says, 'is a nightmare.'

I try to be fair. 'Not everyone agrees with your politics, but most respect your commitment. This must be stressful for you and your family.'

'Which is why I need your help.'

I push my drink away and pull my coat from the chair, laying it over my knees. 'With what?'

'I have my career to consider,' he says, 'but also the welfare of my wife and her children. Jacqueline's boys are still in junior school. They need my support, financially and otherwise.'

'I'm sure they do.'

'I would have supported you,' he says defensively.

'There were too many strings attached. Anyway, Gran left me something.'

'Very little.'

'Enough to allow me to go to university immediately after school. I've always worked. I have savings.'

He places his beer glass exactly in the middle of the coaster. 'You were an intelligent child. I was gratified you didn't waste it; that you completed your education.'

'I have a friend who left school early. She's a farrier, and as smart as anyone I know.' I glance at my watch. 'I'm meeting Pa soon.'

'You still call him that?'

'Most of us do.'

He nods brusquely. 'It must cause confusion with so many foster children.'

'Not really.'

When he stretches out his legs, I move mine to the side. 'There is no evidence that links me to the deposit box,' he finally says.

'So you'll be cleared.'

He laughs without humour. 'When Kate, my wife of over twenty years, was the only person who opened the box? When she gave her closest friend the key?'

I smooth my coat over my knees. 'Mum and Inge are gone. Why would anybody bother pursuing this?'

'If Kate sold confidential information, it was from documents I should have kept secure. At best, I'll be accused of negligence. At worst, I'll be condemned for leaking information in the expectation of reward.'

'From what Matts said, none of this has been proven.'

'Or disproven.'

'Mum was happy before Inge died. She had everything she wanted. Why would she take such a risk?'

He purses his lips. 'Matts told you about the money and your mother's note. He didn't tell you what else was in the box.'

'What?'

'A blue sapphire. It's worth a small fortune.'

The lemon squash glass, wet with condensation, seems very far away. When I wrap my hands around it, I barely feel the cold.

My father often teased Mum about a sapphire ring, telling her it would take a lifetime to save the money for a stone impressive enough to please her. When he gave her birthday or Christmas presents, no matter the size or shape of the parcel, she'd hold them out to show me. 'Sapphire,' she'd whisper conspiratorially. 'I have it at last.'

Robert clears his throat. 'I'm not prepared to protect Kate's reputation at the expense of my own.'

'The sapphire …' My voice is high and shaky. 'It could be a mistake, a coincidence.'

He huffs. 'Kate probably thought it was a lark. Some smooth-talking Argentinian promised her a bauble in exchange for a document I would never know had gone missing.'

I let go of the glass and wipe my hands on my coat. 'What are you going to say?'

'To the investigating authorities? I've said it already. There was no bribe. If information was sold, Kate accessed it without my approval and was presumably paid in cash, and kind, for communicating it to parties unknown.'

My fingernails dig into my palms. 'I didn't expect you to defend her, but …'

He frowns. 'It's by far the most likely scenario.'

Mum used to model for top-end fashion magazines like *Vogue* and *Harper's Bazaar*. She'd say that most successful models were like actresses: they could play a part for the camera. But she was adamant she'd never had that skill. If she felt unhappy, the photographer was stuck with that look. If she felt happy, the images would reflect that emotion. She said her agent refused to send her out on important assignments without first checking her mood. If it didn't fit the brief, the agent would have to warn whoever had commissioned the shoot.

'Mum wore her heart on her sleeve,' I say quietly. 'I don't believe she'd be capable of keeping something like that to herself. In the months before she died …' I clear my throat. 'You didn't see her because you were in London. But Mum found a psychologist she trusted. She was taking responsibility for things she'd done wrong. What upset her most was thinking about Inge. I don't know why, but she thought she'd let her down.'

'I bet she wished she'd got her key back.'

'That's not fair!'

He holds up his hands. 'I withdraw it.' He frowns. 'I was keen to, eventually, return permanently to Canberra and enter politics. Kate was opposed to the idea, much preferring the expatriate life. Perhaps this was a way of getting back at me.'

There are a number of people in the room now, many of them in pairs. A grey-haired couple hold hands across a table.

'Mum had always known you wanted to go into politics.'

'That didn't equate to her liking the notion.'

'Even if she was unhappy, it doesn't make her a liar or a thief or whatever it is you think she was. Inge was always fair about everything. She wouldn't have taken the key if Mum had done something wrong.'

'She probably had no idea about it and, unfortunately, we can't ask her to confirm that.'

'Why do you trust Hernandez? He's the one who's been accused of bribing people.'

'He knew there was a deposit box set aside in my name. Whatever happened, the evidence speaks for itself.'

As they pass, the two men from the bar nod respectfully. Robert raises his hand and smiles. 'Have a pleasant evening, gentlemen.'

'Mum isn't here to defend herself.'

He lowers his voice. 'She put me in this position, whether you care to accept that or not. To minimise the harm, I require my family's support.'

'I'm sure that you'll have it.'

'That's not—' He forces a smile. 'You and I have had our differences, Sapphire, but it might be possible to use this in our favour.'

'How? You know I'll defend Mum.'

He sips his beer before placing it back on the coaster. 'If you and I, particularly given our fractious relationship, can present this matter as a storm in a teacup, others will follow our lead.'

'Do you mean the media?'

'I can't do anything about the official inquiries.'

I smooth my coat over my knees again. My hands are white against the red. 'What do you propose?'

He sits back in his chair. 'Come to Canberra, Sapphire.' He smiles. 'I'd like to introduce you to Jacqueline and the boys. I want us to be seen together.'

'What?'

'Only for a day or two.'

'You want me to play happy families?'

'You're young, clever and extremely beautiful. You're also Kate's daughter. Your presence is likely to elicit sympathy.'

'Wouldn't it draw attention to your connection to Mum?'

'That cat is well out of the bag. Confronting the issue directly is the only way to deal with it.'

The lights from the bar are suddenly far too bright. 'I won't let you use me like that.'

'If Kate hadn't acted as she did, I wouldn't have to defend myself.'

'You don't know what happened.'

He continues as if I haven't spoken. 'After next year's election, I have three more years in parliament. Provided this incident can be contained, a diplomatic posting will follow.'

'I won't do it.'

'It will be an act, nothing more.'

A vase of pink and white peonies sits on the windowsill. The flowers' petals are made of polyester, and their green plastic stems are anchored in resin. Gran didn't like fabric flowers, even the expensive silk ones. 'Our flowers aren't mass-produced,' she'd say. 'Every petal is different, just like the ones in my garden.'

It's hard to talk because my throat is so tight. 'I'm not good at pretending.'

'You're part of my family, like it or not. A picture paints a thousand words.'

'It would be dishonest. My family is in Horseshoe. I have people I'm close to there.'

'You're determined to hide forever?'

'I'm not hiding. It's my home.'

'You currently live at the school, don't you?'

'At the old schoolhouse.'

His sleeves have stiff cuffs. He flicks one button and then the other. His eyes meet mine again. 'I know about the property where your horses are kept.'

'What do you know?'

'You hoped to buy it.'

'I—yes. The council has agreed to sell it to me.'

'Not any more.'

An icy hand grasps my heart and squeezes. 'What?'

'Your option to purchase expired last December. I now have an option.'

I stand so quickly that my hip bumps the table. 'No you don't!'

He looks around before slowly pushing back his chair and standing. 'Don't make a scene, Sapphire.'

I grasp the edge of the table. 'The council knows I want it. I was waiting for the youth centre to open.'

'You had nothing in writing. I made a higher offer. As a public authority, they had to accept it.'

'You can't do this. You can't … they would have told me.'

'I insisted on confidentiality.'

'What? Why would you—' I try again. 'How could you do this?'

'Can you sit down, please?'

My legs are unsteady, so I do as he asks. 'I don't understand.'

He sits too, and puts his hands on the table. 'I suspected you'd refuse to cooperate. This was my fallback position.'

I take a deep breath before slowly exhaling. 'The farmhouse isn't merely somewhere I'll live. It's more important than that.'

'I understand it's in a deplorable state.'

'Who told you that?' My voice catches. 'It was Matts, wasn't it?'

He glances at his watch. 'I arranged to meet him for dinner at seven. Would you care to join us?'

It's hard to think through the ache in my chest. 'Is this how you operate? You take things that people care about in order to force them to do what you want?'

'If you'd agreed to help, you might not have found out that I'd done it.'

'So I've brought this on myself?'

'Be reasonable. I want you to spend a weekend in Canberra. Not imminently—September or October would do. It's not a great deal to ask.'

'Isn't it? To let your advisors put their spin on blaming Mum?'

'Spin?' He counts on his fingers. 'One, there is no truth to the bribery allegation; my conscience is clear. Two, I welcome the investigation, and have cooperated fully with relevant authorities. Three, I was ignorant of my late wife's conduct—'

'You don't know what happened!'

He mutters under his breath, then says, 'Three, regarding my late wife's conduct, the facts are currently in dispute. Four, I have the love and support of my family, including my only child, and we hope to put this matter behind us as soon as possible.' He raises his brows. 'If those points constitute spin, so be it.'

'If I refuse to do what you ask, what will you do with the farmhouse?'

He smiles stiffly. 'I will consider my options.'

'What does that mean?'

'The land can be leased, but I hope it won't come to that.' He leans back in his chair. 'I'll give you a week to decide. In the meantime, I think it's in both of our interests to keep this to yourself.'

It's cold when I step outside, but I don't take the time to button my coat, holding it closed as I run across the road. When I reach the park, I swipe my hand across my eyes and scrabble in my bag for a tissue. I blow my nose and sniff as I walk to the path that circles the pond. In daytime, it's busy with ducks, magpie-larks and ibis. Where are they now? Tucking their heads beneath their wings as they sleep in the rushes?

The tallest reeds cast shadows. I step over them carefully as if they might trip me.

'Sapphire!'

Matts runs towards me. Should I run in the opposite direction? Climb a tree? What would be the point? As I wipe my eyes again, he slows to a jog. When he gets close, he pushes back his hair.

In the darkness, his eyes are black.

Ebony, pitch, jet, onyx.

I bunch my hands into fists. 'What do you want?'

He lifts an arm and drops it. He frowns. 'Why are you crying?'

'Did you know my father had taken it? What did you say to him?'

'About what?'

'The farmhouse.'

'I told him you worked there, and about the horses. What did he take?'

When a gust of wind blows through the park, leaf litter cartwheels towards us. 'The farmhouse.'

'What? You said you had an agreement to buy it.'

'I did, but …' I push the heels of my hands into my eyes. 'My option expired. He's taken out one of his own.'

'Are you certain?'

'Why are you meeting him tonight? Did you know about it?'

His lips firm. 'No.'

'What about the sapphire in the deposit box? You knew about that. Why didn't you tell me?'

'You were upset.'

I wipe my eyes again. I push hair behind my ears, gather my coat around me, spin blindly and follow the path. A car horn blasts in the distance.

'Sapphire, wait.'

'Go, Matts. My father is expecting you.'

'After we talk.' He points to a timber seat near a junction in the path. On the backrest of the seat is a plaque, but I'm too far away to read the words.

'I'm late to meet Pa Hargreaves.'

Does he cut across my path, or do I veer into his? When we collide, my foot slips off the concrete and he grasps my arms. His body is hard. His scent, pine and something else, is unsettling. I squeeze my eyes shut. 'Go away.'

His fingers close and open, press and release. 'What does Robert want from you?'

'He wants me to go to Canberra, to pretend I'm part of his family.'

'I'll talk to him.'

'No!' I pull free. 'He won't change his mind.'

'He can manage the media. He can minimise the harm.'

'That doesn't excuse what he did!' I look past Matts to the pond. 'He sees the farmhouse as a means to an end. I see it differently.'

Another gust of wind sweeps through the park. When I fumble with a button on my coat, Matts mutters under his breath. And then, his movements precise and deliberate, he pushes my hands away and fastens the button.

'Why did you do that?'

'You couldn't.'

He's dressed in black jeans and a pale blue shirt. His dark blue hoodie is unzipped. I grab the fabric with shaky hands and thread the ends of the zip together. I yank the toggle but the zip doesn't catch. A sob works its way up my throat.

'I won't let my father take it away.' I yank the toggle again. The zip glides swiftly, over Matts's abdomen and chest.

What am I doing? My hands still. They drop to my sides.

When he dips his head, his hair touches mine. He fastens the second and third buttons of my coat. Our eyes meet. His gaze slips to my mouth.

There's a rustling from the pond, a flapping of wings. I take a jerky step back and run my hands down my buttons, as if I have to check that they're properly done up.

'You're not my brother any more.'

His jaw clenches. 'I never was.'

'No.'

'I warned you, Sapphire. I told you to call him.'

'It wouldn't have made a difference. He wants to use me. He said I'm young and beautiful and …'

I hear voices behind me. The grey-haired man and woman from the pub walk hand in hand towards us.

The woman smiles. 'It's chilly tonight.'

After the couple is out of sight, Matts walks to the edge of the pond, bends his knees and takes hold of a reed, rubbing it between his fingers.

'You are beautiful, Sapphire. Even more beautiful than your mother.'

'I don't think—' My breaths are wispy and white. 'Her looks didn't help her, did they? Not in the end.'

He straightens and, without touching me but so close I could swear that he was, he runs a finger under my eye. He follows the line of my cheekbone. When his thumb hovers over my lip, a million nerve endings sparkle and fizz.

'Do you ever wear make-up?' he asks.

'Why—' I shake my head. 'Rarely.'

'Do you wear blue?'

'I like other colours.'

'Colours that don't draw attention to your eyes.'

'What's your point?'

'I think you're afraid to be beautiful.'

'I am not!'

'You're also afraid of me.'

I press my lips together. I bunch my hands and put them in my pockets. 'You remind me of things I don't want to think about. You remind me of my past.'

'*Our* past, Sapphire,' he says. 'Yours and mine.'

'It got messed up in other things.'

'So now it means nothing?'

'I've put it behind me.'

'I couldn't.'

'Sapphie!' Pa Hargreaves calls out. 'Is that you, love?'

I step back. 'I have to go.'

Matts nods abruptly. 'I'll see you at the end of the month.'

'What?'

'Check your emails.' He shoves his hands in the pockets of his hoodie. 'I'll be at your committee meeting.'

'What? Why?' I shake my head. 'I don't want you there. I don't want to see you.'

He takes two steps before turning and facing me again. His eyes are hard. His jaw is tight.

'Why not?' he says softly. 'When you say we have no past?'

CHAPTER

9

Sitting on the stool at my kitchen bench with Tumbleweed curled up on my lap, I open my laptop. The email Matts referred to isn't *from* him—it's to him.

Dr Laaksonen,

I refer to recent telephone discussions and correspondence regarding our respective governments' interest in the work of the Ramsar Secretariat.

Horseshoe Hill would be an excellent starting point for your research. The town is situated on the banks of the Macquarie River, a few hours by road from the Macquarie Marshes, and has not only recognised challenges posed by a changing environment, but has acknowledged the need to balance town and agricultural agendas with environmental rehabilitation and enhancement.

As the state government representative on the Horseshoe Hill Environment Committee, I am confident I speak for the rest of the committee in confirming our interest in your project. The committee meets formally twice a year (and informally every month or so). Sapphie Brown, a local schoolteacher, is the chair, and she is copied in on this email. The next meeting (happily a formal one!) will take place at the Horseshoe Hill Community Centre at seven o'clock on 20 August.

Kind regards,

Douglas Chambers, MP

Every one of the hundred reasons I could list for uninviting Matts would be personal. He told me from the start that he was here for work. The committee's public profile is important and Matts's interest in what we do would help to promote that.

It's only one meeting.

The kindling in the fireplace has dwindled to ash, but the small log is still burning brightly. I pick up the tongs and lift another log onto the grate. When Tumbleweed, sitting like a sphinx, extends his claws, hooks them into the rug and inches closer, I hurriedly shut the fireplace door. 'You're close enough, puss. You wouldn't want to get singed.'

Steam fills the tiny bathroom within moments of turning on the water. I lather up the sponge and rub around my neck, then gently press the sponge against my breast. My left side isn't painful, but the skin under my arm and across my ribcage and breast is sensitive.

You're afraid to be beautiful.

'You might have a point, Matts,' I mutter, lifting the sponge and allowing the water to cascade down my side and rinse the soap from my skin.

Alabaster, bleach, translucent, chalk.

Angry, magenta, vermillion, burnt.

My skin is ridged and mottled, but the doctor said I'd been lucky. 'The burns, once healed, shouldn't hamper your physical activity.'

Matts said I was beautiful.

I have my mother's hair. My eyes are distinctively dark blue. I have a nicely shaped mouth. When I was at university and wanted to get my innocence over with, I had no trouble finding men to have sex with. They didn't care, or didn't notice, that I wouldn't take off my top. And I only went out with them once or twice anyway.

If I ever meet someone I want to spend more than a night with, they'll understand. Countless people have suffered much worse.

On my final visit to the hospital, the surgeon said that plastic surgery would neaten up the scarring. And if things had been different, I might have pursued that. But Mum was unwell. Gran had been moved out of respite care and into the nursing home. My father was trying to micromanage my life from London. I was a shitty teenage runaway, angry at the world.

And soon enough, I'd moved to Horseshoe. I liked Ma and Pa Hargreaves. I'd found the farmhouse. I slowly made friends. I was healthy and fit. The scarring didn't seem to matter so much.

As I towel myself dry, my reflection stares back. I love my job at the school. I live in a community where people value and care for me. I don't need anything else to make me happy.

Matts and I shared a childhood and adolescence.

I suspect he broke my heart.

Now it's over.

Tumbleweed is curled up in front of the fire but the logs won't last much longer. I rub under his chin and tuck the throw around him.

At lunchtime on Friday, I leave the staffroom and call the council from my classroom. As soon as I tell Michael, the property officer

I've dealt with for years, that I want to renew my option, he groans into the phone.

'I'm sorry, Sapphie.'

'I would have paid more.'

'I didn't know about it until the deal had been done,' he says. 'The buyer went straight to the CEO. He offered a higher price that couldn't reasonably be refused.'

'What about the youth program?'

'It's a twelve-month option, but even if it's exercised straight away, no access to the farmhouse is allowed for six months, by which time the program will have moved to the new centre.'

'My horses?'

'They've got six months too.'

I end the call and email my father.

Robert,

It appears that Mum knew about the deposit box, but we still don't know that she did anything illegal. I don't think she would steal information, or sell something that didn't belong to her. I don't think she'd risk losing me, or getting you and Inge into trouble.

You're forcing me to do what you want because you have the farmhouse. I know you have a year to exercise the option, but I want this to be over with before that. If you promise that, within six months, you'll tell the council you're not going ahead, I'll let you handle the media and pretend we're in this together. You also have to stick strictly to the facts if you're questioned about Mum. The drugs, the rehab, none of that is relevant.

Sapphie

Five minutes before the bell that sounds the end of lunch, my phone rings.

'Sapphire.'

'Robert.'

'In general terms, I agree to your proposal.'

'But you don't want to put anything in writing. That's why you called.'

'Sapphire! I agree to six months, as you requested. If this can't be contained by then, I'm unlikely to have a career worth saving.'

'What about Mum?'

'I'll do what I can to keep Kate out of it. With one proviso.'

'Go on.'

'You're to pretend that everything is just as it was. No one else wants the farmhouse and when you're ready, you'll negotiate with the council to buy it. My name is not to come up. If the matter is raised, we claim that I am holding the property on your behalf, that I wish to be of assistance.'

'You want me to lie?'

He huffs. 'People believe that you'll buy the farmhouse. Don't disabuse them of the notion.'

'I can keep my mouth shut.'

'When will you come to Canberra?'

'Before the next school holidays. Early October? It'll just be photos, right?'

'I'll select a location we can visit as a family.'

'Matts said he didn't know that you were taking out the option.'

'He didn't. And it might please you to know that I wasn't in his good books. Mind you, neither were you.'

You say we have no past.

CHAPTER
10

On Saturday morning, over two weeks since I spoke with my father, I scramble down the slope to the creek and jump from rock to rock to reach the other side. By the time the farmhouse appears, the clouds have thinned and the sun is warm on my back. I push my hat lower and stretch out my fingers, cosy in gloves, before closing the gate and securing the chain. The late winter grass has shades of sage and cornsilk, with occasional patches of shamrock. I kick at a spiky thistle with my boot, loosening the soil and plucking it out of the ground. When I reach the orchard, I throw the weed into a bin.

The possums and cockatoos have eaten most of the oranges, but I pick the ripest, still tinged with green, to eat with my sandwich at lunchtime. The horses look up as I pass, and Lollopy nickers. Prima is in her usual place under the grey gum and the others are gathered at the gate.

'Won't be long,' I call out.

Within an hour, the farmhouse will be bustling, but for now I'm the only one here. I stand on my toes as I take Gran's keyring out of my pocket and jiggle the key back and forth in the lock. When I open the door, the sun shoots in behind me. A daddy-long-legs spider has stayed overnight. Swinging from a thread, he hovers above a crate of riding hats and boots.

I unfasten the window latch in the room where I make my flowers. Pushing both hands firmly against the window frame, I jiggle to loosen the sash. When I pull the bottom pane upwards, the window opens wide. Banksia roses and vines of honeysuckle and jasmine climb up the verandah posts and creep towards the house. Three old azalea bushes, white, apricot and crimson, are almost as tall as the gutters. At this time of year the buds come out. Soon the azaleas will be irresistibly pretty, but for the rest of the year they don't look much at all. I've thought about digging them up and replacing them with native plants, but something has always pulled me back. Dorothy, Catherine and Lucille Andrews were sisters, and two of them were teachers. They bought the farmhouse when they came from England to work at the school, and planted shrubs and trees that reminded them of home.

'I won't let you down,' I promise the sisters.

I prepare the ponies first, grooming Lollopy and Freckle and checking their feet. As I lead him to the yard, Lollopy shoves his nose against my back and pushes. I laugh as I spring forward. 'Breakfast won't be long.'

In his younger years, Freckle's coat was speckled grey. Now, besides darker markings around his flanks, he's faded almost to white. He's older than Lollopy and, at fourteen hands, quite a lot taller, but he stands back respectfully when I bring biscuits of hay from the shed.

'You're both fully booked today, so you'd better eat up.'

On Saturdays, the ponies do a morning and afternoon shift of equine therapy, mostly with younger children like Barney's brother Archie. Corey, the psychologist who runs the program, also treats older children, teenagers who've been in trouble, many of whom have spent time in juvenile detention. The council agreed to fund the specialists, but Corey needed horses and a venue. I'd already been given permission to use the farmhouse as a temporary youth centre, so it wasn't difficult to extend its use to equine activities.

By nine o'clock, Mary and Amy are threading ribbons through Lollopy's mane and Freckle's tail, Sonnet is saddled and tied to a railing and Strider is in the small fenced yard being groomed by volunteers. By the time I carry an armful of hay to Prima, she's the only horse left in the paddock.

'Don't look so concerned. No one can get to you here.'

I don't manage to get a hold of her halter until I've followed her around the grey gum three times. I clip on a lead rope and run a hand over her back.

'I won't hurt you. When are you going to trust me on that?'

Prima skitters when Joel, a sixteen-year-old local, climbs over the gate. When I lift a hand to wave, he looks away, pulling his hood over his head before leaning against a post. Prima still has one eye on Joel and one on her hay as I unclip the lead rope.

'See you tonight, girl.'

Joel looks like he doesn't want me to think that he's waiting for me, even though he undoubtedly is. He's tall but very thin, with straight brown hair that hangs into his eyes.

'Your appointment with Corey is at ten, right? You're early today.'

'Corey's a waste of time,' he mutters. 'I only said I'd come to get out of juvie.'

'He wouldn't have taken you on if he didn't think he could help.'

'Leading horses around bores the shit out of me. I'm not even allowed to ride.'

'You've only been here a few times.' I tip back my hat. 'Maybe the program will grow on you?'

'I did graffiti at the station and nicked a couple of cars. What's any of that got to do with anger management?'

I pretend an interest in the gate fittings. 'The horses sense feelings—anxiety, fear and anger—from the way we move and speak. They also tap into our responses when things go wrong. Interacting with the horses helps develop emotional awareness.'

'You sound like Corey.'

'I'm learning from him too.'

'Sonnet!' Archie shouts out. 'Sonnet! Hey! Sonnet!'

Archie runs up and down the fence line. Sonnet is toey, but stands relatively still after a handler walks him away from the fence. Barney chases Archie, who's still shouting, and cuts him off, grabbing his arm and swinging him around.

'Shut up, Arch! You're scaring him.'

'It's okay, Barney,' Corey says, 'leave this to me.' He holds out his hand. 'Come over here, Archie. Let's have a chat before we go to Sonnet.'

I turn back to Joel. 'See what I mean? Archie will learn that when he expresses feelings like excitement and impatience in a certain way, it will have an impact on the horses. It'll give him an idea of how others might react.'

'Archie should shut up, like Barney said.'

'When he understands that behaving as he did will spook Sonnet, that both of them could get hurt and Sonnet might avoid him in the future, he's more likely to modify his behaviour.'

'Why can't he learn that stuff at school?'

'Horses sense feelings, like I said.' I put my boot on the bottom rung of the railing and stretch out my calf muscle. 'They don't take things too personally like other children might, or hold grudges. Usually they give second chances.'

'I already know about horses.'

'Your grandfather was a trainer, wasn't he?'

'He took me to the stables and to the tracks. We went to the races all the time.'

Joel's grandfather died a couple of years ago, leaving his dad to care for him on his own. But his father has a gambling problem, and Joel spent most of the previous year in and out of foster care.

'Is that why you're interested in Prima? Because she was a racehorse?'

'Granddad trained a mare like her. His favourite horse he reckoned.'

'She's been mistreated, but I'm not sure how. She won't let men anywhere near her.'

'She's scared of you, too.'

'If I wasn't handfeeding her, I'm not sure I could catch her at all.'

He puts a foot on the gate rung where mine was before. 'Reckon I could help out,' he mutters.

'You've been watching out for her, haven't you?'

'Might've.'

'You have a program with Corey already.'

'That's only an hour.'

'Getting accustomed to having you around will be stressful for Prima. I wouldn't put her through that without the possibility of a positive long-term experience.'

'You want me to hang around, is that what you're saying?'

'To commit. Yes.'

'Gramps taught me how to be patient.'

'Would you be able to come early every Saturday? Will you do what I tell you to do? Do you get a lift to the farmhouse?'

'Or the minibus. Corey sorts that out.'

'You don't think it'd be too boring for you, sitting in a paddock for hours on end? It might take weeks before you can handle her. Assuming we get to that point.'

He sits on the ground and leans against the fence. 'There's nothing else to do anyway. I can wait till Prima's ready, you'll see.'

'All right.' I bend down and offer him my hand. 'You've got yourself a training position.'

He holds back a smile as we shake.

CHAPTER
11

When there's a knock on my door on Tuesday evening, I lift Tumbleweed off my lap, settle him on the couch next to me and stack my lesson plans on the side table. I pull up my woolly socks and check my dressing gown is fastened so my short silk nightdress doesn't show.

'Who is it?'

'Hugo.'

When I open the door he smiles broadly, and holds out a bottle of wine. 'Didn't you recognise my signature knock?'

Hugo Hallstead was brought up in the country, but his hair is streaky blond and scruffy like he lives at the beach. This year he's wearing it long; he runs his hand through it, grinning infectiously.

'I forgot what your signature knock sounded like, just like you always forget that I don't drink.'

'I don't forget, but a true friend never gives up,' he says, hugging me tightly.

'There's nothing wrong with not drinking.'

'Trouble with you is, you're afraid of a drinking problem you've never given yourself a chance to get. It's *grapes*, Sapphie, good wholesome fruit.'

I wave him into the living room. 'Where've you been for the past few weeks?'

'Down in the mountains, saving lives.'

'Tadpole lives?'

'We've all got to start somewhere.'

When I came to Horseshoe, I was a city-girl foster kid who refused to talk about her past. I didn't make friends easily. Hugo was a larrikin at high school, popular and confident, probably the last person I'd trust to even *want* to be my friend. But he'd track me down at lunchtime and ask if I wanted to swap lunches, as if we were six years old. He'd sit next to me in class and ask for my help, even though he didn't need it. I refused to have anything to do with him for months, but then he decided he wanted to be a biologist and started spending as much time in the library as I did. Hugo became impossible *not* to like. We'd study late into the night at school, and spend days down by the river where he'd teach me about the things that lived in it. We went to the same university, four years for me and five for him. Now he works on conservation projects, specialising in critically endangered frogs.

I grew to care for him far too much to ever contemplate having sex with him.

I poke him in the chest. 'Why are you here so late?'

'Nine o'clock?' He laughs as he skirts around me, a duffle bag slung over his shoulder. 'I'm homeless, that's why. Mum and Dad have Andy's kids staying over, and the pub's fully booked.'

'On a Tuesday?'

'A flock of grey nomads flew in this afternoon.' When he throws his bag on the floor, Tumbleweed looks up and squints. 'Why don't they perch in their caravans?'

'How long will you be here?'

'I thought you'd never ask.'

I point to the couch. 'It's almost as wide as my bed if I take the cushions off, but you know how your feet hang over the end.'

Hugo looks at Tumbleweed and raises his middle finger. 'I have to sleep with Killer again?'

I laugh, sitting next to my cat and covering his ears. 'Don't call him that. He's a city cat that lives in the house. He likes steamed fish and slow-cooked lamb.'

'Feral animals, Sapph, can't trust them.'

'When he was a kitten, he was feral. Now he's domesticated.'

'A bit like you I suppose.'

'No!'

When Hugo crashes next to me on the couch, Tumbleweed jumps to the floor. We watch as he stalks towards the kitchen.

'Sapphie? What's up?'

I smooth my dressing gown over my legs. 'It's nothing.'

He bumps me with a shoulder. 'Give.'

I blow out a breath. 'My father's been hassling me, and … other stuff. But now I know what's happening, I'm fine.'

'You know I liked you feral, don't you?'

'I'm not feral now.'

'Nope.' He shrugs. 'You're prickly and domesticated.'

When I spring to my feet and take the wine to the kitchen, he follows, rubbing his arms as he leans against the wall.

'It's freezing in here.'

'That's why I wear a dressing gown.' I pour milk into a saucepan. 'Would you like something to eat?'

'I'm good.' I'm straining to grasp a wine glass from the cupboard above the stove when he reaches above me and gets it himself. He lifts my collar to the side and plucks at the strap of my nightdress.

'What's that shiny stuff you're hiding?' He wiggles his eyebrows. 'Expecting someone?'

'It's acceptable to wear silk at any time.' I push him away and retie my dressing gown belt before filling his glass. 'You didn't say how long you'd be here.'

'Once I'd committed to Thursday, thought I might as well visit my parents on the farm and catch up with friends. Five nights. That okay?'

'Stay as long as you like.' I turn my back as I spoon chocolate into a mug. 'What's happening on Thursday?'

'You're the chair, Sapph.'

'Of the Environment Committee?' I clear my throat, suddenly tight. 'Yes.'

'Dougie Chambers MP tracked me down. He reckons I'm a local boy made good, so I should give back. Told him I'd be happy to, so long as he remembers it next time I ask for funding.'

'I thought the focus was the wetlands.'

'And in the marshes you find ...' He opens his eyes wide and puts a finger either side of his mouth, stretching it out.

'Frogs,' I say, laughing. 'I get it. But I don't have you down as an agenda item.'

'Chambers wants to impress some UN guy. I presume you've put him on your agenda?'

I stir my hot chocolate until there's a fluffy, creamy layer on the top. 'Matts Laaksonen? He was item three but I'll move him down to four.'

Hugo picks up a small coronet, partially wrapped in sprays of wattle. He turns it carefully in his hands. 'You made the flowers?'

'It's for Mary Honey; she's in my class. I'm only halfway through.'

He frowns as he studies the tiny yellow spheres. 'How long does it take to make one of these?'

'Not long.' I shrug. 'Six or seven hours. Maybe eight.'

'A working day. That's a few thousand dollars for a banker, a couple of hundred for a teacher.'

'As if I'd charge my time? It's for Mary's birthday.'

'You are so freaking good to those kids.'

'I like children.' I smile. 'That's why I'm a teacher.'

'Your little kids are okay. But the youth program kids you put up with? They're as likely to spit in your face as thank you.'

'They deserve a chance.'

'Like the horses you rescue? Like that wreck of a farmhouse?'

'I—they've been unlucky as well.'

'You're a bleeding heart, Sapphie, always have been. Why not mix things up a bit? Find someone who puts you first.'

'You sound like Ma Hargreaves. Are you talking about settling down?'

He walks around the bench and wraps an arm around my shoulders, kissing me firmly on the top of my head. 'Why not? You've already chosen where you'll live.'

I force a smile. 'I'm happy as I am.'

He squeezes so tightly that one of my feet lifts off the ground. 'You're still angry with me, aren't you? I'm sorry about the feral comment.'

'I overreacted. It's just …' I bend my knees, escaping his hold, and pick up my mug. 'Don't dare spill wine on my flowers.'

He counts the clusters of yellow, interspersed with grey-green leaves. 'What variety is this? Golden?'

'My grandmother taught me how to make it.'

Acacia pycnantha. Golden wattle.

Kultainen kotka. Golden eagle.

Kissa. Cat.

Matts called me Kissa for a reason. He said that, just like a cat, the more he told me to go away, the more that I came back. But I knew he didn't mean it. I knew he searched for me when I was out of sight. I can't recall why I chose the name Kotka for him. Eagles are powerful and beautiful, rare and often solitary. I must have been only eight or nine when I named him. Did I see those qualities even then?

Last time I saw him, I told him I wasn't afraid of him. But …

The touch of his hand.

His serious mouth.

The shades in his eyes.

I could be.

Matts,
I'd prefer not to have to explain to everyone how we know each other, particularly as Thursday's meeting will be a one-off. Can we pretend we've just met?
Sapphie

Sapphire,
Forget you ever knew me.
Matts

12

The wind finds its way through the gaps between the doors at the community centre, ruffling the papers on the long timber table set up at the back of the hall. I bunch my red coat securely around my legs and stamp my boots on the floor, wishing I'd worn thicker socks.

Almost everyone seated in the first few rows, probably fifty people, is wearing combinations of coat and scarf and gloves. The twice-yearly formal meetings are open to the public, but the same group of people usually turn up. It's odd to see so many faces I don't recognise.

Douglas Chambers, the state MP whose constituency takes in Dubbo and many other smaller towns like Horseshoe, strolls up and down the aisle between the rows, nodding and chatting. I'm filling water glasses for him and the other committee members when he walks to the table. He's a middle-aged cyclist—short hair, super fit, whippet thin.

'Aren't you freezing?' I ask.

He indicates the woollen vest under his suit jacket. 'Not at all.'

I sit on my chair. 'Where did all these people come from?'

'Many have an interest in water management, so Dr Laaksonen was a drawcard.' He smiles politely. 'How widely do you advertise these meetings?'

'I post the agenda on our website, and also the pub and general store noticeboards, and I email it to those who subscribe to our newsletter. That covers everyone in Horseshoe and quite a lot of others.'

He raises his brows. 'We could do more to attract community engagement.'

'The committee members notify people and groups they think could be interested. And we welcome anyone who would like to come along.'

'Excellent,' he says, before walking away.

Hugo, sitting next to me, kicks my boot. 'All Chambers is interested in is attracting more votes. Does he want you to knock on doors like he does?'

The committee member on Hugo's other side, Cassandra Lewis, is a lawyer in her forties. She lives and works in Dubbo, and is active in wildlife preservation. Her hair falls in smooth silver waves either side of her face.

'Now, now, Hugo,' she says, smiling. 'Our local member means well. We're fortunate he hasn't delegated his committee role to one of his staff.'

'You're almost as bad as Sapphie, the way you stick up for everyone.'

Cassie taps his hand with her pen. 'Sapphie keeps us all in check, which is why this committee celebrates what the members, and the interests they represent, have in common. Everyone, our local member included, recognises that Horseshoe pulls its weight—socially and environmentally.'

A fresh blast of wind blows in as Gus Mumford opens the doors. When he struggles to close them behind him, I run to help, shoving the doors shut and fixing one of them with the bolt on the floor.

'They always stick on the threshold,' I say. 'How are you, Gus?'

'Well, thanks, Sapphie,' he says, lifting his tatty Akubra. When he lowers the hat again, his wild and wiry eyebrows almost disappear. 'Sorry I'm late. I was shutting my orphaned lambs up for the night. Even for winter, it's chilly.'

'Thanks for coming out. Did Freddie pick you up on his way through?'

Gus is elderly, and his eyesight deteriorated years ago. He relies on his tractor to get around his property and on friends to get him into town.

'He was running even later than me.'

'Sorry I can't be more help.'

'What? After the shock you had last year? I should be the one chauffeuring you about the place.'

'It's lucky I live so close to everything.'

'You'll be back behind the wheel soon, Sapphie. Just you wait and see.'

I nod woodenly before walking to the table with Gus. Luke Martin, a town planner who works for the local council, has taken his seat and is sorting through the pages stacked in front of him. He has a wide boyish smile.

'Evening, Gus.'

'How's your dad?' Gus asks. 'Heard he's been crook.'

Luke is a little older than I am, and his father is a vet at Dubbo's open plains zoo. 'The virus knocked him around, but he's hoping to be back at work next week.'

'You give him my regards.'

'Will do.'

I hold out a chair for Gus. 'As you can see, we're all here. Hugo as well.'

Gus rubs his hands together. 'What about the Finnish bloke?' He looks around. 'Our MP will want to wait for his illustrious guest.'

As if on cue, the doors open and Matts appears, his hands deep in the pockets of his faded blue hoodie. When an elderly lady, rushing towards the bathroom, almost runs into him, he stands back politely. The stubble on his face is uniformly dark, but his hair changes colour depending on the light, from sable to far warmer tones.

Sometimes I use stains to get the colours I want for my paper. How would I replicate the colour of his hair? Strong coffee for the darker shades. Weak Darjeeling tea for the browns.

Most people have their eyes on Matts, some subtly and others not, as he walks towards the table. He looks neither left nor right, but his hands come out of his pockets. He yanks the hoodie lower, over his jeans at his hips. Compared to the others at the table he's casually dressed, but I don't think he'd care about that.

Mr Chambers holds out his hand. 'Dr Laaksonen? I'm Douglas Chambers, member for Brindabilly. I'm delighted to meet you.'

'Call me Matts.'

I'm sitting at the far end of the table. As Mr Chambers makes his way towards me, introducing Matts to the others, I look down as if considering the agenda. When Matts finally reaches my chair, I stand and smooth down my coat. All the buttons are fastened.

When I look up, it's straight into his eyes. 'Matts.' The press of his palm does odd things to my heartbeat. 'I'm Sapphie Brown.'

He nods stiffly. 'Sapphie?'

'It's short for Sapphire.'

No friendship. No expectations. No *how we used to be*. It's better this way. I watch him walk to the far end of the table to sit next to Mr Chambers.

Hugo bumps my leg under the table. 'Agenda?' he mutters under his breath. 'They're waiting.'

'So ...' I clear my throat and pick up my pen, placing a tick next to the first item on the agenda. *Introduction*. 'Welcome to the meeting, everyone. We'll start with the committee member reports. After a tea break, our guests, Hugo Hallstead, a biologist working on an Armidale University project, and Dr Matts Laaksonen, an environmental engineer who works with the UN-sanctioned Ramsar Secretariat, will speak to us.'

Member reports. I tick again. 'As usual, I've consulted with Leon Lee, the chair of the Horseshoe Chamber of Commerce, and he's given me their report on how businesses in the town are limiting water usage already, and the plans they have to deal with projected water shortages ...'

Mr Chambers's report is next. 'Our local member of parliament will give an update on the state government's current water trading and licensing policies, and the impacts of these on current reserves in the Brindabilly Dam. He'll also comment on the availability of government funding for those already facing hardship.'

Mr Chambers walks up and down at the front of the hall when he delivers his report, arguing that efficient water use facilitates economic activity, and results in more water for environmental use. Most questions from the audience involve criticisms of government policy, but that doesn't seem to worry him. When he's finished, I bring Luke's report to the top of my pile.

'Luke Martin from the local council will talk about existing dam levels and rainfall projections, and will take us through council and state government negotiations regarding water sharing for agricultural, domestic, industrial, cultural and environmental needs.'

Luke stands behind his chair and looks around the room. 'The state government,' he says, glancing at Mr Chambers, 'is responsible for the Brindabilly Dam. The council is concerned that water-sharing decisions made by the government in good times leaves insufficient reserves in dry times such as these. We had reasonable rainfall the year before last. Far more of this water should have been kept in reserve, not sold off to large-scale irrigators for projects unsustainable in climactic conditions that have become the new norm.'

Besides huffing from time to time, Mr Chambers keeps quiet while Luke speaks. But in response to a question from someone in the audience, with a deferential nod in Matts's direction, he says he'll have more to say on water later in the meeting.

Gus never does a written report, just briefs me over a pot of tea. I put the notes of our conversation on the top of the pile as Gus takes off his hat and places it on the table.

'Gus Mumford will summarise how primary producers are dealing with the drier conditions,' I say. 'He'll also speak about the decisions already being taken by farmers. Some have been forced to reduce livestock numbers already, to lessen the costs of the hard feeding that might be necessary in the summer months.'

Grasping the back of his chair with his large, work-roughened hands, Gus stands. He speaks from the heart, and well past his time limit, detailing the difficulties farmers are likely to face.

'That's it from me, Sapphie,' he says finally, plonking his hat back on his head. 'You're up next, Cassie.'

Cassie undoes the toggles of her coat and hangs it on the back of her chair. She's wearing a jumper and cardigan in matching shades of green, and her skirt has a blue-and-green check.

'As most of you know,' I say, 'Cassandra Lewis is a lawyer. But she's also involved with numerous wildlife conservation organisations, and is a passionate advocate for living sustainably. Today she's going to talk about the practical measures we can take, individually and collectively, over the next few months.'

Cassie beams at the audience. 'Each dry day brings us closer to the much needed rain that'—she smiles at Luke—'we're told not to expect until much later in the year. But in the meantime, whether we live on a property of thousands of hectares, a market garden or a vineyard, or keep an apartment in the heart of Dubbo, we must do what we can to preserve the water we have.'

There's a flurry of activity in the tea break as people rush to the counter in the back corner of the hall, where I've set up the urn and china cups, teabags and instant coffee. A CWA member joins us, holding a donations bucket in one hand and a container of homemade chocolate biscuits in another.

When Cassie rings a bell fifteen minutes later, suggesting that everyone return to their seats for Hugo's talk, Matts and Hugo are still deep in conversation at the table. When Matts says something and smiles, Hugo throws his head back and laughs.

'We'd better get back to work,' I say to Gus, as I load the last of the cups into a bucket.

'Sapphie!' Hugo hisses, jiggling my seat before sitting down next to me. 'What sort of chair are you? Did you listen to anything I said in the past fifteen minutes?'

'I—' I pick up my pen and put a tick next to Hugo's name on the list. 'It was enlightening. I thought you only knew about alpine frogs.'

He grins as he snatches the pen and draws a bold blue circle around Matts's name. 'Item four, sleepyhead. Introduce your guest.'

Matts doesn't stand in front of his chair like Luke and Cassie, or behind it like Gus and Hugo. He doesn't stride up and down in front of the audience like Mr Chambers. After I introduce him, hurriedly and briefly, he walks to the front of the hall and turns. He pulls at a thread on the hip of his jeans. The light catches his hair when he lifts his head.

'Good evening.' His smile is confident and personable. Charming. Even though he's never even met these people. Not once in his life. 'I was born in Finland, which is also known as "the land of a thousand lakes". Seventy per cent of my country is forested and water is abundant. In winter, darkness in parts of the country falls two hours after midday. In summer, there is daylight at midnight. So what do our countries have in common? What can we learn from each other?'

It's almost nine o'clock, and many in the audience have a long drive home. But no one is shuffling their feet or checking their watch.

'The Ramsar Secretariat was set up under the Ramsar Convention, of which Australia is a signatory, to encourage the global protection of wetland environments and the sustainable use of water resources. Bogs, marshes, flood plains, peat lands, lagoons, channels, swamps, mires—these shallow bodies of water are classed as wetlands, and thousands are of international importance. Like the Macquarie Marshes, many are noted on the Ramsar List.'

When Matts walks to the table and takes a sip of water, his hand is perfectly steady. He smiles at the elderly lady in the front row and she smiles shyly back.

'The Macquarie Marshes are extensive and diverse,' Matts continues, 'which is why they're important. The habitats within them are unique, and they support nationally endangered bird and fish species, and a variety of other plants and animals. Particularly in times of drought, when other inland wetlands dry out, the marshes serve a critically important role as a wildlife refuge. They sustain many species of flora and fauna that might otherwise die out.'

When Cassie raises her hand, Matts walks towards her. 'You have a question?'

'Your term "refuge" is particularly apt. Thousands of water and woodland birds nest at the marshes. Plant species like river red gum, coolabah and water couch grasslands are vital to the ecosystem and biodiversity.'

Matts nods respectfully. 'Yes.'

'There's a great deal of information available from academia and government, but I have other sources, mostly wildlife and environmental volunteers. Can we meet again? I'd like to share their perspectives.'

'Certainly,' Matts says.

Our eyes meet as he walks past my chair, but there's no hint that he knows me better than anybody else in the room. What does he see in my expression?

Forget you ever knew me.

I turn away, but once he gets back to his spot at the front of the hall, I watch him like everybody else. He puts his hands in his pockets again.

'River and creek diversions, dam construction, pipelines and drainage, a growing population and associated industrial development, have permanently destroyed what took millennia to develop—the natural flow of rivers, streams and other watercourses into wetlands. The secretariat assists signatory countries to restore, rehabilitate and maintain wetland environments, with the aim of returning them to, as far as is possible, their natural state.'

Hugo kicks me under the table. 'Good speaker,' he whispers loudly, raising his thumbs.

I frown and push his foot away. 'Shh.'

Matts's hands go from his hoodie pockets to the front pockets of his jeans. Could he be any more at ease?

'The construction of the Brindabilly and other dams,' he says, 'permanently disrupted the flow to the marshes, not only the amount of water but how it arrived—the patterns of its flow. This had a catastrophic effect on the ecosystem. Irrespective of improvements in the past twenty years, the altered water supply poses a threat to the wetlands.'

'Hear, hear,' Cassie says.

'A loss of any habitat leads to a decline in biodiversity, and of all habitats around the world, wetlands are the most threatened. The marshes contain a—' Matts takes his hands out of his pockets and looks down at them, as if searching for a word that might be in his notes, even though he has none. 'The marshes contain a *mosaic* of habitats. They also provide an important conduit for the movement of native fish and amphibians. Hugo? Could you expand on this?'

Hugo sits forward in his chair and links his hands. 'Movement through the marshes is essential in terms of food and shelter, and also reproduction. Species rely on a variety of habitats in the wetlands to find mates, lay eggs and nurture their offspring.'

Matts turns to the audience again. 'I was invited by your government to advise on a new strategic plan for Ramsar-listed wetlands. As an inland semi-permanent wetland, the Macquarie Marshes are of interest.'

'In our most recent drought,' Cassie says, 'the marshes dried out completely, didn't they?'

'The shortage of environmental water for the towns and rivers had a devastating impact on the marshes,' Matts says. 'Which is why many stakeholders, including your government, are reconsidering water-sharing strategies.' He looks at me. 'Would you like to comment, Sapphire?'

I link my hands in front of me like Hugo did. 'Farmers, busi-nesses that rely on agriculture, recreational fishers, tourists and tourism operators, people who live and work in the towns, they all suffered in the last drought, as did wildlife, livestock and the environment as a whole. We try to give a voice to all interests, and operate on the assumption that what is good for one interest is likely to benefit another.'

'You seek a good outcome for the environment, including the river system, and recognise this has to be balanced by competing cultural, domestic, industrial and agricultural interests.' He glances at Luke. 'Do I have this right?'

Luke smiles. 'Sure do. And as I understand it, river water should end up in the wetlands as well.'

'Water distribution through catchments is highly regulated,' Matts says. 'To replicate the flow that the wetlands once had, in both wet and dry conditions, water must be maintained at mini-mum levels and not distributed to agricultural and other interests at the expense of future environmental demands.'

Cassie nods vigorously. 'That's right.'

Gus's chair tips alarmingly as he gets to his feet. 'What are you getting at, Matts?' he says, crossing his arms. 'Are you blaming the farmers for the rivers running dry?'

'Farmers understand that agricultural production requires a healthy river system,' Matts says. 'Most farmers also acknowledge that adequate environmental water is fundamental, and large-scale farming dependent on irrigation is not sustainable.'

Gus nods. 'Reckon you've got that right. When a man can't feed and water his own sheep and cattle, there's something gone wrong.'

'How long have you lived here?'

'All my life, and I'm going on eighty-two.' Gus looks around the audience. 'Which is why, like a few old-timers here, I like to think

I see both sides of the argument. Some farmers, big corporations mostly, they suck the land dry. The rest of us want what's best for it. We want to see the river like it was, back in the days when my grandpa sat at a desk in Sapphie's old schoolhouse.'

'When the river flooded,' I say, 'it reached the first step of the porch. That's why the new school was built on higher ground.'

Gus clears his throat. 'I don't get to do much reading these days, Dr Laaksonen, my eyes not being what they were, but I listen to the radio and talk to the locals, and I reckon we're thinking along the same lines. You're saying what's good for the wetlands will be good for the rivers. And what's good for the rivers will be good for the farmers.'

'Yes.'

'In that case, Sapphie,' Gus says, winking at me, 'I reckon we have nothing to fear from this Ramsar business.' His hat is on the table in front of him and he straightens it. He smiles at Matts. 'You've won me over, Dr Laaksonen.'

'Matts, please.'

When I pick up my pen, it hovers over the page. What I'd like to write isn't appropriate for the minutes. *Dr Matts Laaksonen is smart, knowledgeable and has excellent communications skills. He is also extremely attractive.*

'Item five on the agenda is question time,' I say briskly. 'Does anyone have any questions? If not, we can call it a—'

Mr Chambers clears his throat. 'Your comments were most instructive, Matts. But I would like to stress that my government is doing its best to ensure that the original functions and values of the wetlands are preserved.'

'Thank you, Douglas,' Matts says. 'But there are a range of out-comes and interests and these often clash. How do we balance them?'

'Through government initiatives.'

Matts turns to me. 'Do you agree with that, Sapphire? What is your committee's position?'

I sit a little straighter in my chair. 'We believe that all views should be taken into account, while recognising they change over time. It wasn't too long ago that some in the community'—I resist the urge to look at Mr Chambers—'didn't believe in global warming.'

'You meet regularly?'

'We chat informally all the time, and try to reach consensus decisions that reflect our different perspectives.' I count on my fingers. 'Gus talks to the farmers. Luke lets us know what's going on in Dubbo and other large regional centres, and keeps us up to date on council programs. I consult with private and public interests in the town. Cassie advises on environmental challenges and wildlife interests. Rain changes everything, but we try to think ahead about the water that's stored and how it should be used in the future. We all care about where we live. More often than not, our interests coincide.'

'Cooperation and consultation?' Matts says.

'Horseshoe is a small town, but this committee works well together, and other towns follow our lead. We believe our government, irrespective of other demands on its budget, should put more money into research and give additional financial support to country areas so we can use allocated water efficiently and sustainably. A number of the improvements the government has funded— river rehabilitation, targeted water distribution, conservation—are attributable to input from local committees like ours.'

'Well said, Sapphie,' Cassie says. 'I second that.'

'Third it,' Gus says.

Luke nods. 'Sure.'

Matts's gaze moves deliberately along the table. Mr Chambers, Luke, Gus, Cassie, Hugo.

By the time his eyes meet mine, I'm tapping my pages on the table to line them up.

'Sapphire?'

I put the papers in front of me. 'Matts?'

'I want to join your committee.'

CHAPTER
13

I hold my pen tightly as I circle item six: *Meeting closed.*

My chair scrapes the floor as I stand and address the audience. 'Thanks for coming out in the cold, and for your support of and interest in the work of the committee. Please thank our speakers, Hugo Hallstead and Matts Laaksonen.'

After the applause dies down, people stack chairs and carry them to the back of the hall. Others chat as they move towards the exit. I sort through papers and file them methodically into my bag.

I want to join your committee.

It was a request.

His words were perfectly clear but I ignored them.

Matts is leaning against the wall, looking at his phone, but straightens politely when he sees the elderly lady walk towards him. He smiles as he shakes the woman's hand. She's halfway down the aisle when she turns and waves over her shoulder.

Mr Chambers joins Matts and beckons to the rest of the committee. I pick up the bucket of dirty dishes before joining them. My bag is slung over my shoulder.

'Thanks for your reports and contributions. I'd like to lock up now.'

Mr Chambers purses his lips. 'Surely we'll respond to Matts's offer to join the committee first?'

I feel Matts's eyes on the side of my face. 'What's the rush?' I say. 'Why delay a decision?'

'Cassie reckons Matts doesn't get to vote like the rest of us,' Gus says, 'if that's what you're worried about. He gets to see how we go about things, that's all.'

'He'd be involved as an ex officio member,' Cassie says, 'observing the committee's day-to-day operations, contributing to our discussions and giving advice.' She smiles at Matts. 'Which we may or may not accept.'

'The Horseshoe Committee is an outstanding example of what can be achieved through local representation,' Mr Chambers says. 'And we'd have an opportunity to contribute to the valuable work of the Ramsar Secretariat. It benefits us all.'

'We're only an advisory committee,' Luke says, 'but Matts's involvement will encourage the authorities to listen to us. It will improve our profile, and might encourage the government to increase funding.'

'No.' My voice is too loud. My tone is too sharp. I clear my throat. 'We should take our time, consider this properly.'

Hugo is staring again. I'm sure he'd kick me if he could do it without being noticed. It's so quiet that I hear my own breathing.

Matts narrows his eyes. But there's no need for him to speak, not when the other committee members are keen to do it for him.

Mr Chambers has the loudest voice. 'I'll take responsibility for the paperwork,' he says. 'I've worked on numerous committees with ex officio members—visiting academics and so on.'

When Hugo pulls at the bucket, I hold it closer. 'Give, Sapph,' he whispers. 'What's going on?'

'You're not even on the committee.' I speak between my teeth.

'You ask me to join it every bloody month.'

Cassie glances at me before holding up a hand. 'Sapphie has made a valid point—there's no need to rush our decision. We'll have another committee meeting soon enough, and we can decide before then.' She smiles at Matts. 'I'm sure you understand.'

Gus blows on his hands and stamps his feet. 'Let's meet in the pub next time. Luke, Sapphie and me are already there for trivia on Saturday nights. Let's get together afterwards.'

'Excellent,' Cassie says. 'I'll put it in the diary for four weeks on Saturday. Eight o'clock?' She smiles at Matts again. 'All going well, perhaps you can join us?'

'Thanks.'

Mr Chambers frowns as he peers at his phone. 'I have another commitment,' he says.

'That's a shame, mate,' Hugo says, shaking Mr Chambers's hand before turning to me. 'I'll call it a night, Sapph. See you later.'

By the time I've herded out the stragglers, turned off the lights and locked the doors, there's no sign of Matts or the other committee members. I'd like nothing better than to go home too. I could climb into bed, pull my doona over my head and pretend that tonight never happened, but Hugo is bound to ask questions.

Not that I can blame him. In a professional sense, there's no reason to turn Matts down. In a personal sense? It's bad enough having to deal with my father without adding Matts to the mix.

The pump for the shower is rumbling when I leave the bucket and my bag on the schoolhouse porch and walk the few hundred metres to town. A group of visitors, probably the grey nomads, walk out of the pub and stroll down the footpath in front of me, talking and laughing. When we meet up at the T-junction at the bottom of the hill, a man wearing a tartan cap touches its peak and nods.

'We're stretching our legs before we turn in,' he says.

'Me too.' I press my hands more deeply into my pockets. 'But I wish I'd worn my gloves.'

There are no cars in sight, but I run across the road to the park. The large oaks and elms in the formal part of the gardens, even bare of leaves, block out the streetlights, but the moon and stars shine brightly. The smaller trees in the shaded areas, rhododendron and camellias, are budding or flowering despite the dry weather. Clumps of bulbs push through the mulch near the cenotaph.

Beyond the gardens are native trees—wattles bursting with new yellow baubles and bottlebrush bushes with vibrant red flowers. When I reach the riverbank, I follow the path. River red gums, many of them decades old, march either side of the river.

The water flows slowly because the levels are low.

The river needs water. So do the wetlands.

Matts wants to join the committee. His profile and expertise would be an advantage. But...

I've left my past behind me.

I lean against a river red gum. The trunk is smooth and cream coloured, but the bark at my feet will be countless shades of brown. The flowers on the gums are coin-sized clusters of fluffy white spikes with lime and yellow centres. Gus used to bring his great-niece April to the river in the holidays, and they'd fish at this spot. She's getting married at the end of October and has asked me to help with her flowers. I'm making Gus a gum blossom for his lapel, and will attach a matching flower to the front of April's card. As I pluck a leaf from the tree, I hear rustling behind me. Four kangaroos bound through the undergrowth. When the leader stops, the others stop too. Only fifty metres away, they stand tall in silhouette, their heads and bodies upright, their tails flat to the ground.

'Are you out for a late-night hop? Stay away from the roads.'

The roos are beautiful but unsettling. I turn and walk away from the river, carefully putting one foot in front of the other as I follow the path to the gardens and the neat rows of shrubs that circle the cenotaph. The main street glows in the distance, as does the pub. The road that leads to the schoolhouse is just out of sight. I skirt around the straw-mulch edges of the rose beds.

One door bangs and then another. A ute is parked across the road from the pub. It's large and black, with six seats in the cabin, a covered tray, fog lights on the bull bar and searchlights on the roof racks. The engine roars to life. Beams from the headlamps stretch down the road and across it.

They swallow me up.

What about the kangaroos?

'No!'

I was too young to have learnt how to drive when I came to Horseshoe. Ma and Pa offered to teach me after my seventeenth birthday, but they were busy with the store, and Pa drove a truck then anyway. When I wasn't at school or at the farmhouse, or travelling to Canberra to see Mum and Gran, I was busy with the horses at Kincaid House.

Hugo and Jet had learnt to drive on their family's farms. Getting a licence to drive on the roads was easy for them, as was driving long distances on difficult roads. They'd pick me up when I needed a lift and they never made me feel guilty about it.

When I left Horseshoe to go to university in Armidale, I was eighteen. Mum died the following year and it took another year before I worked up the courage to get behind the wheel. My driving instructor, a retired steelworker originally from Wollongong, was called Lucky. He was a small wiry man with a very big heart and the patience of a saint. He taught me how to drive competently.

Pa Hargreaves helped me find a small car in Dubbo but I only drove it occasionally. I hardly ever drove at night. I didn't drive in high winds and dust storms, or misty early mornings. I rarely drove when it rained. And I avoided taking passengers unless they were like Gus who, besides humming occasionally, listened to the radio and rarely ever talked. I didn't break the rules and I never got a ticket. Soon enough I was home again in Horseshoe. I kept the car but walked whenever I could.

Late last year, on a Saturday night after trivia, I drove Gus home like I usually did. His property is barely twenty minutes from the town. It was only ten o'clock.

Everybody knows you have to watch out for wildlife at night. Kangaroos and wallabies, possums and wombats run across fenced and unfenced roads. They get spooked when they see lights and then they stop dead.

I'd dropped Gus off and turned left to return to the loop road. I was ten minutes from Horseshoe and on the crest of the hill when my sight was obscured by a solid black form and—

I screamed. A thump. Broken glass.

A kangaroo on the bonnet of my car. Her head was thrown back and her body was twisted.

Lifeless eyes.

I'd thought about how desperate Mum must have been to leave her room at two in the morning to pick up pills from a dealer she didn't know outside a nightclub the coroner said she'd never been to before. I hadn't thought about the last few seconds of her life.

The driver who hit her was an American tourist. He'd left Sydney at two in the morning to attend an Anzac Day service at the War Memorial. The lights were green as he approached an intersection in Kingston. When he saw Mum bent double in the middle of the road, he put his foot on the brake, but it was too late.

Last year I was forced to face the facts.

The kangaroo died a violent death.

And so did my mother.

I had a few panic attacks after I hit the kangaroo, but I haven't had any since I saw the psychologist. I coped reasonably well when Pa and I went to Dubbo in the van. I've even been thinking about contacting Lucky in the hope that more driving lessons might help me face my fears.

I don't remember sitting down, but now I'm aware of everything. The roughness of the stones, the stringy dry grass, the coldness of the earth. As I get to my feet, I wipe my hands on my jeans. 'Ow!' I've grazed my palm again. Did I drop to the ground so quickly?

I make my way to the kerb and look right, left and right again— slowly and seriously like a five-year-old might. Walking up the footpath, taking one cautious step at a time, is like wading through treacle. My throat is scratchy and tight and hurts when I swallow.

'Over there!'

The grey nomads I saw earlier are gathered on the footpath outside the pub. Matts, also on the footpath but further away, is walking quickly towards them. When the man in the tartan cap points to me, Matts breaks into a run and crosses the road diagonally. As soon as he reaches me, he grips my shoulders tightly and peers into my face.

'What happened?'

'What?' I croak.

'You screamed.'

'No, I—I'm okay.'

He runs his hands down my arms to my elbows. He grips them like he has to hold me up.

Is he holding me up? My heart is hammering. My legs are shaking.

The man in the cap catches up. 'Are you all right?'

'I …' My teeth are chattering so violently that I'm scared I'll bite my tongue.

'Sapphire,' Matts says, squeezing my arms even tighter. 'What?'

I shake my head. 'It was the ute. I wasn't expecting the lights.' I take a deep breath as I look from Matts to the other man. 'I'm sorry.'

Matts's hands slide down my arms to my wrists. He turns me so I'm facing him straight on. 'Something happened.'

'Forget it, please.'

His hands slip further, trapping my fingers and stinging my palm. When I wince he loosens his grip, but only for a moment. He cups my hands and lifts them, resting them between us. He's wearing a T-shirt under his hoodie. His hands aren't warm, but they're warmer than mine.

'You're shaking,' he says.

I lower my eyes. 'I'm cold, that's all.'

He's on the high side of the footpath, even taller than usual. As if he reads my mind, he bends his knees so we're the same height. He stares into my eyes. 'Don't lie to me, Sapphire.'

'Think what you like.'

The older man puts his hand on my elbow. 'You've had a shock, my dear, whatever the cause, and you're as white as a sheet to prove it. Where do you live? Come to the pub while we see about getting you home. There's a log fire in the lounge.' He takes out his phone. 'Can I call someone to meet you there? Do you have family close by?'

'I—' I shake my head again. 'Thank you, but—' When I pull my hands free of Matts's, I bump against the man.

He threads his arm through mine. 'Steady, now.'

'I don't live far away. I'm fine to walk home.'

The man tightens his hold and waves to his friends, indicating they go inside the pub. 'Let's walk together.'

Matts walks stiffly by my other side as the man, Gerry, chats about his itinerary and names towns from here to Darwin that he and his friends are planning to visit. By the time we reach the top of the hill, my legs almost feel like my own again.

'Thank you very much, but I'll be fine from here.' I let go of his arm. 'See the signs? That's where I live.'

'At the school?'

'I teach there, but live next to it.'

'Are you a local girl?'

'I spent my last two years of school living here, and came back permanently after uni.'

'It's a welcoming town.' He smiles. 'We're reluctant to move on tomorrow.'

'Then you'll have to come back again—in summer next time.'

As Gerry walks away, Matts moves closer. My heart rate increases again. When he took my hands on the footpath, I didn't object. I take a jerky step backwards and cross my arms.

'Thanks.'

'What for?'

'You thought I needed help.'

'You did.'

'I … maybe.' I look over his shoulder. 'Thanks.'

'Why did you scream?'

'I told you already. Forget it.'

'You were hiding in a tree a month ago. Do I forget that too?'

'That was different.' I uncross my arms and then cross them again. My hand stings. 'We need to talk about the committee, Matts.'

He looks towards the schoolhouse. 'Tonight?'

Hugo will be in front of the television by now. Without knowing our history, he'd take Matts's side and laugh at my objections.

'Tomorrow after school would be better.'

'I'll be in Armidale tomorrow and Saturday. I could see you early on Sunday.'

'Eight?'

'Seven.'

I push my hands deep into my pockets. My fingers are so cold that they hurt when I bend them. 'Nothing will be open.'

'I'll come here.' He walks three steps and then he turns. Even in the dimness, I make out his frown. 'Sleep well, Sapphire.'

Sapphire Beresford-Brown. Sapphie Brown.

How long will he be here? A month? A few months?

How can I trust him?

How can I keep him out of my life?

'Look, Miss Brown!' Mary runs across the playground on Friday morning, her school bag bouncing on her back and a drawstring bag swinging from her wrist. She skids to a stop in front of me. 'I brought some real ones! *Please*, Miss Brown. Can we make them this afternoon? Can you show me what to do?'

I'm holding an armful of folders, a mug of tea, six lost property items and a laptop. 'Good morning, Mary. You can tell me what you'd like to make when we get into the classroom.'

She tosses a plait over her shoulder. 'Did you sleep in?'

By the time I returned home from the horses this morning, it was almost eight o'clock. It's only eight-thirty now, but school starts at nine. I haven't set up the classroom yet.

'Yes, because I had trouble getting to sleep last night. Can you take my laptop while I unlock the door?'

Mary throws her schoolbag on the ground but hangs on to the drawstring bag, following me inside and putting the laptop on my desk at the front of the room. She jumps from foot to foot as I dump the rest of my things next to the laptop and sit in my chair.

'Let's see, then.'

When she releases the string and tips the bag upside down, three long, leafy stems fall in a clump on the table. 'You said we could make flowers in craft,' she says. 'Can we make these? I've seen you do them before.'

'My grandmother taught me how to make them.' I unravel the stems. 'August is early for bougainvillea. This is lovely.'

'It grows on the shed at home. Dad had to get on the ladder because all the red flowers were at the top.'

I touch the papery crimson surfaces. 'The bright parts are called bracts, Mary. The flowers are the tiny white blossoms in the middle.'

'Dad hates the spikes.'

'It will be good to have a real sample to work from.' I point to the paint-spattered trestle table at the back of the room. 'Put the stems in a vase of water, and sit them over there. Take care not to scratch yourself.'

She grins. 'You'll get to look at bougainvillea all day.'

It wasn't long before Inge died that Matts and I sat side by side at her dining room table to do our homework. Matts had moved a vase of bougainvillea, vibrant scarlet bracts with tiny white flowers, to my side of the table, because he'd insisted that, as he was thirteen, he needed more room than I did. When Inge walked into the room and saw what Matts had done, she moved the flowers back to the centre.

'Beauty is precious,' she said softly, her hand on Matts's shoulder. 'We must keep it close. I have told you this before.'

A look passed between them. Matts opened his mouth as if to argue before shutting it again. He rearranged his books to accommodate the flowers. 'Yes, Äiti.'

'I can make flowers just like that,' I piped up. 'Gran taught me.'

'Bougainvillea?' Inge said. 'You must show me how it is done.'

The next day was a Saturday, and I knew that Matts, who didn't rate my flowers, would be at a football match with his father. Dad dropped me off outside the house, and a gardener recognised me and led me through the security gates. When Inge finally answered the doorbell, she looked different than usual because her long fair hair was loose. I wanted to tell her that she looked like Rapunzel, but I held my tongue. *Think before you speak.* My father's constant admonishment rang in my ears. Maybe Inge didn't want to look like Rapunzel?

Inge kissed one cheek and then the other and then the first one again, like she always did. 'Good morning, my little Sapphire.'

I must have looked like Mary often does, jumping from one foot to the other in excitement. 'I came to show you how to make the flowers!' I raced past Inge and flung open the doors to the dining room, stopping short when I saw a man leaning against the table. His suit was dark against the brightness of the vase of bougainvillea behind him.

'Buenos días,' he said, straightening.

Inge came up behind me. 'This is Sapphire,' she said quietly. 'Today she will make me flowers. Bougainvillea.'

'Like these?' He pointed to the flowers on the table. Only he couldn't point properly because he only had a thumb on his hand. He crouched down low and smiled into my eyes. 'I do not believe it.'

I held out my supplies. 'I can teach you too if you want me to.'

When Inge put an arm around my shoulders, I smelt her perfume. It was the same one Mum always wore. She squeezed gently. 'We will show Gabriel another time.'

By the time she returned and sat next to me at the table, her hair was neatly tied up in the chignon she generally wore. I'd brought a small tablecloth from home and I spread it out before setting out paper and scissors, glue and wire.

'What lovely paper,' Inge said.

'It's called maroon,' I said. 'But you can use other colours too, like fuchsia and coral and salmon. Everyone thinks the coloured parts are the flowers but they're not.'

Inge watched me all morning, and we were both still sitting at the table when Matts and his father came home. Inge held out her arm and beckoned them in.

'Look, Leevi, Matts, how clever Sapphire is.'

My paper bougainvillea was barely distinguishable from the real ones in the vase. Mr Laaksonen, who was a number of years older than Inge, graciously complimented my artistry, but when Matts rolled his eyes, a blush warmed my face. I hurriedly pushed the flowers across the table.

'You can keep them,' I told Inge, looking anywhere but at Matts as I scrambled to my feet, stuffed my supplies into my bag and pushed the chair against the table. 'Mum said I have to be home for lunch. I'll call and ask her to pick me up.'

I was dialling the landline when Matts touched my arm. 'I'll walk with you.'

'You don't have to,' I said.

'Give me the phone, Kissa.' When I handed it to him, he placed it firmly in the bracket. 'I like to walk you home.'

Matts walked me home last night.

It wasn't surprising that I was anxious after the meeting. *I want to join your committee.* I wasn't expecting to see the kangaroos or the lights. I didn't have a chance to breathe deeply or rationalise or do any of the things I have to do to ward off a panic attack.

I kneel as I sweep crepe paper scraps from the floor near the trestle table. Making the shapes exactly the same size isn't as important with bougainvillea as it is with other plants, but that's not something Archie wants to know about. His concentration is fierce as he traces around the templates and follows the pencil lines with scissors. Mary and Amy stand either side of him and press the bracts into shape with their thumbs.

'You've done so well today,' I say. 'Next week, I'll show you how to make the flowers.'

Mary sighs. 'I wish we could do this every day.'

When I clap my hands, the children mimic the rhythm. Ahmed and Moses, identical eight-year-old twins with big brown eyes, put down their scissors and glue.

'The bell will ring soon, so it's time to clear our desks. Who's looking forward to the weekend?' I laugh when a sea of hands pops up. 'As you tidy, tell the other children at your table what you're *most* looking forward to.'

Ahmed raises his hand. 'What are you looking forward to, Miss Brown?'

'I ...' When my smile disappears, I force a new one. 'Going to the farmhouse tomorrow, and spending the day with my horses.'

CHAPTER
15

Ma Hargreaves warned me she'd be at the farmhouse first thing in the morning, but I don't expect to see her at seven o'clock, standing on the porch with a broom in one hand. At her feet is a giant Tupperware container filled with chocolate brownies.

'Just let me in, love,' she says, kissing my cheek, 'then go see to your horses. Leave the spring-cleaning to me.'

Ma is going on seventy, with mid-length curly grey hair that's kept off her face with tortoiseshell clips. She's a little overweight because her troublesome knees make it hard for her to exercise. Sitting long hours at the cash register in the store doesn't help either.

When I unlock the door, the sun streams into the hallway. I stand back as Ma bustles inside.

I frown at the spider in the cornice. 'I'd like to say this is unnecessary, but the cobwebs haven't been cleared since your last spring-clean.'

Ma isn't able to bend down low or do heavy work, but her delegation skills are second to none. As soon as Joel, Barney and the other older kids arrive, she tempts them with brownies and puts them to work, refusing to let them leave until they've found somebody to take their place.

By the time I return to the house it's midafternoon and the rudimentary kitchen, hallway, my flower room and the office are much more clean and tidy.

'Looks great, Ma. Any brownies left?'

'I saved you two, love. On the table in the front room.'

'Thanks.' I pick up the brush and pan. 'I can finish up. You get back to Pa.'

'The physical activity is doing me good.' She starts sweeping again. 'Don't you have to supervise outside?'

'We're packing up. Everyone knows where I am if they need me, and Joel is with Prima.'

'He's a good boy, that Joel,' she says through the dust motes. 'Under all his bravado, he has a gentle nature. You can see that from the way he sits with Prima.'

'He arrives early and takes the last lift home. He still won't communicate with Corey though.'

'He'll talk when he's ready,' she says. 'Give him time.'

I crouch with the brush and pan and collect the dust and other bits and pieces that Ma has swept into piles.

'I don't know how it gets so dirty in here.'

Ma pushes the bristles of the broom under the gaps beneath the skirting boards before pointing it towards the flaky plaster ceiling. 'This house is so old, Sapphie, it creates its own dirt.'

'I guess.'

She nods towards the door. 'And you've got twenty kids tramping through on Saturdays. When the youth centre opens, you'll have a lot less to organise and you'll get rid of the gear. You can move in and set this place to rights.'

If I could trust Ma and Pa to keep a secret, I'd tell them about the option on the farmhouse. But I know that Ma would be on the phone to Robert immediately, and she'd also call the council and local paper and anybody else she might imagine could help. Pa would tell his customers and suppliers what my father has done, and ask for their advice. I need my father to be onside, not only because of the farmhouse, but because, like Matts said, he has influence. If it suits his political agenda, he'll protect Mum.

'Stay still for a minute.' I bunch my sleeve in my hand and wipe the dirt from Ma's cheek.

'Ta, love.' Ma is leaning hard on the broom. Her face is flushed pink.

'Maybe you need a break?'

'Don't you worry about me.'

I sneeze. And then sneeze again. 'Maybe *I* need a break.'

We sit on canvas chairs on the front porch with water bottles between us. The weathered floorboards, sheltered by the red gum, are dappled in the sunlight.

'I can't believe it's almost spring,' I say. 'The wisteria will flower soon.'

'Your azaleas are always a delight.'

'Yep.'

Ma can sense tears at ten thousand paces. 'What's wrong, love? You've been out of sorts all day.' She puts her hand on my arm. 'Are you fretting about your driving? Pa said you did well in the van.'

I do my best to smile. 'It's been a long week. I'm tired, that's all.'

'You work full time, keep this place going and put your hand up for everything else. You need another set of hands to help you out.'

'Are you back to telling me that I need a husband?'

'And why not? You're a lovely girl, Sapphie, but you've never had anybody special. And perhaps you're too busy to find him. When you go out, it's to this meeting or that meeting. Last week it was the environment committee, wasn't it? It's a lot to take on.'

Sleep well, Sapphire.

'Sapphie? What is it, love?'

I fumble for my water bottle and unscrew the lid. I wipe an arm across my eyes. 'I never used to be like this.'

Ma pats my arm. 'When your granny passed away, and your mum, you hardly shed a tear. You kept it all inside. It's best to let it out.'

'I guess.'

'So what's brought this on?'

I take a few careful sips from the bottle and then screw on the lid, making sure it's secure. 'My father has been accused of bribery and is worried about the political fallout.' I put the bottle at my feet again. 'I might have to go to Canberra, that's all, so people believe he has my support.'

'Who did he bribe?'

'He's been accused of it, Ma. I don't think he actually did it.'

'All the same,' she says firmly, 'he can't make you go to Canberra, or do anything else you don't want to do. I would've thought he'd understand that by now.'

I walk the few steps to the railing and look towards the road. One of the volunteers raises her hand before she steps into her car. 'See you next week!'

Bright green jasmine shoots curl around the post. Unravelling one, I wind it loosely around my wrist. The shoot is young and fragile, but when it matures it will toughen and harden.

'It's more complicated than that. My mother's name might come up too.'

'Why would that be? She passed away so long ago.'

'She was still married to my father when the bribery happened.'

'You shouldn't have to do this if you find it upsetting.'

'I don't have much choice. This is the best way to protect her, and …'
I settle the shoot back around the post. 'There are other reasons too.'

Someone clumps up the steps at the side of the house. 'Sapphie!'
Hugo yells.

'We're out the front!'

He appears around the corner with tousled tawny hair and an
Akubra in his hand. As he walks towards us, smiling broadly, one
of the boards gives way.

'Fuck,' he mutters, as he jerks to a stop. 'What the—'

'Hugo!' Ma holds on to the arms of the chair and pushes herself
to her feet. 'Watch your language, young man.'

'Sapphie's floor,' Hugo says, as he yanks his foot from the gap in
the boards, 'attacked me.'

Ma puts her hands on her hips. 'You can't blame Sapphie's floor
for your heavy tread.'

Sapphie's azaleas. Sapphie's floor.

'Hugo?' I force a smile. 'Did you want me for something?'

He puts his hat on his head and pushes it back. He grins. 'I
thought we could go for a ride. Fancy a trek to the river on those
reprobate horses of yours?'

After a full day with children and teenagers in the confines of a
paddock, Sonnet and Strider seem relieved to see Hugo and me at
the gate, bridles and saddles over our arms.

Lollopy darts in front of the thoroughbreds. I laugh, pushing
against his chest so we can get through. 'Move over. You'll get your
hay when I get back.'

When I loop my arm under Sonnet's dark brown neck and hold
his mane, he walks placidly beside me to the fence.

'You'd better ride Sonnet,' I tell Hugo. 'He's less likely than
Strider to throw you off.'

Hugo lifts the reins over Sonnet's head so they rest on his neck, then slips the bit into his mouth and fastens the chinstrap of the bridle. 'Sounds like a win to me.'

When I hold out my hand, Strider pricks up his big black ears and snuffles my palm. His eyes are dark and earnest. 'Will you play nice if I take you out with Sonnet?'

Hugo is the first to mount, putting his foot in the stirrup, swinging into the saddle and gathering the reins. Though he never aspired to be a farmer like his older brothers, who swapped horses for motorbikes and quad bikes when they were in their teens, Hugo always liked to ride.

Strider is toey and won't stand still, so I lead him to the old bathtub I use as a feed trough and climb up that way. He prances on the spot as Hugo opens the gate. After we pass through, Hugo swings it shut behind us and fastens the chain.

'Thanks.' I smile. 'I wish you were here every week.'

'Bloody miracle I can ride at all.' He rotates his shoulders. 'How do you sleep in that bed?'

'Exceptionally well. And stop complaining. You're lucky I gave it to you.'

We walk the horses in single file on the road, but trot side by side as we cut across the paddocks to the property owed by Edward Kincaid. It's only fifty hectares, a small landholding compared to many others, but the land is well maintained and I'm aware of most of the dangers like rabbit and wombat holes. The grass is drying out, but the paddocks have been rested for the past few months, so it's in much better shape than neighbouring properties.

We're almost at the bottom of the gently sloping hill when I pull over and point towards the river. 'I usually give Strider his head on the flat stretch down there. Having Sonnet here might cause a problem, but you go ahead if you want to.'

'I'm good,' Hugo says as we walk on. 'By problem, you mean Strider will take off, don't you? Do you reckon you can get him out of that habit?'

'He only does it in company, which isn't surprising when he's spent most of his life as a racehorse. He's a gentleman on a lead rope, so works well in horse therapy.'

'The kids don't have to ride him?'

'Handling is just as important. When the kids are anxious, Strider picks up on it. If they're angry or impatient, we won't let them near him. That means, to have any chance of going to him, the kids are forced to stay calm and quiet and to be patient. He's good for another reason too—being young and beautiful wasn't enough to keep him safe, which is why he was bound for the knackery. Corey tells some of the older kids that he might have been rejected like they've been, but he deserves a second chance.'

Hugo rolls his eyes. 'Bloody teenagers.'

When a flock of cockatoos fly out of a paperbark tree ahead of us, Sonnet shies, skittering into Strider's path. Hugo brings Sonnet under control straight away, but Strider sees it as a challenge. Within moments he's as tense as a spring and bunching his hind-quarters like he's at a starter gate. I sit back in the saddle, turning him away from Sonnet and cantering him in smaller and smaller circles until he settles.

'Good boy,' I say, leaning low to stroke his neck.

'You reckon?' Hugo says as he cautiously pulls in alongside.

'It's been a couple of months since he's thrown me. All I have to do is work on his manners.'

'What is he? Seventeen hands? He's a bloody strong horse, Sapphie.'

'He was trained to race. And after he was sold a number of times, he was mistreated. He might make a good dressage horse, because he'd be in an arena all by himself. There's a chance he'll be suitable for rehoming.'

'So, in addition to Prima, you can buy another crazy horse that no one else can handle?' He loosens Sonnet's rein. 'You shouldn't be out on your own with him.'

'What?'

'I'll amend that—you shouldn't be on your own unless you have a flare and a satellite phone. Otherwise, if he bolts, you've had it.'

'I can handle him. And if he bolts, I'll bail out. I've done it before.'

'And that's supposed to comfort me? When a racehorse runs at seventy k's an hour?'

I push Strider into a trot so we're in front of Sonnet as we veer off the main track to the narrower one that heads to the river. 'Are we checking for frogs today?'

He laughs. 'Why don't we change the subject?'

'Well?'

'Yeah, yeah. Shut up, Hugo.'

Hugo and I dismount and loosely tie the horses to a paperbark tree. Now I'm off his back, Strider is almost as chilled as Sonnet. He rests a back leg, watching with mild curiosity as Hugo and I push through the undergrowth to the river. It's only a few metres across and not very deep because it's been so dry, but the rocks either side are damp with moss and lichen.

Hugo whistles. 'This is great.'

Under the shade of the paperbark trees, boulders, logs and branches have been deliberately placed either side of the river and in the river itself. They trap leaf litter and other debris and form a series of catchments. Additional trees and shrubs, grasses and rushes have been planted en masse. Moisture stays in the ground, even when it's dry.

'Edward's a convert to regenerative agriculture and other environmental initiatives. He's done a lot of work down here.'

Hugo points to the water. 'Look at the aquatic vegetation.'

'Good for frogs, right?'

'Tadpoles eat algae and frogs eat insects. Fish, birds, lizards and snakes eat tadpoles and frogs. They're a crucial part of the ecosystem.'

I link my hands in front of me. 'Frogs live in water and on land, so are perfect for assessing the health of the environment.'

He makes a face. 'Are you having a go at me?'

I laugh. 'You always talk about frogs. But,' I look up and down the river, 'I agree this place is amazing. Shelter for adult frogs, organic matter for tadpoles.'

'So you were actually listening to my talk last week?'

I tread carefully to the water because the undergrowth is damp. 'I don't know as much as I should about the wetlands.'

'They're home to the striped marsh frog, brown-striped grass frog and spotted grass frog.'

I hide a smile. 'What about the crucifix toad?'

'Don't get me started, Sapphie.' He kneels and peers into the water. 'I have nightmares about losing the green and golden bell frogs.'

'Can you see any tadpoles down there?'

He scoops up water, splashing his face and neck. 'The water's not warm enough yet.'

Crouching next to him, I run my fingers through the water, crisp and crystal clear. 'We'll come back again when it is.'

'So long as you do your homework beforehand,' he says, standing and holding out his hands. When I grab them, he pulls me to my feet. If someone came along and saw us like this, we'd look like a couple. He's smart and funny and very good-looking.

But he's not Matts.

Matts? I take a deep breath. We have a history. I find him attractive. But that doesn't mean much. That doesn't bring happiness.

Hugo frees my hands and looks at me suspiciously. 'You read my report after the meeting, didn't you? Why would you bother with that?'

'Because it was interesting and I missed some of it and … if I leave the committee, you might have to take my place.'

'Why would you leave the committee?'

'I've got a lot on.'

'That's never stopped you before.' He crosses his arms. 'It's not because of Laaksonen, is it? The committee would be crazy to refuse him.'

'It's a few things.'

'What the hell? It is him, isn't it?'

'Maybe.'

'I thought he might be an arsehole given his credentials, but he seemed like a regular guy. What's your problem?'

Matts and I fell out as teenagers, which seems a weak excuse for leaving the committee. And I can't tell Hugo about Matts's dealings with my father, because if that got back to Robert, I don't know what he'd do.

'I haven't made a final decision yet.'

'You're so damned secretive, Sapphie.' He lifts his hands. 'When are you going to open the vault?'

When tears spring out of nowhere, I pull away and barge through the undergrowth to the horses. Untying Strider, I throw his reins over his head and face the saddle, fumbling for the stirrup leather. I talk over my shoulder. 'Can you give me a leg up? I have to get back.'

'What's the hurry? It's Sunday tomorrow.'

Matts will be at the schoolhouse at seven o'clock.

I jump when Hugo blows a raspberry onto the side of my neck. 'Don't do that!' I hiccup and sniff. 'Idiot.'

'Hoped it'd change your mindset.'

I croak a laugh. 'It worked.'

'Why are you crying?'

I wipe my arm across my face. 'I'm worried about your corroboree frogs. You didn't even mention them.'

'Northern or southern?' He pokes me in the ribs. 'Before I lift you onto your firecracker horse, I want to know you have vision.'

I scrub my eyes again. 'Yes, I do. Thank you.'

He kicks my boot firmly. 'Lift your leg then, drama queen.'

As a sliver of sunlight sneaks beneath the blind, I yawn and stretch, careful not to slip off the couch.

It was just after dawn when I woke up the first time. I stepped into gumboots in the half-light before running through the cold, damp grass to the toilet. By the time I got back to the schoolhouse, my feet were numb. I had an hour before I had to face Matts. I huddled under the blankets to warm up and ...

A car door slams.

I sit bolt upright and kick the covers to the end of the couch. 'Damn.'

My clean clothes are in a heap on the floor where I left them last night. I yank a long-sleeved T-shirt over my pyjama top and step into jeans.

There's a rap on the door. 'Coming!' I hiss, before tiptoeing to the bathroom, splashing water on my face and brushing my teeth. Searching through a tangle of bedclothes, I find my jacket and throw it across my shoulder. I trip over Tumbleweed, still buried under his mohair throw, as I rush to the door.

Matts is dressed mostly in black—jeans, boots and a V-necked sweater over a white T-shirt. He paces in front of the white picket fence. As I lift my boots from the rack, he crosses the lawn, taking the steps to the porch two at a time.

'Sapphire.'

I smooth my hair, damp when I went to bed last night, and tidy errant strands behind my ears. 'Sorry to keep you.' I glance at the garden. 'Can we talk outside?'

He frowns. 'Why not inside?'

I'd planned to be sitting on a seat in the playground at least ten minutes before he was due to arrive, so Hugo didn't get up and join us. I put my boots back on the rack before blowing on my hands and putting them into my pockets. 'Here will be fine. This won't take long.'

He nods abruptly. 'Go ahead.'

We used to talk for hours about nothing. I could make him smile better than anybody else on the planet. Now I can't read him very well at all.

'The committee, Matts. What are you up to?'

He frowns. 'It has relevance to the wetlands.'

When I cross my arms, my jacket slips from my shoulder and falls to the floor. Matts must notice, but neither of us bends to pick it up. His eyes aren't simply grey, sometimes it seems there are warmer shades as well: golds and dark greens.

'I can recommend other committees.'

'I respect your committee members. I'm familiar with the town.'

A flock of eastern rosellas chatter in the bottlebrush tree near the bus stop. 'Because you barged into my life.'

'I came here to warn you.'

When a breeze rushes up the steps and blows into my face, I twist my hair into a knot at the back of my neck. I wish I'd had time to tie it up.

You're afraid to be beautiful.

'My father will protect my mother if it suits his agenda. You have an agenda too.'

'It's different from Robert's.'

'You had dinner with him. You share information.'

'It's safer to know what he's up to.'

A truck drives past, rattling over the potholes and startling the birds. 'Assuming he tells you what that is. I don't trust him, I can't.'

'You don't trust me either.'

Whispers of dust dance in the sunbeams. 'I don't—' I shake my head. 'No.'

He stalks past me and stands in front of the hooks, gripping them so firmly that his thumbnails turn white. When he faces me again, his eyes are cold.

'After you came to Horseshoe, I sent emails. Did you get them?'

'Yes, but …' I look past him. 'I didn't open them.'

'Before that, I sent letters to your grandmother's house.'

Gran, who always saw the best in what I did, couldn't hide her disappointment when I refused to read Matts's letters. 'It's written by hand,' she once said, holding a postmarked envelope up to the light, 'not typed on a computer.' She traced around the stamp. 'And it's come all the way from the other side of the world. Are you sure you don't want to read it?'

'Please, Gran, just put it in the recycling bin.'

My silk nightie is peeking out from the bottom of my shirt. I roll it up and hide it. 'I didn't read those letters either.'

'I emailed when you were at university.'

'I couldn't—' I shake my head. 'I deleted them.'

Matts stalks back to his spot near the desk. 'And that's why we are strangers.'

I wrap my arms around my middle. 'Strangers with history.' My socks are blue and fluffy. I point my toe and trace a line in the dust. 'I should have told you that I didn't read the letters and emails. I should have told you not to send them any more.'

He runs a finger along the narrow indentation at the top of the desk, and then watches closely as I pull down my cuffs and bunch the fabric in my hands. He bends and picks up my jacket, flicking it against his leg to brush away the dust before laying it on the desk.

He takes hold of my hands, gently but firmly. 'Is that an apology?'

'Yes,' I whisper.

He places my hands between us, flat against his chest. His heartbeats are steady and strong.

'I should have warned you about the committee,' he says.

'Is that an apology?'

He dips his head. 'Yes.'

'I'm happy here.' My voice wavers. 'I'm settled.' I pluck at his sweater. 'I don't know what's happening any more.'

'Sapphie?'

When I lift my face, our gazes lock. 'You don't call me that.'

He hesitates. 'Did I mispronounce it?'

To one side of his scar is a faint silver mark like a pinprick. *Two stitches down, four stitches across.*

I lift a hand, but I'm not sure where to put it. My body is heated. My brain is mush.

'You never mispronounce.'

When he frowns, I rest my palm against his jaw. The bristles are rough, but his hair is silky and smooth. He swallows and I feel it from the ends of my fingers to the tips of my toes. His lips are slightly open and so are mine.

He mutters, 'Sapphie.'

I mumble, 'Matts.'

One hand against his cheek, the other on his heart, I stand on my toes and our breaths mingle sweetly.

How can it be that we have never kissed?

I press my lips to his.

For an instant, he freezes, but then he wraps his arms around me. Our lips connect tentatively, a careful exploration of texture and taste. When I softly exhale, he breathes me in. Our mouths slip, slide, part and rejoin. My lips beneath his. We don't need anything else. Just … this.

My legs tremble. My body burns. The universe wobbles and tilts.

'Kissa.' The word hangs between us.

I touch his bottom lip with the tip of my tongue. It slips inside his mouth when he angles his head.

He growls and pulls me closer. Our tongues stroke carefully. The ache in my breasts is warm and sweet. I open my fingers and feel the contours of his chest. I run my hands up his arms. I cup his face and press even closer, searching deeply for—

A door slams shut. 'Sapphie!' Hugo shouts. 'Where are you?'

Matts lifts his head a fraction. 'Who is it?'

Footsteps in the living room. Another shout. I flatten my hands against Matts's chest but lack the will to push. He kisses me again, circling the tip of my tongue with his. My breath catches in my throat.

'Sapphie?' He speaks against my lips. 'Who?'

I finally find my voice. 'Hugo.'

Matts stills. When I step back, he releases me, shoving his hands in his pockets as he walks to the steps. The sun is behind us and there aren't any clouds, but he tips back his head as if searching the sky.

When the door handle rattles, I dart to the far side of the porch, as far away from Matts as I can get. The air is cold on my mouth because my lips were warm and wet and …

I wipe my face on the arm of my shirt as if that will erase what I've done. I reach for my boots, streaky with dust.

'Sapphire?' Matts asks quietly. 'Why is he here?'

The door opens wide and Hugo, clearly naked except for the towel draped loosely around his hips, stands on the threshold. He glances at Matts, ramrod stiff next to the steps, and then he turns to me, standing on one leg and struggling to pull on a boot.

'You not only need a bigger bed,' Hugo says, looking down as he brushes water from his chest, 'but a new hot water system.'

Hugo's fringe drips onto his face and he brushes it away. He wipes his hand on the towel and holds it out to Matts. 'I thought you'd gone back to Canberra, mate.'

'My flight leaves at ten.'

I pick up my jacket and push my arms into the sleeves. 'You can't go yet.'

Matts's eyes were warm and bright; now they're arctic cold. 'Why not?'

'We haven't finished—'

He smiles stiffly. 'We have.'

I swallow. 'I'll walk you to your car.'

Hugo holds out his hand again. 'Might see you at the pub in a few weeks' time.'

'You'll be at the meeting?' Matts asks.

'No way, mate.' Hugo winks at me and adjusts the towel. 'I go to the pub for trivia and a beer.'

I pull on my other boot. 'I'll be back soon.'

We walk silently to Matts's four-wheel drive, which is parked near the sign for the school. CONGRATULATIONS HORSESHOE HILL

PS DEBATING TEAM! GOOD LUCK IN THE NEXT ROUND! One side of the collar of Matts's shirt has come out of his sweater. Did I do that? How could I have? I had one hand on his cheek and the other on his chest and all we did was—

He points the remote towards the car. *Beep. Beep.* His face is set. 'How long have you known Hugo?'

'Since high school.'

'Will you tell him what happened?'

'Why would I?' I fasten three buttons on my jacket.

He yanks opens the car's back door and takes out a water bottle. 'He sleeps in your bed.'

'Oh!' The rosellas are back in the bottlebrush tree, their red heads bobbing as they hang from the branches by their feet. 'You thought—as if I would have—Hugo is a friend.'

'He doesn't share your bed?'

'I slept on the couch. I don't have sex with friends.'

He frowns. 'Never?'

'Never.'

'You only have sex with strangers?'

I take a jerky step back. 'Why are we talking about this?'

He looks towards the schoolhouse. 'You kissed me.'

My gaze slips to his mouth. Did I imagine it? The tilt in the universe? My throat is suddenly tight.

'Things are complicated enough already without …' I take a deep breath. 'It was a mistake.'

He opens the driver's door and throws the bottle onto the passenger seat. 'It meant nothing?'

'How could it?'

Turning his back, he shoves the key in the ignition before straightening and facing me again. 'Does Hugo know our history?'

My hair is hot on my neck. I lift it and twist it into a coil, but as soon as I let it go, it tumbles down again. 'No.'

'Why not?'

I wave my hand between us. 'What we had ... none of that is relevant.'

'Because you say we are strangers.' He holds his sweater at his hips and pulls it up, bringing it over his head. Without thinking, I tug it out of his hands.

'Don't do it like that.'

The sweater is warm because his body is warm. It smells of him and— *What am I doing?* Not daring to look up, I pull one sleeve the right way through and search for the other one.

He yanks the sweater out of my hands and throws it into the car. His eyes narrow. 'You are not my sister.'

I lift my chin. 'I never was.'

Without another word, he climbs behind the wheel.

The rosellas chirrup and squabble in the bottlebrush tree. Freddie, tooting a hello, drives past as I walk back to the schoolhouse. I vaguely lift a hand as I kick through the leaves on the path.

It was autumn—I would have been fourteen or fifteen so Matts would have been seventeen—when I lay on the grass at Canberra's arboretum and watched the play of light on the bronze and yellow leaves of a maple. He was sitting on the ground and leaning against a tree trunk, a computer on his lap and a dog-eared book, *Romeo and Juliet*, in his hand.

There'd been frost in the morning. Now it was midday but the ground was still cold. He pulled off his sweater and threw it to me.

'Put it under your head.'

'Why do you take your sweaters off that way?' I asked, righting the sleeves and folding the sweater in half before putting it on the grass. When I lay on my side and faced him, the wool was soft on my cheek. 'You're much less likely to get your head stuck if you take your arms out of the sleeves first. And it doesn't turn the arms inside out.'

'My way is more efficient,' he said absently, scribbling in the margin of his book.

'I don't think so.'

He mumbled something and kept on writing.

'Kotka?' I rolled onto my back and stretched my arms above my head. 'Do I talk too much?'

He put his pencil in his book to mark the place. 'Sapphire?' When I turned towards him again, he smiled into my eyes. 'Yes.'

CHAPTER
17

My phone rings as I trudge up the schoolhouse steps the following Friday night. I drop my bag on the floor. 'Hello, Gus. Is everything all right?'

'Sure it is,' he says. 'Can you meet me at the pub for a drink? My shout.'

'I had parent–teacher interviews tonight. I've only just got home.' Tumbleweed winds around my legs and wails for dinner. 'Is it important?'

'It's about our next committee meeting. Thought we'd better get a few things sorted out.'

'The meeting's three weeks away.'

'I'll be here till nine.'

My hair is still damp from the shower when I pull back the heavy timber door of the pub. It's the only place open after five, so serves as a bar, restaurant and café.

Leon, behind the bar, lifts a hand. 'How're you doing, Sapphie?'

'I'm well, thank you.'

Gus gets up from his chair at a small table by the window and pulls out another chair, dusting it off in the same way he does at his cottage when I'm dressed for work and he's worried about dog hair and crumbs.

'Are you sure everything's all right?' I ask him.

'Just wanted a chat, that's all.' His hand, when he holds it out, is callused, scarred and twice the size of mine. 'What can I get you to drink? The usual?'

'Thanks. My shout next time.'

The crowd is mostly local—students from the high school who've just turned eighteen, the local policeman and his husband, and a few farmers who live a little further out.

Gus returns with his beer and my lemon and soda.

'How's my buttonhole flower coming along?' he asks as he sits down. 'Not long till the wedding.'

I show him a picture on my phone. 'What do you think? River red gum flowers are delicate so they're tricky to make, but April likes the colours because her gown is a similar shade of cream, and the leaf colour will pick up the greens in your tie. I'll attach a gum-nut from the river to the stem.'

'I'll be trussed up like a turkey at Christmas.' He winks. 'Maggie would approve.'

Gus's wife passed away well before I came to Horseshoe, but she's still his reference point for scores of things—including formal wear.

'April asked me to make one for her father as well, so you'll have a turkey friend to gobble with.'

He smiles and nods. 'We're on the same table, you and me.'

'April has a lot of family to accommodate. Going to the church would have been lovely; I didn't expect to be invited to the reception as well.'

'What?' He wipes froth from his mouth with the back of his hand. 'With you being a friend, and making the flowers? Course she'd want you there.'

We chat about what's happening with Gus's farm, and the weather forecast, but whenever anyone we know nods in our direction, Gus turns back to me straight away, as if to make it clear we don't need company. After half an hour, I put my empty glass next to his.

'I have an early start tomorrow, Gus, and you're bound to have an even earlier one. Did you want to meet about anything in particular?'

He links his hands on the table. 'You'll be up at the farmhouse in the morning?'

'That's right.'

'I'll see you at trivia at six.'

'I saw Freddie on the way in. He'll pick you up at five-thirty and Luke will drop you home when we're done.'

'As usual, you've got me sorted out.' He leans across the table, raising his brows. 'What about you?'

'What about me?'

He turns his glass in his hand. 'Mr Chambers and the rest of them, they reckon you'll come around to having this Laaksonen bloke on the committee.' When he frowns, his bushy brows almost meet in the middle. 'I'm not so sure about that.'

'He has everyone else's support. And there are more reasons to have him on the committee than not. I see that clearly enough.'

'I'll back you if you didn't think it's the right way to go.'

I attempt a smile. 'Matts is well qualified and has a good public profile because of his Ramsar role. And, as you said at our meeting, what's good for the wetlands is good for all of us here. I'm hoping the politicians will want to impress Matts so much, they'll commit to additional funding and support.'

He scratches an unkempt sideburn. 'So why didn't you want him to join us in the first place?'

'I was surprised. But if everyone else wants him, I'll make the best of it.'

'He's a city bloke, no mistake about it, but that shouldn't worry you.'

'Because I'm a city girl? How long till I qualify as country?'

He puffs out his cheeks in thought. 'You know what, Sapphie? I reckon you're like those flowers you make—they never grew out of the dirt, but no one can tell the difference.'

I laugh. 'Using that analogy, I don't think I'll ever—'

He holds up a hand. 'Some folk end up where they should've started out in the first place.' He nods firmly. 'That's you, Sapphie.'

'Thank you, Gus.' All of a sudden, I'm teary.

He harrumphs. 'Tell me what you think about Laaksonen.'

I clear my throat. 'He's from the city, like you said.'

'Which wouldn't have stopped my Maggie welcoming him to town. Fiona Hargreaves puts the kettle on for magpies, and you're the same these days. But this bloke, he rubbed you up the wrong way. Isn't that right?'

I sit back in my chair. 'Was I that obvious?'

'The rest of us were all cock-a-hoop, and there's our Sapphie, ready to tear out the poor bloke's throat. Haven't seen you like that in years.'

'It—I didn't expect him to say what he did.'

He leans across the table and pats my arm. 'Didn't mean to offend you. Haven't seen you so fierce in a while, that's all.'

I blink. 'Fierce?'

He shrugs. 'The Hargreaves had kids with more problems than you could poke a stick at. You were quiet and courteous most of the time, different to the others, so long as everybody let you be.' He winks. 'Reckon Laaksonen must've overstepped the mark, that's all.'

'I've accepted what's likely to happen. I'll have to put up with him.'

Gus sits back in his chair. 'When I was a young bloke, I did a bit of rodeo work. I met Maggie at a rodeo, as a matter of fact.'

'You rode bulls, didn't you?'

'Roped them too. Which gets us to the crux of the matter. How does a two-legged man bring down a two-ton bull?'

I laugh. 'What are you trying to say, Gus?'

'This Laaksonen bloke, he's a good talker with a flashy job, but that doesn't mean he can trample all over you.'

'You think I should rope him?'

'Like you tackle Mr Chambers every meeting. You work out what'll be best for the town, and find a way for the committee to get to it.'

'So Matts is just like the rest of us?'

'He was the one who put up his hand, so I reckon we should think up ways how he can help us, not the other way around.'

'We all work together as usual?'

'That's right.' He purses his lips. 'You weren't keen on having a full-grown bull in your yard, but that's where he's ended up. You've got to take him by the horns.'

I raise my empty glass. 'I'll do my best.'

Gus puts both hands on the table and pushes himself to his feet. 'Can't ask for more than that. Anyway, you know what I reckon?'

'What?' I say, standing and pushing in my chair.

When he holds out his arm, I take it. His knee creaks as we walk towards the door. 'He's got a thousand lakes in Finland, but what does he do? Leaves them behind for our marshlands over here. He can't be all bad.'

U

Matts's favourite subjects at school were physics, maths and chemistry, and I had about as much interest in them as he had in my flowers. When we were living in Canberra and he was in his final year of school, he caught me trying to look at my finger through the microscope he'd set up on a table in his bedroom.

He held my wrist firmly and pulled my hand away. 'You said you needed help with your homework, Kissa. Stop mucking around.'

'You look at such *boring* things.'

'They're important.'

'Is Lily interested in them? Or is it Brittany this week? How many girlfriends do you have?'

When he turned his back, I assumed he was going to ignore me like he'd been doing on and off for the past few weeks. He walked to the window and opened it, letting in a blast of cold air. His room was on the second floor of the house and there was a large gum in the garden, one of its branches reaching all the way to the window. He leant outside and picked a leaf, before carrying a second chair to the microscope. He opened a box of slides and took a few out.

'Sit down, Sapphire,' he said. 'I'll show you what kinds of things you can see.'

He told me about stomata, the microscopic holes on the outside of a leaf, and explained how they opened and closed. 'Species like gums have fewer stomata, so lower levels of evaporation,' he said. 'It improves their chances of survival in drought.'

My hands touched his as we took turns to look at the leaf and slides. I took my time, enjoying the physical closeness and the fact I had *most* of his attention. His hair fell over his forehead. When he pushed it back, I smelled pine.

'Do you have to shave every day?'

He didn't answer for a while. 'Most days.'

'I get waxed under my arms. Nowhere else though.'

He stilled. 'Do you want to know about the leaf?'

'I wouldn't be sitting here if I didn't, would I?'

'You can detect changes in atmospheric composition by looking at stomata, and measure a plant's response to stress.'

His sleeves were rolled up. I put my hand on his forearm. 'We learnt about that in biology.'

He stood so abruptly that I almost tipped out of my chair. He walked to the far side of the room and stared out of the window.

'Maybe you're not as stupid as I thought,' he said gruffly.

'Now what have I done? Come back, Matts. Tell me something else.'

He didn't sit next to me again, but leant over my shoulder to look through the microscope. He adjusted it carefully. 'Stomata open in daylight to let gases in and out of the leaf.'

'That's photosynthesis, isn't it?'

'Yes.'

'Who is your girlfriend, Matts? Lily or Brittany?'

'At night, or when a plant is dehydrated, the cells close in order to cut down on water loss.'

'Why didn't you answer? Are you two-timing again?'

'I'm seeing Brittany.'

'She turned eighteen last year, didn't she? She's older than you.'

'A few months.'

'She seems really nice, and she's very pretty.' I pushed back on my chair so it was balanced on two legs. 'Will you take her to the formal?'

He pushed the chair forward again, righting it. 'Don't, Kissa,' he said quietly. 'You could fall.'

'My balance is better than yours.' I pushed my shoulder blades hard against the back of the chair, trapping his hands, before smiling up at him and grasping his arms. 'Anyway, I'm fifteen. I can do what I want.'

He didn't smile back. His jaw was clenched. He pulled his hands free. 'You shouldn't be here,' he said. 'Go home.'

I sprang to my feet and stalked to the door, yanking it open before facing him again. His eyes were bright.

'I bet you let Brittany come into your room,' I said.

He pointedly looked at the bed. 'That's different.'

Matts was never my brother.

I was never his sister.

Did he understand that so much better than I did?

A week after Gus advised me to take the bull by the horns, I sit at the kitchen bench with my laptop and send an email.

From: Sapphie
To: Mr Chambers, Cassie, Luke, Gus
Thanks for sending through your thoughts on Matts Laaksonen's request to join the committee. In light of your overwhelming support, I'll issue a formal invitation for him to join us as an ex officio member. Mr Chambers suggested six months.

From: Sapphie
To: Dr Matts Laaksonen
Cc: Mr Chambers, Cassie, Luke, Gus
You recently expressed an interest in becoming a member of the Horseshoe Environment Committee. Assuming you're still interested, the committee would like to have you on board as an ex officio member (from September to March). I attach the relevant documentation for completion, signature and return.

From: Matts
To: Sapphie
Confirming acceptance of your offer to join the committee. Documentation attached.

From: Sapphie
To: Mr Chambers, Cassie, Luke, Gus
Cc: Matts
Confirming Matts's status as an ex officio member. He has been added to the committee's group chat, and will join us for our next meeting later in September.

Cassie: Great to have you on board, Matts!
Luke: Ditto.
Mr Chambers: We are delighted that you are able to serve on the committee.
Gus: Welcome to Horseshoe!
Matts: Thanks.

CHAPTER
18

I drop a clump of ropes and harnesses on the path and push up the arms of my sweater. The air is cool in the mornings and evenings, but the days are increasingly warm.

'Miss Brown!' Mary Honey, wearing jodhpurs and boots and leading her dappled grey pony, waves from the other side of the paddock. 'It's me!'

I laugh as she runs towards me, her pony trotting jauntily by her side. 'You only left school an hour ago. What are you and Mischief up to?'

'Dad brought us. He's helping make the fences. Are you doing climbing today?'

Not all the facilities at the youth centre are open, but we're allowing the kids to use the skate park and have started to run activities at the rock-climbing wall.

'I'll be training our volunteers for the next few Fridays.'

'When will your horses come?'

'The builders haven't finished the office and storage spaces yet. When they do, and the fences are done, the horses can come here on Saturdays.'

'Then you can live at the farmhouse.'

I stroke Mischief's neck. 'I hope so, Mary.'

'Does your finger hurt?'

I hold up my little finger, both joints taped. 'Not if I don't bend it too much.'

Climbing on the unfamiliar wall at the youth centre has given me something other than Matts and my father to think about, but in my final descent two days ago I strained a ligament in my finger.

'Won't it hurt when you climb?'

'I'm teaching climbing today, so I'll stay on the ground.' I check my watch. 'You haven't seen Barney, have you?'

'He's there!' She points over my shoulder.

Barney, a skateboard under his arm, jogs towards the changing rooms. 'Coming, miss.'

The climbing wall is five metres high, mostly under cover and secure, so we can leave the ropes in place when the centre is closed. And as it's twenty metres long, a few pairs of climbers, once they're trained in belaying, will be able to climb simultaneously. The avenue of gums and shrubs the council has planned will eventually screen it from the road.

Barney comes out of the changing rooms, the strap of a helmet and a harness looped over his arm. He scrapes his straggly hair out of his eyes. 'Thanks for taking me on, miss.'

'Thanks for volunteering as an assistant. We'll work through the waiting list quickly once we have a few of you trained up.'

He grins. 'You reckon I'm reliable?'

'Don't prove me wrong.' I cross my arms. 'You're keeping clear of your cousins, aren't you? No more marijuana cultivation?'

'No way, miss. You know I said Mum would kill me? It was way worse. First she cried all over me, then she yelled, then she didn't talk to me at all.' He shuffles his feet, grimacing as he looks down. 'These shoes are way too small.'

I kneel and check his climbing shoes. 'You have to feel your way up the wall with your feet, so they're meant to fit snugly. See what you think after the lesson.'

He glances at the wall. The mostly vertical surface is peppered with irregularly placed holds, brightly coloured bumps where climbers can position their hands and feet.

'It looks freaking high up close,' he says.

I smile encouragingly. 'I'll show you some strengthening exercises, and we'll stretch and warm up. I don't want you pulling a muscle or getting a cramp at an inconvenient time.'

'Me neither.'

A small outdoor gym with bars and other equipment sits to one side of the climbing wall. Barney and I face each other and he mirrors my actions as I stretch my arms and shoulders.

'Climbing is a whole body sport,' I tell him, leaning forward with straight legs and putting my palms flat on the ground.

He snorts a laugh. 'I can't do that, miss.'

'I have to do it to get the stretch I need. You should do what works for you.'

He grips below his knees. 'Hamstrings, right?'

'Then we'll move on to quads and calves. Your legs should do most of the work when you climb.'

I have to clamber onto a crate in order to grasp the parallel bar, but he grips it easily. 'Got it.'

'Hang on tightly and drop,' I tell him. 'A static hang will prepare you for harder climbs, where you might have to hold your body weight.'

He laughs when, after swinging to the ground and doing a series of sit-ups, I clamber back to the bar, taking care of my little finger, for chin-ups. 'I bet Archie doesn't know you can do this.'

'There's not much use for it in the classroom.' I strip down to an old pink T-shirt as we walk towards the wall. 'When the program is up and running, we'll run fitness classes on Friday nights too.'

'Compulsory?'

'Recommended. They'll make you a better climber.' I step onto the edge of the all-weather rubber floor that runs at the base of the wall and extend my arms, walking a line on my toes. 'Did I mention balance? When you move from one hold to another, you need to be aware of your centre of gravity. Your core is important too.'

He squeezes the top of his arm and grimaces. 'I'm not built up, miss.'

'Agility and balance are as important as muscular strength. I do a few exercises and I ride. That's all I need for the climbs I do.'

'You climb real rocks, don't you? Down by the river.'

'Not as often as I did.'

A startlingly white car pulls onto the side of the road and parks behind Peter Honey's ute and float. Mr Chambers gets out of the driver's seat, shielding his eyes from the sinking sun as he faces the grounds.

'What's he doing here?' Barney asks.

'He helped get the funding we needed, so maybe he's checking up on how the building work is—'

Matts slams the passenger door and walks to the front of the car. Is he looking at me? Are his eyes narrowed? Last time I saw him his eyes were bright. And then they were cold. What shade of grey are they today?

Mixing grey and black makes neutral grey, lighter or darker depending on the amount of white. Mixing two colours like blue and orange or red and green produces a complementary grey. More blue or green makes a cool grey; more red or orange makes a warm grey. With primary grey, yellow, blue and red create a flat grey and adjusting the mix varies the tint. Adding black or white affects the shade. Adding a colour affects the hue. And the colours around the grey have an impact too. Matts is wearing black. To create his eye colour, I'd—

'Miss?'

'Sorry, Barney.' I scoop up the harnesses and shake off the dust. 'Let's get to work.'

It takes a while to adjust the harnesses around the tops of our thighs and waists, and even longer to introduce Barney to the intricacies of carabiners, ropes, knots and rappel-belay equipment. 'I'll make sure that everything is safe until you can do that yourself,' I tell him. 'The most important thing is'—I rethread a twisted rope so it lies flat—'always climb in pairs, and if you're unsure of anything, ask.'

'Where'd you learn all this?'

'I've climbed since I was a kid.'

After we moved to Buenos Aires, I competed in gymnastics. But by the time I was nine or ten, I was only interested in doing whatever it was that Matts was up to. We couldn't play football on the same team, but I was naturally flexible and strong for my size so we could climb together.

Peter is laying out fence posts when Matts and Mr Chambers join him. Mary, riding bareback, trots across the paddock towards the men, sliding down Mischief's side as soon as he slows to a walk. When she stands in front of Matts, he holds out his hand.

So formal.

After shaking Matts's hand enthusiastically, Mary waves her arms around as if telling a story, and Matts tilts his head.

Barney fiddles with the straps on his harness. 'Not keen on breaking my neck, miss.'

I indicate the rope in my hands. 'I'm here to hold you up. Not only that,' I say as I jump on the matting, 'this floor cost the council a fortune.'

'You know I weigh more than you, right?'

'Trust me, Barney. That doesn't matter.'

Barney surveys the wall again. He sucks in a breath. 'Where do I start?'

I point to different coloured holds, and show him potential routes. 'Use them to guide you while you're getting used to it.'

Barney tightens his helmet strap.

'Remember the words you say to start us off?'

He nods. 'On belay?'

I check his harness and knot, and then check my own. 'Belay on.'

He faces the wall, putting one hand and a foot on holds. 'Climbing?'

'Climb on.'

Barney puts his other hand on a hold, gripping firmly, but when he lifts his second foot to a higher hold, it slips and he falls. The drop isn't far and I pull him up short, but as soon as I release the ropes again and his feet are on the ground, he punches the wall.

'This sucks.'

I check the rope. 'Let me know when you're ready to try again.'

His face is flushed. 'Didn't know I was scared of heights.'

'You're cautious. There's nothing wrong with that.'

When car wheels crunch on the gravel at the side of the road, he glances that way. 'Like you and driving?'

I'm not sure where Matts and Mr Chambers have gone, but Mary is sitting sideways on Mischief's back while she talks to her father.

'Does everyone know my business, Barney?'

'Haven't seen you drive since you hit the kangaroo, that's all.'

'And ...'

He fiddles with the buckles on his harness. 'My mum was talking to Leon at the pub. Heard you freaked out at the park.'

I knock his helmet with my knuckles. 'Now you've communicated that my driving is way worse than your climbing, are you ready to give this another shot?'

He grins. 'I kept quiet about your mum being a druggie, miss, like I said I would.'

'Thanks for that.'

He glances at the wall before pushing back his shoulders. 'On belay?'

I check the harnesses and ropes again. 'Belay on.'

He faces the wall. 'Climbing?'

'Climb on.'

Barney grasps two holds with his hands, and balances his feet on another two. 'What now?'

'Don't look down in case you worry about falling, and don't look up and think how good it'll be when you get to the top. The best thing to do is to focus on your next hold.'

He moves his foot to another hold and adjusts his hand positions. 'Like this?'

'That's great. But try to point your knees towards the wall. That way, you'll keep your hips close to it too. It makes things easier on your fingers.'

'I feel like a frog.'

'If you lean back and hang on with your hands, you'll exhaust yourself.' I move nearer to the wall. 'You're ready to reach for another hold. Take the closest one, so you don't overreach and lose your balance.'

He looks to his left and extends his arm. 'This one?'

'Push up from your legs if you can, rather than pulling up by your arms.'

'It's easier to use my hands.'

'How many pull-ups can you do in a row?'

'Two or three.'

'That's why you can't rely on your arms. Try to think of your fingers as hooks on the holds. They should keep you balanced but not much else.'

'The footholds should be bigger.'

'It's enough that they hold your weight. If you can, drop your heels lower than your toes.'

He stretches out his right arm. 'Can't reach.'

'What about the hold to the right of your foot? Move your foot onto that and you'll be able to stretch out further on that side.'

He does as I suggest, moving his foot and then his hand. 'Got it!' he says.

'Soon you'll visualise where your hands and feet will go before you start to climb. Foot, foot, hand, hand, or foot, hand, foot, hand. You'll work out a rhythm, relying mostly on your legs.'

Barney is a couple of metres up the wall when he lifts his shoulder to swipe sweat from his face.

I glance at my watch. 'Can you remember what to say when you need a break?'

'Take.'

'If you feel comfortable with one limb off the wall, you've found a good resting place.' I pull on the rope and lock it off. 'Put your weight on your feet and stretch out your arms, one by one, to give your biceps and hands a rest. Always keep three points of contact.'

'A triangle, right?'

'Sapphie!' Mr Chambers calls.

By the time I check the ropes and look towards the path, Matts has his arm out, blocking Mr Chambers's path. I can't hear what he says, but the politician nods and puts his hands behind his back. I focus on Barney again.

'When you rest, it's a good time to reassess your route. You might want to stick to the one you've chosen, or find another one that's easier or harder.'

'Easier would be good.'

I smile. 'You're on the easiest one.'

'My arms are burning. Fuck, they hurt.'

'Give them a shake to dislodge the lactic acid. Other than your language, you're doing really well.'

'My fingers kill too.'

'They'll strengthen in time. And these are just the physical challenges. Don't forget the mental ones. Where will you go next?'

'Up?'

'That's the idea. Set your feet first, and don't forget to bend your knees. Then shift your body weight in that direction. Try to relax, Barney, and not hold on too tight.'

Barney puts one foot on a hold, and then positions his other foot. He grabs a hold above his head.

'You almost moved your hand and foot at the same time, which is really good. Now reset your feet and reach for another hold with your hand.'

He inches his way across and up the wall, wiping the sweat from his hands on his pants when he can.

'I didn't want to complicate things, but next time you climb, you can use chalk. It adds friction between your hands and the holds.'

He gulps a couple of times.

'Try not to hold your breath. It'll deprive your muscles of oxygen.'

'They need all the air they can get.'

'You'll climb faster soon enough. Which means you'll use less energy while working out where to go next.'

'Take!'

I steady the ropes. 'I think that's enough for today.'

'I'm not at the top yet.'

'And you haven't learnt how to come down. Can you remember what you say when you're ready to do that?'

'Get me out of here?'

'It's "Ready to be lowered." Repeat it so you get used to it.'

'You're not going to let me drop, are you?'

'I won't do anything without warning you first.'

He looks down and grimaces. 'Not sure I like the sound of that.'

'I haven't lost anyone yet. Say the words so they become a habit.'

'Ready to be lowered.'

'Lowering.'

'What do I do?'

'You sit back in your harness and let go of the wall. Great. Now put your feel flat against the surface.'

He looks down again, and quickly looks up. 'Sheesh.'

'Take as much time as you need.' As he inches slowly down the wall, I let the rope slip through my fingers.

'Whoa.'

'You're doing really well. If you put your hands on your harness instead of waving them around, you might feel more secure.'

As soon as he gets to the ground he laughs, collapsing in a heap as he undoes his helmet. When sweat runs down his face, he lifts his T-shirt to wipe it.

'That was awesome,' he says, pushing himself to his feet again and picking up his water bottle.

'I'll make a ninja out of you yet.' When I hold out my hand, we high-five. 'Fantastic work.'

Mr Chambers clears his throat behind us. 'Hello, Sapphie.'

I'm still smiling when I turn. Matts's eyes go from my eyes to my mouth, and then back to my eyes. What are his thoughts? What are mine?

Do you remember climbing together? I remember everything. And now there's more. I know what it feels like to kiss you.

'Hello,' I croak.

'Sapphire.'

I wipe my sweaty hands on my pants as I turn to Barney. 'This is Matts, Barney. Though you should probably call him Dr—'

'Matts.'

'Right. You will have seen Mr Chambers at school assemblies.'

Barney is dripping with sweat and hopping uncertainly from foot to foot, so it's not surprising Mr Chambers's hand stays by his side.

'Your first climb?' Matts says. 'Not bad.'

Barney smiles broadly as he bumps his fist against Matts's offered hand. 'Miss Brown was ace.'

Matts smiles politely as he turns to me. 'You're an experienced climber, Sapphire?'

Gum trees? Climbing walls? I take a deep breath. 'Yes.'

Matts and Mr Chambers are still inspecting the building works when Peter leaves an hour later, Mary waving happily out of the window and Mischief standing calmly in the float behind the ute.

I tighten my sweater around my waist and hook my arm through a strap of my bag, bulging with climbing gear, and then make my way to the road. As I pass the building, I cross my fingers. 'Please don't come out yet.'

Within seconds I hear them behind me. 'Sapphire. Wait.'

I stop and turn as Matts veers away from Mr Chambers who, with his phone to his ear, continues on the path towards the carpark. Matts's zipped-up hoodie emphasises the width of his shoulders and narrowness of his hips. Does he know that? Or does he dress to be comfortable? His boots are scuffed.

The sun, fuzzy around the edges, is a fading globe behind him. 'Chambers will drive you home.'

I push the bag further up my arm to my shoulder. 'I'll enjoy the walk.'

'Thanks for letting me join the committee.'

I lift my chin. 'It was a consensus decision.'

When my bag slips from my shoulder, I pull it up again. A ute rumbling down the road trails clouds of dust behind it.

'Sapphire?' He frowns and lifts a hand. 'Are you hurt?'

My bag falls to the ground with a thump as I yank my bra strap and the neck of my T-shirt over my shoulder. I drop to my haunches, open my bag and pretend to search.

'I don't know what you mean.'

'I thought ...'

He couldn't have seen many of the scars. Hair that's come loose from my plait falls over my face. My bra strap slips down again. As I lift my arm, my taped finger catches on the bag handle.

'Ow!' My eyes water and I blink. 'Damn.' Holding my finger tightly in my hand, I stand.

He extends his hand again. 'Did you hurt it climbing?'

'I came down too fast.'

'Where else do you climb?'

'Down by the river.'

A flock of galahs gather by the side of the road, their pink and grey feathers bright against the bitumen.

'When you climbed with my friends and me, you were always first to the top.'

A galah dips his head, his baby pink crest rising up like a fan. 'I had to prove I was capable.'

'Not to me.' He picks up my bag and hands it to me, careful not to touch my fingers. 'The committee meeting tomorrow week. Do I go to the pub?'

As soon as I get home, I send an email.

From: Sapphie
To: Mr Chambers, Cassie, Luke, Gus, Matts
Re: Committee meeting 19 September at 8pm
Looking forward to seeing you all (except Mr Chambers) at the Royal Hotel on Saturday. Agenda attached. The main item for discussion is raising the committee's profile so we can more effectively get our message across to the government. As Gus recently said (in a slightly different context) we have to take the bull by the horns.

CHAPTER
19 .

Prima is becoming accustomed to the sights and sounds of our outings along the road, walking calmly beside me and pricking her ears when we turn at the bend to come home, and nickering a greeting when she sees Sonnet. Her new halter, black with a bright blue headband, looks smart against her light brown coat and dark mane and forelock. I pull up the hood of my jacket to keep out the evening chill as we walk past the farmhouse.

She sneaks a mouthful of grass as I open the gate, chomping happily as I lead her through the paddock to the grey gum. As she snuffles in her hay, Lollopy, who finished his dinner an hour ago, watches longingly. Instead of considering him warily as she would have done a few weeks ago, as if afraid he might approach, Prima turns her back.

Now that Joel's father is doing well with gamblers anonymous, Joel has moved back home and visits Prima daily. When I handed him her lead rope this morning, she stood quietly as she was groomed. Afterwards she followed him, toey but compliant, around the paddock. She looked curiously over the fence at the kids and other horses.

A kookaburra calls out loud and long from the red gum and his family joins in at the chorus. 'It might be time to extend your circle of friends,' I tell Prima as I lift her hoof to check for stones. 'Maybe you'll make a therapy horse after all.'

By the time I arrive at the pub, the trivia game has already started. Gus waves his arm above his head when he sees me at the door. 'Sapphie,' he hisses. 'Over here.'

'Hello,' I whisper to Luke and Ma and Pa Hargreaves. 'Sorry I'm late.'

An hour later, most of the tables are discussing history dates— quietly, so other tables don't overhear what answers they settle on. Hugo, sitting with his brother and sister-in-law, laughs loudly and bangs the table, grinning and making a face when I look his way.

When the door to the street swings wide and lets in the breeze, Ma Hargreaves nudges me under the table. She tidies her wavy grey hair. 'Look, Sapphie. Dr Laaksonen. Gus tells me you'll be seeing him later tonight.'

Matts's hands are in his pockets as he walks past the lounge towards the bar. 'I'll see him at the committee meeting, yes.' I tap the piece of paper in front of her. 'Please, Ma, look at the questions, not him.'

'He's a handsome young man with a very good job. There aren't so many of them in Horseshoe that we can afford to look the other way. Even though'—she lowers her voice—'it's a Saturday night. When I was a girl, men wore a jacket and tie for special occasions. He could have gone to a little more trouble with his outfit.'

'*Please* stop staring.'

'Sapphie!' Gus hisses again, nudging my foot. 'How many men did Horseshoe lose at Gallipoli? What do you reckon?' Gus takes trivia more seriously than most of us, tugging at his hair whenever the scores are close.

'Two men on the beaches,' I say, 'three including the soldier who died a month later in the field hospital.'

'Write that down, Bob. Sapphie says three, and she's the best of us at history.'

Besides a few lean years during the Depression in the 1930s, the Royal has been open for almost a century. I'm not sure how long Saturday trivia nights have been going on, but the tradition was well established by the time I came to Horseshoe.

'Last questions,' the host calls out.

I'm helping Gus—failing dismally to hide his disappointment with second place—separate the tables and tidy the chairs when Matts walks into the lounge. When I hold out my hand, he hesitates.

'Your finger?'

'Fine, thank you.'

His grip is firm, but he holds on to Gus's hand for far longer than he held mine.

The three of us lift one of the larger tables to a nook at the back of the lounge, close to a stained glass window that looks out onto the street. People will return to the other tables later on, but it's relatively private back here.

'Sapphie.' Cassie puts her bag on a chair before hugging me briefly. She stands back and looks me up and down. 'That shirt looks great with jeans.' She touches my sleeve. 'Silk, isn't it?'

The cream fabric has spilled out at my hip and I tuck it in. 'I haven't done my washing this week. I didn't have anything else.'

Cassie's gaze goes to Matts and then returns to me. When she winks, a blush moves up my neck. I *hadn't* done my washing, but …

You're afraid to be beautiful.

Gus pulls out chairs for Cassie and me, before sitting down himself. As soon as Luke joins us, Gus links his hands. 'Let's get to it.'

Matts takes care to keep his legs on his side of the table when he sits opposite me, even though mine are tucked under my chair. Luke sits next to Matts, opposite Gus. Cassie, sitting at the end of the table, takes off her brass-buttoned navy jacket and hangs it over the back of her chair. 'All set,' she says, straightening her scarf.

I take a sheaf of papers from my folder. 'I've already emailed a summary of the main points raised in our last meeting, and here it is again. I thought we could use it as a guide as we think about ways we could raise the committee's profile.'

Gus pulls out his magnifying device and peers at the paper. 'I've got a question straight up.' He sticks out his chin. 'How are the rivers and wetlands ever supposed to get the water they need when the government controls the water flow?'

'In the last drought, water scheduled for the river and marshes was diverted to the towns,' Cassie says.

'Too much land clearing south of the wetlands, that's what I reckon,' Gus says. 'Even when it rains, there's not enough trees to keep moisture in the ground.'

Cassie taps her pen on the table. 'Raising funds for projects that won't bring immediate results is next to impossible.'

My shirt has pulled out of my jeans again. I tuck it in as I turn to Matts. 'When you gave your presentation, you said the secretariat helps countries to restore, rehabilitate and maintain wetland environments. For that, you need community support.'

'Governments won't initiate change without it.'

I flick through the calendar on my phone. 'With the committee's help, I'd like to organise a series of day trips to the river towards the end of October. Showing people, especially city people, what we're up against, is better than telling them about it. We need a long-term strategy, not short-term solutions in response to a crisis. We have to convince the government to fund research and implement new initiatives *before* the next drought.'

Matts leans back in his chair. 'How do you do that with day trips?'

'People get told about dam levels, but showing them what the river looks like, even when we're not in drought, will be instructive.'

'Reckon the farmers would be happy to see you,' Gus says.

'Mr Chambers has contacts with manufacturers and other industries that operate in the towns and employ workers in the region.'

'Environmental groups, sustainable fishing organisations, ornithologists and tourism operators, there are so many interests that simply want to be heard,' Cassie says.

I turn to Luke. 'Any ideas?'

'Landcare groups, farmers and environmentalists are keen to do restorative work, but that gets pushed aside when something more pressing comes up. I can back up your arguments with facts and figures.'

'All the government wanted to do after the last drought was build another dam,' Gus says. 'That's no good for the land.'

Matts folds his page in half. 'Without support from senior levels of government, you'd be wasting your time.'

When Gus harrumphs, I put my hand on his arm. 'Matts might have a point, Gus. Besides Horseshoe locals and the intern at the *Dubbo Daily*, I'm not sure my day trips will garner much interest. But,' I smile at Matts, 'if you were to come with me, people would take notice.'

The pen in his hand is dark grey. Brushed silver? Platinum? He lines it up so it's parallel to the edge of the table. 'How many days?' he says.

'Four or five will be enough.'

'I have an alternative.' He picks up his phone and considers the screen. 'You and I can go to the wetlands together.'

'What?' My heart rate doubles. I swallow twice. 'That's hundreds of kilometres away.'

'You said four or five days.'

'But that's not what—'

'I have unrestricted access to the river and marshes.' He puts his phone on the table and crosses his arms. 'If we go together, it will demonstrate interest in the preservation and improvement of river and wetland environments.'

'Great!' Luke slaps the table. 'That'd be great.' He nudges my foot. 'Sapphie? We can share your posts, not only on our website but other platforms too. When we do a final report, we'll send it out to government and other organisations.'

I keep my eyes on Matts. 'I planned to go to the river near Horseshoe.'

He nods without smiling. 'We do that too.'

'Our river extends to the wetlands,' Cassie says. 'You're a local, Sapphie, and you, Matts, are somewhat more exotic. I think this is an excellent plan.'

'What do you reckon, Sapphie?' Gus shuffles closer, his bushy brows drawing together. 'You're not too keen on hopping in the car these days.'

I have crippling anxiety on the roads.

'I'll drive,' Matts says.

'If you're up for it,' Gus pats my arm, 'I can get your horses taken care of.'

'And I'll cover for you at the youth centre,' Luke says.

Matts is typing on his phone with his thumbs. My phone is on silent, but the screen lights up when a message comes through. My gaze flies from my phone to Matts and back to my phone. I read the group chat again.

From: Matts
To: Sapphie, Chambers, Cassie, Luke, Gus
Macquarie Marshes. Sapphie and Matts confirmed.

The others discuss how a road trip to the wetlands will be beneficial to both our committee and Matts's project. When he's not making informative comments and answering questions, Matts writes neatly on the margin of the page I gave him earlier. Whenever I look away, I sense his gaze on my profile.

I have my bag on my lap when a well-dressed man with thick black hair takes off his smart woollen coat and hangs it on the rack. He walks to the bar and pulls out a stool.

'Evening, mate. What can I get you?' Leon calls from the other side of the bar.

After Leon has served his drink, the man swivels on his stool and faces the lounge. Besides the young couple holding hands near the window, ours is the only table occupied. The man glances towards the smaller table before turning his attention to ours. He looks at Matts for a very long time. And then his gaze goes to Luke, Cassie and Gus. Finally, his eyes meet mine.

He starts and turns away so quickly that his knee hits the bar. He puts a note on the counter and walks quickly to the door.

Gus folds his pages into a square and pushes the wad into the pocket of his shirt. 'Are we good to go?' he asks. 'Anyone want a beer?'

'I'd like an early night.' My hair shields my face as I zip my bag. 'Thanks everyone for coming.'

I glance at the message on my phone again. When I look up, it's into Matts's eyes. 'We have to talk,' I say quietly.

He shrugs. 'Where?'

'Outside.'

Matts, head tilted as he listens to Gus, is still at the bar when I follow Cassie through the door to the footpath and hug her goodbye. I fasten my coat buttons against the cool evening chill, pull on gloves and put my hands into my pockets.

'Miss Brown!' Mary and her sisters are on the opposite side of the road.

'You're up late.'

'We're waiting for Dad.'

Mary is tall for her age, almost as tall as her middle sister, Millie. I watch them, arms securely linked, as they skip side by side like Dorothy and the scarecrow in *The Wizard of Oz*. Molly, the eldest girl, is eighteen. She trails behind the others until, all of a sudden, she breaks into a run. As she gets closer she holds out her arms, herding her sisters away from the kerb. Headlights shine brightly behind them.

I release a shaky breath as a long blue sedan passes slowly.

'Sapphie?'

I jump.

Matts frowns. He points up the hill. 'I'll walk you home.'

I nod—even though I'd much rather prefer to talk out here. Keeping my eyes firmly on the path, neither of us says anything until we're almost at the schoolhouse. When I finally look up, he touches my arm. We stop and face each other.

'What's the matter?' he says.

'I wanted day trips.'

'I wanted wetlands.'

'You set me up.'

'I won't be used.'

When he walks away, I run to catch up. 'Don't do this, Matts. It complicates things even more.'

'How?' His mouth hardens. 'We are strangers.'

The schoolhouse light casts a dim golden glow on the steps of the porch. Hidden in the shadows are the old school desk and the hooks for the coats and satchels. I don't want to take him there.

That's where I kissed him.

Butterfly wings flutter deep in my stomach.

'Where are we going?' he asks, as we cross the garden and walk through the side entrance to the school grounds.

'My house is a mess.' I take off my gloves to work the latch on the gate. 'And this won't take long.'

The narrow path leads to the infant children's playground. A pine log bridge, a metre off the ground, is suspended over an ocean of rubber. To the left of the bridge are two timber panels angled like the bow of a ship with a waist-height platform as the floor. The younger boys and girls play games here.

Sailing ships and pirates. Castles, moats and dragons. Tales with happy endings.

Kotka and Kissa.

When my eyes sting, I spin around and drop my bag. My back to him, I hold onto the platform with both hands.

He mutters something in Finnish, then says, 'You're afraid to be alone with me.'

'I'm …' I run a finger along a crack between the boards. 'I find it difficult. Which is why I don't want to go away with you.'

'We are not who we were.'

'I understand that, but—'

'We're no longer children.'

'We're not colleagues either, or friends or—' His touch on my shoulder sends warmth through my body.

'Turn around, Sapphie.'

When I do as he asks, our breaths, white in the cold, meet in the middle. My hand hovers between us.

'Matts?' My voice is too high. 'What's left?'

He takes my hand. He stares at my mouth. 'You shouldn't have kissed me.'

'I can't take it back,' I croak.

He traces my top lip with the pad of his thumb before running it across my bottom lip. He draws a line along the crease and back again.

'And I can't forget it.' There's need in his voice. And fire in his eyes. He threads his fingers through my hair and watches the strands as they slide through his fingers.

I pull my hand free and grasp the front of his hoodie, bunching it up. He mutters under his breath as he wraps his arms around me and links his hands at the small of my back.

My breath catches. My legs wobble. His heart thumps under my hands. 'Ma said you should go to more trouble to dress up,' I whisper.

He dips his head and whispers back. 'What do you think?'

I mumble against his lips. 'I like the way you look.'

He finds the places with his mouth where his thumb went before. Bottom lip, top lip, along the crease and back again. It's a light kiss, our mouths barely touch, but an aching warmth flows through my veins. My heart beats erratically. Standing on my toes, I stroke the silky hair at his nape. I trace the line of his jaw and the shape of his ear.

His touch, taste and scent. The heat of his body and the strength in his arms. The angle of his head and the texture of his lips. I kiss the silver scar on his chin. For a moment he stills. His hands clench on my waist.

'Sapphie,' he growls, as he pushes me backwards with his movements. He puts his hands either side of my waist and lifts me, sitting me on the platform. My hands settle on his chest again as he traces a finger over my nose and down to my mouth. His lips are damp. Are mine like that too? They must be. He presses softly but deliberately, sliding a fingertip into my mouth.

'So beautiful.'

As moonlight streams through the clouds, lightening his hair, I wrap my arms around his neck. I burrow inside his hoodie to find the warmth of his skin. He runs his hands down my back as his tongue plays with mine. It's a careful exploration, a gentle way to talk.

When he lifts his head, I mutter a complaint. His hands go to my face. He kisses me again, short but hard.

'I want you.'

My heart squeezes tightly. 'I don't know what I want.'

He frowns. But when I inch further forward on the bridge, he tightens his hold even more. I open my legs and he turns side on, sliding between my legs before facing me again. His erection is long and hard and presses on my thigh.

'Sapphie? You understand?'

We are not who we were.

I'm lightheaded with longing and weak with desire. I tighten my legs around him. 'Yes.'

Our mouths meet again, gliding together, apart and together. I rest my hand against his jaw. I find the roughness of his stubble and the beats of his pulse. He threads his fingers through my hair and deepens the kiss. A thick silk ribbon in a deep shade of crimson wraps around my heart.

When I pull at the buttons of my coat, he lifts his head. He undoes the first two buttons but stills my hand when I tug at the third. He groans softly as he kisses my neck and nuzzles under the collar of my shirt.

I shiver.

He yanks my coat closed and forages for my hands, picking them up, rubbing them slowly. 'Where are your gloves?'

'I can't remember.'

He holds my face and presses kisses on my mouth. 'We can't stay here.'

The dip beneath his cheekbones is pronounced. His jaw is tense. When I run my hands over his chest and tighten my legs even more, his breath expels in a rush. His heartbeat drums on the palm of my hand. I've never felt this need before.

Only with him.

I stiffen.

He raises my chin with the back of his hand. 'Sapphie?' His voice is rough like gravel. His eyes are bright. 'What's the matter?'

A whimper escapes from the back of my throat. 'It's all wrong.'

His hands on my body clench and release. He grasps my chin and kisses me again, swiftly but firmly. When he takes my hands and looks down, I smell his shampoo. He lifts our hands higher, stepping closer and trapping them between us.

'Explain what you mean.'

Sapphire Beresford-Brown. Sapphie Brown.

I've kissed him twice. *Just a kiss.* Why does it feel like so much more?

'I—' I shake my head to clear it. 'I don't want this.'

He releases me so abruptly that I sway and grasp the platform. He turns his back and puts his hands in his pockets. When he walks a few steps and kicks a lump of rubber out of the play area, it sits on the concrete, dark and alone.

He turns. 'I'll draft an itinerary. I'll message you.'

'Please, Matts. Don't do this.'

'It's done.' He looks towards the road. 'We shouldn't have come here.'

I slide to the ground. 'I don't know what you want.'

'At your mother's funeral ... you knew what I wanted.'

'You had tissues in your pocket.'

'And you refused them.'

'I hadn't forgiven you.'

'You haven't forgiven me now.'

I wrap my arms around my middle. 'I don't want to feel like I did. I relied on you. I trusted you. You meant far too much.'

I loved you far too much.

A shadow crosses his face. 'You didn't read my letters. You turned your back on what we had.'

'And you haven't forgiven me for that.' I look down, blinking back tears as I pick up my bag. 'So why did you kiss me?'

'I made a mistake.'

The same words I used when I kissed him.

He walks past the roundabout, the slippery dip and the small metal horses on tightly coiled springs. When he reaches the swings he hesitates but then he walks on, past the bubblers, the bottlebrush trees and the noticeboard.

U

I was nineteen on the day of Mum's funeral, and had been living in Horseshoe for over two years. I'd assumed Matts had moved back to Finland, and I suppose that he had, but I was standing outside the church, swallowing tears, when I saw him in the crowd. The service had finished and he was on the lawn with scores of my father's faceless friends. Matts was alone. His hair was brushed back and his arms were stiff by his sides.

When we went to school together in Canberra, I was aware that Matts was handsome. Even girls he didn't know would smile and smooth their hair when he came close. They'd ask me questions. Did I have his number? What music did he like? Did he have a girlfriend? When I teased him about it, he'd ignore me or talk about something else. By the time Mum died and he was twenty-one, I could properly see what others had. His athletic body. His deep grey eyes, his cheekbones and jawline. His bearing. His confidence. The way everything fitted perfectly together. It was painful to look at him at the funeral, but impossible to look away.

When it was his turn to pay his respects he stood directly in front of me, so close he blocked out everybody else. His cheeks were flushed. His lashes were spiky and wet. I stared at the folded tissues in his pocket, starkly white against the darkness of his suit jacket. I pretended not to see the way he held out his hand, palm up, between us. He didn't want to shake my hand—he wanted to hold it. The idea of grasping his fingers, of walking to the gardens together, of wiping my face with the tissues and folding myself into his body, tripled the size of the lump in my throat.

I clenched my fists. I nodded. I thanked him politely for coming.

CHAPTER
20

Trust and mistrust. Love and hate.

If only it were as clear as that. Black and white. Neutral grey.

The universe tilts when we kiss.

I swallow through the tightness in my chest as I kneel in the farmhouse garden. The dandelions have grown so tall that their flowers are tangled together. Digging with a trowel, I pull them out by the roots and throw them into a bucket. I spread spent bark from the red gum over the freshly dug soil.

'That's looking better.'

Prima, tied loosely to a verandah post, looks up from her hay net.

'Thanks for keeping me company.'

When I hear a car, I turn towards the road. The speed limit is eighty, but the car is travelling much slower than that. I recognise it—the blue sedan that passed the Honey girls outside the pub last night. Just before the bend, the driver does a U-turn and parks out the front, pulling over on the far side of the red gum.

I walk to Prima, taking a firm hold of her lead rope and straightening her cotton rug.

The man who gets out of the car is the man I saw in the pub last night. He reaches into the back seat for his coat and then he looks around. When he sees me, he lifts a hand. I check that Prima is tied securely before walking back to the wildly flowering azaleas and picking up my drink bottle.

The man smiles politely as he approaches. He'd be in his late fifties, maybe early sixties, but he's fit. His thick black hair is swept back from his forehead. When he holds out his hand, I take it.

'Gabriel Garcia.' Is he Spanish? Argentinian?

'I'm Sapphie Brown.'

'The hotelier believed I might find you here.' He nods towards the farmhouse and gardens. 'This is very nice.'

'Why were you looking for me?'

'I'd like to speak with you, if I may?'

Not many strangers travelling on their own come to Horseshoe. My father is concerned about the media—is the man a journalist?

I drink from the bottle as he follows me up the steps to the verandah. 'Are you a tourist? We don't get many at this time of year.'

'My sister lives in Melbourne. I see her next week.'

'You're a long way from there.'

'This is what my sister said.' He rubs his hip and glances at the deckchairs stacked under the window. 'May we sit?'

'If you like.' I pull out two chairs and open them, brushing off the dust. 'What's going on, Mr Garcia?'

He smiles. 'Gabriel, please. And you are Sapphie now?'

I stiffen. 'Now?'

'We have met before.'

'When? Why were you looking for me? Who are you?'

'It was many years ago.'

'In Buenos Aires? I don't remember you. What do you want?'

'You are afraid of my motives.' He smiles reassuringly. 'I do not wish to alarm you.'

'So tell me why you're here.'

'I am not a policeman, nor am I from the press. You do not recall me? We met at the Laaksonen residence.'

'When?'

'You were a very young girl. You had come to make flowers.'

I only did that once. And it was the last time I ever saw Inge. When I arrived at the house unannounced, Inge's hair was loose. She introduced me to a tall, dark-haired man. Was it Gabriel? I glance at his hands, one placed neatly over the other in his lap.

'What sort of flowers did I make?'

'Bougainvillea.' He points to the scarlet bracts that climb over the fence near the gate. Only he doesn't point, because the only finger on his left hand is a thumb.

'I remember.' I take a deep breath. 'And I saw you again, didn't I?'

Inge, quiet and modest, had been very different from Mum. But she was a well-respected diplomat's wife and had died young and unexpectedly, which probably explained why the church was packed full. I was waiting for Matts to leave the group of family members gathered around the priest when I saw the man for the second time. I was curious about his hand, but I tried not to stare. He crouched by my side and smiled sadly. Even though he was an adult, I suspected he'd been crying. I thought that was curious too.

'Hello, Miss Sapphire,' he said. 'Did you like the flowers in the church? They were very beautiful, were they not?'

'Yes, sir.'

I get up from the chair so quickly that it clatters on the boards behind me. When I walk to the railing, my legs are unsteady. I balance my bottle on the timber, so weathered that the only vestiges of paint is in the cracks. I trace a line.

'You were at her funeral, weren't you?'

He rises from his chair and joins me. He rests his hands on the railing. 'I was.'

'Why are you here? What do you want?'

'I met your parents many years ago. They introduced me to Inge and Leevi.'

'I won't talk to you about them.'

'I would not ask you to do so.' He glances at the chairs. 'Please, Sapphie. May we sit again?'

After he eases himself into the chair, I sit too, and fold my hands in my lap.

'You offered to show me how you make flowers,' he says quietly. 'This touched me deeply.' He gazes over the railing to the azaleas. 'Inge had spoken of her son, naturally. But also of you. She loved you as a daughter.'

'I loved her too.'

He rests his forearms on the arms of the chair. 'I used to work for Josef Hernandez. You have heard of him?'

I clasp the chair either side of my legs. 'He's tied up with the allegations against my father.'

'Your father has denied that an inducement was received. As this is the truth, the matter might go no further.'

'You know about what happened?'

'Some of it, yes.'

'My father wants to clear his name. My mother isn't here to clear hers.'

His coat is folded over his knees. He smooths the fabric. 'My role also is difficult to explain.'

'Were you involved?'

He hesitates. 'I worked for Hernandez. I knew of these deposit boxes he kept. At this time, I made many, many mistakes.' He speaks quietly, as if to himself. 'May God forgive me.'

'Mum went to the deposit box, but I don't think she would have done anything like stealing documents or taking a bribe. Inge would never have agreed to help her if she had.'

His smile is gentle. 'I saw her son at your table last night. I didn't think … He is staying here in Horseshoe?'

'He'll be in the district for a few months. He's here for work.'

'You will see him again? You will stay in contact?'

'Until the end of October, at least.'

He shuts his eyes. He slowly shakes his head. And then he stands abruptly. 'I should not have come.'

'What do you mean?'

He shakes his head again. 'I had hoped to do more to help your mother, but I am forced to make a choice.' He picks up his coat. 'No, I cannot.'

'You cannot what?'

'This is not the time to tell my secrets.'

'About my mother? What if she's blamed for what happened?'

'There was no crime. I can, at least, reassure you of that.'

'My father insists she did something wrong.'

'I am sorry, Sapphie. I should not have come.' He holds out his hands, palms up. 'And now I should go.'

When he walks down the steps to the path, I follow. 'What if you change your mind again? Will you call me? Can I call you?'

'For now I am—' He frowns. 'What is the expression? Under the radar! I am under the radar. It might be best, for all of us, to forget that I was here.'

'But you won't rule out helping Mum? I won't tell anyone that I've seen you. Will that help?'

'The less people who know we have spoken, the better.'

'All I want … I'd like to know the truth. Mum loved the colour of sapphires. Why was there a stone in the box?'

He opens the back door of the car, laying his coat carefully along the seat before facing me again. He's paler than he was.

'One day, Sapphie, I will confide in you.' He smiles sadly. 'You shall see my dilemma.'

'You're not concerned about my father's reputation, are you?'

'He can protect himself.'

'Please, Gabriel, reconsider. Tell me—'

He touches my arm. 'I am sixty years old, Sapphie, perhaps too old for so many secrets, but I shall keep them for a little while longer.' He reaches into his pocket and takes out his wallet, extracting a card. 'In the meantime, I give you this. If the situation worsens, we will talk again.'

The card is simple and printed with his name, an address in Rosario, Argentina, an email and a phone number.

I watch the car disappear around the bend, a plume of dust behind it. *If the situation worsens, we will talk again.* There's a chance he'll help me so long as I keep quiet. I put the card in my front pocket to keep it safe as I walk back to Prima. A flock of rainbow lorikeets, yellow, red, purple and green, fly across a clear blue sky. When they screech, Prima skitters sideways and I run to grasp her rope. My phone pings as I lead her back to the paddock.

From: Matts
To: Sapphie, Chambers, Cassie, Luke, Gus.
Draft itinerary of Macquarie Marshes trip attached for comment. Sapphie—I'm away next week, but will see you the weekend after next to confirm.

I respond straight away.
I'll be in Canberra that weekend.

CHAPTER

21

I'm not sure what I dread most, the almost four-hour drive—even though Hugo insists it'll only get dark after we reach the suburbs—or dinner with my father and Jacqueline. I hope her twin sons will be there too, but as they're only six years old, they might be in bed.

I glance at the broomsticks lying side by side on the workbench in the flower room. They're roughly the same size, but one is made from a branch of an ironbark tree and the other from a red gum branch, so the colours and grains are distinct. Gus suggested I use willow for the brush, and gave me so many twisted sticks I could've made broomsticks for two Quidditch teams. I've adjusted the lengths of the branches for Atticus and Alex, but in other ways the broomsticks look much the same as those described in the books and seen in the movies.

I run my hands over the timbers, sanded satin smooth and lightly varnished. 'If they don't like Harry Potter, I'm in trouble.'

Sitting on the bench next to the broomsticks is the crown I've made for April to wear at her wedding. Next week, we'll work out the best way to attach it to her head without messing up her hair. I glance at my watch as I pull out my ribbon, combing through my hair with my fingers until it falls smoothly down my back. My overnight bag is sitting at the door. I'm dressed in a clean white shirt, new jeans and my best brown boots, and the broomsticks are ready. Hugo is always late. I should have time to work out where the pins should go before he arrives.

I walk to the mirror that hangs against the wall near the bookcase.

Jet had been sitting on a chair at the workbench as I was laying a crown of jonquils, freesias and daffodils on her long blonde hair when I mentioned I should buy a full-length mirror from the hardware store. 'That way, brides could look at their dresses and hair together,' I said.

'What?' She laughed. 'Get them to admire their reflections in the water trough.'

Jet resembles a young Elle Macpherson, but is unlikely to have spent long enough in front of a mirror to make the connection.

'What do you mean, "them"? You appreciate you're about to be a bride?'

She raised a hand to the crown. Her smile faded away. 'I want flowers for my hair. Finn wants a wedding ring. That's what we care about.'

The next time Jet came to the farmhouse, she had a mirror in the back of her ute. 'You like old things,' she said. 'And you're obsessed with your garden.' She'd bought the mirror from an antique shop in Dubbo. The frame is faded gold leaf with a design of flowers and vines and is so heavy that it took the two of us to carry it inside. She hammered fittings to the wall and we hung it up. 'What do you think?'

I hugged her tightly. 'I love it.'

I peer into the glass as I turn my head this way and that, attempting to see the crown at all angles. The twelve crepe roses are fixed from ear to ear on a narrow wire base, hidden by ribbon that'll match the bridal gown. The roses are cream.

Eggshell, vanilla, seashell, magnolia.

The varieties are old-fashioned.

Hybrid Tea, Bourbon, Floribunda, English.

Each type of rose has a different formation of petal and shape. Some are dense with scores of petals, others are simpler with only ten or twelve. Scattered among the roses are different-sized leaves, emerald, moss and forest green. I walk carefully back to the workbench, pushing aside crepe as I search for the bowl of pins.

'There you are.'

I secure the first few pins. But then I'm distracted by the buttonhole arrangements I've made for Gus and the father of the bride. Last week, I collected gumnuts from the park and used a hot glue gun to attach them to the stems. The crepe for the flowers was white, but I stained it with peppermint tea. I examine the tiny flowers closely. The stem and pod are wrapped in floristry tape. The flowers started out as long strips of crepe, cut myriad times to make a fringe. I wrapped them around the pods to create the delicate feathery blooms. I smile. Gran would be proud of me. And they smell lovely.

When I lay the flowers gently back on the bench, April's crown shifts. I reach for more pins, carefully finding places to hide them. April's version of a bridal waltz is an energetic folk dance and her hair is curly and short. Will the crown survive the turns? I find the old radio under a coil of wire I used for the broomsticks, pull up the antenna and switch it on.

I sing 'Can't Take My Eyes Off You' with Frankie Valli as I twirl around the bench. I spin near the window on the toes of my boots. I waltz towards the bookcase, one arm to the side and the other at shoulder height, as if I have a partner. I pirouette in front of the mirror and glide across the floor. The room spins around me, a blur of colour and—

'Oh!' I'm moving so fast that it takes a few moments to stop. Ma Hargreaves and Matts are standing at the door. Ma smiles and clasps her hands to her breast; Matts leans against the doorframe, one foot in front of the other.

Frankie continues to sing.

'Don't stop on our account,' Ma calls.

My face is warm. I'm puffing quietly. My feet are frozen to the floorboards in the centre of the room. The song comes to an end. Beeps sound over the radio. The announcer's voice: 'It is precisely three o'clock.'

'I …' I focus on Ma. I lift my hair and twist it. 'I didn't want the crown to fall off in the dance.' My words come out in a rush.

'It's for April, isn't it?' Ma says. 'What a wonderful wedding gift.'

I glance at Matts. He's not laughing. Or angry. Or smiling. When our eyes finally meet, he peels off the wall and nods politely as if nothing has happened. He looks around.

'You make these flowers?'

It's only as I follow his gaze that I realise how many flowers are in the room. A garland of crimson chrysanthemums hangs above the door. Bottlebrush and grevillea in vibrant shades of saffron and ruby spill out of a basket near the window. Giant gerbera flowers I made for last year's high school formal are propped up in a corner and reflected in the mirror. The Remembrance Day poppies I'll give to Gus and his friends in November are lined up on the shelves of the bookcase.

'I—yes.'

'Sapphie's grandmother taught her how to do it,' Ma tells Matts. 'It's a family tradition.'

I walk quickly to the bench and switch off the radio. 'That's right.' I take one pin out of my hair, and then another. 'Matts? What are you doing here?'

'I arranged to meet Gus,' he says. 'I also wanted to settle our itinerary.'

'Your expedition is only two weeks away,' Ma says happily. 'Matts was telling me all about it.'

Matts watches closely as I take another pin from my hair. 'I'll have a look at the details,' I say. 'I'll message tonight.'

'I was in the store when Matts found me,' Ma says, 'about to leave for the farmhouse. I told him you'd be here.'

'I didn't expect you either, Ma. Hugo will be here soon. He's giving me a lift to Canberra, remember?'

She limps over to me and touches my arm. 'Are you all right, love?'

I force a smile. 'I'm fine. Your knees are playing up again, aren't they? Can I help with anything before I go?'

'Only the lemons, love. I promised Mike I'd make tarts for Warrandale's fete. You said I could have a bucket from your orchard.'

'I forgot, Ma. I'm sorry. Of course you can have them, but—' I glance at Matts. '—it's not my orchard yet.'

'Only a matter of time, love.'

My hand is unsteady as I pull out another pin. 'I'll take this off and find the stepladder.'

'I'm not in a hurry.'

The next few pins pull out easily. Another I can't get hold of. 'Ma? Could you give me a hand?'

When a car door slams outside, Ma looks out of the window. 'Hugo's here.'

'He's hardly ever on time.'

'Pa's worried about you going all that way. I'll ask Hugo to help with the lemons while you get sorted out here. Turn around, love. I'll see to the pins first.'

'Let me,' Matts says.

Ma beams. 'Thank you, Matts.' She pats my arm. 'Won't be long.'

Matts is far taller than Ma. He stands close while I take deep breaths, trying to steady my heartbeats. He smells nice.

'Try not to touch the flowers,' I say quietly.

Moving methodically from left to right, he pulls out pin after pin and puts them into the bowl.

'Why are you really here?' I ask.

He rests a hand on my shoulder as he feels for pins behind my ear. He hasn't shaved today. Maybe not for a few days. My skin warms.

'I've already told you,' he says.

'You won't have long with Gus, because Freddy won't get him to the pub until after five, and trivia starts at six.'

'I wanted to see you too.'

'You could have called.'

Another pin drops into the bowl. 'That's all of them.' He takes a step back. His hands drop to his sides.

'Thank you.' I raise my arms slowly, taking the crown by the frame, lifting it from my head and placing it gently on the bench. I smooth my hair. When I turn again to face him, he's closer than he was. Our eyes meet. His gaze slips to my mouth.

'It's beautiful, Sapphie,' he says.

We're the only two people in the room. The nation. The world. The universe. I'm not sure who moves first, but all of a sudden my hands are on his chest and my face is in his hands and our mouths aren't quite touching but our breaths are all mixed up.

'Matts?'

'You shouldn't have kissed me again,' he mutters, as his hands slide to my shoulders.

'It was you who started it last time.'

His hands move down my arms and link loosely around my body. 'Forgive me, Sapphie,' he says, before taking my bottom lip between his teeth and drawing it into his mouth. I moan and he releases it.

I take a shaky breath. Rest my head against his chest. 'I couldn't see past my own hurt to yours.'

When he pulls me closer, I don't think he cares that his arm is on the side of my breast and his erection is pressed firmly against my stomach. He knows I understand.

We are not who we were.

He traces a path with his lips from my nape to my ear to my temple. 'Too beautiful,' he mutters, his breath soft and warm on my cheek. I pull his head down and kiss him, sighing in relief when I find his tongue and stroke it with mine. He tastes of peppermint.

He didn't like cakes or sugary food but he liked to eat peppermints. Mum used to keep a packet in her handbag and wouldn't let me touch them. 'No, Sapphire. They're for Matts.'

Our lips are wet and sweet, curious and impatient. My hands explore his chest. They press against his abdomen and cling to his hips. Aching warmth pools in my stomach and seeps to my thighs.

Hugo laughs loudly.

Ma Hargreaves calls out, 'Sapphie!'

The stepladder clangs shut.

When I bunch my hands against Matts's chest, he loosens his arms. 'When are you back?' he asks gruffly.

'Late tomorrow afternoon.'

'Will you stay with Robert and Jacqueline?'

I shake my head. 'At a motel.'

He picks up a lock of hair from my shoulder, kisses it and lays it down my back. He cups my face again, lifting my chin with his thumbs.

'I missed you,' he says.

My hands open and close. Should I bring him closer or push him away?

'The farmhouse,' I blurt. 'You said you didn't know what my father had done. Was that the truth?'

'I don't lie.'

'Sometimes you only tell me what you want me to know.'

He kisses me again, short and sharp. 'Trust me, Sapphie, then you get more.'

I smooth his sweater over his chest before I pull away. 'It's not easy.'

When we face the bench, our arms touch. He picks up Gus's buttonhole and examines the flowers. 'Your grandmother,' he says quietly. 'You blamed me for that too.'

Bending my knees, I take a shoebox from under the bench. When I place April's father's buttonhole on the tissue paper bed, Matts puts Gus's buttonhole beside it.

'What happened with her was messed up with other things.'

'I'll be away for two weeks—until the day before we leave. We have to talk before then.'

'I don't want to talk about Gran.'

'Then we talk about the wetlands.' Without touching me in any other way, he kisses my mouth again, a whisper on my lips. 'It's a start.'

The front door slams against the wall. Hugo shouts, 'Sapph! Get your arse into gear!'

'Coming!'

I put my hair behind my ears with shaky hands. Cutting a length of twine from a reel, I tie the broomsticks together and put them into a cotton drawstring bag, securing it tightly around the sticks but short of the wire that binds the willow. I pull another bag over the top.

Matts watches every move. When I put my hands on his shoulders and kiss his cheek, his bristles are rough.

'Where are you going?'

'Queensland, WA.' He runs his fingertip down my nose to my mouth. He traces a line along the crease between my lips. 'Call me tonight.'

We are not who we were.

CHAPTER

22

'So …' Hugo, says, keeping his eyes on the road but turning down the volume on the radio, 'what was the problem with Prima?'

The seatbelt is a vice across my chest. I bite my lip as a car overtakes on our right. 'There wasn't a problem.'

'Your committee's UN delegate said that's why you were late.'

'The Ramsar Secretariat is UN sanctioned. He's not a UN delegate.' I squeeze my eyes shut. 'Are you trying to make me throw up?'

'Not on my watch,' he says, as he indicates left and pulls into a layby at the side of the road. He winds down our windows and switches off the engine.

I breathe in through my nose and out through my mouth. *Deep breaths. If you don't control the anxiety, it will take control of you.* 'What time is it?'

Hugo peers at the dashboard clock. 'Almost six-thirty.'

'That's why it's dark.'

'Have you just noticed? You've been staring out of the window since we left.'

'I'm telling myself there's nothing out there.'

He puts his hand on my forehead as if checking my temperature. 'We're on the outskirts of the city now. Won't be long.'

'Just give me a minute. If my breathing is okay, I do better.'

'Daylight saving starts next weekend. Maybe that'll help?' He whistles a tune I can't identify. 'Sapph?'

'Hugo.'

'Why'd you go to Prima when we wanted to get here before dark?'

I knew Ma would ask why it'd taken so long to get the pins out of my hair. I didn't want to face Matts again. So after I walked out of the flower room, I left my bags on the steps and ran to the paddock. Freckle nickered and Lollopy rushed to the gate wearing his 'I'm afraid you forgot to feed me' expression. I wrapped my arms around his neck and buried my face in his fuzzy black mane. He smelt of horse and dust and hay, much easier to process than scents of pine and peppermint. 'I'm going to miss you and Freckle when Jet gets back.'

I didn't realise that Joel was still at the farmhouse until I saw him in the paddock with Prima. He'd bridled and saddled her and was leading her around on a rope. He looked up proudly.

'Reckon it won't be long before you can ride her, Sapphie.' Prima stood quietly with Joel at her head as I walked around her, keeping close to her body in case she shied and kicked out. I practiced what we'd been doing all week—Joel holding her steady while I put my hands on the saddle and my foot in the stirrup iron. When I pulled myself up as if I was going to mount, she held my weight calmly. Next week, I'll climb onto her back.

I take another deep breath before I turn back to Hugo. 'Joel was waiting, and I wanted to say goodbye to the horses.'

He laughs. 'Bet they were hanging out for that.'

'You're the one who talks to frogs.'

He puts the car into gear. 'Only the males croak back.'

'Which means girl frogs are much less likely to be eaten.' We turn onto the road. 'I know a lot about frogs because of you.'

He looks at me slyly. 'Matts likes my frogs.'

Within a few minutes, we turn onto the two-lane loop road that leads to the city. There are road signs and traffic lights and round-abouts and pedestrians and rows and rows of houses.

No kangaroos.

I open my fingers, releasing the belt. I link my hands in my lap. 'Matts also likes swamps.'

Hugo grins. 'Give, Sapphie. You didn't want him on the com-mittee. Then you did. When you got back from the horses this afternoon, you couldn't keep your eyes off each other. In a fort-night, you'll be away with him for a week.'

'It's only five days. Anyway, I was roped into that.'

'I'm not an idiot. What's going on?'

'I don't deny he's physically attractive.'

'That's big of you!' Hugo hoots. 'He's not only built like a triath-lete, he looks like a guy who models Swiss watches.'

'He's—yes. But looks aren't everything.'

'He's got a string of degrees and a bloody great job.' He grins. 'I don't know that you've been out with anyone lately, but—'

'I haven't.'

'Which isn't a bad thing, since your relationships never last more than a weekend.'

'That's not true.'

'What's the longest you've been with anyone? You frighten the good blokes away.'

'I don't want to hurt their feelings.'

'You see the futility?' He shakes his head. 'You plan how you'll break up before you've gone out.'

'I ... sometimes.'

'How old were you when you started dating? Eighteen? Nineteen? I've never met anyone you've dated who I liked.'

'I had no idea you were keeping tabs.'

'You don't drink or do drugs. You're beautiful and smart, but go out with jerks. It's not so surprising you dump them.'

'Let's change the subject.'

'You owe me.' When we stop at lights, he turns in his seat. 'I've had no one to talk to for the past three hours. Which is another thing I've been thinking about. There's more to this road fear of yours than hitting a kangaroo, isn't there?'

I shake my head. 'Don't, Hugo.'

'You and the roads have never got on. And that's okay. I know how your mum died. But you got over your reluctance to drive, didn't you? Remember the day you finally got your licence? How we went to the pub and got smashed?'

'*You* got smashed. Jet was tipsy. I drank lemon squash and drove you both home.'

'Whatever. You hit the roo last year, but you're no closer to driving than you were. Why?'

The sob that escapes is a mix of a cough and a hiccup and a gulp, and so unexpected it's impossible to smother. Tears course down my cheeks. I sniff and wipe my nose on my sleeve.

'Jesus fucking Christ.' Hugo pulls over and takes off his seatbelt. He forages in the glove box. 'Tissues.' He dumps them in my lap. 'I'm an arsehole, Sapph. Sorry.'

I shake my head. 'Not you. Me.'

As I scrub at my eyes and blow my nose, he ticks things off on his fingers. 'Something is going on with Matts. It must be. You've had zilch do with your father, and now you're spending weekends with him. You're in the car and it's dark and …' He wraps an arm around my shoulders and pulls me close. 'Don't get snot on my shirt.'

He smells nice. But he doesn't smell like Matts. And that makes me cry even harder.

CHAPTER
23

Gus said my flowers don't grow out of the dirt, but no one can tell the difference. He also said some folk end up where they should've started out in the first place. The renovated houses with manicured hedges, the rows of matching trees on the nature strips, the double garages, fenced backyards, swimming pools and tennis courts ... all of these things should be familiar to me. They *are* familiar. But now I'm a stranger to them.

I don't belong here.

I convince Hugo to drop me off a block away and resist the urge to rub my eyes, already red, as I walk along the footpath. My overnight bag and handbag are in one hand, and the broomsticks are in the other. I must look like ... A runaway? I'm not sure whether the bubble that wants to come up will be a laugh or a sob, so I swallow it down. My father's house, close to where we used to live, is two storeyed and has a long sweep of lawn out the front. Tall lantern lights on black metal poles line the driveway at two-metre intervals. I lower my bag onto the terrazzo porch tiles and lean the broomsticks against an oversized ceramic pot with a cerulean and aqua glaze. I press the doorbell.

Jacqueline, in her late thirties and very attractive with dark brown eyes and hair, opens the door. She holds out her hand. 'Come in, Sapphire. It's a pleasure to meet you at last.'

Her nails match her dress, which matches her lipstick. She's cool, yet courteous. Is she aware I'm here under sufferance?

'Sorry I'm late.' I pick up my bags. 'Robert said his driver would drop me at the motel later on. Could I leave these somewhere in the meantime?'

'Certainly,' Jacqueline says, looking curiously at the bag that contains the broomsticks.

'I've brought outside toys for Atticus and Alex,' I explain. 'I'll give them to them tomorrow if that's okay.'

She smiles a little less severely. 'How kind. Would you mind if the boys joined us in the dining room? Robert wasn't sure whether it would be a good idea or not.'

'I was hoping they'd still be awake.'

'After we've finished our entrée, I'll put them to bed.'

I leave my bags in the foyer, at least half the size of the school-house, and follow her down a carpeted hallway. She indicates the bathroom. 'Would you like to freshen up?'

When I leave the bathroom, my father, dressed in pants and a collared shirt, his grey hair neatly parted, is waiting in the hallway. He kisses my cheek.

'Welcome back,' he says.

Welcome back to Canberra? Welcome back to the Beresford-Brown family? I nod stiffly. 'Jacqueline said I could meet the boys.'

'Come this way.'

Robert sits at the head of the table, fingering the stem of a volu-minous glass containing a moderate quantity of wine. Jacqueline, with Alex and Atticus sitting either side of her, is on his right. I sit opposite. The boys aren't identical twins but look very similar—sweet-faced, dark-eyed and brown-haired. Atticus wriggles incessantly on his chair, sitting, kneeling and standing, no matter how often my father reminds him to sit still. Then, as I reach for my soup spoon, he fires questions at me, asking what countries I know about.

'Should I start with countries beginning with A?' I say. 'Antigua, Austria, Australia, Argentina—'

He interrupts, describing each country's flag in intricate detail. He's articulate and clever. Is he also on the spectrum?

Alex has eyes like his brother, but lighter brown hair. He's painfully shy and speaks so softly that even Jacqueline has to bend her head to understand what he's saying.

When Atticus throws his serviette ring to get my attention, it skitters across my bowl. Sweet potato and carrot soup splashes on the tablecloth.

'Atticus!' Robert says.

Jacqueline stands. 'I'll put the boys to bed.'

'No!' Atticus says. 'I want her to talk to me.'

'Atticus.' I speak quietly. 'If you help me clean up the mess, maybe you won't have to go to bed so soon.'

'No!'

I hold out my serviette. 'Do you think we should dip this in my glass of water? Do you think the tablecloth would be easier to clean with a wet cloth or a dry one?'

He runs around the table. 'I can make it wet! Let me!'

I tip my glass to the side. 'Just put the corner in.'

Atticus does as I ask before industriously rubbing the tablecloth.

'Thank you for being so helpful, Atticus. The stain is much paler now. Do you know any countries with orange in their flags?'

'The Republic of Ireland and the Congo.'

'You're doing a great job.'

'I'm good at cleaning.'

'I agree.' His eyes light up when I plop his serviette ring into my water glass and scoop it out with fork. 'This should shine up nicely.'

'Can I sit with you?'

'Of course you can.' As Robert pushes a clean glass across the table, I pull out the chair next to me. 'I could do with some company.'

'Mum,' Atticus says, 'I can clean yours too.'

As Alex assembles serviette rings for his brother, I look across the table again. 'Alex?'

With Jacqueline's prompting, Alex looks up.

'Atticus has taught me a lot about flags. What are you interested in? What do you like to do?'

'Reading,' Alex whispers. 'I like to do reading.'

'I love to read.' I push the soup to one side. 'Do you have a favourite book? Would you like to show it to me?'

'I've got a book!' Atticus says.

'Two books are even better than one. Could I read them to you?'

'Yes, please,' Alex whispers.

'Now!' Atticus says.

I glance at Jacqueline. 'Do you mind?'

'Not if it wouldn't be too much trouble,' she says.

Atticus is back in a moment, waving *The Highway Rat* above his head. He clambers onto the chair next to me again. 'My book first,' he shouts. 'I always go first!'

Alex pulls the chair on my other side so close to mine that the seats press together. He carefully places a book on my lap. '*The Gruffalo* is my favourite,' he whispers. 'I want that one first.'

I turn to Atticus. 'What letter comes first in the alphabet, Atticus? H for Highway Rat or G for Gruffalo?'

He taps his fingers as he recites the letters. Then, 'G comes first. G!'

'When the children in my class can't decide which book to read first, we use the alphabet to decide. Thank you very much for working out which book starts with the earlier letter in the alphabet. We'll read *The Gruffalo* and then we'll read your book.'

'Yes!' Atticus smiles. '*The Gruffalo!*'

My father leaves the room to take a call as I read and Jacqueline clears the soup bowls.

As soon as I've finished the books, Atticus shouts, 'Again, again!'

'No, Atticus,' Jacqueline says firmly. 'It's time to clean your teeth.'

Atticus throws his book on the carpet. 'I don't want to clean my teeth.'

I sadly shake my head as I pick up the book and hand it to him. 'If you don't clean your teeth, you can't go to bed, and that means we can't go out tomorrow. And that means I won't be able to give you and Alex your presents.'

Alex hops down from his chair. 'We have to clean our teeth, Atticus.'

When I hold up my hand, Alex taps his hand against it. Atticus's slap is a little more forceful, but his eyes shine with excitement.

'Sleep well,' I say. 'I can't wait to see you both again tomorrow.'

Robert, Jacqueline and I make polite conversation in the dining room as we eat our main course and dessert. As Jacqueline clears the plates, my father invites me to join him for a drink in the lounge room.

'I'll leave you and Robert to talk,' Jacqueline says. 'Thank you for your patience with Atticus. It's no wonder you're a teacher.'

I smile. 'Your boys are gorgeous.'

She turns at the door. 'Don't keep Sapphire up for too long, Robert. She's had a long drive today; she must be tired.'

In other circumstances, perhaps Jacqueline and I could become friends. As it is … I hope my father has the capacity to make her happy.

He hands me a coffee. 'A little late in the day for one of these, isn't it?'

'I'm sure I'll sleep anyway.' I perch on the edge of a chair that's adjacent to a long bay window. It faces the front of the house but curtains, café latte—coloured silk, are drawn across the glass.

'Does Jacqueline know why I came?'

Robert, staring at the deep red liquid in his glass as he swirls it around, leans against the back of the couch. 'Presenting a united front is important for various reasons.'

'I was talking about the farmhouse. Does she know about the option?'

He shakes his head. 'As I haven't informed her of it, no. I didn't discount that you might.'

'She wouldn't mind that you'd keep it from her?'

'You're here, Sapphire, as requested. If we can contain the controversy, I will relinquish the option.'

'She's not only attractive, she's obviously intelligent. I'm sure she knows what you're capable of.'

'Take care.' He purses his lips. 'I might change my mind.'

The cup is fine bone china and the handle is slender. I try to loosen my grip. 'You gave your word.'

He swirls his drink around again. 'It won't be easy to defend Kate.'

'I don't want you to make things worse.' I sip my coffee. 'Others have faith in her.'

'Who?' He raises his brows. 'Matts? I don't believe so.'

Putting my cup on a side table, I walk to the window. 'Matts cared about Mum. He wouldn't want to make things worse.' I close my eyes, fearful of hearing the answer but unable to hold back the question. 'What has he said to you?'

'He doesn't need to say anything, not when the facts speak for themselves. Kate had a key and accessed the box. The note to Inge is in Kate's handwriting. *"Don't worry. All will be well."*' He lifts the glass and draws in the scent. 'It's impossible to believe that Kate wasn't, in some capacity, involved in wrongdoing. And then there was the sapphire. No independent person in possession of the facts could defend her.'

I spin around. 'There is someone!'

'Who?'

'He came to see me.'

'What?' He's suddenly still. 'Who was it?'

'He worked for Hernandez. He doesn't think Mum did anything wrong.'

'Someone approached you?'

I take a step back. I shake my head. 'I can't say anything. Not yet.'

'What on earth? Tell me what you know.'

'No! It's—' I face the window again, find the gap between the curtains and open them a crack. Streetlights illuminate the road, the double-fronted houses and precisely mown lawns. When I look through the window at the farmhouse, I see the stars and the moon and the sky and the clouds. I miss the dust and the sheep and the chatter of the possums in the red gum.

'I'm ready to leave now. You said a car would take me.'

'You said *he* worked for Hernandez? Who was it, Sapphire? How can you trust him when you can't reveal his name?'

I shake my head. 'Should I call an Uber?'

He turns away and talks quietly into his phone. He's still frowning when he ends the call. 'The car won't be long.'

'Thank you.'

He smiles stiffly as he picks up his wine glass again. 'Why spoil what you've achieved so far? You made an excellent impression on Jacqueline and, needless to say, the boys.'

'I didn't set out to do that. I'm not good at pretending, any more than Mum was. I like children. I'd like the boys and Jacqueline whatever I thought of you.'

He holds his glass up to the light and peers through the liquid.

Merlot, currant, garnet, port.

Blood.

Why don't I drink alcohol? My mother's addictions? My father's pleasure in an expensive glass of wine? The house is warm but a shiver passes through me.

Robert's phone pings. 'Your car,' he says crisply.

When I walk out of the lounge room, he follows. I stand back as he opens the door. He kisses my cheek, a perfunctory touch.

'I want a name, Sapphire.'

I pick up my overnight bag and the broomsticks. 'You won't get it.'

'We shall see.'

'Is that another threat?'

He looks past me as a car pulls up. 'We'll meet at the War Memorial tomorrow. Ten-thirty? The photographer has booked a room.'

'Can't we go somewhere else? Where we can be outside? The boys might like that too.'

He huffs. 'Where do you suggest?'

CHAPTER
24

The spring air is cool and fresh as I run a circuit, level but lengthy, around Lake Burley Griffin. When my phone buzzes on my thigh, I bend double and unzip my pocket.

'Sapphie.'

'Matts.'

'Oh.'

'Are you all right?'

'Breathless. Running.'

'Not asleep?'

'Too late.'

'It's not seven.' He hesitates. 'You didn't call.'

'By the time I got in it was late, and ...' I stand upright, an arm across my stomach. 'Do you remember when we went to the arboretum?'

'You lay on the grass. I said you talked too much.'

A man, his arm protectively around the baby strapped to his chest, walks past. 'The itinerary looks fine.'

'That's not why I wanted you to call.'

'I ... no.'

Silence. 'How was it?'

'I like the boys.' I study the sky, a metallic shade of pewter. 'I think Jacqueline is probably okay.'

'Robert called this morning.'

The fountain in the middle of the lake shoots a blast of water ten metres high. I walk to the grassy slope and sit, bending my knees. 'Why?'

'He told me about the man who worked for Hernandez.'

Has anything changed since he found me up the tree? What do I feel? Hurt? Betrayal? Pain?

Fear.

'You want information too.'

'Robert said you trusted this man. Why?'

At five this morning, I looked up Gabriel Garcia's LinkedIn profile again, and it confirmed the little information he'd given me. I think I'm a good judge of character. I think he was telling the truth. The photograph on his profile is him and many years ago he worked for Hernandez.

'Did Robert ask you to get the information out of me? Is that why you called?'

Before he has the chance to respond, I disconnect.

By the time I run across the road to the motel, I have a text from Matts.

That was immature. I leave for a conference in Brisbane tomorrow, and then I'll be at wetlands sites in WA. If I don't hear from you earlier, I'll see you on Saturday week.

A few minutes later, a group chat message comes through.

From: Matts
To: Sapphie, Chambers, Cassie, Luke, Gus.
Wetlands itinerary confirmed.

♄

I climb into the taxi just before ten, laying the broomsticks on the floor at my feet. It's broad daylight and we're not on the open road, but the toast I ate for breakfast sits uncomfortably in my stomach.

'Do you mind if I wind down the window?'

'No worries at all,' the driver says.

I tuck my shirt into my jeans. 'It's only twenty minutes to the arboretum, right?'

'Depending on the traffic. You been there before?'

'Many years ago,' I say quietly.

The elderly lady at the information desk promises to look after my broomsticks when I tell her I'm meeting my father at the Himalayan cedar forest. She opens a map.

'That's not too far to walk,' she says. 'But make sure you don't miss our other exhibits. Some of the forests have rare or endangered trees and others have Australian natives. I recommend the Japanese cherry blossom and Canary Islands dragon forests at this time of year.'

I'm at the edge of the forest when Alex and Atticus run towards me through the trees. 'Sapphire! Sapphire!' Atticus shouts. 'We beat you! We're here!'

Atticus and I bump fists. Alex smiles shyly. I hold out my hand and he takes it, clinging on tightly.

'Mum told me a secret,' he says softly, tugging my hand. 'Do you want to know it?'

I crouch down. 'Should you tell me what it is if it's a secret?'

'She said you're like my big sister.'

I squeeze his hand. 'Well, I guess that means …' I hold my other hand to the side of my mouth and whisper in his ear, 'Is your long name Alexander?'

'Yes.'

'Do you like the name Alex better?'

'Yes.'

'My long name is Sapphire, but I like the name Sapphie better. Do you think you could call me Sapphie?'

He smiles. 'Sapphie?'

'Yes.'

'Atticus.' He waves his arms around to get his brother's attention. 'We have to call her Sapphie!'

There are a number of photographers. The one in charge, a middle-aged man with a wild and bushy beard, has a camera around his neck and another in his hand. His assistants wrestle with tripods and large black bags bulging with equipment. Atticus turns his back to the cameras when he gets bored, but once I show him the map of the forests and point out that the trees in each section are from different places in the world, he makes the connection.

'I know the flags!' he shouts. 'I know the flags!'

Late morning sunshine throws light through the trees as the photographers dart back and forth. Robert and Jacqueline, wearing navy, beige and red and looking like a cover couple from *Country Life* magazine, walk arm in arm. The boys and I fall in behind, throwing Alex's tennis ball around and kicking up leaves. As we make our way back to the main path, Robert takes a call. Jacqueline laughs at something one of the photographers says before doubling back to join us.

'I know every flag in the world,' Atticus tells me proudly.

'That's very clever,' I say. 'Do you know about the trees and other plants that grow in those countries? It would be interesting to know about them as well.'

'What about the animals?' Alex asks. 'They're interesting.'

I whistle. 'Alex, you're very clever too. We can think about the trees *and* the animals.'

'And the flags,' Atticus adds.

The photographers spend a lot of time walking backwards as we pass through gum forests and Wollemi pines. When we arrive at the café, I leave the others behind and collect the broomsticks from the information desk. By the time I get back, Robert, his coffee in a takeaway cup, has moved to the bonsai display and is on his phone again. Jacqueline gestures that I sit next to her. The boys sit opposite, drinking milkshakes through cardboard straws.

'Have you got our presents in that bag?' Atticus asks.

'Yes,' I reply. 'You can look inside when we get to the cork oak forest. We can search for acorns together.'

'I'm as curious as the boys,' Jacqueline says.

Jacqueline was an events planner before she married Robert. She still arranges functions, but now raises money for political and charity causes. As she pushes my coffee across the table and smiles, I'm reminded of Alex. Is she more like her reserved son than her appearance and reputation suggests?

I try to drink quickly. 'This is taking much longer than the War Memorial would have, isn't it? The exhibits there are great, but I was worried about being cooped up. I'm not used to cameras.'

'The boys are enjoying themselves here.'

'Robert not so much.'

'A family outing at an iconic Canberra location on a sunny Sunday morning?' She smiles. 'He'll be delighted when he sees the results.'

As if on cue, Robert, still on his phone, appears near the counter. He bends his elbow, raising his brows as he looks at his watch.

I finish my coffee. 'It must be hard work being on show all the time.'

'After three years of marriage to Robert, I'm used to it.' She touches my arm. Her nails are painted a different colour than they were last night. 'I regret I didn't get in touch with you, Sapphie.'

'I didn't respond to your wedding invitation, and I only speak with Robert a few times a year. No wonder you didn't follow up.' I turn my cup slowly in its saucer. 'Anyway, I don't like—' When Atticus throws Alex's tennis ball across the table, I catch it one-handed. Smiling, I roll it back. 'I don't like politics.'

'Or your father.'

'There is that.'

'I should have persevered.'

I blow out a breath. 'It's complicated.'

She smiles sympathetically. 'There was a marriage breakdown. You lost your mother in traumatic circumstances and at an impressionable age.'

'He didn't love her any more.' I regret the words as soon as they're out. 'I shouldn't have said that. He's your husband and you haven't done anything wrong and—'

She holds up her hand. 'This is a difficult time for Robert. I'll do whatever I can to support him.' She looks at her sons. Atticus is studying the map of the forests. Alex's straw has broken in half and he's sucking through two ends.

'He's good to the boys?'

She studies her nails. 'My first husband was abusive,' she finally says. 'When I walked out, I had two children, one with learning and other difficulties, and very little money or support.'

'Atticus has ASD?'

'He's on the spectrum, yes.' She finishes her coffee before taking lipstick out of her bag. 'I wanted stability, together with the trappings of success that I'd previously enjoyed. Robert didn't want another child of his own, but he needed a wife and a family. As it's turned out, he's become fond of the boys, particularly Alex.'

'So the marriage suits both of you?'

'Very well.' She pushes her cup away 'Robert is single-minded. But he's not a bad man.'

'He wants his own way.'

'He's driven and ambitious.' Her lipstick is the same shade as her nail polish. 'As am I.'

'You believe he did nothing wrong in Argentina?'

'He has his faults but in his own way, he's an honest man. This controversy is a nightmare for him.'

I get to my feet. 'I won't let him make my mother a scapegoat.'

She puts her lipstick in her bag. 'He made you come here, didn't he?' She sighs. 'How?'

I look out of the windows and into the distance, beyond the city and suburbs to the hazy green horizon. 'He has something I want.'

Alex points to Robert. 'Can we go and get Daddy?' he asks.

'Remember to say, "Excuse me",' Jacqueline says, her eyes still on me. 'Sapphie? What does Robert have that you want?'

The boys jump excitedly around Robert as he finishes his call. Atticus holds out his map and Robert bends down and studies it too. When he holds out his hands as if he needs help to stand, Alex takes them, his little body straining as he pulls as hard as he can. Robert smiles as Atticus jumps up and down, yelling encouragement.

'Sapphie?'

'Please, Jacqueline, don't tell him that I said anything. It will only make things worse, and it wouldn't be fair to involve you.' I lean forward, scrambling under my chair for my bags. 'Anyway, I'm used to handling things by myself.'

CHAPTER
25

Strider only misbehaves when he thinks he's in a race; Prima shies at her own shadow, prancing and skittering at the slightest excuse.

I pat her glossy neck. 'You're safe with me, Prima. Don't stress so much.'

I've ridden her almost every day for two weeks, ever since I came back from Canberra. As it's Saturday and the paddocks at the farmhouse are buzzing with people, I was going to rest her today. But Joel had drawn up a timetable and scheduled a ride. He's not only taken on a self-appointed role as Prima's trainer, he's helping with the other thoroughbreds too. I didn't want to let him down.

He's leaning against the fence, watching our measured circuits of the paddock. 'You're doing okay,' he says.

'Thank you, boss.' I smile. 'Time for one more round?'

He looks towards the farmhouse. 'Some guy is waiting for you.'

Even though I've been expecting Matts, seeing him ramps up my heart rate. He's standing outside the small paddock where we work with the ponies, leaning against the gate with his forearms casually draped along the top. Archie is mounted on Freckle and one of the volunteers is leading him around. Lollopy has finished his tasks for the day and is angling his head through the wire on the gate.

Matts's shirt is dark blue. His jeans are black. He lifts a boot to the bottom rung of the fence.

I lean low to pat Prima's neck. 'He's early.'

'What's he want?' Joel asks.

'Matts is the reason you're looking after Prima this week.' I undo the buckle on my helmet, loosen Prima's rein and kick my feet out of the stirrups, ready to dismount. 'We're going up north for the environment comm—'

Archie, upset that his session is over, screams at the top of his lungs.

Prima leaps into the air, all four legs off the ground. My hat falls off, hits her in the rump and bounces to the ground.

Another scream, even louder than the first.

Prima takes off at a gallop.

Pitching forward in the saddle, I scrabble for the reins. I search frantically for the stirrup irons. One. Two. My heart thumps in time to the thunder of her hooves as I sit deeper in the saddle, yanking the rein to the left as I try to pull her round. Prima, her neck extended, the bit between her teeth and the wind beneath her tail, ignores every one of my signals. The ground is a blur of greens and browns. My eyes water. When hair whips around my face, blinding me, I lift a hand and swipe it away.

'Sapphie!' Joel calls.

The paddock is a few hundred metres long with a wire fence and a gate at the end of it. The gate is higher than the fence but easier to make out, with a metal bar across the top and another one underneath. I've jumped that height before, but on level ground with horses that knew what they were doing. Prima is unlikely to have done anything but work on the flat.

She's too close to the fence to pull up. And if she goes through it, she's likely to get tangled in the wire, fall and break a leg. I throw all my weight to one side and yank on the rein again, forcing her off balance and changing her trajectory. I crouch low over her neck. The gate looms ahead of us. Prima sees it. She tenses.

'Jump, Prima!'

Her hindquarters bunch under her and she jumps, flying long and high to clear the gate. She plants her front legs on the ground, finds her balance and careens down the track towards the creek. Gravel and dirt, kicked loose by her hooves, flies high into the air.

'Prima!'

She finally responds to the pressure of my legs and my hands on the rein, slowing to a canter before we reach the creek. When I turn her, she slows to a trot. The farmhouse roof with the rooster on the top comes into view. I lean forward and stroke her neck. Her sides heave; her flanks are wet with sweat. She's toey and shaky.

'That was no good.'

Joel, breathing hard like Prima, opens the gate we jumped only minutes ago. Matts isn't puffing. He's standing to one side, arms crossed and lips tight.

'You scared the shit out of us,' Joel says, closing the gate and securing the chain after we pass through. 'Why didn't you bail out? That's what you do when Strider bolts.'

'Strider slows down without a rider on his back. I don't know that Prima would. I was afraid she'd get caught up in the fence.'

A flock of cockatoos flies out of the grey gum. Their screeching would usually upset Prima, but she's far too exhausted to care. One of the volunteers has let Sonnet into the paddock. When he trots towards us, Prima pricks her ears. I kick out of the stirrups and slide from her back, pulling the reins over her head and handing them to Joel.

When I push back my hair, the tangles get caught in my fingers. 'Do you mind giving her a drink and rubbing her down?'

'No problem,' Joel says.

'If she's calm tomorrow, saddle her and lead her around. Act like nothing happened. I'll ride her again next week.'

'No worries,' he says, waiting until I've loosened Prima's girth and kissed her nose before leading her away.

I retie my hair in a ponytail and wipe my hands down my jeans. When I look up, it's into Matts's eyes.

'I'd better get cleaned up.'

He's uncrossed his arms but his jaw is still clenched. 'She could have killed you.'

I take a step back. 'No, I …' My voice isn't as steady as I'd like it to be, and my hands are shaky so I shove them into my pockets. 'Anything can happen with kids around. I shouldn't have ridden her today. It was my fault.'

We're almost at the fruit trees when he steps in front of me, cutting me off so suddenly that I almost bump into him.

He holds out his hands, palms up. 'You take risks, Sapphie.'

His fingers are long and clean. Mine are sticky and grimy but I thread them through his. 'You were early,' I mutter.

A silver scar in the shape of a cross. A worried, serious mouth. Grey eyes like storm clouds.

'You hung up on me,' he says.

'You said my father has a different agenda than you. Asking about Hernandez blurs the lines.'

'You didn't give me a chance to explain.'

'Miss Brown! Are you coming?'

Matts looks over his shoulder before facing me again. I free my hands and wipe them on my jeans before lifting a thumb to smooth the crease between his brows. 'I'm sorry.'

Besides growling a little, he doesn't respond. We walk side by side towards the farmhouse.

Archie, his scruffy blond hair wild about his head, and Mary, her hair tied neatly in a plait and a two-toned pink azalea flower behind her ear, sit next to each other on the steps of the verandah. When Archie bounces to his feet, Mary jumps up too. She grasps Archie's hand and tugs. They walk towards Matts and me.

'Say what Barney told you to!' she hisses.

He yanks his hand free. 'I know!' He walks past me, turns and walks back. 'I have to shut my mouth or I can't ride because you're going to kick me out and I can never come back not for the rest of my life. I won't do it again.'

'Archie.' I bend my knees so we're the same height. 'Thank you for your apology. Did Barney say I'd kick you out? That wasn't right. What I think he meant to say was that the horses will be much happier if you think about their feelings, as well as your own.'

'I wanted to stay on Freckle.' He holds out his hand and shows me his watch. 'I had twenty more seconds to go.'

'Sometimes we have to accept that we can't have what we want— even if we think it's the right thing to happen.'

'Corey said I had to get off.'

When Mary bounces on her toes and raises her hand, I hide a smile. 'Yes, Mary?'

'Next Saturday, Archie can *explain* to Corey what happened, and ask for twenty seconds more.'

'That's a good idea.' I turn to Archie again. 'Freckle doesn't mind if you shout, because he's used to children. It's the other horses who might get scared.'

'They don't like it,' he says. 'Prima ran away.'

'You shouldn't ever shout,' Mary says primly. 'Ever, ever, *ever.*'

I smile. 'It's okay to shout sometimes, Mary.'

She turns to Matts. 'You were at the youth centre, weren't you? Do you remember me? I'm Mary.'

'Your pony's name is Mischief.'

'Yes.' Mary beams.

Matts looks around. He frowns. 'Where is he today?'

She tips back her head and laughs. 'He doesn't come here!'

With Mary, he *pretended* to be serious. With me, it's genuine.

A black and gold butterfly hovers over the azalea bushes. There's a butterfly in my stomach as well, nervously dodging and darting.

Five. Whole. Days.

CHAPTER
26

Sunshine bounces off the bonnet and streams through the windows, but I'm so busy thinking about deep steady breathing that I can barely talk. Every time we hit a straight stretch of road, Matts turns his head. Am I pale? Am I breathing too loudly? *In through the nose and out through the mouth. Through the abdomen not through the chest.* He doesn't drive above the speed limit, but rarely goes below it.

'Sapphie? Are you all right?'

He wanted to drive all this way. It'll be his fault if I throw up all over his fancy car and—

'Stop!'

'What?'

'I need …' I wind down the window. I press the back of my head against the headrest. I close my eyes. I swallow. And swallow again. I slam my hand across my mouth. 'I'm going to—'

The indicator ticks as the car slows and makes a right-hand turn. There are potholes on the road. Saplings scrape the side of the car.

Dust comes through the window. The car stops, my stomach heaves. I wrench open the door and tumble out.

'Sapphie?' His door slams shut. 'What the …?'

The narrow dirt road borders a broad, shallow ditch. My feet hit the ground and my knees buckle and I drop to my hands and knees. But I prefer to be down here where the road isn't moving towards me and I don't feel the need to keep watch. I grasp fistfuls of gravel as I retch into the dirt.

He pulls back the hair that's come loose from my ponytail and tucks it firmly under my collar. He puts his hand on my back. I'm shaky and humiliated but want him here anyway.

'Sairas pieni kissa.'

Sick little cat. I retch again and again, but all that comes up is saliva. And after a while, there's barely even that. I'm in no hurry to explain what's going on, so I turn and face the ditch. I suck in breaths and even through my runny nose, I smell the gum leaves. I draw up my legs and rest my cheek on my knees.

'Don't move.'

Didn't he say that when I fell out of the tree? The rear door slams and so does the glove box. When he comes back, he crouches at my side. He hands me a bottle of water and tissues.

'I have water in my bag,' I croak.

'Take mine.'

I don't seem to be capable of opening the lid, so he prises the bottle out of my fingers and does it for me.

'Drink.'

I press the bottle against my forehead. I lift my shirt and wipe my face. I swish mouthfuls of water around and spit them out. Finally, I drink.

'Sapphie?' He touches my shoulder. 'Motion sickness? You never had it when—'

'I was going to eat but you were early.'

'You get sick if you don't eat?'

When I scrabble to my feet, I slip on the gravel and he takes my arm. His hold is firm but impersonal. Isn't that a good thing?

'I'm fine.'

He leans against the car and looks at his watch. 'Do you want to go home?'

I shake my head. 'It's not even night yet, so I don't know why …' I blow out a breath. 'Pa and Hugo drive differently.'

He frowns. 'I wasn't speeding.'

'No, but …'

'When I proposed this trip, Gus said you weren't keen on going in a car. What did he mean?'

'Do you remember every single thing you ever hear?'

He shrugs. 'Do you want to drive? Would that help?'

I take a step back. 'No.'

'You have a licence?'

'Yes, but …' I take a shuddery breath. 'Last year, I hit a kangaroo.' My voice wobbles. 'It was night time and—'

'I hit an elk.'

Did it lie on his bonnet and stare at him with dark and lifeless eyes? Does he have sleepless nights and panic attacks? I close my eyes but tears slip out. 'You don't understand.'

When he rests a hand on the side of my face, I open my eyes. His thumb slides softly over my cheek. He briefly closes his eyes. 'Fuck,' he mutters under his breath.

'What?'

His thumb is wet with tears; it slips and slides. 'Why didn't you tell me about this?'

'You didn't tell me about the elk,' I croak.

When I blink back more tears, he swears again, turns his back and walks a few paces away. I scrub at my eyes with the tissues, open the door and sit sideways on the seat so my feet rest on the running board. I find a banana and mandarin in my backpack. The door is open, forming a barrier between us, but the window is down. Looking anywhere but at him, I hold out the fruit.

'Would you like one?'

He shakes his head. 'Eat, Sapphie.'

I sniff and peel the mandarin. 'I liked Atticus and Alex.' I chew a segment. 'I liked Jacqueline much more than I liked Robert.'

His lip lifts. 'Are you ready to go?'

'I don't want to eat by myself.'

He reluctantly takes a segment of mandarin and I peel the banana. The sun is slowly sinking.

'Should I slow down?'

'Please.'

It'll take much longer to get to our motel because Matts keeps well below the speed limit. I leave the window down and do my best to focus on the horizon. *Face your fears and push through them.*

'Distraction is good.'

'I should talk?' he asks.

'Yes, please.'

'What about?'

'Before I went to Canberra, you said we should talk about the wetlands.'

He reaches across the gearstick and touches my hand. 'The Macquarie River,' he says gruffly. 'What do you know about it?'

'Assume I know nothing.'

He sighs. 'It runs from Oberon in the south to the wetlands in the northwest, over nine hundred kilometres. The wetlands drain into the Darling River via the lower Barwon River.'

'Brindabilly Dam.'

'When it rains, dams ameliorate flooding in the towns. When it's dry, they act as an additional water supply and assist with irrigation.

But catchments can have a negative impact on the rivers and wet-lands—they restrict the natural flow.'

I nod stiffly.

He glances at me. 'Would you prefer the radio?'

When I rest my head on the window frame, the wind rushes onto my face. My eyes begin to water. 'Tell me about the marshes.'

'The Macquarie River contracts in the north to freshwater chan-nels, streams and swamps, and creates a semi-permanent wetland. If there's sufficient rain, the plains will flood. In the last drought, there was zero surface water.'

'What are we going to look at this week?'

'Parts of the nature reserve, and also privately owned land. This will give me an overview. In the next month, I'll kayak to remote areas that are difficult to access by road or on foot. Eventually I'll get a team in to look at land contours, biodiversity and other things.'

'The wetlands are different than they were, aren't they?'

'Towns, agriculture, mining, dams, drainage. There are many reasons.'

It's not properly dark, but by five o'clock more and more cars have their headlights switched on. A truck comes over the crest of a hill towards us.

'Stop!'

Matts pulls into a layby and I stagger out of the car, putting my hands on my knees and retching into the dirt. He stands back with his water bottle and tissues.

'Sairas pieni kissa.'

CHAPTER
27

My room in the motel on the outskirts of town is sparse but clean, with a double bed, lamps attached to the bedhead, a small wobbly table and two upright chairs. Matts's room is next door. Is he really working? Besides declaring I looked tired, he made writing a report an excuse to eat in his room. When I selected toasted sandwiches and salad from the motel kitchen, Matts did the same.

After I've eaten, I step into the shower. Water is even more precious out here than it is at home, so I turn off the tap while I wash and condition my hair. My nightie is like a petticoat—a simple sheath with shoestring straps that slips over my head. When I smooth the fabric over my hips, it slithers to my knees. Blue silk.

Azure, cobalt, indigo, navy.

Sapphire.

When Mum wore blue, and people complemented her scarves, dresses or shirts, she'd look at me and smile. 'I search for the shade of Sapphire's eyes.'

She didn't seem to mind that I was a tomboy who refused to wear a dress. We were at a school event in Buenos Aires when I overheard a woman telling her I *might* grow into my looks. Matts was with me and I expected him to tease me, but he put an arm around my shoulders and we walked away together. He looked back and glared at the woman. 'Idiootti,' he muttered.

I comb fingers through my hair. It's still damp, but I'm not sure that I can stay awake long enough to dry it, so I go back to the bathroom to clean my teeth. My face is pale except for the smudges under my eyes, and I yawn as I carry the tray to the door and leave it outside. The days are much warmer, but the air is cool at night. On the other side of the parking area there's a jacaranda tree. The lights at the motel entrance shine brightly on the bursts of purple flowers. The scent will be too subtle to smell from my room, but we're not far from the gums that line the roads and dot the paddocks. I stand on the bed and open the window. Now it's more like home.

I'm almost asleep, the covers pulled tightly around me, when a car door opens. It's very close by. Maybe Matts forgot to take something to his room? Was it a map? Did he want to see what the channels and streams and swamps looked like before the farmers arrived and the towns and mines were built and the dams blocked the river and changed things forever?

I'm on Prima's back in a showjumping ring with tiered seating like you see at Olympic events. Which is odd, because I've never competed on horseback. Even so, I sense the crowd's excitement as Prima clears each of the obstacles—a triple combination followed by a water jump, a double post and rail fence, and a jump that looks like the straw house built by one of the three little pigs.

Is my class in the crowd? I think I hear Archie call out and Mary cheering. The final jump is a vibrant red wall with stark white mortar between each row of bricks. Another effort from the three little pigs? The wall is high, but I'm confident that Prima can clear it. I sit forward in the saddle and lower my hands as she shortens her stride, rises up from the ground and—

Mary, with wattle flowers threaded through her hair, sits on the top of the wall. She waves and smiles at the people in the arena. And then she turns to me. She stiffens. Her eyes widen. Her mouth opens.

I'm behind the wheel of my car and I pump the brakes again and again but the car is in the air so the brakes don't work and—

'Mary!' I sit bolt upright. 'No!'

I shiver. I rub my eyes. My face is wet. I shudder with hiccups. Where am I?

My heart pounds.

My head pounds.

The door pounds.

'Sapphie! Unlock the door.'

I fumble with the catch and slide it across.

His T-shirt is hanging out of his jeans. His fringe is in his eyes. He closes the door behind him and puts his hand against my face, sliding his thumb over my cheek in the same way he did yesterday.

When he pulls me into his arms, I press my face against his chest. 'It was a dream.'

He strokes my hair. 'What the fuck?'

'I killed the kangaroo.' My words are muffled.

He puts his hand under my chin and tilts my face. 'It was an accident.'

'Like Mum.'

He freezes for a moment. Then holds me tightly.

My breathing slowly settles and so does his. He smells of soap. One of his hands is firmly around my waist and the other hand glides over my back. He traces the edge of my nightie from one shoulder blade to the other. I look up and his hand stills.

When the breeze pushes through the curtains, they open a little and let in more light. Even so, Matts is only a shadow. A solid shadow with a hard chest and long legs and strong arms. He loosens his hold a fraction.

'You okay?'

I nod, my cheek against his chest. 'Did I scream a lot?'

'Yes.'

His body is tense, like he's about to let me go. Do I want him to? 'No.'

'What?'

I burrow closer. 'Nothing.'

He runs his hand down my spine. 'Sapphie. We should talk.'

'About wetlands?'

'About throwing up.'

'You went too fast, and then it was dark, and …' I blow out a breath. 'I know I need help, which is why I've been talking to my psychologist again. It's anxiety, and the only way to get over it is facing it. It's getting better.'

He indicates my bed. 'Is it?'

'Hitting the kangaroo triggered thoughts about how Mum died. Seeing you again, and my father, has made things worse. Back in Horseshoe they give me time. They understand. And anyway, the dream wasn't only about driving. It had Prima in it.'

He captures my hand and holds it between us. 'That horse is too big.'

'I can handle her.'

'Not yesterday.'

'She hasn't done anything like that before. I rushed her.'

'You don't have the facilities.'

'What would you know?'

He sandwiches my hands between his. 'An idiot could see it.'

Dawn seeps through the window; wedges of light lay stripes on the bed. The sheets are bunched up and the doona is half on the floor. Matts isn't as shadowy as he was. I can easily make out his features, his angular cheekbones and the line of his jaw, dark because of his bristles.

When I raise my face, he kisses my mouth, his lips lingering and briefly caressing. But then he lifts his head. His eyes travel over my body.

'You like to wear silk.' His voice is low and gruff. 'This nightdress is blue?'

'Yes.'

The right strap of my nightie has slipped down my arm, but I'm not sure about the left strap because my hair falls down that side. Would he care if he saw the scars? He knows so much already. He knows too much already.

'Sapphie.' He lets go of my hands and puts hair behind my ear. He steps back. Takes a deep breath. 'You were upset. I should go.'

'I'm okay.'

'You say seeing me makes things worse in the car.'

I put my hand on his chest. 'It's not your fault.'

The silk clings to everything it touches. My breasts rise and fall with my breath. My nipples harden. Warmth seeps from deep inside my body and radiates out. I'm attracted to him. But it's more than that. Want. Need. Every time we touch, I feel it more.

My arms around his neck. His arms around my body. Who moves first? The kiss is bruising and hungry. Our teeth clash. Our tongues spar. He murmurs my name when I grasp his T-shirt. His heartbeat is just as fast as mine.

'Matts.' My voice is a whimper.

'Fuck.' His hand slides over the silk to my breast.

I have a rule about my breasts: Hands off.

Matts doesn't know my rule. But he's touching my right side, not my left. And it feels—my breath hitches as his fingers slip under the strap. He pulls it up and rests it on my shoulder. He runs his mouth up my arm, his lips soft and warm. He lifts his head as his fingers slip under the strap and pull it down again. His eyes are dark and bright.

'I can kiss you here? Yes?'

I swallow. 'Yes.' Just this once.

His kiss on my shoulder is firm. He flicks his tongue against my skin. And then his lips move down my arm as he follows the course of my strap. I cup the back of his head and bury my hand in his hair. My legs are shaky. He wraps an arm around my back. When I arch my neck, he kisses the pulse at my throat.

'Sapphie.'

He pushes aside the neckline of the nightie with his nose and runs his lips along the line of my collarbone. His mouth is warm through the silk, but my body is warmer. When he nudges my nipple, my legs shake even more. I grasp his shoulders as he kisses around the areola. He strokes through the fabric, gently then firmly, firmly then gently. He cups my breast, presses with his thumb, teases with his mouth.

When he takes my nipple into his mouth and softly sucks, I squirm against his body. '*Matts.*'

The nightie is dark but where he's kissed is darker still. His head dips again on a groan, until all I'm aware of is the warmth of his breath and the cool of the silk, the pull of his lips and the touch of his tongue.

My legs are weak when, his hand still warm on my breast, he straightens and kisses my mouth again. His lips are hard and then soft. I stand on my toes to press into his hand. We breathe through each other.

He swaps arms. One supporting me at my back, the other moving up my side and cupping my other breast and—

'No!' I pull away, hitting my thigh on the bed. 'No.' I shake my head. 'Not there. You can't.' I shake my head again. 'You can't.'

'Sapphie?' His voice is raspy. 'What did I do?' He holds out his hands and rests them on my arms, crossed tightly over my middle. He kisses my forehead, a tender touch. 'Did I hurt you? Tell me.'

I want his worried mouth on mine. I want his arms around me. I want the warmth and strength of his body.

I've lost them.

Blinking back tears, I twist away. I lift my bag onto the bed, search through the clothes for my sweater, yank it over my head and push my arms through the sleeves.

'You didn't do anything, Matts.' I pull the sweater down over my hips. 'I hurt myself years ago. It's healed now, but …' I press my left arm tightly to my side and hold it with my right arm. 'I should have explained.'

He steps behind me and puts his hands on my shoulders. 'How did you hurt yourself? How should I touch you?'

Every time he breathes in, I feel his chest against my back. I blink again. 'I find it hard to talk about it.'

'I want to understand.'

If I lean back, I'll feel each of his breaths. I bite my lip and stiffen my shoulders. 'It was an accident, but how it happened … I don't want my father to know.'

'You trust me so little?'

When he lifts his hands, I miss the weight of them. When he steps back, I miss the warmth of him. He strides to the other side of the bed and shoves his hands in his pockets. He faces me again.

'Does Hugo know about it?'

'He knows I have scars.'

He tucks in his T-shirt. 'You told him because he's your friend? You tell your friends secrets.'

'Yes.'

His nostrils flare. 'You only have sex with strangers.'

'Matts ... Don't—'

'Where does that leave me?'

'We didn't have sex.' I force out the words.

'I kissed your mouth. I kissed your breast. That was sex.'

I scoop up the doona and bunch it in front of me. 'In the park, you said I was afraid to be beautiful. Maybe you were right.'

'You are beautiful. I want you.'

'I ... oh.'

'Why would I tell your father you'd been hurt?'

'Because—' I lift my chin. 'I can't tell you. It's personal.'

'That's all you'll give me?'

'Yes.'

'What about the other secret?'

My heart stills. 'What?'

'The man from Hernandez Engineering. What did he want?'

'He didn't want ... I promised not to say anything.'

'Why did he ask that of you?'

I squeeze my eyes shut. 'I don't know, but I trusted him.'

'Yet you won't trust me. You won't even talk to me.'

I turn away, throwing the doona on the bed and smoothing out the creases. My hair hides my face. Like it hid my breast when ...

I face him again. 'I think you should go, Matts.'

He swipes a hand through his hair. 'Go?'

'Yes!'

He stalks to the door but stops before he gets to it. He spins around. 'Where, Sapphire?' His eyes are black. 'Where the fuck do I go?'

'It was you who set this up!' I wipe a hand across my eyes. 'I didn't ask for it!'

He yanks open the door and cold morning air rushes in. Jacaranda flowers form a backdrop when he turns.

'You keep secrets,' he says.

'Sometimes.'

'You take risks.'

'Yes.'

The lights in his hair glisten like teardrops. 'Why not on me?'

CHAPTER
28

The sun is shining brightly by eight o'clock. I throw my bag into the back of the car and climb into the passenger seat. I look straight ahead. *Breathe.*

Matts has barely glanced my way since I stepped outside my room. He puts the key in the ignition.

'I have personal questions.'

'I don't want to talk—'

'Not us. Forget that.'

I turn to the window. Tears sting my eyes. 'Go ahead.'

'You said you have anxiety. You have panic attacks?'

'Yes.'

The engine purrs to life. 'Your heart rate increases. You feel sick. You do breathing exercises to counter the adrenaline?'

'You looked it up.'

'Two months ago at the park, you said the lights scared you. This was a panic attack too.'

'Yes.'

'Wilson is two hundred kilometres away.'

'I'll be okay.'

'We stop at the river on the way.'

'I thought we were going to the river on Thursday.'

'I changed the schedule.'

I smooth down the legs of my jeans. 'You paid for my room. I'll pay you back.'

He watches closely as I fasten my seatbelt. 'Did you eat?'

'My breakfast was on the bill, wasn't it?'

His lips firm as he puts the car into gear. 'Are you ready?'

'Yes.' I wind down the window.

He switches on the radio and finds a news station. So he doesn't have to talk to me? *Because I don't talk to him.*

When I was younger, I talked all the time like Mary does. After we'd moved back to Canberra but before I moved in with her, I'd visit Gran on the weekends. She used to pat my cheek and tell me I could talk as much as I wanted.

'Matts says I never shut up.'

She smiled. 'I haven't heard his name today.'

'He's busy with school and sport.' I rolled my eyes. 'And his girlfriends.'

'Does he walk to school with you?'

'Sometimes I wish he wouldn't. He's so cranky all the time.'

'You still go climbing on Fridays? He must enjoy your company or he wouldn't ask you to join him.'

'He says I don't talk so much when I climb.'

'Matts is seventeen now, isn't he?' She reached across the table for red and pink crepe paper. 'I imagine he's waiting for you to catch up.'

'I climb as well as he does.'

She laid the paper out. 'There are other things, too.'

'He says if I didn't talk so much, I might tune in to what he's thinking.'

'It's Valentine's Day next week,' she said, smoothing out the paper. 'Should we make a red rose?'

Scarlet, raspberry, blush, Ferrari.

'For Matts? He doesn't rate my flowers.'

'You could make a gift for another boy.'

'There is nobody else.'

Other girls my age had boyfriends, but I never did. For me, there was only ever Matts.

I tear my gaze from the window, shift in my seat and look at his profile. He's listening intently to the radio. There are lines at the sides of his eyes.

He didn't mean to do it but he broke my heart. I stuck it together, but it wasn't very strong. To save it I had to hurt his.

He turns. 'Are you all right?'

I look away quickly. Too quickly. A wave of nausea climbs up my throat. He stops the car and I jump out, already bent double. He silently holds back my hair as I rest my forearms on my knees and throw up muesli and fruit. He unscrews my water bottle and hands it to me, watching as I rinse out my mouth.

I'm leaning against the car when he produces an apple. 'From the motel,' he says.

I'm too afraid of throwing up again to eat the apple, but I keep it on my lap. And, when we turn off the highway onto a two-lane road, I lean my elbow against the window frame and rest my chin on my hand. I thread hair into my plait but it escapes, flying wildly around my face. The land is cleared either side of the road; the car bumps over the potholes.

'Ten minutes,' Matts says.

We turn onto an even narrower road. When we pass a tower-ing gum, shedding bark in long brown strips, Matts breaks hard, slowing the car to a stop. He reverses before turning left at an old iron drum mounted on a post and painted red. A shimmery apricot haze hangs like a cloud up ahead. I taste dust.

'Oh!' I wind up the window. 'I should have done that earlier.'

He glances at me. 'Keep it open.'

'I'm okay.' I undo the buttons on my cuffs and roll up my sleeves. 'During the day it's much easier.'

'We'll be back before dark tonight.'

'Is that a car ahead?'

'Yes.'

'I thought we were going to the river.'

'We are.'

We follow the green four-wheel drive to the top of a rise. When it turns off at a gate that leads to a paddock dotted with blue gums, we pull in behind it. There's a National Parks logo on the rear door. When the passenger door opens and Hugo steps out, I sit forward so quickly my seatbelt locks up. I wind down my window again.

'Hugo?'

He tips his Akubra to the back of his head, lifts a hand and grins. 'G'day, Sapphie.'

As Hugo opens the gate, I turn to Matts. 'Why is Hugo here?'

'He knows this part of the river.'

'He doesn't work for National Parks.'

'Lisa Stanhope is with him. She does.'

After we've passed through the gate, Hugo walks to Matts's side of the car. When Matts winds down the window, the men shake hands.

Hugo rests an elbow on the roof. 'See that ridge over there? Drive in that direction. In a few hundred metres, we'll ditch the cars and walk. ' He smiles at me. 'How're you doing, Sapph?'

'I didn't expect to see you.'

'I didn't expect to be here. Matts only called this morning.'

When it becomes difficult to find a route between the shrubs and rocks, the other car pulls over near a large boulder. Matts does a three-point turn and reverses, parking his car close by.

Lisa, probably a few years older than me with short blonde hair and extremely long legs, steps out from behind the wheel. She's wearing a standard-issue park uniform of green pants and a matching cotton shirt tucked in above a wide leather belt.

'Hello,' I say, smiling as we shake hands. 'I'm Sapphie.'

'Hugo tells me you're a teacher at Horseshoe. I bet they loved getting someone as young as you out there.'

'I was lucky the position came up.'

She loops her thumbs through tabs on her belt. 'I like to stay connected. Dubbo and Tamworth are about as country as I get these days.' She smiles at Matts and holds out her hand.

'Dr Laaksonen, I presume?'

'Matts.'

'I couldn't believe it when Hugo called with the invite. I've heard so much about you. I've read your PhD thesis, for God's sake.'

Hugo laughs. 'If you haven't already guessed, Lisa is a fan.'

Smiling, Lisa puts a hand on Matts's arm. 'I'm doing post-grad studies in environmental engineering. You're living my dream career, no doubt about it.'

Hugo slings an arm around my shoulders. He flicks my plait. 'What's with your horse tail, Sapph?'

'It's a braid.'

As Lisa opens the back door of her car, Hugo winks at Matts. 'I hope she didn't puke in your car, mate.'

'Let's go.' Matts turns abruptly.

We walk along the ridge for half an hour, before heading down a slope towards the river. The tree cover is a multicoloured canopy of green and there's a constant hum of bird chatter. As the land levels out, glimpses of water filter through the spindly tree trunks and undergrowth. The branch and leaf debris and the rocks that line the riverbank create a series of catchments and ponds. Water cascades at the narrowest point of river to the wider stretch beyond.

I walk along a dam of fallen logs, crouch and peer into the river. 'I can see right to the bottom.'

'This is how the river is supposed to look,' Lisa says. 'It's not rocket science, either. Don't use pesticides or overstock the land, and leave things as they used to be.'

Water rushes through the deeper channels between the ponds. 'Are there fish here?'

'And frogs,' Hugo says.

I smile up at him. 'I guess the water will be warm enough for tadpoles by now.'

'Smart-arse.'

'Hugo?' Matts calls. 'You ready?'

For over an hour, Matts, Lisa and Hugo discuss current and projected flows, environmental water allocations from the dams to the river and wetlands, and the ways in which the river and marsh environments are interdependent. As Hugo kicks aside ground cover to check for ant nests, he and Matts argue about the pros and cons of earthwork operations to replicate natural and changed environments. We form a semicircle that faces the river when we sit for a break. I'm at one end and Matts is at the other.

Hugo, sitting next to me, nudges my boot with his. 'What've you been up to while we've been knocking heads?'

'I've taken photos and drafted a post for the committee's website.'

'Still working on my frog article?'

'Since you haven't sent me anything, you don't deserve a byline.'

He grins. 'Don't be like that, Sapphie.'

'I want to illustrate how frogs are relevant to the river and the wetlands.' I scroll to a document on my phone. 'Can I ask you a question?'

'Go for it.'

'Burrowing frogs, in extended dry periods, can live underground. But what happens when the wetlands dry out altogether? In *simple* terms, can you clarify aestivation?'

He speaks deliberately slowly. 'Aestivation is when the metabolic rate slows dramatically and the frogs are in a state of dormancy.'

'They create a cocoon of dead skin cells around their bodies, don't they?' Lisa asks.

Hugo grins appreciatively. 'They burrow into soil with their back legs and once they're there, they store the moisture they have.'

'They come out of their dormant state when it rains?' I ask.

'You got it.'

'What's your role on the committee, Sapphie?' Lisa asks.

I open my bag and take out my water bottle. I'd like to eat a piece of fruit, but don't have enough for everyone.

'I'm the chair and do most of the admin. Unlike Cassie and Luke, I don't have any special expertise, but I pass on the town's concerns and put together our reports. Gus gives the farmer's perspective and Mr Chambers explains and defends what the government is up to.' I glance at Hugo and Matts. 'We get input from outsiders as well.'

Hugo laughs. 'Why'd you look at me? I'm not an outsider. And Matts is an ex officio member, isn't he?'

'Insiders, then.' I shrug. 'We use the reports for lobbying government and non-government organisations.'

'You're from Finland, Matts?' Lisa says. 'I've been to Sweden but nowhere else in that part of Europe. What a fascinating place to grow up.'

Matts smiles politely. 'My father was a diplomat. I spent much of my childhood elsewhere.'

'Really? Where did you live?'

Even from here, I sense that he stiffens. 'Four years in Brasilia in Brazil. Seven years in Buenos Aires in Argentina. Two and a half years in Canberra. Then I returned to Finland for military service and university.'

'Have you come back since?'

'Once, for a funeral.' He glances at me. 'I didn't stay long.'

Pressing my lips together firmly, I look down. And see a small native plant with a delicate, orchid-like flower. *Caladenia caerulea*. One of us must have stepped on it because the stem has snapped. I pick it up, examining the spiky purple-blue petals and single narrow leaf.

'What is it?' Hugo asks.

'Its common name is eastern tiny blue china orchid. It's also known as blue fairy.'

Matts extends a hand. 'Can I see?'

When Lisa reaches over Hugo, I pass the flower to her. She moves so close to Matts as she gives it to him that her arm drapes casually over his thigh.

Hugo nudges me with his elbow. I feel his gaze on the side of my face. When we drove to Canberra, he suspected there was something going on between Matts and me. Does he expect to see pain in my eyes? Or to share a joke? I ignore him.

When Matts bends his knees, Lisa's hand goes back to her lap. But their shoulders touch as he considers the flower. He's comfortable with women, but that's not surprising. He had a lot of girlfriends when he was growing up, and I don't imagine that anything would have changed. This morning when he touched my breasts he was—

'Is there anything like the flower in Europe?' Lisa asks him.

'In Switzerland, there's a blue flower called fairy's bell, but they're a different shape.' Matts turns to me. 'Do you know their colour, Sapphire?'

'Fairy's bell?' Heat creeps up my neck. 'It's a much lighter blue.'

Arctic. Sky. Cornflower. Periwinkle. Baby.

When Hugo passes the flower back to me, I find paper in my bag and carefully wrap it up. Matts stands, and I stand too. A scatter of tiny stones tumbles down the slope and plops into the water.

'Is it time to go?' I look at the sun, still bright through the gaps in the trees. 'It'll take a while to get back to the car.'

We take a different route on our return, walking along the river before scrambling up the rocky slope to the far end of the ridge. The cars are dots in the distance. Matts and Lisa are twenty metres ahead and climbing through a fence, and Hugo is close behind them. When a breeze whips up behind me, I spin around and face it. The river beneath me threads through the trees like a ribbon.

Just as it does in Horseshoe.

Has Prima recovered from her steeplechase? What if she'd bolted to the creek? It's in the same catchment as this river and—

The breeze stirs up dust. No matter which way the wind is blowing at the farmhouse, the weathervane on the roof will be pointing northeast. The rooster and weathervane haven't rusted, but the mechanism is corroded and worn. I should climb a ladder, take the weathervane down and ask Mike Williams, Warrandale's blacksmith, if it can be repaired.

I'll do it when the farmhouse is mine. When my father relinquishes the option.

Matts and Lisa are walking side by side. They've barely stopped talking. Is this what he's like now? Serious yet sociable?

I can't be jealous, can I?

Yes, I can.

'Sapphie!' Hugo puts his fingers in his mouth and whistles. 'Get your arse over here!'

By the time we turn into Wilson's modest main street, I'm tired and dusty and my throat is stiff from swallowing. The sun is still out but slowly sinking.

Besides saying, 'Should I pull over?' a number of times, Matts has barely spoken.

The hotel, built a hundred years ago after floods wiped out the town, is a handsome two-storey building of mellow red-brown bricks and white-painted render. A verandah with a green balustrade wraps around the first floor. When Matts turns into the lane that leads to the carpark, I unclick my belt. As soon as the car stops, I open the door and plant my feet on the asphalt. I lean forward with my hands on my knees and take deep breaths.

The driver's door slams. Matts crouches next to me. He lifts a hand as if to touch my shoulder, but then puts it back to his side. 'Fuck,' he says.

'Yes.'

He mutters another curse before standing and leaning against the car with his legs stretched out. I count slowly to fifty and then I straighten too. There are quite a few four-wheel drives here, a couple of open utes and a white late model sedan, dusty but clearly well maintained.

Matts looks at his watch. 'I'll tell Chambers we'll meet him at seven-fifteen.'

I scrape hair off my face. 'What is he doing here?'

'He's a member of parliament with an interest in my work. He's on your committee and has access to funding.'

'Did you call him this morning, like you called Hugo?'

'You don't have to join us.'

'You don't want to be alone with me, do you?'

'Or drive with you.'

'I'm ...' I take a breath. 'I'm sorry.'

'Are you? When you said that seeing me again had made you worse?'

'I wasn't blaming you!'

He reaches past me to the glove box, taking out the apple he gave me this morning and handing it to me. 'I don't want to lie.' He slams the passenger door, walks to the back of the car and opens the boot.

'I don't make you lie.'

He drops my bag at my feet. 'If Lisa had asked if you'd been to South America, what would you have said?'

I shake my head. 'I don't know.'

'You would have denied it. That would make me a liar too.'

He walks away, not looking back as he lifts the remote over his shoulder and presses the button to lock the car.

CHAPTER

29

I'm only in the shower long enough to wash the dust away, but by the time I wrap myself in a towel and return to my room, I have two missed calls and a message from my father.

Sapphire. Please call.

My phone is almost out of charge, so I plug it in before securing the end of the towel under my arm and pressing play on the TV remote. I sit on the end of the bumpy double bed and rub my hair with the hand towel.

The national news is on. Robert, dressed in a blue pinstriped suit with his special pin on his lapel, his grey hair neatly cut and combed back from his forehead, stands in one of the courtyards at Parliament House. There's a Japanese maple behind him, its branches aflame with burnt orange leaves. I recognise Robert's advisors, the man and woman standing either side of him, from the arboretum. In front of the three are journalists and cameramen—twenty at least.

My father brings the journalists up to date: Hernandez, as the head of his group of companies, has been accused of bribing government and non-government organisations. Hernandez's defence is that gifts or gratuities, not inducements or bribes, were given to business associates as a means of thanking them for their assistance. In regards to the Swiss bank deposit box allocated to Robert Beresford-Brown, Hernandez believes that the money and precious stone it contained was merely a gift.

'Under Australian law,' one of the journalists says, 'gifts must be declared, particularly valuable gifts like this one. Why wasn't a declaration made? Why weren't the contents handed over? Whether a gift or a bribe, the law has been broken.'

'Until I was contacted by the Argentinian authorities,' Robert says, 'I had no idea this deposit box existed.'

'So how do you explain it? And its contents?'

'Firstly,' Robert says, 'there is no evidence that the Hernandez companies received an advantage from my then employer, the Department of Trade. Secondly, I categorically deny having knowledge of any transaction that might have taken place. Thirdly, I have cooperated fully with Argentinian and Australian authorities and will continue to do so.'

A young female journalist pushes through the crowd. 'The deposit box, Minister. Why did it,' she draws quote marks in the air, '"have your name on it"?'

One of Robert's advisors touches his arm and he looks her way. He nods. 'I had no knowledge of this box,' he says to the journalist. 'But my late ex-wife, Kate Beresford-Brown, was aware of it.'

'Don't.' My hands clench the towel. 'Please, don't.'

'Your ex-wife, Minister?' the journalist says. There's a murmur of interest from the other journalists. 'Could you expand on that?'

My father nods graciously. 'I lived in Argentina with my first wife and our daughter for a number of years. It is possible that Kate passed information to Mr Hernandez or one of his associates. There is evidence that she accessed the deposit box described by Mr Hernandez.'

'You take no responsibility for this?'

'None.' He frowns. 'In the last few years of her life, Kate was deeply troubled.'

'Can you clarify that, Minister?'

'She had drug and other addictions. It was a very difficult time for my family.'

'Bastard.' I brush away tears.

'Surely she shouldn't have had access to confidential information?'

'It hasn't been proven that she did. In any case, the Department's protocols are now quite different.'

'But that doesn't change—'

'To preserve my daughter's privacy, I am unable to go into further detail. Except to say that, within a few years of this incident, I was awarded sole care and custody of my only child.'

'Her name is Sapphire?'

'It is.'

'Like the gemstone deposited in the box?'

'Correct.'

'That's got to be more than a coincidence.'

Robert purses his lips. 'Sapphires were Kate's favourite stones, but the rest is conjecture.' He looks into a camera. 'I have the support of my wife, Jacqueline, and my two delightful'—he smiles—'if extraordinarily energetic, stepsons. My relationship with my daughter has never been stronger. As a family, we wish to put this unfortunate incident behind us.'

I was aware of the photographers that followed us around Canberra's arboretum, but I didn't realise that one of them was filming.

At the end of the bulletin, the newsreader crosses to a clip. The boys are on their broomsticks—Alex on the red gum branch and Atticus on the ironbark—'flying' along a leaf-strewn path fringed by towering oaks. I'm standing at the side of the path and holding out a tennis ball, the 'quaffle', and an acorn, the 'snitch'. As the boys approach, I laugh. My face tips up to the sky; my hair falls down my back to my waist. Jacqueline and Robert stand to one side. They're arm in arm and smiling at the boys, the bright spring leaves of the oak trees behind them.

I turn off the TV, unplug my phone and put it in my lap; my hands are so shaky that I can barely dial.

My father answers immediately. 'Sapphire.'

'How—' My voice breaks. 'How could you do that?'

'You've seen the interview? I was forced to bring things out in the open to end the melee. I called to warn you.'

'I don't understand how ...' I wipe an arm across my eyes. 'You loved her once, you must have done. You didn't have to say those things. She was always kind. She wouldn't deliberately hurt anyone.'

'I took steps to protect Jacqueline and the boys.'

'You did it to protect yourself! Your career!'

'And why shouldn't I?' He lowers his voice. 'I wanted the media off my back.'

'So you blamed Mum.'

'The evidence is overwhelming.'

'Is it? You said it yourself—you don't even know that she accessed your documents.'

'I've said my piece, Sapphire. I won't say more. In a few weeks, Parliament will close for the year. By the time it sits again, I hope this will be forgotten.'

'Not by me!' I walk to the window and pull aside the curtain. Once the sheer fabric would have been white; now it's smoky grey. Fingermarks smudge the glass. 'It's not the first time you've used me.'

'We should be united as a family.'

'I could go to the media. I could tell them you lied about Mum.'

'I didn't lie, Sapphire. And you know as well as anyone that I could have said more. She sent her child, *our* child, to buy drugs on the street to feed her addiction. Is that what you'll take to the media? Or will I be forced to inform it of that fact in order to defend myself?'

'She was desperate.' I force the words through. 'You never understood, you never even tried.'

'I'm a politician, Sapphire. I know what I'm doing. Don't cross me on this.'

Mr Chambers is a politician too. He's standing on the footpath below me. Matts walks towards him and they shake hands.

'Did Matts—he didn't know about this, did he?'

'I hope he gives me credit for keeping Inge out of it. Not that she deserves any less.'

Matts looks up. Can he see me? I twist away from the window and lean against the wall. A faded print hangs near the door. A child rides a dark bay draught horse, a Clydesdale. The water in the river is high and the skies are leaden with steel grey clouds. The fields are bottle green, the earth is umber and the trees are graceful willows. It's an English scene. I think it's a Constable.

'I want the farmhouse, Robert. I did what you wanted.'

'Did you? What about this man who approached you?'

'What about him? It all means nothing now anyway. You have to relinquish the option.'

'It's too late to do so.'

'What do you mean?'

Silence. Then, 'I instructed my solicitor to exercise it a number of days ago.'

My knees crumple as I slip slowly to the floor. 'You've bought the farmhouse?'

'Correct.'

I put my forehead against my knees. 'I could tell the journalists that you took out the option in order to blackmail me. You went back on your word.'

'I could far more convincingly say that my daughter had her heart set on a property. As she had failed to take adequate steps to secure it, I did it for her.'

'That's a lie.'

'It's a demonstrable truth.'

'I trusted you.' My voice breaks. Tears stream down my face.

'Sapphire. Listen to me. There's bound to come a time—perhaps when I leave politics—that I have no use for twenty hectares of land and an uninhabitable house.'

'You'd silence me until then?'

'Your mother was deeply flawed. Your grandmother, while she did her best, was unable to adequately care for you. You've held onto this resentment for too many years.'

Mum couldn't go to Gran's funeral because she'd just been admitted to rehab again, so the next time I visited from Horseshoe, she got a day pass and we caught a bus to the cemetery. It was better that way anyway, without my father and his colleagues milling around and looking at their phones. We were arranging roses in a vase on the grave when Mum smiled sadly. She pulled a thorn from the stem. 'I couldn't love you more,' she said. 'But Gloria loved you better.'

'I loved her too.'

'You're a lot like her.'

'The flowers?' I said.

'She was kind and loyal. You have those qualities.'

I hold the phone away from my ear, swipe at my eyes and rub my face on the towel. 'You want me to forget everything that happened?'

'It's time to move on.'

'I did that. I went to Horseshoe and found the farmhouse.'

'Once you see things more clearly, assuming you still want the farmhouse, we can negotiate.'

The rooster on top of the weathervane. The azalea bushes and the red gum tree. The track that leads to the creek. The lemon trees in the orchard and the horses in the paddock. The room where I make my flowers and the timber sash windows that stick. The chilly winter draughts and the warm summer breezes.

My chest is so tight that it hurts to breathe. I roll onto my knees before standing. I wipe my face again. My phone pings. A message from Matts.

We're in the bar.

If Gus were here with me now, he'd take off his hat. He'd twist it around in his work-roughened hands and tell me what Maggie would say. 'Tomorrow is a brand new day. Let's get this one over with.'

I've lost the farmhouse but Horseshoe is still my home.

I refasten my towel and walk to the bathroom, splashing my face and pulling my hair into a bun. Digging to the bottom of my bag, I find my short-sleeved yellow dress. It's not too creased, so I slip it on. I shrug into a pale blue cardigan with yellow buttons, and wrap a yellow ribbon around my bun. I wasn't expecting Mr Chambers to turn up, but he's here and he's powerful. As chair of the committee, I have to present our perspectives. Gus remembers when the river was so high that it lapped at the steps of the schoolhouse. Cassie's wildlife needs access to clean water. Hugo's frogs can't reproduce unless water forms puddles on the ground. And Matts? He cares about the wetlands—bogs and swamps and flooded plains.

I slip into brown leather flats as I study the picture of the horse and the river. When my eyes begin to sting again, I squeeze them shut and bite my lip.

Matts and Mr Chambers sit opposite each other at a table next to an unlit open fireplace. The mantle and surrounds are timber, stained rich mahogany red. There are pinecones in the cast iron grate, pale green and plump.

'Sorry I'm late.' I force a smile.

Mr Chambers stands and takes my hand. He kisses my cheek. 'Sapphie. You look very pretty. It's nice to see you out here.' He rubs his hands together. 'What can I get you? I'm having a beer. Matts is drinking soda.'

'Lemon squash with ice, please.'

Matts stands too. He takes my hand but doesn't shake it. He peers into my face. 'What's the matter?'

Mum and Inge used to laugh and say, 'He has a sixth sense with Sapphire.'

'I can't tell you now.'

There are three middle-aged couples in the bar, talking and laughing. It's bird-nesting season so maybe they're here for that. Mr Chambers talks to the barman and smiles and nods at the tourists. He and Matts discuss climate and politics as they eat steak, salad and chips. I fork chicken around my plate and make notes.

'Sapphie?' Mr Chambers says. 'You're quiet tonight. What are your thoughts?'

I take a sip of soft drink. 'The rain we had last year broke the worst of the drought. Besides environmentalists and locals, people stopped worrying so much. We have to show them that the problems with the river and wetlands haven't gone away.'

By the time we've finished our meal, Matts and I have given Mr Chambers a lot of facts about the river and wetlands, and he's dictated them into his phone. He's also promised to actively support research initiatives and proposals in need of funding.

'Sapphie,' he says, as he drains his glass, 'I'd like you to draft a statement to be released by the committee. You can give details of everything I've—'

Matts pushes back his chair. 'We have an early start tomorrow.'

'Yes, of course,' Mr Chambers says. 'I'll send Sapphie a note.'

When Matts's phone vibrates on the table, he glances at the screen and so do I. *Robert Beresford-Brown.*

As he answers, I walk away.

I close the door to my room and pull the ribbon out of my hair. I glance at the painting but can barely see the horse because of the tears in my eyes. I tip my face to the pressed metal ceiling, blinking furiously until I can make out the stains on the paint. I'd told myself I wouldn't cry any more—at least until I was back at home in Horseshoe—so hold back more tears as I take shorty pyjamas out of my bag. I pull them on and put a faded pink sweater over the top.

I'm cleaning my teeth when there's a knock on the door. 'Sapphie.'

I spit out and rinse.

Another knock, much louder this time. 'Sapphie. Let me in.'

I pluck tissues from the box and blow my nose. When I open the door, Matts scans my face.

'Fuck.' He lifts his arm and drops it. He focuses on the bed before his gaze comes back to me. He blows out a breath. 'Can we go to my room?'

'Why?'

'It's bigger.'

'So?' I sniff and shuffle my feet. 'You didn't know what he'd done, did you?'

'No,' he says, kicking the door closed before standing stiffly in front of it. 'He leaves tonight for Vietnam. I want to see him face to face. We meet on Friday week.'

'He uses everyone. Including you.'

His lips clamp together like he's biting back words. But then: 'You were fifteen years old. That was different.'

'He insisted he acted to protect me against Mum. And later, to protect me against Gran.' I turn and face the bed, pick up my dress and fold it precisely. 'In his warped view, this is the same.'

'Will you challenge him?'

'He threatened to say more about Mum if I did.' I wrap my ribbon around my hand and lay it on the dress. 'Anyway, I don't want to hurt Jacqueline and her boys. I don't want to be like him.'

Matts walks to the bathroom and plucks more tissues from the box. He hands them to me over my shoulder, careful not to touch.

'I didn't trust him, not properly, but I hoped ...' I wipe my eyes and blow my nose, then bunch the tissues in my hand. 'If he does say anything else, or pretends I'm part of his family, I'll stick up for myself.'

'Turn around, Sapphie.'

I shake my head. 'Gus always says tomorrow's a brand new day.' My voice breaks. 'I want to go to bed and—'

'What about the farmhouse?'

'I'll have to find somewhere else to live.' I sniff again. 'I won't allow him to hold it over me. I won't let him manipulate me.'

He steps closer. Touches my shoulder. 'Sapphie.'

As soon as I feel the warmth of his body against my back, I close my eyes. Push and pull. Matts and me. He rests an arm across the tops of my breasts, his fingertips brushing my neck. His other arm lies across my hips. When I breathe out in a shuddery rush, he tightens his hold. He rests his chin on the top of my head.

'I'm sorry, Kissa.'

The strength of his body, the steadiness of his breath, the scent of his skin. He lowers his head and his jaw, rough with bristles, rests against the side of my face. His cheek will get wet.

'I don't want to leave you alone.' He speaks softly.

'I'll be okay.'

He exhales. And then he grasps my hand, snatches the key from my bedside table and walks to the door—so quickly that I don't have time to object. When he slams the door behind us, I'm barefoot in my pyjamas, my hand still tightly held.

'Matts! Give me my key.'

He tugs my hand and strides down the corridor, only letting me go to open the door to his room. It isn't much larger than mine but instead of a window, it has doors that lead onto the verandah. The curtains blow inwards like silken white butterflies.

He points to two deckchairs outside. Once upon a time, one would have been navy and the other bottle green. Now they've faded to sky blue and sage.

'Sit, Sapphie.'

I sit upright in my chair, but he leans forward in his. The floorboards slope towards the railing. There are ten streetlights, five on each side of the road. Besides an old cattle dog lying on the footpath, probably waiting for its owner to finish his drink downstairs, the street is deserted. The moon, a shining silver ball, hangs in the sky with the stars.

My pyjama shorts are very short. I pull them down over my thighs. 'I don't want to think about my father.'

He looks at my face before his eyes slip to my body. He looks away. His jaw is tight. 'I care about you, Sapphie.'

'I care about you too.'

He mutters something in Finnish before putting his hands on the arms of the deckchair, standing abruptly and walking to the railing.

He leans his forearms on the timber and links his hands. He bends a knee and slips it between two of the posts. From a distance he'd appear to be relaxed but he's as tense as a tightly coiled spring.

'You don't trust me.'

'I don't know how I feel.'

'You say you can't go back. That's the problem.'

When he doesn't say anything else, I get to my feet and stand next to him. 'After I left home … I'm sorry I hurt you, Matts.'

'You were young.'

'You visited Gran in the nursing home. You wrote to me. You came to Mum's funeral. I was seventeen, eighteen, nineteen by then. I should have done better.'

'Yes.'

I like his mouth—even when it's tight. I like his cheekbones. I like his scar and the colour of his eyes. I like his honesty. I even like how he's blunt.

'I *should* trust you, shouldn't I?'

'Not tonight.' He closes his eyes for a moment. 'First the roads, now this …' He shakes his head. 'I shouldn't have brought you in here. You should go back to your room.'

Across the road from the pub is an antiques shop, a narrow-fronted terrace sandwiched between a hardware store and a bank. In the front window are two tall bookcases crammed with books— a lot of books for a tiny town with trickles of tourists.

I swallow. 'Can I stay here?'

Silence.

'Not—' I shake my head. 'Nothing intimate or anything.' I pull my sweater further down so it covers my hips. I look over my shoulder to the bed, a double like the one in my room with a candlewick bedspread that's probably older than me. 'I can sleep on the floor.'

He walks to the lattice and turns. 'Why do you want to stay?'

I open my fingers and squeeze them shut. 'It's hard to explain.' I pull hair from under my collar. 'We're not friends like we used to be, but …'

'What?'

You mean more to me than anyone. You've always meant more to me than anyone.

When tears spring up again, I walk quickly to the door and push aside the curtains. 'I'll be downstairs for breakfast at seven. I'll see you—'

'Wait.'

I pick up my key from where he threw it on the bed and fumble with the latch on the door. But the moment I get it open, he reaches over my shoulder and clicks it shut it again. He walks to the other side of the room.

'Sleep here while I work. I have a report due early evening Geneva time.'

'Is that where you live?'

'Mostly.'

'What time is it there now?'

'Mid afternoon.'

The door is old like the pub. Its surface is uneven and patchy with layers of stain and paint. It needs to be carefully sanded back and—

'Take the bed, Sapphie. Go to sleep.'

CHAPTER
31

When I went to sleep, I was lying on my side on the edge of the bed and facing the door. There was plenty of room, two-thirds of the space, for Matts. I'm no longer clinging to the edge of the bed. I think I'm slap-bang in the middle. It makes sense for the verandah to be on a slope—when it rains, the water has somewhere to go. Under the roofline is different. So why does the floor slope in here? I can't hear the tapping of keys on Matts's laptop any more. One of the last things I remember was when he switched off the overhead light. He sat down at the desk again, and worked from the light above the sink in the bathroom. Now that light is turned off too.

Where is he?

I slowly roll onto my back. He's sitting in an upright chair with his feet on the end of the bed. His shoulders are broad. His T-shirt is white. He's looking straight at me.

He sighs. 'Did I wake you?'

I roll again, grasping the edge of the bed and wriggling towards it. 'Sorry.' My voice is muffled. 'The bed is on a slope.'

The mattress shifts when he lies down. 'Stop it,' he says.

I try to be smaller. 'What?'

'You'll fall.' His touch on my arm is light. It's simply a warning. So why do I jump like he's poked me with a cattle prod?

'It's four am.' I'm sure he's speaking through his teeth. 'I have two hours to get some sleep.'

'Were you working all that time?'

'I finished thirty minutes ago.' He holds my arm more firmly. 'Can we fix this?'

'What do you mean?'

'Let go of the mattress.'

He's lying on his side. As soon as I do as he says, his hand slides down my arm to my waist. He pulls me towards him and holds my body in place. His chest is on my shoulder blades. Our waists are lined up. My bottom is pressed to his thighs. One of his legs finds a gap between mine and pushes through. It shouldn't feel right. But somehow it does.

'Oh.'

'We share the middle.'

I loop my arm over his and feel the soft fine hairs on his forearm. I try to span his wrist, but my fingers aren't long enough. They stop short at his pulse and I count the beats.

'Two hours isn't long.'

'No.'

'You'd better go to sleep. I didn't think I would, but I did.'

He sighs deeply against my back. 'I'll talk to Robert.'

'I've thought more about it. I think he wanted to teach me a lesson.'

'What for?'

'You know.'

'Tell me.'

I didn't plan to be here, lying in bed with his body wrapped around me, but here I am. 'I was much closer to my mother than my father. He was distant. You knew that, didn't you? Your father was different. Even though he was just as busy with work.'

He strokes my arm. 'He always put my mother and me first.' He holds my hand.

'I was picking up drugs on the streets. Anything could have happened, so it was natural for my father to put a stop to it. But he used it to punish Mum, to get rid of her. He didn't know me well enough to see how much that hurt me too.'

Matts's grip tightens. He breathes deeply into my hair.

'I grew up a lot when I went to live with Gran. I started to see Mum more objectively; I knew I could help her in safer ways. But then Gran's kitchen caught fire. It was the same thing all over again.'

'Sapphie—' He cuts himself off, swallows down words. 'She couldn't cope on her own.'

'Gran didn't wander, and even after the fall she was well in a physical sense. The social worker at the hospital set everything up—food deliveries, cleaning, a carer to visit when I was at school, and to take her shopping—but Robert refused to agree to it. Even though she'd made such sacrifices for him, and he knew how much she loved her garden. I told him she wouldn't adjust to life without her home, but he wouldn't listen.'

'He wanted you in London.'

'Which is why he sent Gran away.'

'You told him the fire was your fault. He didn't believe you.'

'He used my lie against us. He said Gran had *made* me cover for her. It was … it was the opposite of the person he knew her to be.' A kookaburra calls out and others join in. It reminds me of home. 'Gran always thought she'd married well—even though there was no Beresford-Brown money left, and the name meant little in the end. Grandfather was so angry when the university retrenched him, he refused to work again.

'She worked, didn't she?'

'Full time at David Jones for thirty-one years. She paid her boys' school fees because Grandfather insisted they go to the same school as their forebears. She supported Robert when he did postgrad at Harvard, and helped Uncle James buy his property. But whenever they visited, they criticised her TV shows and magazines. They said she should stop wasting her pension on craft supplies.'

'Your father believed she'd undermined him.' Matts draws a circle with his finger on the inside of my hand. 'I got leave from military service every six weeks. I wanted you in London too.'

I close my fingers tightly around his hand. His arm between my breasts heats my body through. 'If I tell you something,' I say quietly, 'you won't tell my father, will you? He could use it against me, especially now. Do you promise?'

He whispers into my ear: 'Yes.'

'Gran had already fallen when I got home from school.' His breath is warm on my neck. He turns his hand and links his fingers through mine. 'She didn't need so much oil to fry the rissoles; she'd forgotten what to do.'

'She was cooking?'

'For my birthday.' My voice wobbles. 'It was my fault. I'd prepared the food and was going to cook when I got home.'

He pulls his fingers free and gets up on an elbow. 'Sapphie?'

'I'm getting to it.'

He rests his cheek on my shoulder.

'I turned off the gas. I picked up the pan. I didn't notice there was water in the sink. It—' My voice breaks.

He presses down on my shoulder and rolls me onto my back. He lays a hand on the side of my face. 'You were hurt?'

'Robert was already suspicious that the fire was Gran's fault. If he'd known about the burns it would have been more ammunition, not only against Gran, but Mum, because he held her responsible for me refusing to live with him. That's why I didn't tell anyone.'

'What?'

'The nerves were damaged. That's why there wasn't much pain at first.'

He opens his mouth and closes it again. 'Your breast?'

I lift my arm and run a hand down my side. 'Mostly down here, and across. It's not too bad really, just a lot of scarring. But I was sixteen and I'd developed late. I was self-conscious. And later … My skin is numb there. It feels weird when it's touched.'

His frown is clear, even in the shadows. 'Kate, your grandmother, the burn. You said what had happened with your mother was messed up with other things. Is that what you meant?'

'I couldn't rely on Mum. Gran was in the nursing home. I wanted nothing to do with my father. And you …' I clear my throat. 'It was all tangled up.'

'So you ran.'

His hair is dark in the shadows, but glimpses of light catch the traces of gold. I push back his fringe.

'When I came to Horseshoe, I didn't know who I was.' I run the tip of my finger along his eyebrows, the curved dark lines. It's tempting to kiss him. But he didn't want to be alone with me yesterday. 'The Hargreaves trusted me to work it out for myself.'

He looks troubled. 'That's what you did.'

I lie on my side again, facing the door. 'Do you remember my geography assignment? The one about the eagle?'

He lies down behind me like before, but not as close. When he puts his arm around my waist, I pull it higher so it rests between my breasts again.

'Wedge-tailed,' he says gruffly. 'The males and females pair permanently and both look after the eggs. After they hatch, the male feeds the female and the chicks.'

I thread my fingers through his. 'You never forget anything.'

He breathes into my hair. 'I missed you, Kissa.'

I squeeze his hand. 'I missed you too.'

Matts said he'd only get two hours sleep. That means he planned to wake at six.

No alarm goes off. His breath is soft on my neck. The movements of his chest against my back are steady and even. His arm crosses my front and I hold his hand. I dip my head and run my lips across his knuckles. What would he do if I turned around and woke him? Would he let me kiss his sleepy mouth?

A television is on next door. The national news jingle filters through the wall. Will my father be on the screen? Will I be there too, playing happy families with Atticus and Alex on their broomsticks?

Whenever I think about my father and the farmhouse, my chest aches. There's a deep well of sadness in my heart. I'll have to move out. Gus's shed is bigger than his house; he'll let me store things there. I'll ask Edward Kincaid if I can keep my horses on the land at Kincaid House until I find somewhere more permanent. My flowers? I take a shaky breath.

'I'll work something out,' I whisper.

Matts's arm tightens and he nuzzles my neck. One of his legs is wedged between mine. I squeeze my thighs tightly around it.

He stills. 'Sapphie.' A warning.

I put his finger in my mouth and gently bite. 'Matts.'

He makes a sound between a growl and a groan. He presses even closer, his erection long and thick against my lower back. He pulls his fingers free. His hand slides slowly down my arm to my waist and then to my hip. He cups my bottom. His hand slips beneath my shorts. He traces the lacy edge of my underpants with his fingertips.

I bite a little harder. 'Mmm.'

'Fuck.' He sits bolt upright. 'Fuck. Fuck. Fuck.'

I sit too, my legs curled to the side. 'What's the matter?'

His gaze rakes over me. He runs a hand down my leg and takes hold of my foot, trails his thumb along my instep. He's looking down so I can't see his face.

'I want you, Sapphie.'

I stroke his hair. 'Yes?'

When he looks up, our eyes lock. But then his gaze swings to the door and he swallows. He rolls off the bed. There's only a metre of space either side of it. Something hits the wall. An elbow? A knee? He curses again.

I check my pyjama top. The buttons are all lined up. I straighten my shorts and pull down the legs as far as they'll go. My face is hot and so is my neck. I plant my feet on the floor and look around for my sweater and my key and …

The mattress dips. He mutters under his breath as he crawls across the bed behind me. Without touching me in any other way, he kisses the side of my neck. His mouth is open. His tongue is wet. 'Sapphie?' he growls. 'Turn around.'

I squirm on the bed, just as aroused as I was. I clench my fists and shake my head. 'I don't know what you want.'

'I told you what I want,' he says, wrapping an arm around my front. He leans over my shoulder and tips up my chin. 'I want you.' He runs his thumb along my cheek. He lowers his head and kisses my mouth. It's a kiss full of promise. His tongue finds mine, but only for a moment. He lifts his head.

'Matts?' My voice is husky with need.

'I want you. I've waited.'

'Then why …?'

He steps off the bed and kneels in front of me. He kisses me again. Briefly. Possessively. He sits back on his heels and takes my hands.

'I've waited.' He squeezes my hands so tightly it hurts.

'Ow.'

He loosens his grip a little. His jaw is clenched. He prises it open before closing it again.

'Matts? What's going on?'

He runs his thumb over my fingers. 'You said you have relationships with strangers. Nothing long term?'

'I—no.'

'We were friends once.'

'Yes.'

He looks over his shoulder to the bed. 'I've waited.'

'You've said that three times now.' His fringe is messy. I tidy it. 'What have you waited for?'

He kisses my wrist, the movement of his lips soft against my skin. 'I want you to take a risk on me. I want you to trust me.'

I hesitate. 'I trust you much more than I did.'

He stills for a heartbeat. He returns my hand to my lap. 'Sex won't be enough.'

'No, but …'

He glances at the bed again. He gets to his feet and pulls me to mine. 'I want more.'

CHAPTER
32

Matts wants me to take a risk. He wants me to trust him.

The universe tilts when we kiss. That's not friendship, it's …

I freeze at the bottom of the stairs.

Is it time to put a name to it? Am I in love with him?

We arranged to meet in the courtyard where the hotel serves breakfast. What will we talk about? Rivers. Wetlands. Frogs and birds. Droughts and floods.

More. What is that? Commitment? Short term? Long term? Forever?

What about my home?

'Are you lost, love?' Last night's barman is wearing a red-checked apron and carrying a basket of bread. 'You looking for breakfast? He points to a door at the end of the corridor. 'The others are already there.'

The courtyard is paved with bricks, the perimeter marked by rectangular planters. The mint, parsley and rosemary are thriving, but the coriander is wilted and yellowed. Shaggy, bright green carrot tops burst from the pot closest to the table where Matts is sitting. His back is to me, but Cassie sits opposite him. She waves.

'Sapphie! Good morning!'

Matts turns in his chair, but I'm not yet ready to face him. I lean over the table to hug Cassie. 'This is a surprise.'

'Very last minute, but Matts thought having another committee member might help to take the load off you. We had no intention of gatecrashing breakfast, but Ray'—she smiles at the middle-aged man wearing a Crocodile Dundee hat sitting next to her—'wanted to meet up early.'

Ray stands and holds out his hand. 'Ray Bainsbridge. Nice to see you again.'

'You're an ornithologist, aren't you? From Bathurst?'

'That's me.' He smooths his neat goatee beard between his thumb and index finger. 'Thanks for having me along.'

Matts stands. He smiles stiffly. 'Sapphie. Can we talk?'

His jaw is perfectly smooth. His shirt is tucked in. I walk to the far side of the planter box with the carrot tops, much deeper than the one I have outside my classroom. I run my fingers over the lacy fronds.

Matts frowns as he stands in front of me, blocking the others from view. 'I didn't know they'd be here.'

Less than an hour ago, he was tousle-haired and ... I clear my throat. 'You asked them to meet us later this morning though, didn't you? Cassie said it was very last minute.'

'I called her the day before yesterday.'

'When you called Hugo and Mr Chambers? Is your whole life like this, Matts? You click your fingers and people come running?'

He kisses my lips so swiftly that they barely have time to soften. 'Not you,' he mutters.

My skin heats. 'They're waiting for us.'

When he crosses his arms, it pulls his shirt tightly across his shoulders. 'I want to tell the truth, Sapphie. That we grew up together.'

The orange part of the carrot is the root. *Some folk end up where they should have started out in the first place.* For me, that's Horseshoe.

'Why is it so important?'

'It's our past.'

He's not touching me, but I wish that he would. I wish we could go back to bed so he could hold on to me and I could hold on to him. We could think things through together. We could tell the truth.

I clear my throat. 'I talked to Gus about you, but I didn't tell him about our childhood. Gus is like you—he values honesty. I'd want to tell him first.'

Cassie's laughter peels out. 'Ray!'

'We have to go.'

He takes my hand as if I haven't spoken. 'You're pale, Sapphie. You're tired.'

'It's you who stayed up all night. I'm okay.'

'Your father, the roads ... Today won't be easy.' He turns my hand in his. 'Do you want to stay here? I'll come back as soon as I can.'

I shake my head. 'It's better to be busy and ...' When my hand flutters, he tightens his hold. 'I've come all this way.' I try to smile but it wobbles. 'I might as well see your wetlands.'

His lip lifts. 'Yes.'

When we return to the table, Ray shuffles over on the bench, so I slip into the seat next to him. He offers me the bread basket and I take a roll, sprinkled with poppy seeds and shaped into a knot. I dip a spoon into a jar of marmalade.

'I ordered tea,' Matts says. 'Is that what you wanted?'

'Thank you.' I lower my gaze as I break the roll in half. Poppy seeds, scores of black full stops, spray across the plate and onto the table.

Cassie smiles. 'That reminds me. How are you progressing with Gus's Remembrance Day flowers?'

'I'm almost done.' I spread marmalade on the roll. 'He needed extra poppies this year, because there are so many children, grandchildren and great-grandchildren attending the services in November.'

'Sapphie makes crepe paper flowers,' Cassie tells Ray.

Matts's head was bowed, but he looks up. 'You make poppies?' he asks.

The memory dances between us. A Remembrance Day afternoon tea was held at the Governor-General's residence in Canberra every November. I'd agreed to attend with my father not only because I knew that Matts would be there, but because it would be one less thing he could hold against Mum. Dad hadn't gone into politics yet, but often mixed with MPs. By then I was fifteen, and understood what was required. I had to listen closely, nod with interest and answer questions politely.

There was a vase of fiery red poppies on each of the tables. It would have been too late in the year for poppies to grow in Canberra, so they must have been grown in a greenhouse or flown in from Europe. They're an old-fashioned flower, so it was surprising that Gran and I had never sat at her laminated table and made them together. I took one of the poppies from the vase and walked to a shady spot to examine it more closely. I'm not sure why my father followed me, but by the time he'd caught up, I'd carefully pulled the flower apart and was pondering the shapes of the petals, filament and anther. He was telling me off for destroying an emblem of courage and sacrifice by the time Matts joined us. He took the pieces of the poppy out of my hand and shoved them into his pocket as if to hide evidence. 'Sapphire wouldn't intentionally offend anyone,' he said to my father.

Matts had been avoiding me all afternoon. Is that why I was as furious with him as I was with Robert, who hadn't given me a chance to explain? As soon as my father walked away, I turned on Matts. 'Why did you do that?'

'To get rid of him.'

My fists were clenched. 'Why do you care how he treats me?'

'You think I don't?' He glared. 'When will you grow up?'

Walking away, he swung a foot as if booting a ball and a clod of earth flew into the air. When he came back, his hands were shoved into his pockets. I was midway through my growth spurt, but he was seventeen and far taller. We stood toe to toe and he looked at my mouth. His lips were slightly apart. He dipped his head and I lifted my face. For a fraction of a second I thought that we'd …

I keep my eyes firmly fixed on my poppy seed roll, the knot untied and the soft white bread sticky with marmalade. Even though I'm still waiting on the tea, I turn the cup in its saucer, pick it up and put it down again. It's taken a long time to work it out, but now I know.

Matts had wanted to kiss me.

I'd wanted to kiss him back.

The following week, my mother was taken away.

My plate is awash with poppy seeds by the time I've finished my roll. As the others talk around me, I lick my thumb and press it against the tiny black dots, picking them up in twos and threes.

'Sapphie.' Matts's brows are drawn.

I take my thumb out of my mouth. 'Yes?'

He opens his mouth and slams it shut. His gaze slides to my thumb. His colour deepens as he leans across the table and puts a blue-and-white striped teapot to the left of my plate.

'Drink your tea, Kissa,' he says under his breath. 'It's almost time to go.'

CHAPTER

33

Cassie's car, an old troop carrier, is parked next to Matts's car in the hotel carpark. By the time I've run to my room and brushed my teeth, she's behind the wheel. As I throw my bag into the back of Matts's car and he slams the boot, Ray appears. He takes off his hat before pulling the strap of his satchel over his head.

'I want to pick your brains about the Ramsar criteria,' he says to Matts. 'And while I'm at it, I can answer your questions about the waterbird breeding cycle. I'll fill you in on the Australasian bittern too. It's been on the critically endangered list for a number of years now.' He opens the front passenger side door and throws his bag on the floor. He smiles. 'Cassie says she's happy to go on her own. Okay if I hitch a ride with you?'

'No,' Matts says.

Ray's smile disappears. 'Why not?'

'Sapphie gets car sick.'

Blunt. Misleading. I put a hand on Ray's arm. 'We'd like to have you with us, Ray, but would you mind sitting in the back?'

'No problem,' he says, smiling again as he scoops up his bag. 'One of my daughters gets car sick.' He opens the back door as I climb into the front. He sits in the seat in the middle and fastens his seatbelt. 'Have you tried nibbling on a piece of ginger? Joy swears by it. Or drinking lemon and ginger tea before you set off?'

'It's a recent thing.' I clip up my belt. 'I hit a kangaroo last year. It's made me anxious on the roads.'

'Valerian will do the trick then. That's a relaxant, but not on the prohibited substances list as far as I'm aware.'

Matts looks into the rear-view mirror. 'She doesn't need advice.'

I attempt a smile. 'I'm much better than I was.'

'Wind down the window,' Matts says quietly as he releases the handbrake. 'It'll take over an hour.'

As soon as he pulls out of the carpark, I tip back my head and take deep breaths. The anxiety *is* much better than it was. Matts is helping with that. He takes note when I swallow more than usual, or link my fingers so my hands shake less. He slows at the blind corners and on the crests of the hills. He follows my gaze when he can, as if to communicate that he's also aware of the dangers out there.

After a couple of failed attempts, Ray leaves me out of the conversation. 'The Macquarie River doesn't run out to sea, it runs inland,' he tells Matts. 'And fifty kilometres north of Wilson, depending on rainfall and environmental water allowances, it runs into watercourses that create thousands of hectares of wetlands, a nirvana for birdlife. At the northern end of the wetlands, the channels unite to form a river again, and the Macquarie meets the Barwon, which eventually flows into the Darling, and then Victoria and South Australia's Murray River system.'

Ray's vowels are long and drawn out and his syllables and sentences run together. When Matts occasionally gets a word in, he speaks precisely, his sentences short and direct.

'The sheep and cattle farms up here do quite well,' Ray says, 'and other agricultural interests such as cotton farming give a boost to the local economy.'

'Irrigation is unsustainable,' Matts says.

Ray's smile falters. 'We need a certain amount of it.'

'Without policies to guarantee environmental water for the wetlands, you lose the reed beds, essential for birds and other wildlife. Thousands of hectares have already been lost.'

I hold my breath and grip my belt when a four-wheel drive with a loaded trailer thunders towards us. Matts veers onto the side of the road. He glances at me.

'Okay?'

I nod jerkily. 'Yes.'

Ray leans forward. 'How about tourism?' he says brightly.

Matts mutters under his breath. 'Not without water management.'

'But surely—'

'The river's flow is fucked—upstream and downstream.'

I look for Ray's reflection in the visor mirror. 'I suppose that's one way of putting it,' he says, his lips tightly pursed.

When the road narrows to a strip of bitumen, not wide enough for two cars to pass without one moving onto the reddish earth, Matts slows even more. We pass a dead kangaroo. Within a kilometre, there's another one and then another two.

Ray whistles through his teeth. 'For a road barely used, there's a lot of road kill.'

'People shouldn't drive through here at night,' I manage.

Matts glances at me. 'Do you need a break? Should I stop?'

I remind myself that the country is where I belong. And that means dead kangaroos at the side of the road are a part of my life. The sadness and regret I'm feeling is natural. I didn't hit these kangaroos and whoever did hit them didn't do it deliberately.

My mother died in an accident on the road but this has nothing to do with her.

'I'm okay,' I croak.

Coolabah trees with thick straight trunks throw circles of shade on the ground. The grasses are greener here, and the low scrubby plants more numerous. Handsome glossy cows—cream, russet and chocolate brown—look up cautiously up as we pass. Many have calves by their sides.

Matts slows even more. 'Ray,' he says, 'look up ahead.' He points to two white, black and grey birds swooping in front of the car.

'Black-shouldered kites!' Ray exclaims. 'Magnificent!'

Within a few kilometres, Matts checks his odometer and turns off at a nondescript gap in the fence. Driving over a cattle grate, he heads towards a group of grey gums. Cassie's car and another four-wheel drive come into view. A tall, well-built man, dressed in a khaki shirt with sleeves rolled to the elbows, sits on the bonnet and chats to Cassie. He tips his Akubra forward and ties his curly black hair into a bun at the nape of his neck.

'Hello, mate,' he says, as Matts steps out of the car. 'Rory Ablett. Welcome to the marshes. My boss tells me you're a big shot.'

Matts returns Rory's smile as they shake hands. 'Not out here. Thanks for taking us out.'

I'm undoing my seatbelt when Rory crouches and looks through Matts's window. 'Sapphie Brown, right?' His white teeth sparkle. 'Thought it must be you. My niece was in your class a couple of years back.'

'Georgie Ablett? Is Missy your sister?' When I get out of the car, he offers his hand. 'Georgie never stopped talking about her Uncle Rory.'

'Only good stuff, right?'

I laugh. 'Teachers get to hear a lot of things they shouldn't. Missy moved to Brewarrina to be closer to your mum, didn't she?'

'You got it. Georgie still wants to be a teacher because of you.'

'Give her a hug from me. I'm looking forward to seeing Missy at April's wedding.'

After Rory opens the gate marked STRICTLY AUTHORISED ACCESS ONLY, we drive single file along a roughly graded and increasingly soggy road, past hectares of reeds and grasses as tall as the car. There are gums and coolabahs dotted around us, with thick stands of trees in the distance.

Ray leans forward in his seat. 'In the eighteen-twenties, the white settlers followed the river up from Bathurst. When they saw the water stretch out in front of them, they thought they'd found an inland sea.'

We drive away from the reeds onto an expanse of floodplain. Water laps around the tyres of the cars in front. Matts glances at me. He smiles reassuringly as he stops the car.

'There's a mob of emus to your left.'

At least twenty emus sprint across the shallows, their strong and sturdy legs supporting thickly feathered bodies, long straight necks and small heads with broad dark beaks. Silver spray shoots into the air behind them. Smaller birds, adolescents and larger chicks, run along behind.

I unbuckle my belt and rest my arms on the dashboard to watch, only straightening again when there's nothing left of the emus but a blur in the distance.

I turn and smile at Ray. 'They looked like they were running through a cloud.'

He rubs his hands together. 'Over a hundred species of birds can nest here. Wait till you see the eagles, cormorants, brolgas, snipes and spoonbills ...' He recounts the highlights of his visits to the wetlands, interrupting his narrative only to point out birds. He asks us questions and answers them himself. He sets out scenarios and posits solutions. When we turn off the track and follow a path to higher ground, I glance at Matts and smile.

When he smiles back, it's not a formal smile or a fake charming smile or a stiff and censuring smile that doesn't meet his eyes. It's not the world-weary smile he picked up as a teenager, a cynical lift of his lip on one side.

His smile lightens the grey of his eyes and creases the sides of his mouth.

My heart flips.

He smiles again.

U

Watery plains and channels and reed-covered swamps surround the raised clearing where we stop for lunch. Matts and I brought water bottles, sandwiches and fruit from the pub. Cassie, Ray and Rory have thermoses of tea and coffee, as well as their lunchboxes. It's after midday and the temperature has dropped; steely clouds block out the sun and hover low over the wetlands. I take the teabag out of my cup and put it in our rubbish bag before perching next to Cassie on a log.

She blows steam from her coffee. 'I can't believe I've lived within a day of this place most of my life and never been here before.'

'It's like a secret garden.'

Her eyes widen and she points. 'Which ibis is that?'

Long-legged birds with black heads, dark-feathered bodies and long thin legs wade through the water.

'If I were Ray …' I look over my shoulder. Ray is peering through binoculars at a flock of birds flying in formation above us. 'I'd go through the ibis options.' I count on my fingers. 'I'm pretty sure it's not the white ibis, because we get them in the park at

Dubbo and I know what they look like. It could be the glossy ibis, but their feathers are a shiny bronze shade, and I think they have different-shaped bodies to the others. That leaves the third option, the straw-necked ibis.' I tip back my hat. 'I believe the fluffy feathers on the birds' necks clinches the matter, but we could ask Ray for confirmation.'

Cassie laughs. 'Let's leave him in peace with his—' She looks up, trying to identify the birds he's watching.

'I think they might be plumed whistling ducks. Don't quote me, though.'

On the far side of the ibis, hopping in a helter-skelter line, are a small band of grey kangaroos. When the leader stops, the others stop too, their long tails laying flat on the ground behind them. The lead roo lowers his head to graze and the others follow suit.

When I turn back to Cassie, she's looking thoughtfully at Rory and Matts, their heads close together as they study a map. Rory is nodding intently at something Matts is saying. Matts takes a different map out of his backpack, snapping the folds into place before spreading it out. He looks across the wetlands and gestures to the map on Rory's lap.

'He's concerned,' Cassie says quietly, 'isn't he?'

'Things have got much worse in the past few years.'

'Only someone who cared passionately about the environment would do this type of work. The Ramsar connection is prestigious, but I imagine he could make more money doing something else.'

'He seems to spend a lot of time lobbying.'

'Chasing funds from governments that refuse to acknowledge how bad things are and how much worse things could get.' Cassie drains her cup. 'Beneficial outcomes from significant environmental projects are almost impossible to cost. Convincing governments to think long term, let alone challenge established interests or look outside their borders, is inherently difficult.'

'It's all politics, isn't it?'

'A lot of us care about the planet, and in sufficient numbers at grassroots level we can make a difference. But achieving major structural change to climate policy is difficult. Matts plays that game well. He got the briefing to advise the federal government. He's working on the state government via Douglas Chambers.'

'The parks authorities are on side.'

'Which is telling in itself.'

'Doesn't it make sense they want his input?'

'Yes, and no. In the original Ramsar listing, these wetlands were more extensive, and in much better shape in terms of number and diversity of species. Matts's report will not only highlight the decline, but will likely point the finger at what a mess the government, and at times the parks authorities, have made of the rivers and catchments.'

The wetlands below us are a mosaic of swamps and billabongs, reeds, grasses and shrubs. Thick trunked gums grow either side of the channels.

'Matts is worried about the flow of the river,' I say.

'We had good rain last year, but what happens if we don't get rain next year?'

When she holds out her hand, I pass my cup. 'I've always looked at Horseshoe's immediate needs. We have to go beyond that, don't we? We need long-term solutions for the river and the wetlands.'

Cassie glances at Matts again. 'What do you think of him, Sapphie? In a personal sense?'

'I … I'm getting used to him.'

She laughs. 'He made no effort to hide his displeasure at seeing Ray and me at breakfast this morning.' Her brows lift. 'That's unusual. He's generally so self-contained.'

Matts wasn't *always* self-contained when we were growing up. Sometimes, particularly when we spoke about Inge, he found it impossible to hide his emotions. Mr Laaksonen couldn't hear Inge's name without his eyes misting over, so Matts had no chance of talking to his father. Thinking about Inge upset Mum too, but when we were in Buenos Aires, she answered whatever questions he had.

Did Äiti like champagne with strawberries? *Yes, darling, but not as much as I.*

What was her favourite book? *I'm not sure, something Finnish, I think. Her favourite play was* Romeo and Juliet.

Was she happy? *When she was with you, always.*

What about when she was with Isä? *She loved your father very, very much.*

Why don't I have a brother or sister?

Even at twelve and thirteen, I knew about the miscarriages Mum'd had, and I'd told Matts about them. When tears filled Mum's eyes, I put my hand on Matts's arm. 'Shh,' I hissed.

Ignoring me, Mum took Matts's hand. *Had she lived, Inge would have loved another baby.*

Matts nodded stiffly and walked outside to the courtyard. He wiped his eyes with the heel of his hand.

I'd been making gardenia petals and had scraps of white crepe in my pocket. 'You can use this,' I said.

He scrubbed at his eyes.

'It's not a tissue, Kotka. It's crepe paper. You're rubbing much too hard.'

His voice was thick with tears. 'Go back inside, Kissa.'

'No way.' When I threaded my arm through his and leant against him, he found my fingers and linked our hands together.

CHAPTER
34

It's after three by the time Matts and I walk along the track to the cars. We've spent the past two hours in the northern part of the marshes. Ray, Cassie and Rory are ahead of us, Ray searching for the nesting grounds of the intermediate egret, and the others peering into the reeds, hoping to make the sound recording of the barking marsh frog that Hugo requested.

There's a sea of reeds to our left. The long green stems are almost as tall as I am, and the fluffy frond flowers are taller than Matts.

'They look healthy, don't they?' I say.

'They were far more extensive,' Matts says.

'You're disappointed with everything, aren't you?'

'Climate conditions have changed. Without the wetlands, we lose the biodiversity of ecosystems like this. Agriculture and towns will also suffer.'

'The wetlands need more water from the river.'

'And programs to keep the water in the rivers, streams and land for longer.'

Being careful to avoid the mud that claimed Cassie's boot at the last stop, I take hold of a thick glossy stem.

'This is the common reed, isn't it? *Phragmites australis*.'

'Yes.'

I point to our right, where river red gums line up like old friends, their branches gnarly and thick. '*Eucalyptus camaldulenis*.'

'You know a lot.' His expression is serious.

'I know that wetlands are like sponges, soaking up water and hanging on to it, then releasing it gradually downstream.'

'What else?'

'They can improve groundwater quality. They filter out sediments and pollutants. They're nurseries for Ray's birds and other species, like the reptiles Cassie's been searching for all day.'

'Which ones did you see?'

'A goanna with thighs as thick as mine and, thankfully from a distance, a red-bellied black snake.' I take off my hat and loop the strap over my arm. I brush back the hair that sticks to my face and retie my ponytail.

He lifts his hand. Hesitates. But when my eyes stay stuck on his, he brushes my cheek with the backs of his fingers. He collects the hair I've missed and puts it behind my ear. When he smiles, my heart turns backflips.

'Tell me more,' he says.

I take a deep breath. 'Hugo's frogs adapt to wet and dry conditions in the wetlands, but the wetlands should never have been allowed to get as dry as they did. That's why you and Rory are particularly worried about your reeds.' I fiddle with my hat toggle. 'It's also why you were short with Ray, isn't it?'

'He was offended?'

Two flys buzz between us. 'You were blunt.'

When I wave the flies away, Matts captures my hand and studies it. 'Roots in the reed beds should be protected by mud.'

'And there was no mud in the drought.'

'The beds had been here for thousands of years.' He kisses my thumb before releasing my hand. 'Many were lost.'

I put on my hat again. 'Luke is drumming up support with his network, and encouraging others to get involved.' I point to my bag. 'I've taken reams of notes and plenty of photographs. We'll engage with environmental groups and communicate the facts.'

'Do you have flowers in your bag?'

I smile. 'That wasn't what today was about.'

'No?' He grasps a reed. 'What would you make out of these?'

I tip my head to the side as I study his face. 'I could braid them together and make you a wetlands crown.'

'What colour would it be?'

'I think you're asking what shade?' I consider the reed seriously. 'It's more chartreuse and lime green than pistachio and olive green. It's not bottle green or pear. I'd say it's emerald.'

He places his hands on my shoulders, dips his head and looks straight into my eyes. 'Sapphire.'

Sapphire Beresford-Brown. Sapphie Brown.

I start at the rustle in the undergrowth. A small brown snake, its diamond skin a mosaic of tan and mocha, slithers out of the reeds.

'Oh!'

Matts squeezes my shoulders. 'The sun's going down. We'd better get back.'

'When I get home ...' I blow out a breath. 'I have to move my stuff and find somewhere for my horses and—'

He runs a thumb along my chin. 'Are you going to cry again?'

I sniff. 'I hardly ever cried before you turned up.'

'Friday week I see Robert.'

'My father won't budge.'

The touch of Matts's mouth on mine is soft and sweet and sensual all at once. It's a tender, thoughtful, toe-curling kiss. A spiky bolt of heat shoots straight to my heart.

We're standing next to a swamp. We're sticky with sunblock and insect repellent. He doesn't belong in Horseshoe. He's arrogant and bossy and protective.

I might have fallen in love with him.

'Matts? Have you invited anyone to dinner tonight? Mr Chambers, perhaps? Or Ray?'

'No.'

I'm not a child any more, standing back and deferring to him. I'm not fifteen either, missing out on kisses I should have seen coming. I take hold of his shirt and stand on my toes and, when he wraps his arms around me, I kiss him firmly on the mouth. I slide my hands over his chest and find the skin at this throat. His pulse beats quickly like mine. When I touch his lip with my tongue, he groans.

Our breaths are uneven when he pulls back a little. He talks against my mouth. 'Early dinner. Bed.'

A gust of wind blows through the reeds, whistling and whispering secrets.

Ray calls out, 'Come along, slowcoaches!'

Matts lifts his head and mutters. 'Send him back with Cassie.'

'No.' I tidy his collar. 'Even though Ray doesn't approve of your swearing, his feelings would be hurt if he didn't get a lift back to Wilson with you.'

When we see the others, we're walking so close that we could be hand in hand. Rory, grinning broadly, looks up from his phone and puts it in his pocket.

He slaps Matts on the back. 'We'd better get going, mate.'

'Where to?'

'Four days of sodden boots, snakes, leeches and mozzies. But first, we pick up a shitload of gear and get a few hours' sleep.'

Cassie smiles. 'What Rory is communicating, Matts, is that your kayaking trip has been brought forward.'

My backpack is suddenly heavy. I drop it at my feet. 'What's going on?'

'It's drier out here than I thought it'd be,' Rory says. 'There's no rain forecast, so by next month the water levels will drop even more. I didn't think I'd get the go-ahead straight away.' He pats the phone in his pocket. 'But my boss called. The landowners and parks authorities have okayed an expedition up north.'

Matts glances at me. 'Sapphie and I had plans. Can she come?'

I bounce on my toes like Mary would. 'I'm not too keen on snakes, but who is? I'd need to borrow gear, but I'm way stronger than I look. I'm fit and—'

Rory holds up a hand. 'I've got no worries with you hiking and sleeping rough, Sapphie, but the kayaking is a killer. They're one-man boats, loaded with gear, and a lot of the time we'll be dragging them through reed beds to find paths through the channels. How do you reckon you'd go? You got runs on the board in a swamp?'

I tip my hat further forward to shadow my face. 'I've kayaked once, and that was on a lake. I got blisters on my blisters.'

'The kayaks are heavy, they have to be.'

'Could I do some of the trip?'

'The wetlands are a shocker to negotiate, and we'll be way off route. I can't see how that'd work.'

'Sapphie?' Matts puts his hand on my arm. 'We could delay this until—'

'No.' I pick up my bag and smile bravely. 'You can't delay it. And it's not like I was expecting to go on a kayaking trip anyway.'

'Why don't you join me?' Cassie says, walking to my side and smiling encouragingly. 'I'll be touring the river for the next few days. I plan to get back to Dubbo on Friday.'

A goanna, a metre long at least, scampers from under Matts's car and runs on short stiff legs towards the reed beds. Ray stares through binoculars at the birds that fly overhead. Matts looks from Rory to Cassie.

'Give us five minutes.'

'I'll get my things out of your car.'

I'm leaning over the tailgate when Matts reaches past my shoulder and drags my bag towards us. As I take the handle, he puts his hand over mine.

'Sapphie? I can ask Rory to put it back a day.'

'So we can have dinner together?' I lean against him. It's not the time or place for lust, but I feel it from my head to my toes. 'We can do that when you get back.'

He puts his chin on my shoulder. 'Fuck.'

I smile. 'Don't let Ray hear you.'

His lips move softly on my neck. 'What about the roads? I could drive you home tonight.'

'I have to face my fears, remember? I'll go with Cassie. I'll be fine.'

'I've got meetings scheduled from Friday night until the following Friday, when I meet with Robert. I won't be back in Horseshoe until Saturday week.'

'You don't have to—'

He spins me around. His eyes narrow. 'Saturday week.'

One of his buttons is undone. He draws in a breath as I fasten it. 'I know my father, Matts. He won't change his mind.'

'Let me try.'

'I'll be at the farmhouse in the morning. I have April's wedding in the afternoon.'

'If I have reception while I'm here, I'll call you.'

Ray smiles and waves when he catches my eye over Matts's shoulder. I check Matts's other buttons. All done up.

'You'll be careful, won't you? Don't get bitten by a snake.'

He kisses my mouth. 'Don't take risks.'

What about a risk on you? 'Cassie is a very careful driver.'

Rory's four-wheel drive, engine running, waits at the edge of the clearing. Matts's car pulls up alongside him as I throw my bag into the back of Cassie's car.

Ray climbs into the middle seat and does up his belt. 'Off we go, ladies!' he says.

Cassie, sitting behind the wheel, hides a smile as I climb into the passenger seat. 'We'll say a sad farewell to Ray when we leave him behind in Wilson,' she says, 'and then we'll head down south.'

'You sure it's okay that I tag along?'

She laughs. 'Thelma and Louise, eat your heart out!'

CHAPTER
35

On the far side of the riverbank is a scribbly bark gum with a pale pearly trunk. A flock of cockatoos with bright yellow crests fly into the branches and line up in rows like Christmas tree lights.

'Ray would be impressed,' I say.

Cassie, sitting next to me on the ground, smiles gently. 'I think he would.'

'I learnt a lot from Ray. I think I'll invite him to be a guest of the committee in February, at our next formal meeting. Rory might come as well. It'd be great if I could get him to talk to the senior kids about all he gets up to.'

'Good idea.'

It's Friday, my final day on the road with Cassie. Last night we stayed at a town in the mountains where the Macquarie River begins its journey north. This morning, we've hiked three hours down a track to photograph the river. The air is alive with birdcalls.

The water gurgles as it tumbles over rocks. The sky above us is a washed-out turquoise blue.

'It's lovely,' I say, 'but I have to get back.'

'What? You don't like my driving?'

'Your driving is great.' Cassie is almost as sensitive to my anxieties on the road as Matts, and she's been kind in other ways as well. The controversy with the deposit box has been in the papers all week, but she hasn't mentioned it since I told her I'd rather not talk about it.

She puts her hand on my arm. 'I was teasing you, Sapphie. You'll be missing your home.'

'And Tumbleweed and my horses.'

I've also missed Matts—more than I would ever have thought possible. Does 'more' mean a long-term commitment? How many risks am I prepared to take?

Cassie picks up her hat. 'You called Mrs Hargreaves last night, didn't you? But not Matts?'

The cockatoos, screeching and squawking, lift in unison and fly from the tree. 'I'd spoken to him the night before last.'

'When I wanted to leave you in peace, you blocked the door.'

'It was after ten by the time he got mobile reception, and you were wearing a nightie. You could have frozen to death outside. Anyway, we only talked about the wetlands. It wasn't a private conversation.'

'I've never heard a more stilted one.'

I scrape the heels of my boots down the bank, making two shallow channels. 'We'll have dinner together when he's back from Canberra.'

She laughs. 'Finally an acknowledgement. What's going on with you two?'

'It's a very long story.'

She bends to retie her laces. 'Dot points will do.'

I rest my chin on my knees. 'Matts and I knew each other when we were growing up. I hadn't seen him for over eight years but then he turned up in Horseshoe.'

'You became reacquainted?'

'I like him … a lot. But I don't know what will happen. We're very different. I'm local and he's global.'

'You have a common interest in the environment.'

'You like him too, don't you?'

She laughs. 'He's so *Finnish*. Never has a man used so few words so darned attractively. You could do worse.'

'You sound like Ma. He's good-looking, eligible and smart. Is that all it takes?'

'It's not a bad start. And don't forget, you happen to share those attributes.'

I stand and brush dirt from my jeans. 'You live happily on your own. Why do I need something different?'

When she holds out her hands, I pull her to her feet. 'How old are you now?' she asks.

'Almost twenty-eight.'

'By your age, I'd ruled family life out. I don't think you have.'

Serious little children with dark hair that lightens in sunshine.

'Maybe not.'

'You not only chose teaching as a career, you spend weekends with the region's delinquents. Despite your own childhood, and it can't have been an easy one or you'd never have been placed with the Hargreaves, you love children. You'd have to.'

'I'd like my own children, but I have to be careful.'

'In what way?'

I'm in love with him, but…

'I want to end up where I should have started out in the first place.'

'If that means what I think it does …' She smiles as she touches my arm. 'You'll get what you want, Sapphie. I'm certain of it.'

We're still two hours away from the car when we see a dark shape on the track. The path is narrow, winding between a steep and heavily treed slope on one side, and a tall sandstone cliff on the other. Cassie, walking in front of me, breaks into a run.

'Oh my god!'

A man, a climber with a harness and helmet, lies on his side. 'Help me,' he moans. 'My leg.'

The man's tibia, the main bone in the lower leg, is not only broken but has pushed through the skin. Red-rust blood stains his leg from his knee to his ankle and seeps into the ground. His face is whiter than white.

Cassie kneels next to him and takes off her backpack. She runs her hands over his upper body. 'What's your name?'

'Damien.'

'My name's Cassie,' she says. 'And Sapphie's here too. We'll get help. You're going to be fine.'

I take out my phone. 'There's no reception.'

Cassie grimaces. 'We lost it hours ago.'

'How is he really?' I whisper.

Not good, she mouths.

I kneel on Damien's other side as Cassie pushes up his shorts and wraps her jacket around his leg.

'Can I take off his helmet?'

'Try not to move him as you do it.'

His eyelids flicker. He's only young, maybe early twenties. He moans again. He passes out.

'He must've have been here for hours,' Cassie says. 'He's cold, the blood …'

I touch his arm. 'He's gone so still.' I take off my jacket and lay it over his chest.

Cassie looks around. 'Shit.'

There's still plenty of light, but the sun is lower than it was, the tree cover is dense and the shadows are darkening. The cliff is around fifteen metres tall, but I glimpse a railing at the top.

'The road's up there somewhere. He probably abseiled from the carpark.' I stand to take a better look. Midway down the cliff is a narrow ledge. Beneath it, the cliff slopes sharply inwards. 'His rope might have snagged.'

Cassie takes Damien's wrist and feels for his pulse. She frowns as she checks the pulse at his throat. 'It's slowing.'

I unlace my boots. 'Right, then.'

'What are you doing?'

'Running flat out, it'll take well over an hour to get to the road.' I tug off my boots and stuff them in my backpack as I face the cliff. 'I can climb much quicker.'

'Without all your gear?'

I carefully study the wall. Further along the path from where the climber fell, the cliff is vertical, but only for four or five metres. There are pockets and outcrops, footholds and edges. Above the vertical section is what looks like an ironstone seam that bisects the sandstone. If I can follow the crevice the seam has created, it'd get me much higher, to the trees where the angle of the cliff eases off. I should be able to scramble up the incline from there. It's a bit risky, but …

I glance at Damien, lying so still. 'I don't see why not.'

I haven't climbed a natural rock wall for a couple of months at least. I stretch out my hands, my arms and shoulders, willing them to loosen up quickly. I lean my hands against the cliff and warm up my Achilles and hamstrings as I picture where I'll place my hands and feet.

'Please take care, Sapphie.'

I smile reassuringly. 'I'll be fine.'

I'm unfamiliar with this climb, but the techniques for an out-door climb are similar to those I teach the kids who climb at the youth centre. Hips close to the wall. Rely on your legs and rest your arms. Keep your balance and find a rhythm. Three points of contact when you can. By the time I reach the seam, I'm sweaty and dirty with aching fingers and a scrape on my elbow.

I wedge a foot between the ironstone and sandstone. I find a ridge for one hand and a crack for the other. Following the crevice is easier and quicker than climbing the cliff, but two metres from the trees I dislodge a clump of dirt and my foot slips off the edge.

I don't watch the scatter of stones tumble, but I hear Cassie swear and call out. I close my eyes and breathe deeply, taking twelve more steps before clinging onto a tree branch and swinging to the ground at the top of the cliff. My legs give out and I sit, relatively secure in a tangle of tree roots.

'I'm fine, Cassie!'

My sock is shredded, exposing a rough and bloodied scrape across the inside of my foot. I press remnants of sock against the skin. The scratches aren't too deep, but extend across the arch to my toes. To keep my balance on the steeply sloping ground, I loop an arm around a root as I take my boots from my bag, prying the laces open as wide as they'll go. My eyes water when the roughness of the leather scrapes against my skin.

It's only as I bend over my boot to tie the lace that I notice my hands. A scraped knuckle and two nails split to the quick. My little finger is sore and stiff.

It could be worse.

I'm no use to Damien if I get lost, so I create a route through the undergrowth of ferns and grasses, spiked bushes and fallen branches, in a direct line to the road. I put my hands on my knees and draw breath before following the railing to the layby. Cassie's car is there, as is a beaten-up Subaru. I look at my phone again, holding it up as if that might make a difference. Still no reception.

But I've already worked out what I have to do. Cassie has hidden her key between the back bumper and tow bar of her car all week. I find it immediately, open the doors, sit behind the wheel and push back the seat. I check my phone again.

Nothing.

My heart is racing. My chest is tight. I feel nauseous. And all of that is related to adrenaline. Which is all related to fear. I have to push past the anxiety. I fasten my belt, turn on the ignition, release the handbrake and put the car into gear. I check my mirrors, indicate left and pull out onto the road.

Ambulance and paramedics. Fire and rescue officers. Police. Helicopter.

Damien is airlifted to Sydney for surgery. Not long afterwards, the rescue team winch Cassie up the cliff. I drove safely to the top of the hill, but once I'd called for help I didn't think I should push my luck by driving back down again. I left her car where it was and ran down the incline to the carpark.

'Could you give us a lift to Cassie's car?' I ask the police officer. 'It's only two or three kilometres.'

He grunts. 'How about to a hospital?'

I try not to hobble so much. 'I think my foot has swollen up. Other than that, it's—'

'I'll escort you to the Emergency Department.' He puts his hands on his hips. 'Bathurst or Dubbo?'

'Thank you, Constable.' Cassie firmly takes my arm. 'We'll follow you to Dubbo.'

From: Cassie
To: Sapphie, Chambers, Luke, Gus, Matts
You might have heard the news reports. Sapphie is sore but comfortable at Dubbo Base Hospital ED.

My arms and legs, protected by my shirt and pants, have minor scratches. The scrapes on my hands and elbow have been thoroughly cleaned and neatly patched with tape. We've been in the Emergency Department for a couple of hours, me on a bed and Cassie on a chair close by. Whenever a nurse or doctor pushes aside the curtain, Cassie starts and her eyes spring open.

'You're exhausted,' I say once again. 'I'm worried about you. Please go home.'

She points to my foot, raised high on a pillow. 'They won't let you leave until you have an X-ray.'

'If I'd broken a bone or if it was fractured, the pain would be much worse. It's a few superficial cuts and a minor sprain, I'm sure of it. I've promised Pa Hargreaves I'll call him after the X-ray. He's waiting by the phone and he'll pick me up.'

The curtain pulls aside. 'I'll stay with her.'

Cassie looks up but I don't need to.

When he was pushed from the wharf and cut his chin, I gave him my blue cotton hat to press against his wound and we went to the hospital together.

Two stitches down, four stitches across.

CHAPTER
36

It's only been four days, but his face is much more tanned than it was. He has a series of faint scratches on the side of his face, as if a tree branch has swiped him. His sleeves are rolled up. He has bites on his arms. His boots are muddy. His clothes are dusty.

'Sapphie.'

He walks past Cassie's chair to the bed. He lowers his head and kisses my mouth. He looks from one of my hands to the other. Two fingers on my right hand are taped together so he takes the left one. I squeeze his hand tightly as he runs his fingers over my knuckles. He glances at my foot.

'The Emergency Department?' he says quietly. 'What the fuck?'

'I thought you were going to Canberra.'

He shakes his head. 'I'll get you home first.'

One hour and two X-rays later, a young nurse with hazel eyes and sea-green eyeliner patches the broken skin on the inside of my foot and straps it up. She insists on pushing me in a wheelchair to the patient pick-up area. 'You'll have plenty of opportunities to hop next week.'

When Matts's car, filthy with mud and spattered with bugs, appears around the bend, I hold onto the arm of the chair and stand. 'Thank you very much,' I say to the nurse.

As I limp slowly to the kerb, Matts slams the door and strides around the car. 'I asked you to wait.'

'My foot is bruised, not broken. I'm fine to—'

'Kissa,' he mutters, holding my arm as I climb up to the seat. 'Shut up.' He hands me my seatbelt before shutting the door.

I'm fastening my belt when he gets behind the wheel. He glances at me. And then he jumps out of the car.

When he opens my door again, I twist in my seat and face him. 'Matts? What's the—'

He steps onto the running board and leans against my legs. My hair, pulled into a ponytail for the hundredth time today, sits untidily over my shoulder. He runs the strands through his fingers and smooths out the tangles. His jaw is clenched. His eyes are dark.

'Don't ever shut up,' he finally says. 'I want you to talk.'

I put my hands on his chest and feel for his heartbeat, then speak through a yawn. 'I'm a bit tired for talking.'

He leans across me and checks my belt. 'Horseshoe.'

It's almost midnight. There are no other cars in the hospital laneway, but before we turn onto the side road, I glance at Matts. He pulls over and switches on the hazards. He carefully takes my hand.

'Cassie said you drove her car.'

'I had to.'

'The climber had a transfusion on the track.'

'He's only twenty-one.' My voice breaks.

'You saved him.'

'Could Mum have been saved?'

I don't know where the words come from. I'm not sure he does either, because he stills before lifting our hands. His eyes stay on mine as he kisses the base of my thumb.

'Not that night.'

'She would have been scared when she saw the headlights.'

'Not for long, Sapphie.'

I'm sitting in a car with my seatbelt done up. But when I close my eyes, for the first time in months, I don't see an image of my mother, cheeks wet with tears and stained with mascara, staring back.

She's wearing a royal blue dress with apple red buttons and sitting on a bench in a park in Buenos Aires. Matts and I are probably too old to be on the swings, but we're swinging so high that our feet touch the sky. I think it's spring or early summer because there are fresh green leaves on the deciduous trees and scented yellow flowers on the rosebushes. One of the flowers drops to the ground and Mum picks it up. The inner petals are soft and velvety; the outer petals are faded and dry.

Perfect imperfection.

'Sapphie?' Matts squeezes my hand and puts it back in my lap. 'Are you ready to go?'

'Yes.'

He puts the car into gear and pulls out. The indicator clicks when we turn onto the highway. As the car accelerates into darkness, I lean against the headrest. My eyes flutter closed.

'Yes.'

U

'Sapphie.' I'm in the car but the engine is off and my door is open. Matts stands next to me and unclips my belt. 'We're at the schoolhouse.'

'I must have gone to sleep.' My head is filled with clouds of cotton wool. When I rest my face on his chest, he winds an arm around me and pulls me close. I yawn and close my eyes again. 'This is nice.' I sniff. 'You smell of mud.'

'You smell of hospital.' He rubs his cheek on my head. 'Should I carry you?'

'Let's stay here.'

The flyscreen door creaks on its hinges. 'Bob!' Ma Hargreaves calls out. 'They're home.'

I lift my head. Blink. 'Still asleep.'

'Do I carry you?'

'No, thank you.' When I shuffle to the edge of the seat, my hands are stiff and clumsy. My foot doesn't want to come with me. I shift position, lose my balance and pitch forward.

Matts grasps me by the waist and hauls me back to the seat. He turns me and lifts, putting one arm under my shoulder blades and another behind my knees. 'I'll carry you.'

As soon as Matts steps over the threshold, Tumbleweed stalks out of the kitchen and wipes his brindle stripes against his legs.

'Bring her through here, love,' Ma Hargreaves says. 'I'll put her to bed.'

Matts sits me carefully on the end of the bed, making sure I'm steady before letting me go.

'Ma?' I yawn. 'I want to have a shower, but I'm not allowed to wet my foot.'

'Where do you keep your plastic bags?'

'I don't have any.'

She looks concerned for a moment. 'Bob will work something out.'

When Pa finds a roll of bubble wrap in his van, I wind it around my foot, prop myself against the wall in the shower, soap my body and wash my hair. My cream silk pyjamas are laid out on the bed when I come out of the bathroom. I sit on the end of the bed where Matts put me earlier, and button up the short-sleeved top. Through the closed door, I hear every word.

'Sapphie should stay with us,' Pa says.

'No, Bob,' Ma says. 'She'll want to sleep in her own bed.'

'She can sleep in the bed in her old bedroom.'

'What? When Matts insists on staying and has offered to take the couch?'

'I'm warning you, lad,' Pa says, 'Hugo hates that couch.'

'I can sleep anywhere,' Matts says.

'It can't be too uncomfortable,' Ma says. 'Or Hugo wouldn't keep coming back.'

'We have two spare rooms, Fiona. I can't see why they can't both bunk with—'

'Come along, Bob. It's past time we went to our own beds.'

I shout through the door, 'Thank you for everything. Sorry to worry you and to keep you up so late. I'll see you tomorrow.'

'Sleep tight, love.'

On my third attempt to push my bandaged foot through the leg of my pyjama shorts, I miss completely and my heel hits the floor.

'Damn!'

'Sapphie.' Matts taps on the door. 'Can I come in?'

I sigh. 'Yes.'

He opens the door and glances at my shorts. He kneels in front of me and takes my hands. 'You're tired, kultsi. Let me do it.'

'What does "kultsi" mean?'

'Gold.'

'Why would you call me that?'

'It's a name.'

I look at him suspiciously. 'What type of name?'

He lifts a shoulder. 'An endearment.'

'Oh.' I study our hands. 'Kultainen means golden, doesn't it?'

'You remembered that?'

Tumbleweed walks through the door. 'Did you meet my housemate?'

When Tumbleweed sits next to Matts and looks up at him adoringly, Matts scratches under his chin. 'He likes me.'

'He's cross with me because I went away.'

'He's old, isn't he?'

'I found him before I left Canberra.'

When I fish for my shorts with my good foot, Matts picks them up. Without looking at me once, he eases the legs over my feet. When the shorts reach my thighs, he helps me to stand on my good leg so I can pull them up.

'Thank you.'

He turns away. 'Can I use the shower?'

'There are clean towels in the rack near the sink. The toilet is outside at the end of the path.'

He rubs around the back of his neck. 'Mrs Hargreaves showed me.'

His shirt is hanging out of his pants at one side. He grasps the fabric and pulls, freeing the rest.

CHAPTER
37

I'm lying on my bed facing the window when he walks out of the bathroom. I don't need to turn around to know he's standing between the door and me.

'Sapphie?' His voice is gruff. 'Should I turn out the light?'

'You can fit here too.'

'No.'

I roll onto my back and, taking care of my bandaged foot, push myself into a sitting position. I stretch out my sore leg, bend the other and lean against the headboard. I look up.

Swallow.

His hair is wet. His T-shirt is black and sticks to his skin. His chest is broad, his hips narrow. His boxer shorts are darkest blue.

Prussian, indigo, dusk, cobalt.

Steel.

I pull my gaze away. 'If you won't sleep here,' I say, 'I'll take the couch. That's what I usually do with Hugo.'

'You don't sleep together.'

'No way.'

He takes a deep breath and sits on the end of the bed. 'Only with strangers.'

'I want …' I blow out a breath. 'I slept with you when we stayed at the pub.'

His eyes narrow. 'So you do sleep with friends?'

'Only you.'

He wraps his fingers around my ankle. 'You're not good on the phone, are you?'

'No.'

'But I am your friend?'

I'm pretty sure I'm in love with you. 'Yes.'

He looks pointedly at my foot. 'You're hurt.'

The doona cover is white with a floral pattern woven into the fabric. I trace around the flowers.

Parchment, cornsilk, antique, vanilla.

'I'll go straight to sleep.'

He stands and walks to the door. I see the tension in his shoulders and his fists.

'Matts? I promise.'

As he turns, he grabs the hem of his T-shirt and yanks it over his head, folding it in half before rolling it into a ball and throwing it into the corner of the room.

'This is how I sleep.'

His nipples are flat and brown. His abdominal muscles are clearly defined. He switches off the light and slams the door with his heel. He lies flat on his back as I wriggle down the bed from the bedhead. I hold my arms close to my sides and count slowly to ten. A breeze whispers through the leaves of the gums in the playground.

'Do you remember when we looked at the leaf through your microscope?'

'Yes.'

'You told me how levels of evaporation let some trees survive better than others.'

'Drought-tolerant plants release less moisture.'

'The roots have a role as well, don't they?'

He turns his head on the pillow. 'Why are you asking these questions?'

'Do you know the answer, or not?'

'Roots can shrink and lose contact with the soil to minimise water loss.' He bends his knee and then lays it flat. 'In drought, some plants form an embolism.'

'What?'

'It's a bubble of gas. It stops water flow and allows the plant to live longer.' He bends his knee again. 'Is that enough?'

I roll onto my side and face him. 'You said you'd like me to talk.'

He grunts. 'Go to sleep.'

I washed the curtains after I moved to the schoolhouse and they shrank in length and width. During the day, sunbeams stream through the gaps. Moonbeams and starlight filter through at night. Matts's profile is clear. A lock of hair has fallen on his forehead. His nose is straight, his jaw is strong. When I walked from the farmhouse on the night he arrived, there was a half moon hidden by clouds.

I smother a gasp but not quickly enough.

'Sapphie?' Matts comes up on an elbow. 'Do you need a pain-killer? What's the matter?'

'It's …' I clear my throat. 'The farmhouse. I have to work things out.'

He touches my shoulder. 'Wait, Sapphie. Next week I'll see Robert.'

I press my hand over his mouth. 'Not now.' My hand slips to his jaw. When he leans against me, I feel the movement of his chest against my breasts. He smells of my soap, but the scent is different on him. His hair near his ear is damp and cool.

When I lift my head off the pillow, he puts a hand behind it. His other hand trails over my shoulder and down my side to my hip.

My body warms. I ache with need. And, even in night's monochrome, I see colours. The darkness of his lashes when he closes his eyes. The warm hints of gold in his hair. The blush of his mouth. His skin glows silver in the moonlight.

At first our kisses are tender, as if we're afraid that we'll lose what we've found. But as the heat builds, our tongues search more deeply. I'm breathless with need. He shakes with restraint.

I trace the line of his shoulder and the ridges of his sternum and ribs. I feel the strength in his muscles and the texture of his skin. I try to pull him closer. He resists.

'Please, Matts.'

'I want you, Sapphie. So long.'

I lift my bandaged foot and rest it on his thigh. 'Yes.'

He lifts his head. 'Fuck.' His arms stiffen. He swallows. 'Can't.'

He's drawing away when I push with all my weight and roll him onto his back. My leg drapes over his hips; his erection presses against the inside of my thigh.

'Define "can't".'

'You know what I want.'

I lay my head on his chest. 'Trust?'

'I told the Hargreaves I'd look after you.'

I tighten my arm around his body. 'You think Ma would mind this?' When I look up, he gently pushes hair from my face. 'She didn't give you sheets for the couch, did she? She didn't offer you a pillow?'

'Hospital.' He runs a finger under my eye.

'Are you sick?'

When he doesn't respond, I push against his chest until I'm sitting.

'You promised,' he says gruffly.

'I promised I'd go to sleep and I will.' I straddle him, take his wrists and press them down on the pillows. 'After you've kissed me goodnight.'

'Sapphie …'

'If you try to get free you might hurt my foot or my fingers, and you'd never do that.'

'You know me this well?'

I release his arms. 'We're friends.'

His erection is long and hard against my back. When I sit a little straighter and wriggle, he moans. He holds my hips tightly. 'Not fair.'

'Your sentences are very short.'

He pulls my head down and kisses me, looping his tongue around mine and stealing my breath. He runs his hands up my thighs. He follows the hemlines of my shorts with the tips of his fingers.

'Sapphie.'

I stretch out my legs so I'm lying on top of him. 'I like that name much better.'

We roll onto our sides with our heads on one pillow. I stroke his hair, the stubble on his jaw, his mouth. He traces my lips.

'Beautiful,' he says.

When I hold his thumb and gently bite the pad, he groans and runs his hand down my arm to my waist. He lowers his head to my breast but when I stiffen, he hesitates.

'Only this one,' he mumbles.

'Yes.'

He plays with my nipple through my top, stroking and teasing. I arch my back; sink into the warmth of his touch and the heat of his body. He puts his hands inside my shorts and undies and cups my bottom.

'Sapphie?'

I draw back a little. 'Matts.'

His voice is not quite steady. 'We can stop now.'

'Why?'

'I didn't want to …' He shudders a breath. 'You aren't …'

'What? Experienced enough for you?'

'Fuck,' he mutters. 'Fuck.'

I put a hand against his face. 'I haven't done this for ages, and even when I did … I'm not on the pill or anything like that.'

He growls as he rolls me over, laying me on my back. He looks over his shoulder to check where my foot is before pinning me down with a leg. He kisses me again while he strokes my stomach and hips. He draws shapes on the insides of my thighs—circles and ovals and paisleys. When I press against his hand, moaning my need, his fingertips slip inside my shorts. He's gentle and teasing then firm and possessive. His breaths become harsh as he nuzzles my neck and kisses my breast. He licks and sucks through the fabric.

'Sapphie?'

'Mmm.'

He frowns as if he's lost his train of thought. And then he remembers. 'I want more.'

'What does that mean?'

He pulls off his boxers and throws them onto the floor. 'Long term.'

Helsinki?

Geneva?

Horseshoe?

'But—'

'Long term.'

I smooth the crease between his brows. 'Yes.'

When I lift my bottom, he eases my shorts and undies down my legs. His chest is firm, his stomach flat. I stroke his erection and he groans. He covers my hand.

His voice is strained. 'You're sure?'

You asked me to trust you.

I love you.

'Yes.'

He rummages in his toiletries bag before coming back to bed. We sit side by side, arm against arm and thigh against thigh, as he rolls on a condom. He glances uncertainly at my foot before lying on his back and positioning me carefully on top.

He runs his hands over my shoulders. He cups my breast over my pyjama top. 'You're beautiful, Sapphie.'

I push back his hair. Trace the contours of his face.

He looks into my eyes as he plays where we join. I rock slowly back and forth as I take him in. His skin is slick, he clings to my hips.

I grasp his arms and his shoulders. The slide of our bodies. The press of our tongues. Desperate, caring, tender and rough. It's new and frightening, wild and fierce. Our breaths are harsh as we search for release.

The tightrope snaps.

Our colours explode.

Orchid, fuchsia, cherry and ruby.

I moan and taste salt on his skin. He follows my lead in a shuddering rush.

Afterwards, his kisses are lazy but deep. I lie against his body and he drapes a leg across my back. He pushes hair off my face and twists it around his wrist. He holds me up by my shoulders as he studies my mouth.

'What?'

His lip lifts. 'Beautiful.'

I slump against his chest again. 'Mmm.'

He shadows me when we walk to the outhouse, but scoops me up and carries me on the way back. I rub my cheek against his shoulder. 'You can do this just this once.'

When we go back to bed he strips off again before pulling me into his arms. He runs his hands over my body and kisses my head. 'Long term,' he mutters.

I sink into his body. The hardness and softness. The colours and shades. The scent of his skin and the deep steady beats of his heart.

CHAPTER
38

Matts lies on his side behind me—his arm warm and heavy on my waist. His forearm is between my breasts and his hand is held tightly in mine. Moonlight casts shadows on the walls and in the mirror that stands in the corner of the room.

Long term.

I haven't had relationships that last much more than a weekend. Does long term mean the months that he's here—or something else?

I love him.

He breathes gently against my back. I lift his hand and kiss his thumb. 'We'll sort things out when you wake up,' I whisper.

He nuzzles through my hair and kisses my neck. 'Sapphie,' he mumbles.

'Shh.' I stroke the soft hairs on his arm and he goes back to sleep.

My foot aches. I should ice it.

When I slip out of his arms and wriggle to the edge of the bed, he mutters, but then he quietens again. I don't think he'd mind if I stared at him naked, but I draw the sheet over him and pick up my pyjama shorts.

'I'll be back soon.'

He rolls onto his back as I hop to the door, but by the time I peek through the crack, he's fallen asleep again.

As I hobble across the living room, Tumbleweed uncurls from the couch. He follows me through the kitchen door and waits by the fridge, rubbing against my legs as I take out the milk and fill his bowl. I sit on a stool at the kitchen bench and rest my foot on another stool, positioning the icepack on my instep. My phone is on the bench.

Cassie has sent a message.

From: Cassie
To: Sapphie, Chambers, Luke, Gus, Matts
Confirming Sapphie is back in Horseshoe. I'll circulate draft blog posts and press releases by the end of the weekend.

There's a text from a number my phone doesn't recognise.

Dear Sapphie. I hope that you are well. Did you receive my email of two days ago? Regards, Gabriel Garcia

My heart flutters nervously as I open my laptop.

Dear Sapphie,

I have been called to give evidence to the inquiry into the Hernandez group of companies. My legal representatives inform me it is likely I will be questioned about the deposit box linked to your parents. If this is the case, I will be forced to reveal more about this matter than I would wish.

As I have returned to Argentina, could we speak by video call? May I call at 8pm on Monday evening (Sydney time)?

I request that, for now, communications between us remain confidential. Involving others, specifically your father and Matts Laaksonen, would complicate matters and could cause harm. You will understand my dilemma after we speak.

Kind regards,

Gabriel

By the time I've read the email for the tenth time, Tumbleweed is sitting on my lap and the icepack has softened. I hold my cat to my chest as I hop two steps to the freezer and open the door.

Tumbleweed settles back in my lap as I sit at the bench again.

Gabriel,

Thanks for you messages. It's early Saturday morning here. Could we talk earlier? If not, I'll speak to you on Monday night.

Sapphie

He responds immediately.

Dear Sapphie,

This is the earliest time I can arrange. I'll call by Skype on Monday.

Kind regards,

Gabriel

When I silently open the door, Matts, still lying on his back, looks directly into my eyes. Dawn creeps through the gaps beneath the curtains, casting soft golden stripes across the sheets. A rooster crows the morning.

'Sorry. Did I wake you?'

He sits and holds out his hand. 'What's wrong?'

Matts has a sixth sense about Sapphire.

I push the thought out of my head, aiming for a smile as I sit on the side of the bed. I take his hand. 'You always think something is wrong.'

You will understand my dilemma after we speak.

My father has blamed Mum. If I tried to defend her, things could get worse. Sending a child to pick up drugs. There's no defence to that. I can't turn my back on the one person who hasn't condemned my mother. I owe it to her to listen to what Gabriel has to say.

After that, I'll tell Matts everything.

'You loved Mum too, didn't you?'

'Yes.' He puts hair behind my ear. 'You were a long time.'

'I iced my foot.'

He hesitates. 'I heard you typing.'

'I checked my emails.' I sandwich his hand between both of mine. 'My foot's a little stiff.'

'But that's not what's worrying you. What is it, Sapphie?'

'You didn't approve of what my father did, did you? Talking to the media?'

He turns his hand and captures both of mine. 'They're not likely to clear Kate. You know that?'

I pull my hands free. 'Even if she did take a bribe, I want to know the truth.' I inch away when he reaches for me.

'Don't, Sapphie.'

I clear my throat as I fold my hands neatly in my lap. 'You want me to trust you, don't you?'

'Yes.'

'There are some things I don't want to tell you, but that doesn't mean ...' I undo the bottom button of my shirt. 'I can show you this.'

He puts his hand over mine. 'That's not about trust, Sapphie. You don't have to show me anything.'

'You don't want me to?' My voice is too high. My fingers tremble under his.

He closes his eyes and when he opens them, I can't read them at all. He's frowning and tense and ...

'I don't know what you want,' I whisper.

'I want you.'

A tight knot of need unfurls in my heart. When I kiss his mouth, he groans and kisses back. I put my hands on his chest and pull back a little.

'I want to get this over with.'

I undo the next button and then two more. When I reach the top button, I fumble.

He covers my hand. 'You've told me how you were hurt. I don't care about the rest.'

My breasts are still hidden. 'How do you know that?'

He pulls me down so my head is on the pillow. His tongue strokes and caresses and curls around mine. The kiss is possessive. He gathers me closer, his erection pressed between us. He runs his hands across my shoulders, his touches whisper soft. I'm warm and needy, aroused.

He rolls me onto my back again. Keeping his eyes on my face, he puts his hands inside my pyjama top and trails his fingertips down my sides.

I freeze.

He buries his face in my hair and talks against my neck. 'Tell me how to touch you.'

I swallow. 'That was okay.'

His palms glide softly. On my right, the skin is smooth. On my left, it's rough and bumpy. I breathe deeply as he strokes.

'Sapphie?'

When I look up, he stares into my eyes. Grey and blue. Blue and grey. He kisses me again, short and hard. He undoes the final button, opens my top and eases it back. I look at the ceiling as he looks down. He cups my cheek and puts his thumb on my chin, turning my face towards him.

'How long before you got help?'

'Two days. That's why the scars are so bad.'

He dips his head. He kisses the nipple of my good breast, an open-mouthed kiss.

I almost shoot off the bed in surprise. 'Matts!'

He holds me firmly by the tops of my arms and kisses my nipple again. He sweeps his tongue around it. He looks at me innocently. 'What?'

'You … you—' I glance down at his erection. 'Nothing.'

This time I watch him. He cups my right breast. And then he cups my left. The scars end a millimetre from my nipple. He circles the areola with the pad of his thumb.

I squirm. 'Matts?'

'Is that uncomfortable?'

'It's embarrassing, but … No.'

He licks the nipple and sits back. 'Tell me when to stop.' He puts the pad of his thumb on the dampness. He frowns and kisses my nipple again, this time with his tongue. Afterwards, his thumb glides easily.

'What—what are you doing?'

He kisses my right nipple and my left. His lip lifts in one of his almost smiles. He looks from one breast to the other. He kisses them again like he's known me this way forever.

'Beautiful.'

By the time he kisses my mouth, I'm hot and shaky with lust. I yank down my shorts and he eases them over my bandage.

'You okay?'

'Mmm.'

When I lie on the pillows, he fans out my hair and props my bandaged foot on the cushion he finds on the floor. He kneels at the foot of the bed and kisses my ankle above my bandage. He kisses my other ankle. He kisses my calves. He lifts my good leg and bends it so he can access the back of my knee. He kisses up the insides of my thighs with soft, wet lips.

'*Matts*.'

He smiles. 'More?'

My toes curl into the sheets. The rooster starts up again, pealing long and loud. I groan. 'It must be getting late.'

He mutters appreciative sounds as he kisses the insides of my legs. He makes patterns with his tongue as he kisses higher.

I moan his name. I stroke his hair. 'Please.'

He kisses around me and inside me, teasing and playing until all I'm aware of is the movement of his lips and the strokes of his tongue, the rumble of his voice and the touch of his hands. I groan and I pant and I climax.

'Matts!' I reach for him.

He crawls up my body, puts his hand between my legs. He nibbles my neck as if pleased with the tremors. When his fingers slide inside me, I tighten my thighs around them.

'Please, Matts.' My voice is husky. 'Do it properly.'

Making love last night was falling over a waterfall and plunging down a river —exciting, dangerous, intoxicating. This morning is a stroll by a gently flowing stream. We hold hands and face each other. Our eyes are wide, our mouths are soft, our movements slow. When he climaxes, he mumbles words into my mouth. I wrap my legs around his hips and hold on to him firmly. He carries me into the sunshine.

Honey, dandelion, bumblebee, butterscotch. Gold.

The edges of his face are softer when he sleeps. I trace the arcs of his brows. I trail my thumb across his cheekbone.

'You're beautiful, too,' I whisper.

The front gate squeaks on its hinges.

Children's chatter. Footsteps on the stairs. A tap on the door. 'Miss Brown.' A girl's voice. 'Are you awake yet?'

CHAPTER
39

By the time I reach the front door, there are two sets of knocks. I open it to see Mary, her hair neatly tied in two long plaits, bobbing up and down on the doormat. Archie, looking at his feet but smiling, stands next to her. Barney leans on the gate next to the kangaroo paw bush. The flowers are deep tones of mustard, bright against the fence.

'Dad said you hurt your foot,' Mary says, looking at the bandage and frowning momentarily. 'Gus tried to call but you didn't answer so he called Dad. He'll be here at eight o'clock.'

'Gus or your dad?'

'Gus.' She grins. 'Dad's ploughing early because he thinks it's going to rain soon so he took me to Archie's house. But his mum had to go to work too, so Barney is taking me and Archie to the horses.'

I look over her head to Barney. 'It's only seven o'clock.'

'They were driving me nuts so I said I'd take them early.'

'They need supervision. I'll tag along with whoever Gus gets a lift with, but the other volunteers won't be there until nine.'

'That's why we came here first.'

By the time Matts appears, dressed in jeans and the T-shirt he threw into the corner of my bedroom last night, Mary and Archie are sitting at the kitchen bench eating toast and Vegemite, and Barney is sitting on the floor near the fridge with a bowl of Weet-Bix in his lap. Tumbleweed is curled up next to him on his mat. I put a hip-length waterproof jacket over my pyjamas before I answered the door. Matts glances at it and raises his brows.

'Good morning, Sapphie.'

'I know you!' Mary says, licking Vegemite off her finger before holding out her hand like Matts did when he introduced himself in the paddock at the youth centre.

He shakes her hand solemnly. 'Good morning, Mary.' He looks around and frowns. 'You have forgotten Mischief again?'

She grins. 'He had to stay home.'

When Barney puts down his spoon and holds his hand above his head, Matts high-fives it.

'How's the climbing?' he asks.

'Better than it was.'

'Who are you?' Archie asks Matts.

'His name is Matts,' Mary says. 'He was at the farmhouse when you got into trouble for scaring the horses.'

'Where's he from?' Archie asks, hopping off his stool.

'I'm from Finland,' Matts says.

'Finland makes Nokia phones,' Archie says. 'Do you make Nokia phones?'

'Matts is an engineer,' I say. 'You like building things too, Archie. That might be something you and Matts can talk about. Would you like to introduce yourself before you ask any more questions?'

'My name is Archie.' He jumps up and down on the spot. 'Finland is the biggest manufacturer of paper in the world.'

Matts talks to Archie, in a very serious way, about renewable pine forests. And he's no less serious when he says goodbye to the children and Barney and tells me he'll see me at the door. When we step over the threshold to the porch, I close the door behind me. His overnight bag is at the top of the steps.

'Don't go to the farmhouse,' he says.

'I go there every Saturday.'

'Your foot is painful.'

I lean my bottom against the desk. 'I'll ice it before I leave, and restrict myself to the office once I get there. I can put it up on a chair.'

We stare at each other, but I don't know that either of us knows what to say next. I look away first, facing the desk and running a finger along the indentation at the top.

He comes closer, leaning over my shoulder to straighten the collar of the waterproof. When the tips of his fingers brush my neck, warmth seeps through my veins.

'I don't want to leave like this,' he says.

'You were supposed to be in Canberra yesterday. What time is your flight?'

'When I cancelled, they put me on the next one. Ten.'

A flock of lorikeets rise up from the trees in the playground and fly towards the creek. Will they squawk all the way to the farmhouse?'

'What are you thinking about?'

'Things …'

He strokes my hair, wraps a lock around his wrist. 'The farmhouse?'

'It's always meant a lot.'

He releases my hair and puts his hands on my shoulders. 'I could stay here until the end of the week.'

'What? When I have to be back at work on Monday morning?' I shake my head. 'Anyway, I don't need to be looked after.'

He growls as he turns me around. 'That's not what I'd be here for.'

When I stroke the crease between his brows, he kisses my wrist. 'I'll miss you, Matts, but you're already later than you thought you'd be. And you have meetings all this week, don't you?'

'I can reschedule.'

'Your schedule was arranged months and months ago.'

'Don't do anything about the farmhouse until I've seen Robert.'

It's tempting to lean against him. He'd wrap his arms around me. He might even tell me that things will work out. The desk nudges the tops of my legs when I step back.

'My father plays games. He makes deals. I refuse to do that. I'll have to find somewhere else.'

He runs his hand through his hair. He walks to the other side of the porch. 'If I go,' he says, 'I won't be back until Saturday night.'

'I know that already. I'm fine on my own.'

He mutters under his breath. 'Long term, Sapphie. Remember that?'

My throat tightens. 'I need to think things through.'

In two long strides, he's standing as close as he was. 'Be more specific.'

An old truck, open at the sides, honks as it turns off the loop road. It's Freddie and Gus so it must be eight o'clock. I glance at my waterproof and the hems of my cream pyjama shorts.

'I have to get ready. You have a flight.'

The sun streams onto the porch, so why are his eyes so inky and dark? He takes my hands. 'Reassure me.'

I thread our fingers together. I stroke the back of his hand. I lift it and kiss the scratch on his wrist. 'Last night and this morning was ...' My skin warms. 'It was—I've never had anything like it. I'll miss you and I hope that ... It's just that ...'

He rests his forehead on mine. 'You're worried about the farmhouse and what your father might say about your mother. And whatever it was that scared you this morning.'

'I wasn't scared.' I push back his hair. 'But I can't tell you about it and you resent that.' When I kiss his cheek, his bristles are rough. 'It'll be settled by the time you come back. I'll tell you everything then.'

'One day, you'll trust me.'

I nod bravely. 'I'll see you next Saturday.'

His car is parked a little way up the road, under the ironbark tree. Fallen leaves, green, brown and grey, are sprinkled all over the bonnet. He runs down the steps, lifting a hand to acknowledge Gus and Freddie. He shades his eyes from the sun and then he turns to me. He doesn't wave. I don't think he smiles.

Dark hair that lightens in sunshine.

CHAPTER

40

I was fast asleep when we drove onto the loop road last night. Today, sitting between Freddie and Gus in the truck, I feel ...

'Not too bad.'

Gus takes off his hat and puts a hand to his ear. 'What's that, Sapphie?'

'Just talking to myself.'

Freddie didn't have safety seats for the children, so I asked Corey to pick them up from the schoolhouse on the way to collect Joel. The minibus hasn't arrived yet, but a four-wheel drive with a Dubbo zoo logo on the door is parked at the side of the road.

'Who is that?'

Gus grins. 'Who do you reckon?'

Keep away from the flowers or else! This is Miss Brown's (Sapphie's) room. Private!

When I push open the door to the flower room, Jet is bent over double and sweeping under the bench. She spins around, her sparkling eyes as brown as mine are blue.

I burst into tears.

She doesn't say anything, but hugs me tightly. She brings me a chair and sits opposite. And then she gets up again, returning with a box of tissues and balancing it on my knees.

Jet isn't much older than me. She was only seventeen when her father died and much younger when her mother passed away. When we first met, I was secretive and unhappy. I wanted to be left alone to work out who I was. She didn't ask about my family, or why I'd left the city. I didn't ask why she bit her nails, or never rode her horses.

She's thoughtful and smart.

I sniff. 'I thought my life was sorted, but—'

She pulls her chair closer and plucks tissues out of the box, pressing them into my hand. 'It's not your foot, is it?'

I blow my nose. 'No.'

'That's a pity.' She smiles sympathetically. 'I could do something about your foot.'

I smile and cry at the same time. 'Yes.'

'And if I couldn't help, Finn could take a look.'

'You married an excellent vet.'

Jet would never ask why I'm crying. Which has the effect of making me tell her. 'My father has bought the farmhouse.' I blow my nose again. 'He wants to make sure I don't talk out of turn for a few more years. Everyone's worked so hard to fix this place up and I have to tell them I've made a mess of things.'

She touches my arm. 'No one's worked harder than you. And what do you mean, he's bought—'

'You can't say anything, Jet. There's something else as well. I'm not sure what to do about someone. Someone I like a lot.'

'Is he tall?' She sits back in her chair and crosses her arms. 'With billboard good looks and the weight of the world on his shoulders? I saw him here earlier.'

'Matts?'

'He was leaning against the fence and lecturing Prima.'

'What?'

'He introduced himself to Finn and me.' She scuffs her boots on the floorboards. 'Then he left.'

I wipe my face with the tissues. 'Do you remember our *Pride and Prejudice* conversation? It was after Finn came to Horseshoe.'

She smiles. 'I paraphrased Mrs Bennet, didn't I? I said no one could be as good and kind and pretty as you without a good reason.'

'And I told you that I only ever have sex with men I never want to see again.'

She nudges my good foot with her boot. 'Do you want to update that?'

'He said he wanted long term. What do you think that means?'

She laughs. 'More than one night.'

I press my hands between my knees. 'I was happy before. I was happy at the farmhouse. I was happy with the horses. I was happy at school and on the committee. I was happy making flowers.' The headdress and buttonholes I made for April's wedding are lying on the bench where I left them. Only a week has passed since we went to the wetlands. It feels like a lifetime.

'Will you see him again?'

'Next Saturday night, assuming he's still talking to me after this morning.'

We look towards the door when we hear footsteps. Finn is six foot two, thirty-three and extremely good-looking.

'Is this a private conversation?' He's Scottish, but has a posh English accent.

Jet stands and smiles. 'It is.'

I hobble to Finn and hug him. 'Thanks for coming to help today.'

'It's good to see you, Sapphie.' He glances at my foot. 'Well done on the rescue.'

'We could have done with your help.'

'Is the climber all right?'

'I think he will be. When are you home?'

'By Christmas.' When Jet holds out her hand, Finn takes it. 'Jemima and I are looking forward to it.' He smiles into her eyes and kisses her. 'Freckle needs a trim and Strider needs shoes. I've put your tools in the yard.'

'Duty calls,' Jet says as she walks to the door. 'Finn will keep you company.'

When Finn holds out a chair, I sit down again.

'Besides your injuries, are you well, Sapphie?'

'Are my eyes red?'

'Slightly.'

'I have a few problems.'

He leans forward so his arms are on his knees. 'I'm listening.'

I sniff. 'You and Jet … It wasn't easy for either of you, was it?'

He frowns, as if uncertain how to answer. But then he shrugs. 'I loved Jem from the beginning. Now I love her more. But, no, it wasn't easy.'

'I'm used to being on my own. Jet and I had that in common.'

He smiles as he holds up his ring finger. 'I like this.'

'You convinced her to marry you in Horseshoe and in Scotland.' I smile. 'Admirable.'

'Laaksonen,' Finn says quietly. 'How well do you know him?'

'I—pretty well.'

'Before we met this morning, I knew him by reputation. He's intelligent, ambitious, hardworking.'

He's more than that. He's honest and protective. He's thoughtful and passionate. He's steadfast and patient.

I'm in love with him.

I can trust him.

U

Pa's not picking me up until five, but I lock the farmhouse up at four, leaning on one of Ma's old walking sticks as I hobble into the garden.

The azaleas are shooting hunter green leaves now that the flowers are spent. Wisteria blooms, like bunches of grapes, clamber up the lattice on the wall near the chimney. I shade my eyes as I peer at the weathervane. When I found it buried in a clump of blackberry bushes near the rusted water tank, I bent it, more or less, back into shape. I propped an old timber trellis against the house, climbed onto the roof and fixed it to the chimney with baling wire. Was the wind so strong last week? The weathervane has tipped even more and the rooster lies almost on his back.

What will my father do with this place? The land can be leased easily enough, but without consistent work to cobble things together, the house will disintegrate further. I lean heavily on the stick as I stand at the gate. I do my best to be objective. What is worth saving? The verandah posts and floorboards should be replaced. The roof needs substantial repair. Inside the house, there's rewiring and re-plumbing and ...

A baby pink banksia rose, wild and tangled, climbs the fence. Old-fashioned roses in traditional colours are massed near the path to the paddocks. The orange trees were early with fruit; the lemon trees were late. I've neglected the vegetable garden because there's been so little rain, and the only thing that flourished in the greenhouse this year was Barney's marijuana crop. I snap off a bushy stem of mint that's taking over the parsley patch.

Prima nickers as Joel, a biscuit of lucerne hay in his hand, walks to the gate. Instead of hiding under the grey gum, she's been at the fence all day, looking over the railing as if concerned she's missing out on something. At lunchtime she took carrots from Mary and Archie. She let Barney take off her rug, groom her and lead her around the paddock.

'You're doing so well with her, Joel. I can't believe how much she's improved in the past few months.'

He grunts. 'Gramps said if a horse'd had good rearing, they could be saved. I reckon Prima's like that. She got bad treatment after she broke down.'

I stroke her neck as Joel climbs through the fence. 'You've been here every day, haven't you? I should never had doubted your commitment.'

'I like working with horses.'

'I saw you on Sonnet today. Corey's finally letting you ride?'

'He talks less shit than he did.'

I laugh. 'I'll pass that on.'

'I've left school,' Joel says, as he loosens hay from the biscuit and it scatters into the trough. 'I'm going to a technical college in town. I get to do horse management and agriculture, bookkeeping, stuff like that.'

'That sounds like a good move.' I lean against the gate. 'How much riding experience do you have?'

'I was okay when Gramps was around. Not so great now.'

'Can you find other rides as well as Sonnet? He's a similar size to Prima, but as steady as she is flighty. It wouldn't be fair to put anyone on her back unless they knew what they were doing.'

He nods repeatedly. 'Reckon I could get some more rides, Sapphie. One of my mates has a horse.'

'I'd never been on a horse until I was about your age, so you're one step ahead of me. Lessons could help. I'll speak to Corey about that.'

Joel almost skips to the road, his skateboard under his arm. I open the gate to the paddock and sit on a patch of dry grass near the trough. Prima looks at me curiously.

'I heard Matts came to see you,' I say. 'I will talk to him, I promise. After I've found out what Gabriel has to say.'

CHAPTER
41

When Gabriel Garcia appears on the screen, it's eight in the evening in Horseshoe and six in the morning in Argentina. So why am I the one fiddling with my ear pods and adjusting the angle of my laptop like it's me who's just got up? I've googled him interminably. He's been an engineering consultant with his own firm for many years. From what I can see, he's reputable and respected. He was well presented and neatly dressed when I saw him in Horseshoe. Seeing him looking like that again shouldn't surprise me.

But his confidence at turning up unannounced at the farmhouse and asking me to keep quiet; his unwillingness to compromise on the timing of the call. Is he like my father? Should I trust him?

I push my laptop further back on the kitchen bench. 'Why couldn't we do this earlier?' I ask.

He smiles uncertainly. 'My lawyer received additional documentation last night. He called,' he looks at his watch, 'very late last night.'

'It's Sunday morning over there. Why are you wearing a tie?'

He raises his brows. 'Despite my many sins, and those of my church, I am a Catholic. I will attend Mass later in the morning.'

I sit back on the stool. 'I didn't mean to—'

He holds up a hand. 'Please, Sapphie. I understand your suspicion. I have to lay my cards on the table. Correct?'

'I—yes.'

'If you will excuse me.' He reaches for a glass of water and sips. 'I shall start from the beginning. At least then you will, if not forgive me, understand the circumstances.'

'Take as much time as you want.'

'I turned sixty a few months ago,' he says. 'I was born and raised in Rosario and after university I worked as a design engineer with a company in Buenos Aires. I was forty when the firm closed down.'

'You went to work for Hernandez?'

'I was surprised and flattered when Josef Hernandez called me personally and offered me a role in one of his companies. The Hernandez group work all over the world—bridges, roads, manufacturing plants and mining operations.'

'Was he corrupt?'

He raises his brows. 'Good and bad, Sapphie. There are many variations of this. In the few years I worked at Hernandez, part of Josef's unofficial business model was to give gifts to those with the power to decide which company would be awarded a contract. I was aware of this and did nothing to prevent it.'

'The gifts were bribes?'

'Gifts, inducements, bribes … the law in Argentina, unlike your laws in Australia, did not differentiate these things as strictly as they do now.'

'Did you deal with my father?'

'It was made clear that, to do my job as well as was expected, I should get to know him more closely. Through his social network,

I met your mother, Kate. As your parents were close to Leevi and Inge Laaksonen. I also became acquainted with them.'

'Did you give my father anything?'

'He was in charge of receiving tenders for a substantial government project. Josef suggested I reward him for his consideration of our bid.' He takes another sip of water. 'Josef subsequently believed that a gift, an inducement, had been given to your father.'

'Had it?'

'I did not want to cross Josef. For personal reasons, I wanted to stay in Buenos Aires. The money was never paid to your father, but I led Josef to believe that it had been.'

'How? Did you take the company's money?'

He shakes his head. 'Let me explain more clearly. Josef was—still is—a man of substantial means. He did not know what money was going into and coming out of what he called his "kitty", a slush fund kept for these purposes. He did not want to know the details.'

'So he thought you took the money, but you didn't?'

'Correct. I paid your father nothing. In consequence, he accepted nothing. I did not admit to this at the time. I have not admitted to it since because I believed there was no reason to do so.'

'Until my father was named as one of the recipients?'

He runs a hand through his thick black hair. 'The deposit box in Geneva. This was my undoing.' He takes another sip of water. 'As I said in my email, the prosecutors have called a number of ex-employees in the hope that more facts come to light.'

Tumbleweed walks through the cat flap and across the linoleum to the fridge. He sits and waits.

'You said my father did nothing wrong. How does my mother fit in?'

'In addition to his kitty, Josef kept keys to deposit boxes. Gifts were left there, and keys handed to whoever had accepted a gift.

After that, all links to the Hernandez companies were lost. It was up to the recipient what they did with the key.'

'My mother accessed a box.'

He presses his hands against his face. There are gaps where his missing fingers should be. He takes his hands away. 'Yes.'

'Tell me.'

'Of course.' He looks directly at the screen. 'I had a key in the drawer of my desk, the one that Josef had given to me. I used that key, Sapphie, not for business reasons but for personal ones. I put the items in the box and it was opened by your mother.'

'You said she was innocent.'

'Kate opened the box on her friend's behalf. The money and sapphire belonged to me. It was a gift for her friend.'

'But that could only be ...' I'm suddenly shaky. 'Inge?'

He nods solemnly. 'Inge.'

'So she wasn't looking after the key for Mum? It was hers?'

'Have you a glass of water, Sapphie? I find I am in need of a top up.'

I take out my ear pods and fill my glass from the bottle in the fridge. Tumbleweed miaows plaintively when I close it. 'Later, puss.'

I face Gabriel again. 'Why did you give Inge a gift?'

'Leevi controlled her bank accounts. She couldn't leave him with no money.'

I hold tightly to the bench and force myself to speak. 'Were you having an affair?'

He slowly nods. 'We were in love.'

'She was—she wouldn't ...'

He sighs. 'Sapphie, let—'

'No!' I take a deep breath. 'Why did my mother look in the box?'

'She was Inge's dearest friend,' he says quietly. 'She knew Inge was not always happy in her marriage. She knew we had developed something stronger than friendship. With reservations, Kate supported our union.'

'How long did this go on for?'

'Inge and I were friends in secret. Much, much later, for only six months, we became intimate. Two years in total.'

'Why didn't she leave earlier?'

'It wasn't commonly known, but Leevi's posting in Argentina was due to end the year that Inge died. It was only after her death that it was extended. Once the family had returned to Finland and Matts was enrolled in school, Inge believed it would be safe to leave her marriage. Leevi could be posted overseas, but it would be much more difficult for him to take Matts if he were settled. Her son came first, always.'

'What would you have done?'

'I would have lived in Finland. I would have gone anywhere to be with her.'

'Why was it Mum who went to Geneva? Why did she look in the box?'

'She thought if Inge had financial security, she could make an independent decision whether to separate from Leevi or not. Kate was adamant the gift be given freely. If at any time Inge changed her mind about me, the money would be hers. I agreed willingly.'

'You still haven't explained.'

'This matter of money was upsetting to Inge, but Kate was firm. She said she would check that I had done what I had promised to do, to leave the money in the box. Then she would open an account in her own name, deposit the money and transfer it to Inge. But.' He sighs. 'She saw the sapphire. She wanted Inge to find that for herself. When she returned to Argentina, she gave Inge not only the key, but a ticket to Geneva.'

'Mum—' I clear my throat. 'Mum would have thought that was romantic.'

Gabriel searches his pockets. He pulls out a handkerchief. 'This is true.'

'Are you married now?'

He shakes his head. 'There was only Inge.'

'Why a sapphire?'

He refolds the hanky. 'Inge and I met in September. It was also the month of her birthday. This was her birthstone. It was to be a ring.'

'You kept this secret for all these years?'

'And would have continued to do so.'

'You were going to tell me about it when you came to Horseshoe? Why didn't you?'

He looks down and lines up something on his desk. 'You saw me in the hotel, the pub, the evening before we spoke, yes? Matts Laaksonen was with you.' He smiles sadly. 'He is an accomplished young man, is he not? I understand he has a good relationship with his father. The truth would be hurtful, certainly, but in the interests of clearing your mother of blame, I thought he could bear it.'

'What made you change your mind?'

His eyes fill with tears. 'How could I ever have been a father to Matts? I could not, he had one already. But I imagined that, in time, he would see how deeply I cared for his mother. I hoped, I prayed, that we could be close. But—' He dabs at his eyes with the hanky. 'When I saw him that night, I did not see the man I expected to see. I saw the boy that Inge loved above all else. I saw the stepson I could have had.' He holds up his hands. 'You see how foolish I am?'

'Did you want to protect Leevi as well?'

He smiles sadly. 'I deserve reproach, Sapphie, nothing else. But Inge and I deeply regretted the hurt that Leevi would suffer. He was traditional in his views of a wife, but he loved her too.'

'Did he find out about the affair?'

'When Inge was in the hospital.' Gabriel's eyes close briefly.

'Did she tell him?'

'At first she was unconsciousness. After that, she was on life support. She couldn't.'

'Then how did he find out?'

He shakes his head. 'I think you have heard enough, Sapphie.'

I look outside, to the treetops in the playground. I know where I belong now, but for many years I didn't. I swallow the lump in my throat.

'Inge died when I was ten. After that, we were in Buenos Aires, then Canberra, but nothing was the same as it had been. Mum changed and I want to know why. I was told that Inge had an infection. Did she? What happened?'

He dabs his eyes again.

'Please, Gabriel.'

Finally, he nods. 'After Matts was born, Leevi, unlike Inge, did not want more children. I was forty-two and had never fathered a child. Inge was thirty-nine. It would make matters more complicated, certainly, but what a blessing ...'

'Inge was pregnant,' I whisper.

'Inge and Leevi had not been intimate for many years. The baby could not have been his.'

'Mum once said ...' *Had she lived, Inge would have loved another baby.* 'Inge was happy about the baby, wasn't she?'

'Deliriously so. We both were.'

I wipe my face on my sleeve. 'Mum knew too, didn't she?'

He blows his nose. 'Sapphie, my dear. If I am forced to give evidence, I will tell them the money was mine, as was the sapphire. I have bank records and a receipt to prove this.'

'They know Mum went to the deposit box. They know that she and Inge were friends. They'll ask why you put those things there.'

'There was no crime.'

'Inge's death was particularly hard because Mum knew about the baby. That's right, isn't it?'

His hands are shaking. He puts them in his lap out of sight. 'I saw your father's statements. This was unfair to Kate. I should have done more to support her.'

'How? What do you mean?'

'I was selfish in my guilt. Kate was lonely in hers. I should have persevered.'

'She did feel guilty, but I never knew why. Tell me, Gabriel. Please.'

'Kate had a burden.'

'What? Why?'

He looks straight ahead, but through the screen, not at it. 'I was on a building site off the coast of Chile,' he says slowly. 'Inge was eight weeks pregnant. She'd had pain the previous night, and the bleeding began that morning. She was afraid to go to the hospital because she had a driver from the embassy. Leevi would find out.'

'She called Mum?'

'Kate had some knowledge.'

'She'd had miscarriages. I know that.'

'She told Inge there was no need for a hospital, that this baby was not meant to be. She told her she should rest and wait for Kate to come to her. Kate was at a school function, a luncheon. She was delayed. There was a traffic jam.'

'But ... that's not how Inge died, is it? It can't have been.'

He wipes his face with the hanky. 'The blood was not from miscarriage, but from internal bleeding. Inge had an ectopic pregnancy. Her fallopian tube had ruptured. If she'd had medical treatment earlier, perhaps ...'

My throat is full. My tears blur the screen. I wipe my face with my sleeve.

Once upon a time, Mum loved my father. She loved me. She loved Matts. And she loved Inge.

Gabriel comes closer so his face fills the screen. 'Your foster parents, Sapphie. I think they live nearby. Please go to them.'

When Tumbleweed jumps onto my lap, I stroke his brindle fur. Kookaburras laugh from the gums in the playground. 'Mum didn't tell anyone, did she?'

'She believed she had let Inge down. She blamed herself. She wanted to make amends but she could not.'

I swallow a sob. 'The things Mum asked me to do. The drugs. It was wrong, but … I was stronger than she was. I knew that.'

'Inge loved you as a daughter, Sapphie. Kate loved Matts as a son. She wanted to protect him from innuendo, from gossip. Most importantly, Matts had an image of Inge as a loving mother and wife. Kate kept Inge's secret.'

Tears run in streams down my face. 'She kept Inge's secret.'

CHAPTER

42

To: Sapphie, Cassie, Luke, Gus, Matts
From: Chambers
Great work on the press releases and other information, ably led by
Sapphie and Cassie. Sapphie—as arranged I'll call early tomorrow
morning (Thursday) to finalise the roll out.

From: Matts
To: Sapphie, Chambers, Cassie, Luke, Gus
Sapphie—others in the group are getting through on your phone. I am
not. Please call.

U

My foot doesn't hurt when I wear boots and keep to level ground, so after I call Mr Chambers, I walk slowly to the farmhouse by road. I *could* drive. Yesterday I borrowed Pa's van. I sat behind the wheel and fought my anxiety all the way to the end of the loop road and back again. I don't imagine I'll be driving at night anytime soon, but one day I will.

Mum wouldn't want me to run scared. She did enough of that for both of us.

The farmhouse looks much the same from the outside, but most of the furniture and equipment, the desk, filing cabinets, boots and hats and halters and bridles and saddles that were stored in the hallway and office, have been taken to the youth centre. Edward Kincaid has given me permission to keep my horses on his land at Kincaid House until I find somewhere else, and I can store their gear in Jet's shed. Gus's working bee, his annual community project where we help each other out, is a big December event. When I told him the farmhouse had been sold to my father, he cussed and cursed for an hour. And then he pulled out his small spiral notebook and wrote my name on a list.

'Don't see why Beresford-Brown should get the lot,' he said. 'You'll be wanting your flower bench and mirror and your other odds and ends for when you find another place. We'll move them to my shed.'

I've packed all my crepe paper—the scores of rolls and scraps I kept in the bookcase—into containers. I've stored my glues and scissors and wires as well. The boxes will take up all the living space in the schoolhouse, but I want to have them close. I flick through one of Gran's exercise books. She wrote in pencil to record the patterns she thought she'd use again, but she rarely referred to her notes. She'd either remember what she'd done the first time around, or decide to try something new. She liked to make flowers she'd never made before. 'Look, Sapphie,' she'd say, peering at the petals through her glasses. 'The perfect imperfections.'

Inge seemed to be perfect. She never raised her voice. She was modest and kind and thoughtful. She always kept fresh flowers on her dining room table.

I move Gran's books aside and put my phone on the bench. I pull up a hardback chair and find Matts's number in my list of missed calls.

'Sapphie.' He doesn't exactly bark my name, but it's close.

'I'm sorry.'

Silence.

'Are you still there, Matts?'

'Hold on.'

There are muffled voices in the background. Is he in a meeting with the Water Resources minister? Or an environmental lobby group? Or farmers, irrigators and organic crop producers? The UN High Commissioner?

'I can call back.'

'No.' A door clicks shut. 'What the fuck, Sapphie?' Louder now.

'Shout at me then.'

'I never would.'

'I know ...' The box of tissues I used when Jet was here is on the bench. I pluck two and wipe my cheeks. 'I know that.'

Silence again.

'Matts?' I sniff. 'Are you still there?'

'Are you crying?'

'A bit.'

'That's unfair. *Fucking* unfair.'

'I'm—' My voice breaks. 'I don't want to hurt you again.'

He sighs so loudly that I hear it. 'Has your father upset you?'

'Nothing new.'

'Have you injured yourself again?'

'No.'

'Why are you crying?'

When I fold the tissues and put them on the table, it not only reminds me of Gabriel's handkerchief. It reminds me of the tissues

I gave Matts at Inge's funeral. And the tissues he wanted to give me at Mum's.

I shudder a breath. 'I wish you were here.'

He mutters under his breath. 'Saturday, Sapphie. My flight leaves Canberra at five. I won't get to Horseshoe much before eight.'

'April's reception ends at seven.'

A breeze skitters under the windowpane. The tissues lift and fall to the floor.

Voices in the background.

'I have to go,' he says.

Matts might be older and physically stronger, Mum would remind me, but he needed someone to watch out for him in the same way he watched out for me.

My mother kept Inge's secret. Should I?

April's wedding is held at a church a few kilometres out of town. On an adjacent parcel of land is the reception venue, a large barn-like structure with gardens of native trees and shrubs. The barn is crowded with people and music and movement. Most of the guests are standing now, laughing and talking as they wait for the final dances. The DJ, jumping around on a raised platform at the rear of the parquet dance floor, turns up the volume. Hugo drapes an arm across my shoulders.

'Anyone swiped right yet?'

I smooth down my new dress, dark blue, short sleeved and slinky. It falls demurely to my knees, but there's a split to the thigh on one side.

'You're drunk, Hugo.' I elbow him in the ribs. 'Stop leaning on me.'

He peers at my sneakers. 'You been working at the farmhouse?'

'I hurt my foot, remember?'

He grunts. 'Gus said you gotta move out.'

'I don't want to talk about it.'

'You okay?'

Matts was supposed to see my father yesterday, but he didn't call last night or this morning. He hasn't called tonight. Maybe, like me, he's waiting until we see each other in person.

I still haven't decided whether to tell him about Gabriel.

I shake my head. 'No, I'm not okay.'

'Your father's an arsehole. And I'm not drunk.'

'So why are you leaning on me?'

He doesn't answer, just looks pointedly over my shoulder to the dance floor. I follow his gaze to ...

'Is that Patience Cartwright?'

'Unless she's got an identical twin I don't know about.'

Patience is ethereally lovely, like a storybook fairy with wavy blonde hair. She's dancing with a group of women, but even in heels she's the smallest by far.

'She's back?'

He drops his arm. 'Not for long.'

'Hugo? You can't possibly still—'

He looks down at his shoes. 'Don't want to talk about it.'

I touch his hand. 'I'm sorry.'

His smile goes nowhere near his eyes. 'You did a good job on April's head thing.'

'It's called a crown.'

'Whatever.'

April, the crown of twelve old-fashioned roses pinned to her short curly hair, holds Ranjit's hands and smiles into his eyes as they cross step, sidestep, gallop, slide and spin to a folk dance. Gus stands on the edge of the floor, clapping and tapping his foot. The gumnut buttonhole sits neatly on his lapel, the fringes of the flower bright against the blue.

Mary darts in front of me, holds out her dress and curtseys. 'Dance with me, Miss Brown! It's the last dance!'

'I'd love to, Mary.' I straighten her wattle coronet, at an angle because she's tugged her braids loose. 'But I'm supposed to rest my foot. School starts again next week.'

I wait until April and Ranjit have waved goodbye to their guests before I follow Gus out to the carpark. He's arranged a lift to our homes with his neighbours, but I ask them to let me out of their car at the bottom of the hill near the park.

'You sure, Sapphie?' Gus asks.

I push up the sleeves of my cardigan. 'I'll enjoy the walk.'

I've only just crossed the road from the park when I see Matts on the footpath outside the pub. He's wearing a dark-coloured hoodie and his arms are crossed. The grey-haired man he's talking to has his back to me, but when he squares his shoulders, he's easy enough to identify.

My father slices his hands through the air. Matts shoves his hands into his side pockets. His back is straight, his chin is up. As soon as he sees me, he spins away from my father and runs across the road. I'd imagined throwing myself into his arms and kissing his mouth and—

As he steps onto the kerb, I take a backwards step. 'Why is Robert here?'

Matts glances at my hands, so tightly clenched that my nails dig into my palms. He lifts an arm and drops it. He looks into my eyes. Can he see the shades?

Sapphire, cobalt, indigo, navy.

Bruised.

CHAPTER
43

When I was fostered by the Hargreaves, I promised to maintain contact with my father and to see a counsellor. Angela, a psychologist, lived on the outskirts of Dubbo, and I'd catch the bus to her house every second Monday. We talked about trust not long before Mum was killed.

'A lack of trust makes it difficult to express emotions,' she said. 'Why do you think that might be?'

'You don't want to tell people how you feel in case they let you down.'

'Trusting people makes us vulnerable. Keeping our distance and avoiding interactions with others protects us from harm.'

'I talk to people when I have to.'

'When we're distrustful, unexplained actions can be seen through a magnified lens. They can appear to be threatening. Intimacy and relationships become difficult.'

'I've made a few friends.'

'You're very pretty, Sapphie, exceptionally so. Boys must ask you out.'

'I don't want ...' I linked my hands tightly in my lap. 'I'm busy with other things.'

'You're doing well.'

I glanced at the screen of her iPad. 'Then why'd you tick so many boxes?'

Angela closed her iPad and draped her hand over the top. Her nails were acrylics, painted red, green and silver for Christmas. She smiled encouragingly.

'We'll talk about trust again next time we meet.'

Matts offers me his hand when I step off the kerb, but I pretend not to see it. He stands next to me when I face my father on the other side of the road.

'Sapphire.' Robert nods formally, making no attempt to kiss me. 'You look lovely.' He's wearing a suit and a royal blue tie patterned with burgundy triangles.

'What are you doing here?'

'I wanted to speak with you.'

Matts mutters, 'He said he'd come tomorrow.'

'And that's supposed to make this better?'

'Don't, Sapphie.'

'You should have warned me!'

Robert, frowning, glances towards the pub. Mike Williams and Artie Jones, both from Warrandale, are sitting at a table by the window. Mike lifts his hand, large and rough from a lifetime of work.

'Do you think we could retire to somewhere more private?' Robert asks.

When I walk past my father and open the door to the pub, Leon looks up from the bar.

'By the look of your finery, you went to April's wedding,' he says. 'Good celebration?'

'It was a beautiful wedding. Is it okay if we use the private dining room?'

'All yours. Lemon squash?' He looks past me. 'G'day, Matts. How're you doing? Soda water?'

Matts nods stiffly. 'Thank you, Leon.'

'I'd like a single malt whiskey on ice.' Robert takes out his wallet and hands over a note. 'Drinks are on me.'

Leon smiles. 'I'll bring them out to you, Mr Beresford-Brown.'

I leave coins on the bar. 'For the squash.'

The dining room at the back of the pub, often booked for birthdays and special occasions, seats twenty at a rectangular table. Robert sits at the long end near the door, I sit opposite and Matts sits next to me, clenching his jaw when I shift my chair further away. No one speaks until Leon bustles in with a tray, sets down coasters and places our drinks in front of us.

'Enjoy,' he says, before closing the door quietly behind him.

Robert swirls his whisky over the ice. 'As I appear to have caused a ruckus by bringing this meeting forward, perhaps I should start?'

Matts glares. 'Yes.'

'Sapphire?' Robert says. 'You're well aware of my motivations in respect to the farmhouse.'

I clasp my hands together. 'You want to control what I say.'

'I desire to encourage discretion.'

'I've moved out.'

'What?'

'Most of the stuff has gone already. My furniture should be out in a couple of weeks, my horses after that.'

Matts frowns. 'I told you to wait.'

'And I told you I wanted nothing to do with him.'

Robert turns to Matts. 'I believe I require your assistance.'

Matts angles his chair towards mine. 'Robert has a proposal. How you respond is up to you.'

'I played happy families and he went back on his word. I want him out of Horseshoe.'

Robert huffs. 'I will transfer the farmhouse to you,' he says, 'for the exact sum I paid for it. Effective immediately. In exchange, I want information.'

'What information?'

'As the Australian authorities refuse to hand down their findings until the Argentinian inquiry is complete, I find myself in limbo.'

'You're still working.'

'I've been stood aside from ministerial responsibilities. I have the media at my throat. The cartoonists are having a field day.'

'It might be a year before the Argentinian authorities bring Hernandez to trial,' Matts says. 'After that, months could pass before the judgement is handed down.'

I sip my lemon squash. On the second attempt to swallow, it goes down. 'I don't see how this involves me.'

'I didn't take a cent from Hernandez,' Robert says, 'and I suspect authorities on both sides of the southern hemisphere know this very well. But no one is prepared to speed things up. They're investigating years of potential bribes before making findings on any of them.'

'Didn't you know this before?'

'New allegations, nothing to do with me, have been brought against Hernandez.' He drinks, then returns his glass to the coaster. 'There's a general election next year. If this matter drags on, I'll lose preselection. It will be the end of my political career.'

'This must be hard for Jacqueline.'

I watch as he bites back a retort. He turns his glass on the coaster. 'You, Sapphire, were approached by an ex-employee of Hernandez. I want you to give me his name.'

'No.'

He pulls a piece of paper from an inside pocket of his jacket. 'In the two years I dealt with Hernandez, these men were employed in senior management. My lawyers believe it would have been one of them who approached you. If he is reputable, and provides a sworn statement confirming my non-involvement, there can be no case against me.'

'Against you? What about Mum? You've been adamant she's done something wrong. Isn't there guilt by association?'

'This contact, according to you, attests to Kate's innocence.'

'Surely your lawyers have called these men already?'

He nods abruptly. 'Some profess ignorance of my case. Others refuse to talk. They will only give evidence if compelled to do so at the trial.'

'So you need one of them to put their hand up for you? You want me to encourage them to do that?'

'Exactly.'

'I know of no one.'

'Sapphire!'

I stand. 'What about the deposit box? Your lawyers would need to explain the contents, wouldn't they?'

'I have no idea how fifty thousand euro and a sapphire worth twice that could be explained.' He smiles stiffly. 'Your contact might be able to do so.'

'Sapphie?' Matts stands too. 'If this man could defend Kate, this helps you both.'

When you know the facts, you will see my dilemma.

I scrabble in my bag, but can't find a tissue. Matts's chair hits the wall as he pushes it back. He opens drawers in the sideboard and finds serviettes. When he hands one to me, our hands touch. Our eyes meet. I look away.

'This man's explanation.' I swallow. 'At first he told me to wait. And now ... now I know that others are involved.'

'You've seen him again?' Matts asks.

'I spoke to him.'

'When?'

'It doesn't matter.'

Robert pushes away his glass. He stands. 'This is your final warning, Sapphire.'

'Don't threaten her,' Matts says.

'I'll do as I please.'

Matts walks to the door and opens it. 'Get out, Robert.'

Robert holds Matts's gaze as he straightens his jacket. He picks up the piece of paper, slowly folds it and puts it into his pocket. He's at the door before he turns and faces me again.

'I leave this hotel at eight tomorrow morning,' he says. 'Give me a name, Sapphire, and you'll get your farmhouse.'

'I won't be bought. And I don't trust you.'

'In which case, I have nothing to lose. If it's in my interests to do so, I'll announce that Kate was an addict and she used her child as a courier. In other words, she was capable of anything.'

I cling to the table. 'She changed after Inge's death.' My voice wavers. 'Only then.'

'So now you blame Inge?' he says. 'Shame on you.'

When I can't hear my father's footsteps any more, I walk to the tall, narrow window at the far end of the dining room. Across the courtyard, three old stables have sets of double doors.

Matts puts my drink on the windowsill and stands close but not touching. From the corner of my eye, I see the rise and fall of his chest. 'He was meant to come tomorrow.'

I cross my arms around my middle. 'So you said.'

'I was going to warn you tonight.'

'I shouldn't have yelled. I'm sorry.'

When he places his hand on my forearm, my heart skips a beat. 'Robert is a manipulative bastard, Sapphie. You owe him nothing. But if you refuse to do as he asks, you lose the farmhouse.'

'If I give him the name, others will get hurt.'

'What others?'

Matts has lost his mother once. If I tell him the truth he'll lose her—his innocent childhood memories of her—all over again. Mum understood that. So should I.

When I turn and lean into his chest, he wraps his arms around me. 'Robert was wrong, Matts. I wasn't blaming Inge. I never would.'

He buries his face in my hair. He runs his hands down my sides. His touch is lighter on the left than the right. He knows the scars on my body. He knows the scars in my heart.

'I missed you, Sapphie.'

I don't even open my eyes. I simply lift my face and find his mouth. Our lips are happy and sad and sorry and hungry all at once. I stroke his hair and the stubble on his jaw. I trace the line of his ear. I burrow under his shirt. Skin against skin.

I need him.

But what does he need?

He lifts his head. Cups my face. Looks into my eyes. 'What's wrong?'

I love you and I trust you. 'I don't want to hurt you.'

He kisses a trail from my lips to my cheek to the pulse at my throat. He puts his tongue against it. He mumbles, 'Long term.'

'But—'

He lifts his head. He runs a finger down my nose. 'Why do you trust this man?'

I step cautiously back. 'He was telling the truth.'

His arms drop to his sides. 'How do you know?'

I wipe my hands down my dress, the soft, clingy fabric. 'I just do.'

'Tell me about him.'

'What? Why?'

'I won't say anything to Robert.'

'That's not what—No.'

'When did you speak to him the second time?'

'Monday afternoon.'

'You knew something on Saturday morning, didn't you?' His eyes are troubled. 'I asked what had scared you.'

'He'd sent an email.'

'Why didn't you tell me about it?'

I press my lips together.

'Talk to me.'

To one side of the stables are bins with different coloured lids. Red. Blue. Yellow. The primary colours. The Wiggles. I swallow the lump in my throat. Leon is good with his recycling. He won an award from the committee and proudly displays the trophy in the bar with his premium bottles of whiskey.

'Sapphie?'

I drag my eyes from the courtyard. 'I didn't expect to see my father tonight. I thought it would just be you. I didn't ...' I shake my head. 'I need to think things through.'

'You said that last weekend.' He puts my glass on the table. His expression is shuttered. 'When we slept together, what did it mean to you?'

'You know what it meant.'

'Do I? When you don't trust me with other things?'

'You think if I tell you what you want to know, it will prove that I trust you.' I link my fingers together. 'It's like a test.'

He stills. 'What if it is?'

'If you don't have faith in my judgement, it means you don't trust me. That's unfair.'

'Unfair?' There's a ring of condensation on the sill. He runs his thumb through it. 'Unfair is assuming I set you up. Unfair is telling me you do things on your own. Unfair is ignoring my calls.'

'Don't.'

He draws another line through the condensation, making a cross. 'Unfair is having sex with me—and then giving up.'

A wave of sadness drowns out my words. I swallow. 'Are you done?'

'Unfair is denying the truth. Denying we were friends. Unfair is forcing me to lie.'

I shake my head. 'Please don't.'

'You said we were strangers. Cassie, Gus, Luke, Hugo. Even Chambers. They praise you for what you do, but mostly they value your friendship. And then they warn me, "Sapphie won't talk about her past." *I'm* your past, Sapphie. How do you think that makes me feel?'

My father left the door open. The jukebox hums. 'Raspberry Beret'. 'Purple Rain'.

I blink back tears. 'I'd lost you. I couldn't rely on Mum. Gran was dying. I had to start from scratch.'

He opens his mouth and slams it shut. He walks two steps and turns. The swirls on the carpet swim before my eyes.

'You've given up on the farmhouse. And on Kate. Tell me why.'

I shake my head.

'Give me a name.'

'Or what?' My voice breaks. 'Will you threaten me?'

'Like your father? Is that what you think?'

'No.' I hold tightly to the back of my chair. 'That was unfair.'

At the threshold, he turns. 'You know what else is unfair?' He's in the shadows. His eyes are black. 'You never lost me, Sapphie. You never could.'

CHAPTER
44

His message comes through in the early hours of Sunday morning.

From: Matts
To: Sapphie, Chambers, Cassie, Luke, Gus
Leaving tomorrow for Finland, then Switzerland. Back in Canberra late November.

Gus thought Matts might be warning us that he wouldn't be able to respond to our messages. But he continues to contribute, bluntly but usefully, to our group chats. He thanks Mr Chambers for supporting additional funding for Rory's wetlands project. He introduces Cassie to a government minister so she can lobby him about koala habitat rehabilitation. He sends Gus a link to a Swedish environmental group that records farmer's recollections of their land. He supports Luke's push for a new inquiry on the Murray–Darling river basin.

For so many years, I tried not to think about him. Now I read and re-read every word that he writes. I use an app on my phone to keep up to date with the weather.

Horseshoe: Low of 21 degrees. High of 32. Clear and dry.
Geneva: Low of 3 degrees. High of 7. Morning drizzle; overcast.
Helsinki: Low of -3 degrees. High of 1. Rain and sleet. Snow/slush.

Matts left almost two weeks ago, on the second of November.

Ten weekdays. One weekend.

Soon it will be summer.

'Miss Brown!' Mary's sister Millie, who usually plaits her hair, has been away on camp. Mary's wattle coronet sits at a jaunty angle on her head, but keeps most of her hair off her face. Standing at the workbench at the back of the classroom, she's waving a wad of scarlet crepe. 'We're ready to make poppies!'

When I raise my brows, Mary bites her lip. She raises her hand.

'Yes, Mary?'

'Can me and Amy make poppies like you made for Remembrance Day?' She presses her hands together. '*Please?*'

'You may cut out the templates for the petals.'

Archie, sitting at a desk covered with small timber puzzle pieces, raises his hand. 'The guns and bombs killed all the plants, but then it rained and poppies grew on the battlefields.'

'They did.'

'Lieutenant Colonel John McCrae wrote a poem called "In Flanders Fields".'

'Yes, Archie. The poem was about the World War One poppies.'

Archie picks up a piece of the puzzle. 'I'm going to be an engineer.'

Matts liked to know how things worked. And he liked to look into a microscope. What is he doing in Finland and Switzerland? Thinking about dams and weirs and catchments? Working out the different requirements of gaining streams and losing streams for water distribution? Modelling ideal conditions for marshes, mangroves, bogs and swamps?

He said the flow of the river was fucked.

He said I'd never lost him. That I never could.

Our pasts and futures all mixed up.

A few days before she died, Gran was propped up in a reclining chair in the nursing home. I was sitting on an upright chair next to her with a rickety table by my side. Its surface was covered with paper and the other things I'd need.

'Roses and gerberas,' Gran said, her words soft with memory, 'baby's breath and delphiniums.'

I laid out crepe paper and templates. 'I like to make native flowers best.'

She leant over the arm of her chair to have a closer look. 'What are we working on today?'

'One of the flowers you taught me how to make.'

'What a lot of paper you have. All those different yellows.'

Flaxen, amber, canary, gold. *Acacia pycnantha*. Golden wattle.

Kultainen kotka. Golden eagle.

Kultsi. Gold.

I use glues to join the petals of my flowers. What do I use to join the pieces of my heart?

U

By the time the last of the children have left the classroom and I've organised my materials for Monday, it's well after four o'clock.

I walk through the side gate to the schoolhouse. A car, clean, large and white, is parked on the verge at the side of the road.

When the driver's door opens, Jacqueline, wearing a floaty floral dress and nude-coloured high heels, steps out. I close the gate and walk across the garden. I force a smile as I hold out my hand.

'Jacqueline.'

'I'm sorry to turn up unannounced like this.'

'How are Atticus and Alex?'

'I didn't dare tell them I was coming.' She smiles uncertainly. 'They often ask about you. The broomsticks remind them.'

'I imagine that annoys Robert.'

Her bubble of laughter is genuine. But then she sobers. 'I was afraid you'd send me packing.'

'You'd better come in. It's hot out here.'

We're almost at the door when she doubles back to the car. She leans into the passenger side and picks up a buff-coloured folder.

My flower supplies are neatly stacked in the living room. There's a narrow path between the boxes from the front door to the bathroom and bedroom, with a right-angle turn to the kitchen. Stacking the boxes on top of each other would give me more room, but I wouldn't be able to find anything.

'Sorry about the mess,' I say, as I clear strips of blue crepe from the kitchen bench.

'They're beautiful colours, Sapphire.' Her brow creases. 'I should have said they're beautiful colours, *Sapphie*. What are you making?'

'A native flower—the blue fairy.'

We talk about the weather as the kettle comes to the boil. I put a selection of teas on the bench. 'Which one would you like?'

'Earl Grey, please.'

I make a pot of ginger and lemon tea as well. Jacqueline perches on a stool, the skirt of her dress draped elegantly over her knees.

'Those boxes,' she says, 'were they previously kept at the farmhouse?'

Ray Bainsbridge recommended ginger for nausea. I fill a cup from the pot and blow crystal clear steam from the top.

'Your car is a rental from Dubbo. I guess you flew in this morning?'

'Yes.'

'You've had a long day. Ma Hargreaves never lets anyone leave Horseshoe without a cup of tea.' I sit opposite her. 'That's why I invited you in.'

'You haven't spoken to Matts Laaksonen, have you?'

'What about?'

'He said he wouldn't tell you. He wanted it to come from Robert.' She glances at the folder. 'There's paperwork to be finalised, naturally, but Robert will sell you the farmhouse.'

I wrap my hands around my mug. 'I won't do what he wants.'

'There are no strings attached.' She opens the folder. 'As I understand it, you sign the transfer and give it to your solicitor to register at the lands office. In the meantime, you pay the money into Robert's bank account.' Tapping the folder, she pushes it across the bench. 'It's all here.'

'He must want something.'

'Not from you.' She sips her tea again. 'Matts refused to give details, but assured Robert your Argentinian contact had given him the entire story. Robert and your mother did nothing wrong.'

I blow small even breaths on my tea. One. Two. Three. 'My contact. How did Matts find out who he was?'

'Leevi Laaksonen knew nothing about the controversy involving Robert but, as I understand it, he gave Matts a lead about something else.'

'I see.'

'Matts wants to keep whatever happened secret, as does your contact. He won't give Robert the statement he wanted. This means Robert will be forced to wait until the Argentinian inquiry, and possibly the trial, are over. He's likely to lose preselection. He won't be able to contest his seat.'

'So why did he agree to sell?'

She raises her brows. 'He's a political animal—one door closes and another one opens. When Robert refused to return the farmhouse to you as Matts had demanded, Matts's father stepped in.'

My breath catches. 'Mr Laaksonen got involved?'

'Very much so,' Jacqueline says. 'Robert had always envisaged a career beyond parliament, preferably one in diplomacy.' She uncrosses her legs before crossing them again. 'Leevi is a career statesman, with innumerable contacts in the international community.'

'Did he force Robert to do this?'

She takes a tissue from her bag and pats her lipstick. 'Now that Robert has had an opportunity to reflect, I believe he would say that Leevi, acknowledging his former friend's desire for an international posting in the future, persuaded him that it would be in his best interests to return the farmhouse to its rightful owner.'

I can't see the farmhouse out of the window, but I can see the hill in the distance. My heart thumps in a confusion of hope and uncertainty.

'Why did you come here, Jacqueline? You could have emailed.'

She lifts the teapot, swirls the tea around and pours a little more into her cup. 'I wasn't aware of what Robert had done. Why didn't you tell me about the option when we met in Canberra?'

My tea is much cooler now. I sip it slowly. 'Robert supports you and the boys, doesn't he? And you know what kind of man he is. You'll put your sons' interests first. You won't let him trample all over you.'

'I will continue to be a good wife to him.' She nods thought-fully. 'On my terms.'

'That's what I thought. My relationship with my father is different from yours. I didn't want to make things difficult for you.'

When our eyes meet again, she smiles. It's a small smile, but a genuine one. 'I rather like the idea of an overseas posting.'

'Atticus will enjoy it too.'

'Why Atticus in particular?'

'He'll get to see a lot of different flags.'

She smiles again. 'I wish only good things for you, Sapphie. I hope—' She runs a perfectly manicured fingernail around the handle of her cup. 'I hope you'll find peace at the farmhouse.'

U

It's almost midnight here, so it'll be late afternoon in Europe. Tumbleweed is fast asleep at the end of the couch when I send a text.

Can I call?

I still have my phone in my hand when it rings. My heart skips a beat. 'Matts.'

'Sapphie.'

'Where are you? Are you all right?'

'Geneva. Yes.'

I stand up and sit down again. 'Jacqueline came to see me.'

'Not Robert?'

'No ... She said you'd spoken to Gabriel. I ... What did he say? How much—'

'The affair,' he says quietly. 'The pregnancy.'

If he were here, I could hold him. 'I'm sorry.'

'Garcia, the deposit box, this whole fucking mess. Why didn't you tell me?'

I hold the phone even closer to my ear. 'I care about you, Matts. I didn't want to hurt you.'

'You were protecting me?'

'Like you've always protected me. Even after we argued, you helped me get the farmhouse back. Jacqueline told me everything.'

'I don't want what we had when we were children.'

I curl my legs on the couch. 'You said I couldn't lose you. What did you mean by that?'

'I think you already know.'

'When do you come back?'

'That's up to you.'

When I close my eyes, I see the shades in his.

Charcoal, flint, graphite, dove.

Shadow.

CHAPTER
45

After last week's rain, water dances over the rocks in the creek. Prima skitters when an echidna burrows into the softened earth at the base of a sandstone boulder. Further upstream, the creek leads to the river, which flows to the wetlands. The kangaroos and birds. The reeds, red gums and coolabah trees. The frogs and fish. Weeks ago, Jacqueline said she hoped I'd find peace at the farmhouse.

'I *should* be happy.'

When Prima's ears twitch, I lean forward and run my fingers through her mane. She trots as we climb the incline to the paddock, but slows to a walk as we reach level ground and the farmhouse comes into view.

Morning sun bounces off the corrugated roof. The rain has washed the dust away; the leaves of the lemon and orange trees sparkle in the light. There's more water in the dams than there was. Soon enough, the grasses will shoot and the stock will have feed in the paddocks. Jet and Finn will be home for Christmas and we'll spend the day with the Hargreaves.

I miss him.

New water tanks sit proudly near the vegetable patch. The sinks are plumbed and soon there'll be an inside toilet and shower. First thing on Monday morning, the electrician will finish the basic rewiring. I glance at the roof. The rooster still lies on his back. Short term, I need to have the roof patched and the gutters and floorboards repaired. There are gaps beneath the skirting boards and the windows don't seal. Long term …

I want more.

By the time I arrive at the pub the following Friday evening, Gus is already there, sitting at the table by the window and peering at his notebook. Leon lifts a hand.

'Hello, Sapphie. Your drink is on Gus. I'll bring it over.'

I sit heavily in the chair opposite Gus. 'Sorry I'm late. I can't believe how many kids turned up to climbing tonight. And we're fully booked for the equine activities tomorrow morning, so I had a pile of paperwork to finish. But now all I have to do is get Sonnet and Strider to the youth centre by eight. Peter Honey will pick up Freckle and Lollopy in his float.'

Gus harrumphs. 'You're meant to be winding down for the holidays, not picking up the pace.'

'I like to be busy.'

'My Maggie would say you're too busy. And the committee's giving you more work than ever. Raising funds for this and lobbying for that.'

'It's the others who do most of the work.'

'You're the one who brings it all together. ' He sips his beer and wipes foam from his mouth. 'Haven't seen Matts in quite a while. Is he back from the continent yet? What's he been up to?'

'I think he's in Canberra again.'

'It's about time he came back to Horseshoe, to see what it's like in the summer.'

'I'd like to see him too.'

'Well, then?'

I seem to have a permanent lump in my throat. 'What do you think of him, Gus?'

He scratches his head. 'Reckon he knows more about rivers than the rest of us put together. He's a bit stiff, but he's always courteous and respectful. I like him. Maggie would've liked him too. Reckon he's an honest bloke. A good steady bloke.'

A group of grey nomads gather on the footpath in hats and sturdy shoes. There's a couple holding hands. When the man tips back the brim of the woman's hat and kisses her soundly on the mouth, she laughs.

'Does he fit in here, do you think?'

'Reckon he could fit in anywhere, a man like that. Why do you ask?'

You never lost me, Sapphie. You never could.

Peter Honey walks into the bar with Molly, his pretty eldest daughter, and gazes right and left as if on the look out for trouble. Leon catches my eye and lifts a glass, asking if I'd like another drink. I shake my head and turn back to Gus.

'I thought, once I had the farmhouse, I'd be happy. But something's missing.'

Gus nods wisely. 'It'll be like having a baby, I reckon.'

'What?'

'For the nine months she carried him, Maggie hankered to see our first child. But once he arrived'—he winks—'there were things she hadn't taken into account.' He links his hands on the table. 'You've put a lot of time into that place already, Sapphie, but there's plenty more work to do yet.'

'What I meant was … *someone* is missing.'

Gus nods slowly. 'Ah. Now I see.'

'What do you see?'

He sits back in his chair. 'No bloody idea.'

There's an ice cube in the bottom of my glass and I poke it with the straw. 'Matts says I take too many risks.' I push the glass away, put my hands on the table and stand. 'But I don't see a way out of this one.'

From: Sapphie
To: Chambers, Cassie, Luke, Gus, Matts

Clause 6.8 of the committee's code of conduct states: 'To guard against potential conflicts of interest, relationships (both professional and personal) between members of this committee must be disclosed to other committee members.'

When I was seven years old and Matts had just turned ten, our mothers became best friends. For eight years, first in Buenos Aires and later in Canberra, Matts and I saw each other almost every day.

I loved him.

We had a terrible argument when I was fifteen. By the time I'd turned nineteen, Matts had accepted that I'd turned my back on our friendship. Earlier this year, he found me at the farmhouse and over the past five months …

I've fallen in love with him.

Good corporate governance dictates that I put this disclosure on the record. So that it may be minuted appropriately, please acknowledge receipt.

Gus: Maggie would approve.
Cassie: You deserve the best.
Chambers: Receipt acknowledged.
Luke: Ha!
Matts: Noted

CHAPTER

46

Twenty-four hours have passed since Matts wrote *Noted* in response to my message.

Not a word since.

A few people smiled at me shyly at the youth centre today, and the Hargreaves barely complained when I told them I wouldn't be attending trivia tonight, so I suspect Gus might have said something. After I ride Sonnet and lead Strider back to the farmhouse, I shower and change in the refurbished bathroom at the end of the hallway. I haven't moved into the farmhouse properly yet, but it won't be long.

The westerly wind is picking up so I stand on tiptoes at the flower room window, push my palms against the frame and press down. It *almost* closes.

'That will have to do.'

I straighten the mirror, stand back and straighten it again. My hair was wet so I'd left it loose, but it's hot on my neck so I plait it, securing it with a piece of ribbon left over from April's headdress, and throw it down my back. The bookcase is bright with stacks of crepe and shoeboxes. I search one of the lower shelves and find my small curved scissors.

Myriad strips of crepe are strewn across the bench. The blue fairy flower I brought home from the river, softly faded now, lies in a tissue-lined box. It has one dorsal sepal, two lateral sepals and three petals, each of them long and narrow like the points of a star. The labellum, a tiny pouch, sits in the middle of the petals.

Jacqueline said the colours of the crepe were beautiful.

Midnight, royal, navy, peacock, sapphire.

I've made five flowers, each a slightly different shade. I line them up on the bench. 'Now you need something to hold you up.'

I wind green tape around floristry wire to make the stems. For the elongated leaves, I use a template to cut the crepe into shape, lay a fine piece of wire down the spine and glue it into place. I stick another leaf-shaped piece of crepe on top.

Moss, army, grasshopper, jungle, olive.

As I lay the stems and leaves on the bench next to the flowers, there's a knock on the front door. I look up as the key turns.

'Sapphie?'

I take a deep breath. 'I'm in here.'

The door clicks shut. Footsteps in the hallway. Matts stands just inside the door, his blue linen shirt light against the black of his jeans. He hasn't shaved today. His mouth lifts in an *almost* smile as he holds up Gran's old keyring. The enamelled rosebuds are pale against his fingers.

'I let myself in.'

Good-morning kisses. Laughter and tears. Wading through water in sunshine. Children and ponies and flowers. Is that what he wants too?

The red gum rustles. The window rattles. Wind sneaks through the gaps in the frame. Crepe paper flowers fly across the bench and flutter to the floor.

Matts gets to them first, carefully picking them up and putting them back on the bench. He glances at the window.

'Should I shut it?'

'It sticks.' As he walks to the window, I back away. 'I have to wash my hands.'

By the time I get back, he's standing at the bench and looking closely at the flowers. When he holds out his hand, I take it. Our palms press together as we stand side by side. He links our fingers.

'Eastern tiny blue china orchid,' he says.

'Or blue fairy.'

'You found one at the river.'

I look down at my jeans and boots. Should I have worn something prettier? 'I'm surprised you remember. Lisa had her hand on your thigh.'

'Sapphie?' He puts his hands on the tops of my arms and I turn and face him. 'I only wanted you.' His serious eyes search mine. 'Always.'

When I lay my hand on the side of his face, he kisses my wrist. 'I'm sorry about Inge, Matts. Did Gabriel call you? I didn't think he would.'

He frowns. 'I hadn't talked about my mother in front of my father for eighteen years. That meant we never talked about Kate— even after my father had found the key. But after I left here, I stayed with him in Helsinki. One day at breakfast, he asked why I'd been a bastard for the past few days.' He kisses my forehead. 'I told him I was missing you.'

I put my head on his chest. 'Sorry.'

He wraps his arms around me. 'I also told him what Robert had done. And by chance I asked whether he knew anybody from Hernandez Engineering.'

'Oh!' I look up. 'Did he know—'

'In deference to my father, Garcia had stayed away since my mother's death, but my father had suspected it was him. He'd tried to forget.'

'He wanted to remember Inge in the way he'd always known her. Your father loved her very much.'

'I'd asked him a direct question. He's an honest man. He couldn't refuse to answer.'

'You're like him.'

'He gave me Garcia's name but nothing more. I called him.'

I blink. 'He told you?'

Matts nods. 'I asked for proof. He showed me a copy of the withdrawal slip, and a receipt for the sapphire.'

'He didn't want to hurt you, Matts. That's why I knew I could trust him.'

'My father should have told me.'

'He was protecting you too.'

He presses his lips together. 'Kate paid the price.'

I don't want to leave the circle of his arms for a tissue, so I wipe his eye with a fingertip. 'No one knew how bad it would turn out. Mum didn't—' I shake my head. 'She didn't want help, from my father or anybody else. She refused to share her burden.'

'I was with you and Kate every day. She was forced to remember.'

'She wanted to remember. Inge was kind and gentle and caring. It must have been so hard for her to—'

'Be unfaithful.'

I take his hands and yank until he looks at me again. 'You weren't a snob like my father. You respected my grandmother.'

'You remind me of her.'

'She talked about perfection. When we made flowers together, she said I was far too fussy, that it was the imperfections that made the flowers perfect. Bruised and faded petals, softly bowed heads and crinkled leaves, that's what made them real. People are like that too.'

'This is my mother?'

'Perfect imperfection. My mother too.'

He runs his thumb over the tops of my hands. 'Garcia had no letters from Inge, but he told me she gave him a gift.'

'Oh.' I whisper. 'What?'

'In Inge's personal items, my father found the key to the box, but also cards, jewellery, mementos and the flowers you made.'

'The bougainvillea?'

'Garcia had one too.'

'I didn't give him—'

'She was pregnant and he was going away. She sent him a flower.'

'He kept it.'

'Yes.'

I grasp his shirt with one hand and put my other hand on his cheek. 'She loved you, Matts, more than anything else in the world. Nothing changed that.'

His eyes still shadowed, he steps back. He takes my hand in his. 'And you, Sapphie?' he says quietly. 'What do you feel?'

'Didn't you read my message?'

He touches my mouth. 'I want to hear it.'

'I adored you.'

He growls and pulls me close. 'Not that.'

I repeat the words he used the last time we spoke: 'I think you already know.'

He kisses me swiftly but firmly. And then he kisses me again, running his lips over mine and warming my body. I open my mouth and sigh. Our kisses are careful then careless, savage then sweet. We're both breathing deeply when he lifts his head.

'As a child you were fearless.' He loops his finger through my ribbon and lifts my plait over my shoulder. 'You sat still only to make your flowers. Anyone you met—my classmates, babies, old people—you were their friend. You were physically beautiful, but that held no meaning. You wanted to be known for other things.'

'I followed you around like a kitten.'

'When I came back, I told myself we would have little in common. You taught young children. You lived a quiet life.'

'That's true.'

'You totalled your car.' He tightens his arms. 'You ride wild horses.'

'Not wild.'

'*Disobedient* horses. You scale cliffs without ropes.'

'Rarely.'

'That first night, why did you climb the tree?'

'I thought you might be up to no good.' I undo one of his buttons before fastening it again. 'You need me to keep an eye on you.'

'We climbed well together.' He's very serious.

'I was more flexible. Your reach was better. We complemented each other.'

He puts his hands over mine, still on his chest. 'I had a choice of twenty committees, Sapphie. I couldn't go past yours.'

'They're good people.'

'The land, the river, the wetlands. I work from the ground up too.'

'Are you saying we do have things in common?'

'Too much.'

'We always did.'

He narrows his eyes. 'Tell me our age difference.'

'A little under three years.'

'Two years, eight months and four days. I had to wait.'

'You had so many girlfriends.'

'You should have had boyfriends.'

'So you could be jealous too?'

'I wanted you to be certain. I wanted you to choose me over the others. You never did.'

Strong and sensitive. Arrogant and vulnerable. I stand on my toes and wrap my arms around his neck. 'I didn't want the other boys.' I kiss his mouth. 'I only ever wanted you.'

CHAPTER

47

As if afraid to let go, we hold hands as we walk down the hallway. When I lock the door, he stands behind me, an arm across my breasts. I put the keyring in my bag and he takes my hand again. It's dark now. Eucalyptus perfumes the air. There's scratching in the red gum.

'That will be the possums.'

When I turn towards his car, he pulls me back. 'Can we walk?'

Once we're away from the shadows of the house, it's easy to see the path. The moon, a shimmering sphere, hovers over the hill.

Silver, brilliant, argent, pearlescent.

There's mint in the herb garden but very little else. I have to replace the old lemon trees, mulch the vegetable garden and have the glasshouse repaired …

The farmhouse alone won't make me happy. I need him too.

'Matts? Can you explain what you mean by long term?'

He squeezes my hand but says nothing.

When we reach the paddocks, Lollopy leaves Freckle to nap and bustles to the fence. He tips his head sideways and pushes it through the wire.

I laugh as I scratch under his forelock. 'You have to wait till breakfast.'

Sonnet and Strider stand on the far side of the paddock. Strider nickers a greeting. Prima, ears pricked, walks cautiously to the fence and stands next to Lollopy.

'Hello, girl.' I turn to Matts, still holding my hand. 'She's much more confident than she was.'

When he extends his hand, Prima lowers her head and brushes her muzzle against his palm. 'Don't fucking bolt again,' he mutters.

'You'll get used to—' I frown up at him. 'You didn't answer my question.'

He tugs my hand and we walk towards the creek, but just before we get to the gate he reaches for me. I lean my back against his front. We face the farmhouse together, his arms around my middle. He kisses my temple and trails kisses to my jaw. He nuzzles my neck.

He smells nice. His body is hard and warm against my back. Desire ripples over me in waves. But when I try to turn, he holds me still. He kisses my neck again.

'Do you want my answer?'

I take a deep breath. 'Please hurry up.'

He rests his chin on my head and points to the farmhouse. 'The weathervane was at a thirty degree angle. Now it's at ninety. Why?'

'It was years ago I tied it to the chimney. The wire must have loosened.'

'You need a new roof.'

'It can be patched.'

'It can't. The house needs gutters, downpipes, drainage and solar panels. It needs new floorboards and better ventilation. New posts and boards for the verandah. The windows, skirtings and cornices have to be replaced.'

I spin around. 'I've spent all my money. I've *borrowed* money. I have to save up.'

'I'll pay for it.'

'You can't do that!'

'Marry me.'

'To get my roof fixed?'

'So I don't fall through your floor.'

'It's not a good enough reason.'

'Will you make flowers for your hair? Will you dance to that song?'

I laugh. '"Can't Take My Eyes Off You"?'

The light is fading but his eyes are bright. 'I love you, Sapphie Brown. Marry me.'

Good-morning kisses. Laughter and tears. Wading through water in sunshine. Children and ponies and flowers.

I smooth his dark, glossy hair where it kinks behind his ear. I press my palm against the bristles at his jaw. I feel the texture of his mouth and his breath on my fingertips.

I stand on my toes and softly kiss his mouth.

U

As I fumble with the lock of the schoolhouse front door, Matts kicks off his shoes and puts them on the rack with my boots. He pulls his T-shirt over his head and throws it onto the desk.

'Matts!'

His skin glows bronze in the shadows. His nipples are dark, his muscles defined. There's a thin line of hair from his navel to his jeans.

His lip lifts. 'Hurry up.'

'I'm doing my—'

Tumbleweed meows.

Matts is sitting on the end of the bed, still half naked, by the time I feed my cat and close the door to the bedroom. His knees almost touch the wall, but when he opens his arms, I sit sideways on his lap. He holds me firmly around my waist as I breathe in the scent of his skin and stroke his hair. I run my hands over his shoulders and chest.

I clear my throat. 'We don't have to get married straight away.'

'We do.'

I touch his mouth with shaking fingers. 'But living here ... I want to be with you, that's the most important thing. Horseshoe is so far away from Switzerland and Finland.'

'Not so far.'

I look through the window to the treetops near the playground. 'Gus once said that even though I didn't come from Horseshoe, I ended up where I was supposed to start out in the first place.'

He runs his lips over the inside of my wrist. He looks up at me with dark sombre eyes. 'You love me, yes?'

I tug my hand free and wrap my arms around his neck. 'Always.'

'I am meant to end up with you. We live here.'

The warmth in my veins seeps straight to my heart. I trace his scar. 'I have long holidays. And Jet will look after my horses. Tumbleweed can stay with the Hargreaves. I'd like to see Switzerland.' I kiss his shoulder. 'Mostly I'd like to see Finland.'

'The mangroves and swamps?'

I smile against his lips. 'The thousand lakes.'

The touch of his mouth is new yet familiar. He takes my lips and tongue and breath and gives his own to me.

When I lift my arms, he pulls my T-shirt over my head. He kisses down my cleavage as he unclasps my bra. His eyes are heated as he cups my breasts. Our eyes meet. He must see the uncertainty in mine. He kisses one nipple and then the other. 'Only you,' he says.

We're the same as we were. We're nothing like we were.

Kissa. Cat.

Kotka. Eagle.

Our hands are impatient as we pull off our clothes. At first we move slowly and savour each moment. And then we move swiftly and search for release. He groans my name against my neck. I sob his against his mouth.

When the colours have faded, he sleeps against my breast. I hold him inside me. I trace his lashes, dark against his cheeks. I kiss his mouth and catch his breath.

What colour is this?

The silvery leaves of the gum trees and the orange-brown dust of the roads. The bright green rushes and grasses and the glistening patchwork of stars. The black cockatoos, the finches and kestrels and kites.

The grey of his eyes and the blue of my own.

The water that pools at our feet. Azure, aqua, ocean and turquoise.

The sunshine that rests on our shoulders. Saffron, lemon, amber and gold.

The perfect imperfections of our hearts.

ACKNOWLEDGEMENTS

Thank you to my publisher Jo Mackay from Harlequin, for your faith in my stories and the way I love to write them. And thank you to Annabel Blay, senior editor from Harlequin—it was a joy to work with you again on *Starting From Scratch*. Many thanks also to Kylie Mason, my editor, for your insightful suggestions. To the Harlequin team, in particular Sarana Behan, Adam van Rooijen and Johanna Baker, thank you for all you do behind the scenes in sales, marketing and publicity to allow readers to find my books.

The environment has been a theme in most of my novels, but I've been able to explore environmental issues in two of them in particular—global warming in *In at the Deep End*, and the protection and preservation of wetlands in *Starting From Scratch*. I'd like to thank Dr Hope Ashiabor and Dr Patricia Blazey, my long time legal colleagues at Macquarie University, for fostering my early academic interest in international responses, legal and otherwise, to climate change and the environment. Australia was one of the early signatories of the Ramsar Convention on Wetlands of International Importance, and one of the first nations to place wetlands on the Ramsar List. I have changed town and other names, and geographic locations in *Starting From Scratch*, but the Macquarie Marshes in New South Wales does indeed appear on the Ramsar List. These wetlands, like other wetlands both locally and globally, are under threat as a result of many decades of water management and mismanagement, and the drying of our planet. The regulation of water resources and climate policy are extremely complex and dynamic issues, but I have endeavoured to portray them (of necessity often in outline) as faithfully as possible. Any inaccuracies or omissions in this fictional work are mine—and creative license.

To my writer's group, the Ink Wells. What can I say? Pamela Cook, Joanna Nell, Laura Boon, Rae Cairns, Michelle Barraclough, Terri Green and Angella Whitton. Your support and encouragement in the year I was writing and editing *Starting From Scratch* was inspirational, hilarious, intelligent, informative, and all round blue balls brilliant. Thank you from the bottom of my heart.

Many thanks to Dr Margaret Janu who is not only a medical specialist but also married to a surgeon who knows all about stitches. You are the best friend a writer could have. And thank you to my fabulous colleague and friend Alma Urbiztondo, who introduced me to Rica and Paul Nyberg, experts on all things Finland. I hope you approve of Matts's last name!

My friend Vani Gupta, a speech pathologist who specialises in the treatment of children, generously read and discussed various scenes in this book. Her insights into the learning challenges many children face was instructive and invaluable. And to Liz Dibdin, the third member of our Broody Café clique, thank you. Our writing discussions are inspiring, our friendship very special.

To Victoria Purman, thank you for not only writing wonderful novels yourself, but for your friendship, advice and wisdom (and thank you for the cover quote!). To my many talented and generous friends in Romance Writers of Australia, you constantly inspire and amaze me.

To my beautiful sister Julie, thank you for your sustained encouragement (and your wonderful company) during the writing of this book, and to my brother-in-law Christopher, thank you for the cupcakes and finger buns (white icing with sprinkles). Many thanks to my thrillseeking and adventurous son-in-law Scott for generously sharing your knowledge and expertise in all things rock climbing. Thank you to my daughter Michaela for introducing me to Canberra's arboretum (and for keeping my laptop alive). Thanks also to my friend Michelle—now you've added a masters in forensic mental health to your other degrees, your continued assistance with my character's psychological health and wellbeing is assured (and will be greatly appreciated). To my parents, Ann and Philip, thank you for telling me as a child that I had a way with words. My parents' love and commitment to each other is, and always has been, romance-novel worthy.

Which brings me to my husband Peter (he of the titanium bicycle, skis and ribs). We met as eighteen year olds as law students at the University of Sydney and shortly thereafter fell in love. Thank you for encouraging me to take risks, making me laugh and maintaining my faith in happily ever afters.

Last but by no means least, thank you to my readers. If not for you, I wouldn't have the privilege and joy of creating characters I love and sharing their stories.

Turn over for a sneak peek.

Clouds on the Horizon

by

PENELOPE JANU

Available January 2022

CHAPTER

1

Stripes of silver hang in the air and rivers of water crisscross the track, but Camelot, black as the clouds, treads confidently over the uneven ground. Leaning forward in the saddle, I stroke his rain soaked neck. I breathe in eucalyptus and the dampness of the earth.

My face is wet, as is the hair that's come loose from my plait. Between the tops of my knee-high boots and the leg flaps of my oilskin coat, my jodhpurs are sodden. I run a finger inside my collar and re-fasten a press-stud, shivering as we skirt around the tree roots. Notwithstanding my gloves, pins and needles prickle my fingers as I clench and unclench my hands. When I push Camelot into a trot, my body warms, but the wind is cold on my cheeks.

Camelot, as happy as a platypus swimming in a stream, breaks into a canter at the top of the rise, and I laugh as I pull him back. 'Not today, boy.'

A rumble of thunder sounds in the distance as we pass Mr Riley's shearing shed and sheep pens. The water tank is shrouded in mist.

When Camelot shies, edging off the path and into the bush, I increase the pressure on my outside leg to bring him back to the track. He complies but tosses his head as I guide him towards the copse of gums and the narrow dirt road that leads to the churchyard and home. He shies again, skittering sideways. I steady him, patting his neck, when he takes a tentative step.

'What's the—'

A long dark shape lies across the track, blocking our path. I kick my feet free from the stirrups and slide to the ground, my heart thumping hard. I bring Camelot's reins over his head and loop them through my arm.

The man lies on his front with an arm thrown out to the side. One of his legs is bent at the knee and the other is straight. His pants are dark; his white shirt sticks to his skin. Kneeling at his side, I touch his shoulder. Even through the rain, my gloves and his shirt, I feel his body stiffen.

He spins and rolls onto his back.

'Oh!' I sit back on my heels.

He's in his late twenties, maybe early thirties. He has a straight nose and a strong jaw. Blood trickles from his temple to his ear. 'Hvem er du?' he whispers.

I lean over him. 'What?'

He's shivering so hard that his whole body trembles. His eyes flutter closed. 'Who are you?'

'Phoebe. Who are you?'

His eyes open again and he blinks as if trying to focus. 'Phoebe Cartwright.'

'How do you know that?'

He lifts an arm and drops it. He shakes his head. With a shuddering exhalation, he passes out.

I pull off my gloves and rest my fingertips against his neck, counting carefully through the fear that tightens my chest. His pulse is faint. Breathing laboured and shallow. Skin cold and pale. Sight, hearing, touch, taste and smell. It's my job to know about the senses, but this is beyond me.

When his eyes spring open, I jump. 'Telefon,' he mutters.

'There's no reception here.'

He's cleanly shaven. His thick, dark hair looks recently cut. He's wearing a business shirt and suit pants. His shoes are city shoes, leather with narrow eyelets and long thin laces. Why is he in the middle of nowhere, alone and icy cold?

How does he know my name?

I touch his cheek and he flinches. 'Who are you?'

He shakes his head. 'No.'

'You've bumped your head. You're freezing. Tell me your name.'

He utters a string of words I don't understand. Danish? Swedish? I *think* it's Scandinavian. Another shudder takes over his body. He stares at me and swallows. 'Get my phone.' He lifts his hand, but just like before it drops back to his side. 'Find it.' His voice disappears but I read his lips. 'Pocket.'

'We have to get out of the rain.' I look towards my home, a kilometre away. And then I look up at my horse. Now that the shape on the path has taken human form, Camelot is curious. When he lowers his head, only half the length of the rein separates us.

I turn to the man again. 'I don't suppose you can ride?'

'Motorsykkel?'

'A thoroughbred.' By the time I indicate Camelot behind me, the man's eyes have drifted closed again.

He shakes his head. 'No.'

'I don't think you could get onto him anyway. Can you stand? Can you walk?'

His eyes open and his brow creases, as if he's considering my questions. And then, as if in slow motion, he rolls onto his front. He moans as he comes up on his hands and knees. He's slender but his shoulders are broad. The muscles on his arms and chest are clearly outlined through his shirt. I'm average in height, but there's no way I could carry him. I don't think I could drag him either.

Mr Riley hasn't sheared in his shed for years, but he keeps winter hay, tools and other paraphernalia here. It's likely to be weather-proof and even if it isn't, it'll be safer than being outside. I put my hand on the man's shoulder.

'There's a shed twenty metres away. We can go there. Other-wise, I'll have to ride home and call an ambulance on the way.'

'Telefon.'

A bolt of lightning splits the sky and thunder breaks it open. 'That settles it.' Getting to my feet, I take hold of the man's arm with both hands and pull as hard as I can. 'You have to help. You have to stand.'

It takes a minute at least for the man to get off the ground. I pull his arm around my shoulders. Even stooped over, he's tall. When Camelot nudges my back with his nose, I stumble.

'Cut it out, boy.'

'Telefon,' the man whispers, as blood drips on his shirt. Another bolt of lightning, closer than the last.

'Why won't you tell me your name?'

'Nei.'

I don't know what he's up to or where he's from, but he's far too weak to cause trouble. I adjust his arm over my shoulder. 'Let's get out of the storm.'

When I take a step, the man stays rooted to the spot. He holds out a hand and Camelot sniffs it.

'Vakker hest.'

He speaks nicely enough, but I have no idea what his words mean. When he sways towards Camelot, I pull his arm more tightly around my shoulders.

'You have to walk.'

Leaning so heavily on me that I'm forced to brace my legs to stay upright, the man takes slow, leaden steps to the shed. Camelot, his footfalls soft on the rain-soaked track, walks patiently behind us.

The shed isn't locked, but the bolt is stiff and I can't work it while supporting the man. I balance him against a wall. 'I won't be long.'

A moment after I release him, his knees buckle. I shove my shoulder against his chest to support him as he slides to the ground and slumps against the wall, his head tipped onto his chest. Another flash of lightning illuminates the bolt, but even two handed I can't pull it back, so I rifle through the grass and find a brick. I whack the curved end of the bolt until it slides clear of the barrel. I pull against the doors and they swing outwards. The shed smells of hay, wool and dust and it's even gloomier in here than it was outside. Camelot baulks at the doors, but after I double back and pat his rump firmly, he walks tentatively over the threshold. When I loop his rein through a sheep pen on the far side of the shed, he stares back with big black eyes.

By the time I return to the man, he's facing the wall, pressing both hands against it as he works his way up. He leans on me as we inch towards the shed, but when we get to the doors, he reaches out and grasps the frame. He looks inside. Sways.

'Nei.'

'Yes!'

When I push him through the doors, he staggers towards a stack of hay bales, dropping to his knees just before we get to it. The doors crash shut, plunging us into darkness.

A whimper works its way up my throat.

I swallow compulsively, stilling the memories, the old, relentless fears.

'It's not locked,' I say aloud, my voice thin and high.

My eyes adjust. The windowpanes are filthy but rain streaked. I can see the outlines of gum trees through the glass. Light filters through the six half-doors behind the shearing platform. Shearers would have pushed freshly shorn sheep through the doors to scramble down the ramps and quiver in the pens.

I can breathe.

Camelot's bit jangles. When he shifts a leg, his shoe scrapes the concrete. I make out a stirrup iron, glistening dully in the darkness. Another gust of wind rattles the doors on their hinges.

I can get out.

I step carefully to the doors and push them open, ignoring the gusts of icy wind and rain as I kick the half-brick under one of the doors, creating a wedge. By the time I get back to the man, he's flat on the concrete. Concussion? Hypothermia? Either way, he has to warm up. Dragging six bales of hay off the stack, I lay them out like a bed.

'Can you get up there?'

He doesn't have the strength to stand, but I yank until he kneels and, pushing and shoving, roll him onto the bales. He lies on his back, groans and loses consciousness again. My hair sticks to my face. Rain or sweat? When I feel for his pulse, even weaker than it was before, I see a card through the pocket of his shirt and slide it out. The cardboard is wet through but the words, black on white, are clear enough.

> *United Nations First Committee*
> *(Disarmament and International Security)*
> *Sindre Tørrissen*

He doesn't have a title, but the string of initials next to his name suggests scientific qualifications. There's a UN email address and two telephone numbers.

'Sindre?'

His eyes briefly flicker open. 'Sinn.'

Whoever he is and wherever he's from, he won't warm up if he's wearing wet clothes. My fingers are stiff and clumsy as I pull his shirt free of his pants. After I fumble over the top two buttons of his shirt, I grasp the front panels to rip the remaining buttons through the holes.

'Sorry about that.' I undo his cuffs before rolling him onto his side to pull off the shirt, then push him onto his back again. Thunder rattles the roof and lightning brightens the shed. His chest is firm, his abdominal muscles clearly defined.

When I exhale, my breath is white. 'Your pants are wet too.'

I peel off his socks and tug at his shoes. I undo his belt buckle and button, and unzip his fly, exposing his underpants. 'I'm not looking. I promise. And those can stay on.'

I focus on the hay as I pull off his pants, dropping them onto the pile with his other wet clothes.

Opening the press studs of my oilskin, I shake off the worst of the moisture. I pull the man onto his side, spread the coat out behind him and, brushing off the hay that's stuck to his skin, roll him onto the coat. I draw the thick cotton lining around his body. The coat covers most of his legs and torso, but isn't wide enough to wrap around his chest, so I take off my sweater and smooth the wool, warm from my body, from his waist up to his neck. I gather the coat around his sides. A drip from his hair rolls down his cheek, joining a trail of blood trickling across his throat.

Taking off my T-shirt, I fold it in half and rub his hair, shivering when drips fall from the end of my plait and down my spine. He blinks.

'Du er vakker.'

'I can't understand you,' I say as I hastily pull my T-shirt back over my head. The fabric is damp. I shiver again and rub my arms. 'I'll see what else I can find.'

Camelot's saddle blanket is warm and mostly dry. I remove his saddle and rest it over a railing before wrapping the padded rectangle around the man's feet, tucking it under his heels to secure it. I frantically search the perimeter of the shed before finding a stack of hessian sacks on the shearing platform. They're clean and thick, rough against the insides of my arms when I pick them up. I shake them out and layer them on top of the man, then I free the cape of the oilskin from under his shoulders, lift his head and lay a folded sack beneath it, positioning it like a pillow.

He's trussed up like a mummy, but he'll be warmer. So why, all of a sudden, is he so frighteningly still? Shivering is the first stage of hypothermia. After that, the body preserves energy for the vital organs—the lungs, heart, brain and kidneys. I burrow through the sacks and coat and touch his side. His skin is as cold as marble. I search for the pulse at his throat but can't find it.

'Please don't—'

Feathery beats. One. Two. Three. Four.

I take a shaky breath. 'Thank you.'

I feel down his side again. He's dry now. Any heat he produces, he should keep.

When his head jerks towards me, I jump. He murmurs something unintelligible and I put my hand on his cheek. I push back his hair. 'Sinn?'

'Ja.'

'Are you Swedish?'

'Norsk.'

'Norway?'

He swallows. 'Telefon.'

I pick up my phone from a hay bale and hold it out. 'I've already told you. No reception. That's why I have to ride home.'

He grasps my hand. 'Satellitt.'

'I think you have hypothermia. If you warm up too quickly or move around, you could go into cardiac arrest. I should get a signal around five minutes from here, and I'll call an ambulance. It'll take an hour for it to get here from the hospital, but Camelot and I will race home. I'll get my car and come back with blankets and something warm to drink. You can't move while I'm gone. Do you understand?'

'Satellitt.'

'There are no doctors in Warrandale, so the ambulance will be the quickest way for you to get help. I'll be back in thirty minutes, maybe less.'

I try to prise my fingers free, but he holds on. He opens his mouth and shuts it again. Besides 'telefon', I haven't understood much of what he's said since I brought him into the shed. I put my other hand over his.

'You have to let me go.'

He shakes his head. 'Nei.'

I pull my hand free. 'I'll be back as soon as I can. Don't move. Please.'

'I have ...' His brow furrows as he whispers the words. I bend closer to listen. 'I have a satellite phone.' His dark gaze focuses on my face. He swallows. 'I have reception.'

When he does speak in English, he barely has an accent.

I use the torch on my phone to find his clothes and lift them to the hay bales before feeling the weight and shape of his phone through his shirt. The phone is zipped in a pocket that must have sat at this hip. It's not chunky like the satellite phones I'm familiar with, but black and slender like a regular phone.

The hessian sacks lift as he raises his hand. 'Here.'

When I give him the phone, he holds it up. It glows, highlighting his features. His face is attractive. Exceptionally attractive.

He doesn't dial or do anything else. I don't know that he'd be capable of it. His hand drops heavily to his chest and he closes his eyes.

'De vil komme,' he whispers.

I roll his shirt into a ball and press it against the gash on his head. 'I don't understand.'

He mutters. 'They will come.'

I didn't hear anyone on the other end of the phone, so how does he know that they'll come? Who is 'they'?

When his eyes close, the phone slips from his fingers. I make sure my sweater covers his chest, wrap the oilskin up and over his sides again, and secure the hessian sacks. I press the edges of the cape around his ears and brush back his hair.

'I wish you'd stop moving around.' I lean a hip against the hay bales as I pick up his phone and push the buttons at the side.

'Phoebe.' He croaks my name. When I look down, it's straight into his eyes. A shudder passes through him. 'Leave it.'

I put the phone back on his chest. 'I can't get anything on the screen anyway.'

He frowns as if he's lost his train of thought. 'Go home.'

'Leave you here? After I've gone to all this trouble? You said they were coming. Will there be a doctor?'

'Forget this.'

Camelot's shoes scrape on the concrete when he pivots and faces the rear of the shed. I run to him, afraid he'll pull back, dislodge the pen and panic. I put my hand on his neck, quivering with tension. 'Easy, boy,' I say as I untie him. 'What's the matter?'

Rain pounds on the roof and the wind howls though the trees. But there's another sound as well. At first it's a whir. Then it's a roar. The incessant thump of helicopter blades directly above us.

I tighten my grip on the rein and lead Camelot, toey but compliant, to the hay. *They will come.* Who are they? Who is he?

'Sinn?'

He opens his mouth before closing it again.

'That is your name, isn't it? Sinn Tørrissen. You work for the UN.'

Silence.

'You know my name. Why can't I know yours?'

He shakes his head. 'No.'

The helicopter isn't overhead any more, but it's still very loud. Mr Riley grows corn and canola crops on cleared land to the west of the shed. A helicopter could easily land there.

I touch Sinn's arm. 'Has the helicopter come for you? Should I go outside and tell them that you're here?'

He's shivering again. He attempts to roll onto his side, but when I put a hand on his shoulder and gently push, he collapses onto his back. I lean over him, securing the hessian beneath his arms.

'You have to stay still.'

When another shiver passes through him, he clenches his teeth. They're even whiter than his face, and perfectly straight. I press the backs of my fingers to the skin at his neck. He swallows and shudders again. But I'm certain he's warmer than he was. I rewrap his feet with the saddle blanket.

'Do you come from Norway? That's what you said before.'

'Gå Hjem.'

'I don't understand.'

His eyes are brighter than they were. 'Go home.'

The doors open wide and I jump. Squinting, I try to look past the broad shaft of light that spills into the shed. Camelot skitters, his reins rushing though my fingers. One of the men standing on the threshold is extremely broad shouldered and dressed in city clothes. The other man has brutally short hair and is wearing grey fatigues. He has embroidered patches on his arms and a badge on his chest. When he shines the light into the shed again, I turn away and hold a hand above my eyes.

'Who are you?' My voice isn't as steady as I'd like it to be.

'Lower the torch.' A woman's voice. Dressed in black and carrying a bag, she says something else to the men before pushing past them and striding confidently towards me. Her hair is short and fiery red and her face is peppered with freckles. 'Sorry that took a while.'

I stand between her and Sinn. 'Who are you?'

'I'm not here.' She smiles and holds out her hand. 'Who are you?'

My hand lifts automatically. 'Phoebe.' We shake briefly. 'What do you mean—'

She jerks her head towards the men. 'Politics.'

Sinn's eyes are closed; he's deathly white.

'Are you a doctor?'

'I'll check him out and then we'll get him to one.'

I step aside but stay close to Sinn as she drops the bag at her feet and pulls out a stethoscope, blood pressure equipment and a lunch box–sized container that rattles as she puts it on the hay bales. She pulls on gloves and pushes aside the hessian to take Sinn's hand and feel for his pulse. When she addresses him, she tips her head to the side.

'This'll teach you to jump from a moving van.'

He grunts before looking from the woman to me. 'No names.'

'I got the directive,' she says, listening to Sinn's heart before pressing both hands down his arms, torso and legs. She moves the shirt from his head and touches the cut before lifting his eyelids and shining a torch into each of his eyes. She places a thermometer into his ear.

'He slips in and out of consciousness,' I tell her. His head is bleeding again so I press his shirt against the cut. 'He can walk and doesn't seem to be in too much pain, so I guess no broken bones. He was freezing. I took off his clothes to warm him. I think he's better than he was, but he could have concussion. You'll take him to hospital, won't you?'

'We'll do what needs to be done.' The woman squints at the thermometer. 'Thirty-five point six. Could be worse.'

The broad-shouldered man walks towards us, looking cautiously at Camelot as he skirts around him. 'Okay to butt in here?' he says in an American accent, smiling as he runs a hand through his dark blond hair. He'd be in his early thirties.

'Looks to be a superficial head wound,' the woman says, 'but I'll sort out a scan just in case.'

'I found him on the track,' I say. 'He wasn't making much sense.'

'Being cold and wet in freezing temperatures will do that to you,' she says. 'You did a great job with him.'

'Did he really jump from a van?'

She glances at the broad-shouldered man. 'Eight hours ago.'

The man, still keeping well clear of Camelot, stands at Sinn's head and squeezes his shoulder. 'Hey, buddy. You gave us a hell of a fright back there.'

Sinn swallows. 'They didn't see me.'

The man and woman wrap a large silver blanket around Sinn. By the time they've finished, his eyes are closed. His breathing is deep.

'Is he going to be okay?' I ask.

A sleeve of my sweater peeps out from the top of the blanket. The woman moves it aside to check the pulse at Sinn's neck before tucking it in again. She smiles reassuringly. 'All good. Exhausted, that's all.'

The man at the door calls out. 'Stretcher is on its way, lieutenant.'

As he brushes hay from my oilskin, the broad-shouldered man considers my T-shirt and jodhpurs.

'You must be cold yourself.'

I reach for my coat. 'Yes.'

He smiles. 'Thanks for your help. Really appreciate it, but ...'

'You weren't here, right?' I shrug into the coat and fasten all the press studs. 'I can't know your names and I get no explanation.'

He smiles apologetically. 'You got it.'

I lay the saddle blanket over Camelot's back before turning to the woman. 'Are you in the navy, lieutenant?'

The woman and man exchange looks. 'No comment,' she says.

'My sister Patience is in the navy. She wears the same camouflage as the sergeant over there.'

'Is that right?'

'Are you in charge?'

She grimaces as she glances first at Sinn, still asleep, and then at his colleague. 'Not the boss of these two, that's for sure.'

'Sinn's with the UN, isn't he?'

The other man attempts to hide a frown. 'Did he tell you that?'

When Sinn mumbles, I put my hand on his arm. His lashes, inky-black crescents on his cheeks, open for an instant before they drift closed. He probably has a family that cares about him. A wife or partner. What if he'd died so far from home? Repressing a shiver, I bunch my hands into fists and put them into my pockets. I stamp my feet, suddenly frozen.

'I offered to call for help, but he only wanted you. Why was that? Why so secretive? Why can't I talk? What is he hiding?'

The woman's face is expressionless as she peers closely at the bruise on Sinn's forehead. The hair at his temple is thickened with blood.

'Take it from me,' she says, 'you can trust him. He'll be grateful for your help.'

'What was he doing all the way out here? How did he know my name?'

The American's brows lift. 'What *is* your name?'

'Phoebe Cartwright.'

He whistles a breath. 'Is that right?'

'Have you heard of me too?'

'Can't really say.'

I pull Sinn's card from my pocket. 'Are you from the UN like him?'

The man plucks the card out of my hand. 'Where did you get this?'

'Besides his phone, it's all he had on him.'

'We'd really appreciate your cooperation with keeping a lid on this.' The man's smile is strained.

'Because you've finished here? I won't see you again?'

'Say nothing, Phoebe.' The man looks at Sinn, still asleep. 'When he's back on his feet, he'll be in touch.'

talk about it

Let's talk about books.

Join the conversation:

 facebook.com/romanceanz

 @romanceanz

romance.com.au

If you love reading and want to know about our
authors and titles, then let's talk about it.